DISTANT
VALOR

DISTANT VALOR

C. X. MOREAU

A TOM DOHERTY ASSOCIATES BOOK

NEW YORK

DISTANT VALOR

Copyright © 1996 by C. X. Moreau

This book is printed on acid-free paper.

A Forge Book
Published by Tom Doherty Associates, Inc.
175 Fifth Avenue
New York, N.Y. 10010

Forge® is a registered trademark of Tom Doherty Associates, Inc.

Book Design: Michael Mendelsohn of MM Design 2000, Inc.

Library of Congress Cataloging-in-Publication Data

Moreau, C. X.
    Distant valor / C. X. Moreau. — 1st ed.
       p. cm.
    "A Tom Doherty Associates book."
    ISBN 0-312-85941-4 (acid-free paper)
    I. Title.
  PS3563.07723D5   1996
  813'.54—dc20   96-16746
                             CIP

First Edition: November 1996

Printed in the United States of America

0 9 8 7 6 5 4 3 2 1

This book is dedicated to the Marines and sailors
who served in Beirut, Lebanon, during the deployments
of 1982–1984.

Et pour nos frères, mort pour la France.

ACKNOWLEDGMENTS

I would like to thank my literary agent and editor, Andrew Zack and the Andrew Zack Agency. Had it not been for Andrew's belief in this book, his insight as an editor, and his perseverance in presenting it to various publishing houses, this project would never have been brought to fruition.

Special thanks also to Tom Doherty, Camille Cline, and the people of Tor/Forge for taking a chance on an unknown writer.

Any acknowledgment would be incomplete without a special thanks to those friends who assisted me in the technical preparation of the manuscript, who encouraged me in its writing, and whose belief in me as a writer was unwavering.

And, most important, thanks to those of you with whom I served during the long months in Beirut. The privilege was mine.

Semper Fidelis

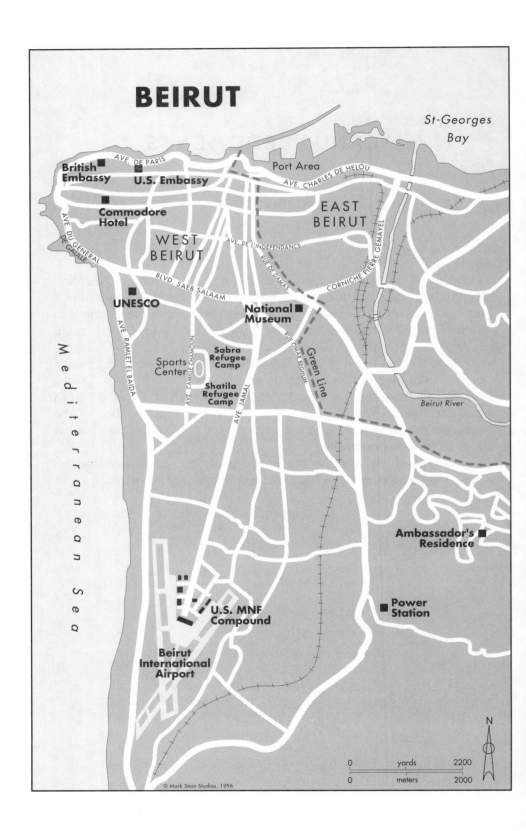

BEIRUT

St-Georges Bay

British Embassy

AVE. DE PARIS

Port Area

AVE. CHARLES DE HELOU

U.S. Embassy

Commodore Hotel

AVE. DU GENERAL DE GAULLE

EAST BEIRUT

CORNICHE PIERRE GEMAYEL

WEST BEIRUT

AVE. DE L'INDEPENDANCE

RUE DE DAMAS

BLVD. SAEB SALAAM

UNESCO

AVE. RAMLET EL BAIDA

National Museum

M e d i t e r r a n e a n   S e a

AVE. CAMILLE CHAMOUN

Sports Center

Sabra Refugee Camp

RUE OMAR BEGHUM

Green Line

Beirut River

Shatila Refugee Camp

AVE. JAMAL

Ambassador's Residence

U.S. MNF Compound

Power Station

Beirut International Airport

0   yards   2200

0   meters   2000

N

© Mark Stein Studios, 1996

UNITED STATES MNF COMPOUND
(AIRPORT TERMINAL AREA)

MAIN AIRPORT HIGHWAY

MSSG HQ

MAU HQ

BLT HQ

Airport
Terminal

Airport
Towers

Beirut International
Airport

N

0   yards   550

0   meters   500

© Mark Stein Studios, 1996

DISTANT

VALOR

PROLOGUE

"In such dangerous things as war the errors which proceed from a spirit of benevolence are the worst."

—Karl von Clausewitz (1780–1831)

Eastern Mediterranean, 1982.

In the darkness the American and French naval vessels alter course for the second time in as many hours and make sail for the port of Beirut. The commanders of the ships gauge their speed so as to arrive at dawn, the hour when the warring factions are most likely to be at rest.

Below decks, in the berthing areas, old hands feel the change of course and rouse their sleeping troops. Before orders can be relayed to those in the ranks, platoon sergeants are checking the weapons and gear they know their men will need once ashore in the hostile city. Ammunition is passed out and weapons are given a final check by sergeants too young to have ever seen combat. As the helicopter assault platoons are designated and formed up, the Marines stage their packs in the narrow gray passageways of the ships. Hours before dawn the spaces closest to the flight decks are lined by Marines too nervous to sleep who sit in silence and wait for the arrival of the helicopters that will ferry them to shore.

In the cavernous well decks of the amphibious assault ships other Marines form into landing parties and align themselves in symmetrical rows next to the small flat-bottomed boats that will carry them ashore onto the beaches south of the city. Few sleep, many play cards or write letters home in the dim light and dank air of the well deck. Before loading into landing craft the Marines are given short briefings by junior officers regarding the morning's mission.

On the hangar decks of the American vessels, ground crews work unceasingly through the night to prepare their aircraft for flight. As each aircraft is made ready, it is lifted to the flight deck by the heavy elevators

13

that hang precariously over the dark waters of the Eastern Mediterranean. Pilots sit in ready rooms and study the aerial photographs of the city they will fly over in the morning, noting the positions of the warring armies and the numerous antiaircraft emplacements of both sides.

The first streaks of light begin to form on the eastern horizon as the smaller ships of the fleet carrying the majority of the Marines alter course just off the coast of Lebanon and head south toward the beaches where the Marines will come ashore. The remainder of the fleet, including the French vessels, steers north and slips into the channel leading to Beirut's once magnificent port. Those on the bridge and above decks are treated to a spectacular view of the sun rising over the mountains that ring the city. The desolation of the port is enough to remind them they are entering a war zone of some eight years.

Everywhere around the harbor are the rusting, pitted hulks of merchant vessels destroyed by the fighting. Warehouses lining the port show the signs of heavy fighting, and fires burn unchecked in many areas of the docks. Railroad cars sit on their sidings, some apparently undamaged, others totally destroyed. Lookouts on the vessels fail to spot a single living being. In the predawn calm even the ever-present gulls do not disturb the quiet.

Although most of the sailors, Marines, and French legionnaires are unaware of it, the city is slowly succumbing to eight years of violence and civil war. In the heights above the city lies the Israeli army. Trapped within the city are the remnants of the PLO, which has harried Israel's border with Lebanon since the last invasion in 1978.

Three months earlier, in what many judged to be a repeat of the 1978 invasion, the tank columns of the IDF lunged across the Israeli-Lebanese frontier. Finding the forces of the PLO vulnerable and in disarray, the Israelis pursued their foes to the gates of the city. Once satisfied that the PLO had been run to ground in Beirut the IDF drove east of the mountains and hammered the regular forces of the Syrian army, arranging to seal off any escape by the PLO with the help of the Christian Phalangists who occupied the mountains north of the city.

For some three months the IDF had pounded their foes in Beirut with every weapon in their arsenal. To the east the Syrian army had been beaten back within its own borders and an uneasy cease-fire had taken hold. Israeli aircraft flew unimpeded above the city and selected their targets at will, attacking with virtual impunity.

Although badly beaten, the PLO remained a force to be reckoned with as long as it remained within Beirut. Battle-hardened Israeli commanders knew the cost of house-to-house fighting and preferred to stand off and let the air force and heavy guns batter the PLO while their infantry encircled the city and cut off its lifelines. Israeli engineers pumped mud into the gigantic pipes that delivered fresh water to the city, and the residents resorted to digging wells through the concrete of their sidewalks. Electrical power was also easily eliminated, and candles became scarce in Beirut as hospitals struggled to treat the wounded in operating theaters using emergency generators to power lights and machinery.

While a horrified world looked on the Israeli army slowly and effectively tightened its grip on the city. The PLO shifted its gun positions, placing them near hospitals, schools, and any other target that might facilitate gory pictures of maimed civilians should they be hit by errant Israeli bombs. Determined not to loosen its death grip, the IDF continued to shell Beirut, seemingly oblivious to the clamor of the world press for some form of mediated peace.

Amid the protestations of the United Nations the Israeli government finally conceded to allow the PLO to withdraw from the city. The Israelis insisted, however, that no heavy weapons be allowed to exit with the fighters, and that they be evacuated through the port of Beirut by non-Arab shipping.

Halfway around the world, the American secretary of state was by now virtually frantic to loosen the Israeli stranglehold on the Lebanese capital and quickly agreed to arrange the evacuation of the PLO. Neutral shipping for the evacuation of the Palestinians was arranged, and U.S. naval vessels routinely sent to the Mediterranean were ordered to land their Marines beside French legionnaires and safeguard the withdrawal of the PLO.

Within days U.S. Marines were standing beside their French counterparts in the Foreign Legion as thousands of PLO fighters boarded ships for destinations in North Africa. Although the Palestinians did not attempt to bring out their heavy weapons, American and French commanders were hopelessly outnumbered and planned a fighting withdrawal to their vessels in the harbor should hostilities have broken out. The PLO for its part seemed content to don new uniforms, arrive at the port in whatever semblance of order they could manage with their heavy weapons in tow, and fire their remaining ammunition into the air.

By week's end the PLO had abandoned the city amid the chaotic sounds of its ammunition arcing skyward and the cheers of the Lebanese civilians only too happy to endure this final danger to be rid of their uninvited guests. The PLO leadership, including Yasir Arafat, retired to Tripoli, Lebanon, some distance to the north.

The Americans and the French, having accomplished their task without the loss of a single life, were only too happy to quit the city and return to their vessels. As the fleet pulled away from the pier the IDF prepared to enter Beirut from the south as their Christian allies secured the port and harbor.

While the IDF slowly began to consolidate its positions in the city the Christian Phalange plotted its revenge against its old enemy, the PLO. The Phalangists had not forgotten the PLO alliance with the various Muslim factions that had sought to remove the Christians from power during the Lebanese civil war in 1975. Indeed, had it not been for the intercession of Syria, the PLO and its allies, the Lebanese Muslims might have virtually wiped out the Phalangists during the height of the fighting. As it stood, several Christian villages had been the focus of PLO massacres, most notably Damour, just south of Beirut.

The code of Lebanon now called for the Christians to exact their revenge. The massacres at Damour and the other villages had gone unanswered. Now that would be changed and the honor of the Christian fighters restored.

Young Israeli tankers stood helplessly by as vehicles bearing dozens of Christian Lebanese entered the Sabra and Shatilla refugee areas and the killing began. Those who understood Lebanon, and there were a few in the Israeli command who did, knew that this night would mark another chapter in the Lebanese tragedy. By morning hundreds lay dead and the stage had been set for the next round of fighting. Israeli troopers and commanders stared in horror at grinning Lebanese militiamen who left the camps smiling amid the carnage.

Within hours the story of what had taken place began to reach the world, and the United Nations once again publicly called on the IDF to withdraw from Lebanon. Behind the heavy mahogany doors of the security council chambers the American representative was asked to answer for the actions of the Israelis.

As the information began to filter back to the White House the National Security Council advised an aging American president to act in a decisive manner. The United States, they argued, would be held responsible for the actions of Israel to varying degrees by the rest of the world. In fact, the United States was the only country with any hope of exerting influence over the Israelis, whose army now sat astride the Lebanese capital and its warring factions. To avoid another bloodbath and possibly a broader Middle Eastern war, the United States would have to act quickly. The European dailies were already editorializing that the United States and France had assumed responsibility for the safety of the remaining Palestinians by entering the port two weeks earlier.

The president of the United States sat alone in the Oval Office looking at the first reports of the massacres as the U.S. representative to the UN Security Council assured its other members that the United States was prepared to act. Even now, he told them, an American and French fleet was headed toward Beirut, and within hours U.S. Marines would land to take up positions between the Israelis, the Christian militia, and the families of the Palestinians.

CHAPTER

$$1$$

G riffin groaned inwardly and leaned back on his pack. He scanned the patrol route associating map features with landmarks and road junctions as the staff sergeant continued to brief the squad. He mentally walked the eleven kilometers of the day's patrol and concluded that the fate of first squad could have been much worse. Not too many tight twisted streets or tall buildings that could block radio transmissions and isolate the sixteen-man patrol in a sea of hostile faces. He cursed silently over the fate that had made him part of this insignificant footnote in Marine Corps history, in a place he hadn't known existed only five months ago. The battalion had waded ashore in Beirut with an ill-defined mission that fell well short of Griffin's expectations.

It wasn't like the old man's war. No chance to be a real Marine and measure himself against a real enemy. Instead he was involved in a half-baked intervention as a "peacekeeper" in another squabble between the Arabs and Israelis. He wondered what his father would think of this, and gave an involuntary smile. At that moment, the staff sergeant asked if he had anything to add. Griffin exchanged glances with the older man and asked the squad radioman, "Is comm up?"

The Marine nodded that the radio was up and working and Griffin said, "We're ready then, Staff Sergeant Whitney." At twenty-five, Griffin regarded the staff sergeant as an old hand. Whitney had double Griffin's time in the ranks and it showed in the way he handled himself and the platoon. He noted that the staff sergeant quietly inspected each Marine, checking their weapons and equipment. Griffin liked the staff sergeant, he was the real thing. Two tours in Vietnam sufficed to earn him the respect of the Marines in his platoon, including Griffin. As the squad leader for first squad Griffin was directly subordinate to the staff sergeant. He had gotten to know him in the past months, and he respected the man for his quiet demeanor and professionalism.

Griffin ran a hand through his short cropped hair and gazed across the grassy field with its coils of razor wire separating the Marines from the village. He searched the muddy village for some sign that would alert him to danger. Seven years in the Marine Corps had hardened his body, and the past months in Beirut had served to make him wary. Easily the biggest man in the platoon, he worked constantly to maintain his physical edge. Griffin understood, intuitively, that physical strength is an inherent element of leadership in an infantry squad.

"Get 'em moving, Sergeant Griffin," said Whitney. "I'll be monitoring your radio traffic from the company head shed."

Griffin nodded and said, "Let me have the corporals. First squad, we move in five minutes. Lock and load on my command as we leave the company wire. Keep 'em apart out there. I want five paces separation all the time. Any questions?" said Griffin looking over the Marines that formed his squad.

Griffin didn't really expect any questions. In five months on the ground in Beirut the squad had mounted countless uneventful patrols. Endless walking past increasingly hostile faces. In the past two weeks he had noticed the obvious return of military-age men and adolescent boys to Hay-el-Salaam, as the section of Beirut near the Marines' firebase was called. At times these young Arabs would taunt the Marines with shouts of "Khomeini good!" and "Iran good!" Griffin longed to respond as he had been trained to do. Instead he stifled his own impulses and carried out the official policy of nonconfrontation with the locals, dutifully noting their hostile taunts and gestures in every patrol report.

The three corporals formed a loose semicircle in front of him and waited for him to speak. Contrary to his usual habit he lowered his voice, speaking so as not to be overheard. "Okay, this is the drill. Keep 'em alert. The staff sergeant says that the other two squads are reporting a lot of activity near the café at phase-line red, so let's be heads up out there. I don't want that passed around. Everybody is jumpy enough already, and I don't want anyone to lose it out there and lean on a trigger. Just stay awake and make sure your fireteams do the same. Any questions?"

"Yeah, it's getting late, let's get the hell out of here so we can make it back before dark," said Downs.

"That's not a question, Corporal Downs," snapped Griffin. "Get 'em ready to go, and make sure the Doc is in the middle of the squad." Griffin looked on as Downs and the other corporals walked off toward the squad in order to make their final preparations. Goddamn Downs, he thought, he should have been a lieutenant as much as he worries. Griffin watched as Downs inspected the other three members of his fireteam, then checked his own gear. With his blond hair, fair complexion, and easy manner, Downs was a curiosity among the dark-skinned Lebanese. Downs would be the first man in the patrol, followed by his fireteam, then the other two fireteams and the machine gunners, all of which composed the squad. Downs positioned himself at the head of the squad and scanned the buildings at the edge of the village through his binoculars. Griffin watched approvingly as Downs searched each window and doorway for movement or sign of an ambush. After concluding his search Downs caught Griffin's eye, pointed to the wire, and let the bolt go home on his rifle, signaling he was ready to step off. Griffin stood and said, "Let's do it, first squad." He joined the squad near its center as it shook itself out and moved to the wire. He gave the command to lock and load and noted that the bolt went home on each rifle, then asked the M-60 gunner if he was ready.

"Born ready," came the sarcastic reply from the squad's smallest man, nicknamed Tiger by the others as much for his flaming red hair as his small stature. Griffin watched as Tiger slung the heavy machine gun over one shoulder, adjusted the weapon on its sling, then checked to see that the ammunition was still in place and ready for use. After exiting the wire, the squad moved north along perimeter road, a dirt track circling the western boundary of the airport and marking the outer boundary of the Marine defenses. Following perimeter road to a point about midway along Bravo Company's section of the line the squad turned almost due east along a smaller road and headed into the village jokingly known as "Hooterville" among the Marines for the inhabitants' custom of sounding their horns before negotiating an intersection or corner. The road junction was covered by a .50 caliber machine gun, and this had been strengthened by the presence of a tank. The tank, though, as was often the case, had been withdrawn so as not to present a tempting target to an ambitious Arab armed with an RPG.

The squad moved past the gun emplacement and Griffin exchanged greetings with the gunner. Other members of the squad had nodded their hellos, but none had spoken. Griffin reserved that right for himself, feeling that any conversation by the squad only served to distract them.

The Marines headed toward checkpoint 35, a platoon position about three hundred meters east of perimeter road. Before reaching the position, Downs, the point man, peered around the corner of a building, assured himself that no ambush had been set, then stepped around the corner and into the street. Griffin watched as the slack man, MacCallum, a dark muscular boy, maintained his distance from the squad's point. Griffin wanted to assure himself that MacCallum didn't hurry to regain visual contact with the point, and thereby set off a chain reaction that would put the whole squad in motion to maintain tactical dispersion. As the squad in front of him disappeared around the corner man by man, Griffin felt his stomach tighten. No place for an ambush, he thought. He hated having Downs and MacCallum out on point. Although both of them were good Marines, he knew that it was wrong to have one of his corporals walking point. It should have been a senior lance corporal, or even better, one of the more expendable privates. For all the necessity of having a skilled point man he was most often the first man down in a house-to-house situation. Griffin knew that his younger Marines lacked the survival instincts of Downs, and he trusted that MacCallum, Downs's inseparable companion, would do his utmost to extricate his friend in the event of an ambush.

Rounding the corner Griffin signaled to the radioman and said, "Phase-line green." The man called in the squad's position to the company headquarters. The patrol would be plotted on the company situation map by the company clerks, while radiomen relayed the position of the squad to the higher headquarters at battalion. At battalion the procedure would be repeated, and react forces would be standing by in the event of trouble. All of this was little comfort to Griffin who knew that a well-placed ambush could cripple the squad in seconds.

The Marines rounded the corner and left the protective cover of the checkpoint and Griffin felt the hot angry stares. A few months earlier it had all been very different. The locals had been grateful to the Marines for interposing themselves between the warring factions and the Israeli invaders. The Marines had arrived and the fighting had stopped, or at least moved to other areas.

Griffin thought of all this as his eyes constantly searched the maze of buildings the squad was moving past. No building stood without some form of battle damage, and many of these appeared to be little more than rubble held together by a connective skein of mortar. None of the windows had glass, and the shadowed interiors presented perfect cover for a sniper or enemy squad. Hooterville appeared to the Marines as some sort of real-life recreation of World War II Europe, complete with bombed-out buildings and rubble-strewn streets. The only thing missing from the picture were the hordes of grateful civilians waiting to be liberated.

Griffin's eye left the buildings and ran over the men in front of him. He saw Downs nod and speak to an old woman standing in her doorway. Of all the members of the squad only Downs had managed to pick up a few words of Arabic. Griffin knew that Downs now spoke enough to carry on rudimentary conversations, and could make simple inquiries if it was required. His hand went to the small PRC-68 radio in the top right pocket of his flak jacket, used for intrasquad communication by the four NCOs, and he said, "Corporal Downs, keep your mouth shut."

"Roger that," Downs laughed back. Although Downs had been with the squad over two years he remained something of an enigma to Griffin. Downs had the combination of education, looks, and probably family that spelled success on the outside. For Griffin, joining the Marine Corps had been the natural thing to do after graduating from high school. He hadn't wanted to join the union like his father and brothers, and college hadn't really been a possibility. Something about the Marine Corps had appealed to him for as long as he could remember. On his eighteenth birthday he had gone into the recruiting office and signed the papers while his father waited outside. Griffin had never even spoken to any of the recruiters from the other services. In his mind it had been the Marines or nothing.

Downs appeared to him as more the college type. His speech and manners were different from the other members of the squad, and at times Downs struck Griffin as a little too refined for the infantry. Griffin suspected that there was some personal reason why Downs had chosen the Marines over college, but that wasn't so unusual. Although Downs interested him more than most, and had earned Griffin's grudging respect, he kept his own counsel, and Griffin knew little of his life prior to the Marine Corps. Even more intriguing to Griffin was Downs's obvious ability to handle himself in a fight. Downs had never hesitated to challenge any member of the platoon physically, once even Griffin himself. Griffin had beaten him soundly, but Downs had remained quietly defiant and never made any move toward a personal reconciliation. The two eventually reached an agreeable peace, but it was on a plane closer to equality than Griffin would have preferred. Griffin knew that no infantry squad has room for more than one leader, and only Downs's instinctive longing for solitude allowed him to remain in Griffin's squad.

The Marines wound through the warren of streets that comprised their patrol route encountering a variety of reactions from the local inhabitants. The battalion had been in Beirut long enough for the novelty of their presence to have worn off, and the majority of the Shiite residents gave them only passing notice. An exception to this were the young boys who, although at first fascinated by the Marines, were now beginning to test them. A favorite game among these boys was to allow a heavily armed patrol to walk by while the boys waved or saluted. Once half the patrol had moved past, the bravest among them would toss an empty can into the path of the patrol. The usual reaction was a shout of "Grenade!" and the whole squad would go to ground before the can had finished its hollow roll into the street. Once the ruse had been played out the patrol was subjected to the laughter of the boys, who instantly disappeared down an endless maze of narrow alleys.

Lately however, a new and maddening twist had been added to the game. The can would be filled with dirt or sand to lend a more authentic sound when it struck the surface of the dirt street. Even more frustrating for the Marines was the deliberate attempt to play this drama out in front of the bemused eyes of the boys' older brothers who had returned to the village after their safety was guaranteed by the presence of the Marines. As they rose from the dirt where they had taken cover the Marines felt the laughter of the young men, and their resentment burned inside them. Griffin knew that his squad was coiled and ready to respond to the taunts, and any signal from him, no matter how slight or indirect, would unleash five months of frustration and anger.

He moved to the center of the narrow dirt track to more clearly observe the movement of the squad down this section of road. The Marines were correctly spaced five yards apart and walking on alternating sides of the street. The progress of the squad was slowed by the fact that only a narrow single lane was left to allow for the passage of traffic in the street, with cars parked haphazardly on either side. Pedestrian traffic moved down both sides of the street as best it could. In some spots a narrow, yard-wide sidewalk existed, but was broken by storefronts and porches of the one- or two-story buildings that lined both sides of the street. Shiite women and children moved in and out of the Marines' path, and all manner of business was conducted from the open storefronts as the patrol moved past.

From his vantage point in the center of the roadway, Griffin was able to observe the whole squad as it wove its way down this fairly straight length of road. He looked forward first, noting Downs some twenty-five meters ahead of him and hugging the left side of the street. As he turned to observe the rear of the squad, Griffin removed his helmet and wiped his forehead with a sleeve, motioning Tiger out into the street and around a parked car. As he put the helmet back on, he automatically canted his head rearward to settle the webbing into place. Griffin saw an arm, silhouetted against the sky, appear from behind the facade of the building to his rear. As the hand opened and the grenade sailed clear Griffin drew breath for the warning shout and gathered himself for the lifesaving leap back to the side of the road. He knew instinctively that this grenade would not be a prank. Even had he not felt it viscerally, his eye had detected the small trail of heavy black smoke that hung in the air as the grenade arced to the road below, and his ears discerned the faint hissing of the fuse burning.

The grenade bounced once after hitting the packed earth of the roadway, then detonated. Griffin's warning had served to give sufficient time for Tiger to throw himself over the hood of the car he had been moving past, but he was well within the five- to six-yard killing radius of the grenade.

As he jumped onto the hood of the car Tiger rolled away from the blast, exposing as little of his body as possible to the effects of the explosion. Even before Griffin had signaled, Tiger had followed his eyes and seen the expression on his face and correctly guessed what was to follow. Shrapnel from the grenade peppered Tiger's flak jacket, buttocks, and the rear of his legs as the blast lifted him off the hood of the car and threw him against the wall of a nearby building. The brunt of his impact against the wall was absorbed by his knees and the M-60 machine gun that he cradled across his chest. He came to rest at the bottom of the wall in the fetal position he had assumed on the hood of the car.

D'Amico, a hulking heavily muscled rifleman appropriately nicknamed "Samson" by his fellow Marines, was walking just ahead of Griffin as the grenade took its short, deadly bounce. A long nail-like splinter had entered the sole of his boot, pierced the foot, and exited the top of the boot only to reenter his leg at a point just below the knee.

As he gave the warning, Griffin had wheeled on his right foot, taken one step, and lunged over the trunk of the car closest to him. He had just clambered across the trunk and plunged headfirst to the ground below when the explosion rocked him. His head rung from the concussion and the acrid smoke burned his nostrils. The explosion had been so close that Griffin could taste the acid bitter air in his mouth and feel the heat from the blast. Even before his head cleared he was conscious of the prostrate form of Tiger, crumpled against the wall behind him. Without thinking he yelled "Corpsman up!" The call was immediately echoed down the length of the squad by others who had been farther from the point of detonation.

Good, thought Griffin, not more than one or two men down and everybody is functioning. As he moved toward Tiger in a low, crablike motion Griffin gave the commands that would set the squad in motion. "Fix bayonets!" he screamed. "By the numbers!" Griffin knew that in the confined spaces the squad was now in a bayonet could be a deadly weapon. He also hoped to avoid the squad's instinctive reaction to spray the area with automatic fire. This would not only waste valuable ammunition, it would doubtlessly result in the meaningless death of civilians.

Just as they had rehearsed it a thousand times the squad now set about fixing their bayonets "by the numbers." This involved one predesignated man from each of the squad's three four-man fireteams attaching his bayonet while the others held their position. The tactic was designed to prevent the whole squad from lowering their weapons simultaneously while the six-inch blades were fastened to their rifles.

Although he already felt that the grenade had been thrown by an individual who had then fled, Griffin knew the squad would have to remain in place while the casualties were checked and radio contact was made with the company.

"Rifleman, cover the rooftops!" he ordered. Again Griffin's command was picked up and echoed down the squad. The one designated rifleman in each fireteam now scanned the roofs while the other members searched windows, doors, and alleys for signs of movement.

Griffin rolled Tiger away from the wall, noting the dark blotches of blood spotting the back of his camouflage trousers but correctly judging them not to be serious. As the navy corpsman scurried up, he knelt beside the inert Tiger and asked, "How's it look?"

"Dunno," answered Griffin, "check him for concussion."

"You got it, Sarge," said the corpsman. Griffin acknowledged the corpsman with a grunt and resisted the instinctive temptation to remind him that "Sarge" was not a term applied to sergeants in the Marine Corps. As he turned away from Tiger he heard the diminutive machine gunner curse and ask, "Doc?"

"Yeah, Tiger. It's me, the Doc. Be quiet a minute, okay?"

"All right, but don't touch me. My mother told me when I signed up that all sailors are queer."

Griffin moved toward the front of the car to decide what his next move would be. "Samson?" he asked.

"Yeah, Sergeant Griffin. That little bitch got me. I'm okay though."

"Doc," said Griffin as he continued to check the position of the squad, "Samson is next."

"Roger that, Sarge," came the reply.

Griffin stifled a curse as another Marine begin to wrap a pressure bandage around Samson's calf. Griffin looked on angrily and asked, "Can you walk on that, Samson?"

Samson glanced at him and answered, "I don't know. I think so." Griffin noted the last announcement with some concern. Samson's position had been very carefully arranged within the squad. Being large, well muscled, and uncomplaining, Griffin had deliberately saddled him with extra ammunition for Tiger's M-60 and positioned him just ahead of the gun. Now Griffin confronted the possibility that Samson's ammo would have to be given to another Marine. Not very serious in and of itself. But if Samson couldn't walk then the heaviest man in the squad, other than Griffin himself, was going to have to be carried out. That would require two men at worst, none if he could walk out. With a total force of only fifteen Marines and one navy corpsman Samson was destined to become walking wounded if at all possible. As the corpsman darted across the road to check Samson, Griffin flinched as another call of "Corpsman up!" rang out. He turned to face the direction of the call and asked, "Who now?"

"It's not one of ours, Sergeant Griffin. There's a kid under the car behind Tiger, and she ain't moving. I just noticed her," said Samson.

"Okay," said Griffin, "Tiger, hold your position." He circled the car, moving past Tiger and along the wall, noting that Tiger appeared to be okay. Without allowing himself to look down, Griffin knelt beside the car and attempted to locate the child by touch alone. Samson, just to the rear of Griffin, looked over and attempted to give aid. "She's on the other side, closer to the street," said the big Marine.

Griffin circled the car, gave the small body a quick visual inspection and reached under the car to grab an arm and pull her out. To his astonishment the child inched away from him, seeking refuge farther under the car. Griffin noted the alert, frightened look in the child's eyes then lunged under the car, catching her by an ankle, and unceremoniously dragged her out.

Griffin held the child as the Doc scuttled over. He listened as the corpsman gave the status of Tiger and Samson. "Tiger is okay, but he's got some shrapnel in his legs and ass. No concussion as far as I can tell. A real doctor will have to look at him once we make it back to the battalion. Samson's foot is fucked up, and I'm afraid to take the boot off to look at it. It will probably swell and we won't be able to get it back on."

Griffin nodded as the corpsman then turned his attention to the child. He peered at the squad sprawled along the narrow street and realized again the vulnerability of remaining where they were. "Samson! Give your ammo to somebody else. You're walking out of here. Got that?"

"Yeah," said the big Marine. Griffin hoped that by letting Samson know he was expected to carry on he wouldn't ask for any assistance. He also made a mental note to observe Samson once the patrol moved out and consider giving him some help before allowing him to slow the patrol too much. Griffin glanced over at the corpsman and asked, "Doc, what's the story on the kid?"

"She's okay. Scared shitless, but then ain't we all?"

Griffin ignored the sarcastic jibe and asked, "Doc, did you see where this kid came from?" An incredulous "shit" was his only answer. Griffin turned and looked down the length of the street, noting the closed doors and shuttered windows, as if expecting to see an aproned mother holding her arms out to the child. Seeing nothing more than closed doors and half the squad nervously scanning every building, Griffin knew he had to do something. The thought occurred to him that the squad had been motionless now for almost five minutes, plenty of time for an unseen enemy to arrange another ambush, or complete this one.

He looked at the frightened child. She was perhaps six years old, with curly black hair and big dark eyes set in a round face. Silent tears ran down either cheek as she attempted to press farther into the back bumper and trunk of the car they sheltered behind. Griffin remembered the lack of struggle once he had grasped the slim brown ankle. It wasn't that she was frightened, it was more a quiet resignation on the part of the little girl, as though she had sensed her inability to decide her own fate. The child's complete lack of expression and listless crying also disturbed him. Griffin noticed that one hand held a round foil-covered disc, containing the waxy chocolate that was standard fare among the combat rations of the Marines. Fucking Downs no doubt, he thought. He had probably seen the little girl as the patrol passed and given her the candy when he should have had his mind on his business. He made another mental note to speak to Downs about it, then said quietly to the corpsman, "Okay, Doc, we're gonna put the kid in that house," nodding to indicate an ancient faded blue wooden door. "Follow me."

Griffin opened the door and he took a quick look inside. Seeing no one, he motioned the Doc up, who then deposited the silent child in the room. She continued to stand where the corpsman had left her and stare after them as Griffin reached in and closed the door. His last image of the child was one of her standing immobile and doll-like on the stone floor of the empty room, arms at her sides as her eyes followed him out of the room before the door cut her stare.

The Doc moved off to resume his position in the squad as Griffin fingered the radio in his pocket. "Downs!"

"Yeah."

"We gotta get the fuck out of here. You ready?"

"We're set. Mac's got the map out and it shows an open field about two clicks from here big enough for an LZ if we need one, but we have to leave the patrol route. Anybody down bad?"

"Maybe," answered Griffin. "Samson's foot is fucked up, but he should be able to make it eight or nine clicks back to the wire. We can't get the company up on the radio. How does the route look to this LZ?"

"Okay, I guess. Map shows a built-up area. Same shit we're in now."

"All right, give me the grid, then get ready to move." As Downs read off an eight-digit grid coordinate Griffin plotted the position on his laminated map and marked it with a small black circle. He made a mental note of the sparse map features so as to have an idea of the squad's position as it moved. He was also aware of the effects the Israeli invasion had had upon the village. What appeared as a village or town on the map often turned out to be little more than mounds of rubble. Even worse, the maps were so old that often what was marked as clear areas on the map had since become a small village, or an extension of a larger one. The best "maps" available to the Marines were actual aerial photographs taken by reconnaissance aircraft then superimposed with grid lines. Although awkward, they provided up-to-date information not available on maps issued to the squad leaders. For reasons incomprehensible to Griffin and his peers, these photos had become the prized possessions of the lieutenants who invariably chose not to accompany their squads on the long, hot, usually monotonous patrols.

The Marines picked themselves up and moved off, and Griffin recalled the complete absence of civilians on the street prior to the grenade's explosion. He made a mental note to check with his corporals to see if any of them had seen anything that could be interpreted as a prearranged signal for the locals to clear the street.

Griffin's biggest concern by far was his lack of radio contact with the company. Even under the best of conditions the PRC-77 radio carried by the squad was of doubtful quality. Until the squad moved into an area clear of buildings tall enough to block transmission they were out of touch with the company, and any chance for timely relief if they needed it. Once contact was reestablished the resources of the battalion could be mobilized to lend whatever assistance was necessary.

Griffin grimaced as he thought of the reaction of his superiors to the attack. They would no doubt blow the whole incident out of proportion, he was sure. He was also sure that a reaction force would be sent to relieve the squad and bring it safely back to the Marine perimeter.

Griffin found the prospect of this type of "relief" humiliating and therefore dreaded the moment when contact would be reestablished with battalion. The patrol had left the wire under its own steam and, even taking Samson into account, it was fully capable of returning without assistance.

Seven years ago when Griffin had gone to Parris Island for boot camp, the Marine Corps had been a different animal—leaner, harder, less a place of refuge and more a home for the capable who chose its Spartan lifestyle. Staff NCOs and officers who hadn't proven themselves in the steaming jungles of Vietnam had quietly left or been relegated to out-of-the-way units in the air wing. Griffin and his peers had been trained by men who didn't need to rely on worn phrases emphasizing their ability to impart lessons that could "save your life one day." Their lessons had been brought home with a quick, sharp blow to the solar plexus, or worse, a contemptuous stare. Their credentials came from nameless battles and lesser firefights in Vietnam. Griffin knew that the officers who now awaited his contact report at the battalion command and control center were, for the most part, too junior to have seen action in the Vietnam War. He resented what he felt would be their unwarranted intrusion upon the conduct of his patrol, and it awakened the frustration and anger that lay buried deep beneath his professional demeanor.

The patrol swung west, heading for the spot selected by Downs and MacCallum, clearing the buildings that had been blocking radio contact. Griffin listened in silence as the radioman read off the contact report including the number and severity of casualties. Almost immediately the battalion operations officer's voice crackled over the speaker and ordered that the patrol's "actual," or ranking NCO, be put on the radio. As Griffin took the handset from the man he chafed at the breach of procedure. In theory something as small as this ambush should be handled by the officers at company level, with the information and relevant requests for reaction forces being relayed to the battalion operations center. As Griffin had anticipated, with the first word of the ambush arriving at battalion, all thought of proper procedure so rigorously insisted upon by the battalion officers at other times had been abandoned. Instead, a rush to be a part of the action was made by each officer then manning the battalion combat operations center. The net result was the abandonment of the chain of command and established procedures for the flow of information from the unit making contact to its parent unit. Griffin's company commander, known to his troops as "Captain Rock" due to a rather prominent jawline, now listened to Griffin relay an incredibly expanded version of the initial report directly to the battalion operations officer.

Normally such information would have been passed by radio operators with the rank of private first class or lance corporal. As Griffin wound up his version of the contact report he informed the operations officer that the patrol was now heading for a possible LZ, and gave the locating grid coordinate.

The voice of the officer shot back over the radio ordering Griffin not to leave the designated patrol route. Griffin sighed and avoided making eye contact with the radioman, although the two were physically linked by the pigtailed cord of the radio handset. Although he appreciated the conventional wisdom of not leaving the patrol route and thereby avoiding the possibility of the patrol being "lost" to battalion, he had resigned himself to the inevitability of relief by the react force. Accepting this, he and Downs had figured the easiest and least complicated means of extract for the patrol. The LZ selected would facilitate removal of the wounded by helicopter while not taking the squad too far out of the way. Griffin and Downs were also familiar enough with Hooterville to know that the area chosen could be fairly easily defended if that became a necessity.

As these thoughts raced through his head the tinny voice of the operations officer again came over the radio. Griffin was given the grid for another LZ selected by the officer and told to proceed there with all possible speed. As he gave the handset back to the smirking radioman he avoided the temptation to voice his opinion of the battalion's officers in general, and of the operations officer in particular.

Griffin was well acquainted with the inequities of the system in the Marine Corps. He had lived with the disparity between the ranks and the staff NCOs and officer corps for years. He accepted the system because he knew it was necessary, and because it worked. Griffin also knew, from prior experience, that the operations officer would have the last word, and that he had no choice but to obey the order. He was silently amused that in the compressed atmosphere of Beirut the operations officer, with the rank of major, would make decisions that would otherwise be made by corporals and sergeants.

Griffin's amusement faded into resentment as he gave Downs the new grid. Every Marine in the squad knew the operations officer had ordered the change to demonstrate his own abilities to handle a crisis. Only Griffin and Downs viewed it as a personal insult.

CHAPTER

2

"Hey GI, you want boom-boom maybe?" piped MacCallum as he jumped heavily into the bunker occupied by Smith, Ferris, and Downs. He was greeted by a flurry of obscene gestures and vulgar suggestions. "Does that mean no?" he asked innocently.

"Eat shit and die, asshole. How are Samson and the other fallen heroes?" asked Downs.

"Doc says they'll live, but Samson has been flown out to the *Iwo Jima* so the real doctors can peep out his foot. How else are they gonna get their Navy Achievement Medals?"

"Jesus, Mac, you're a salty bastard. You been hanging around that boot Downs too much," said Smith.

"My protégé," chimed in Downs, "so when will we see those other skates, Mac?"

"Company gunny says they'll all be back tomorrow. But we're not due for another patrol until Saturday. So I guess we got tomorrow off." All the Marines looked at each other, then burst into laughter.

"Shee-it! With that sandbag-happy bastard we got for a first shirt, I'd rather make a patrol, even if I have to volunteer for it," Ferris said, shaking his head in amazement and contemplating Mac's optimism. "Man, we haven't seen a day off since Christ was a corporal, Mac. I'm not even sure they really exist anymore."

"Yeah, they exist alright," added Downs, "but only for those with the rank of Staff NCO and above."

"What exists for Staff NCOs and officers?" asked Griffin, as he appeared in the narrow sandbagged entry to the bunker.

"A day of rest and recreation for us, Sergeant Griffin," Mac said. "I asked the company gunny what the patrol schedule was and he said the poop at the head shed is first platoon has tomorrow off. Sort of a mini liberty call, Beirut style."

Griffin shared a conspiratorial grin with Ferris before addressing the group further. "Well, I hate to interrupt your liberty run, Mac, but the first shirt has arranged a little party for us tomorrow. And the last time I checked the chain of command, the first shirt was still in charge of the company, Staff Sergeant Whitney was still in charge of the platoon, and I'm still in charge of first squad. The company gunny will take whoever he needs from first platoon to fill sandbags, but our squad has drawn the listening post for tonight. Corporal Downs, your team is going out. Have them ready by nineteen-thirty tonight. See me about comm gear, flares, and anything else you think you'll need. We'll go over the set up a little later."

Downs acknowledged Griffin with a nod and withdrew from the conversation to think about the night's assignment. Although initially flattered that Griffin had selected his fireteam for the listening post, he couldn't be sure it was not due to the fact that Griffin wanted to spare his senior corporals the monotony of a night spent on an LP.

Downs silently considered the wisdom of a listening post. The strategy was to place a four-man fireteam a short distance in front of the company's night defensive perimeter. The purpose was to provide the company with advance warning of an enemy attack, with the listening post directing supporting arms onto the intruders if possible. Downs judged the reasoning sound, but the assignment itself difficult and possibly extremely dangerous. Although he didn't really expect any trouble from the villagers, or even the various militia, Downs hated having his fireteam positioned directly in front of their own perimeter. If the company came under attack its outgoing fire would be aimed primarily in his direction.

Forty-five minutes after exiting the company perimeter under the watchful eyes of Griffin, Downs had selected a spot he felt reasonably secure, below the company's line of fire, and settled the team. He made the required comm check with the company command post and mentally prepared for a long night. Speaking in the lowest possible whisper he leaned toward the other three Marines and said, "Everyone awake until midnight, then Mac and I will take the first two-hour shift. We'll alternate that way until dawn." As soon as he had finished he felt foolish. He had gone over the conduct of the watches before leaving the wire, and no further explanation was needed, especially here when the slightest sound could betray their position.

Downs flattened himself against the ground and faced the village some four hundred yards to the east. He noted with approval the actions of the three others. All of them had pressed themselves into the hard-baked earth and sparse knee-high grass. Anyone passing within six feet of them would probably walk past without being aware of their presence.

He turned to his left and nodded slightly to Mac, less than a yard away, sprawled comfortably on the ground, rifle across his forearms. Mac smiled back, but Downs could only make out the whites of his teeth and eyes. The rest of him appeared only as an indistinct dark silhouette, somehow more dense than the shadows forming the background. To Downs's right sat Ferris, then Smith. Ferris caught his eye and gave a slight thumbs-up motion. Downs acknowledged it with a nod, and had to make an effort not to smile. The other two members of the four-man fireteam were lean, good-natured cousins from Georgia. They had enlisted almost three years before on what the Marine Corps referred to as the "buddy plan," a recruiting gimmick designed to allow buddies to stick together throughout their first tour of duty.

Downs allowed himself a grin as he contemplated Ferris and Smith. The two of them seemed to accept whatever conditions they found themselves in without complaint. They didn't question the reasons for the Marine Corps' involvement, and hence their own, in Lebanon. They simply did what they could to accomplish the task at hand without serious questioning or contemplation.

In both demeanor and looks the cousins were a great deal alike. Each of them was well over six feet tall and more than once on a battalion forced march Downs had envied them their ground-eating stride. No amount of hardship ever outwardly affected the two, and even in the worst of circumstances Downs had listened as they laughed over some shared experience from their childhood in Georgia. Both of them had been Marines longer than Downs, and he had thought this might be a source of resentment when he had been promoted to corporal over them. Instead, both Ferris and Smith had congratulated him, chiding him about being a "boot" corporal at length.

The four remained on an informal first name basis that Downs knew grated Griffin. He and Mac had come through boot camp and Infantry Training Regiment together, and Mac remained his only confidant in the squad. Downs looked again at Mac, noting that Mac was facing away from him, scanning the village for signs of movement, listening for sounds that might mean someone from the village was approaching. With his soft-spoken manner Downs knew that Mac would leave the Marine Corps without ever becoming an NCO. He was a quiet boy who had joined to prove something to himself, and Downs understood that his friend, although proud of being a Marine, would leave upon completing his enlistment.

Downs realized that he knew the members of his fireteam better than boys he had grown up with, or even his own brothers. He knew that if he were to leave this minute and not see them again for years, he would still recognize their silhouettes in the dark, or the rhythm of their steps in a quiet hallway. As the darkness crowded around them, Downs felt the village quiet down for the night. Engine noises from cars gradually ceased, and the murmur of voices died away. The only noise beyond the usual night sounds was the soft click of Mac pressing the transmit button on the radio receiver to make his periodic check with the company.

At 0200 Downs woke Ferris and passed the radio to him. After allowing a few minutes for Ferris and Smith to become fully alert, he began to relax. He felt sleep coming on as Ferris whispered his first comm check. Downs rolled onto his back and gazed at the stars, comforted by the steady breathing of Mac. As he retreated into his own thoughts he remained alert to the sounds and smells around him, but his mind drifted to another place.

He allowed himself only a few minutes each day to think of her, always hating himself for it. He husbanded these moments carefully, his mind playing back scenes of her. He needed the comfort these images provided, resenting himself for being weak and needing her. Lying there on his back, his eyes no longer focused, he saw only her. Every detail of her came back to him, her scent, the clothes she wore, the slightly crooked smile, her frailties, the grace of her movements. The daydream absorbed him and for a few minutes he was a different

Downs, unencumbered by the heavy boots, flak jacket, and rifle. His own callousness, discovered at Parris Island, melted away. He no longer felt the need for the ordered existence the Marines so readily provided. She smiled her mysterious smile and he smiled back.

They had spent the summer before he left for the Marine Corps together. He had known her his entire life, and for as far back as either of them could remember they had shared a silent understanding. They had never actually had a first date, they had merely remained together as they grew up, their shared childhood merging slowly into something different. Nothing could have been more natural. She had always been a part of his day, and a part of his thoughts.

Downs blinked as a familiar sound registered vaguely in his brain. Familiar and nonthreatening, but alarmingly loud in the stillness of the night. She disappeared and Lebanon returned with a rush. Downs heard a low chuckle from the direction of Ferris and Smith and concluded that the noise had been that of air rushing into the vacuum of a soda can. Before he could realize his worst suspicions, the unmistakable smell of warm beer reached him. Muttering a low "shit" he glared at the spot in the darkness where he imagined Ferris to be. "I can't fucking believe you two! Now pour that shit out! Jesus fucking Christ!" he said in a harsh whisper. Ferris smiled into the darkness, took a gigantic swallow of warm beer, and belched. Smith chuckled and Downs swore, "Pour the shit out now!" he said.

"Relax, Steve. It's just a beer, man," drawled Ferris.

"I don't give a flying shit. Pour it out, man. I don't need this bullshit, and since when do you bring fucking beer on post, you asshole?"

"Christ, Steve, it's just my lousy ration of beer, man. I ain't drunk and the Lesbos are all crashed for the night." Ferris's voice reached Downs, low and husky, but with a chiding quality that wasn't lost on him. He knew that he was being tested by the cousins who had more time in the Marine Corps than he did. He also knew that one beer each wouldn't affect the performance of Ferris or Smith, and both of them considered the whole idea of an LP asinine and useless. To their minds they were simply making the best of a bad situation. Downs restrained a sigh of relief as he heard the remainder of the beer gurgle out of the can and onto the ground. "Thanks, asshole," he muttered.

"No problem, Corporal Downs," came the sarcastic reply from Ferris, "although I do hate to waste perfectly good beer." For the remainder of the night Downs fumed in silence. Although he knew that Ferris had intended no harm he was furious that he had brought beer on post. He was also resentful of being placed in the dilemma of what to do about the whole matter. To do nothing might only encourage the cousins to pull similar stunts in the future. If he chose to report the incident to Sergeant Griffin he was relieved of the responsibility but probably at the cost of harmony within his team. Downs also knew that Ferris and Smith felt a bond of kinship, a fraternal affection formed during long forced marches and shared hardships. He hated to betray that bond by reporting them to Griffin. The easiest thing to do would be to assign them some sort of extra duty, but that couldn't be done without attracting the attention of Griffin. As dawn broke Downs was still undecided as to just what action to take.

The team made radio contact with Griffin who met them at a predesignated spot in the company wire. As the four filed past, Griffin attempted to catch Downs's eye and ask how things had gone. "Boring," was the only reply from Downs, who carefully avoided looking into Griffin's face. Griffin was quick to catch the unsure tone in Downs's voice as well as the hasty exchange of glances between Downs and Ferris. As the other three moved off to drop their gear and find a few hours sleep Downs felt Griffin bearing down on him. "What happened out there that I should know about, Corporal Downs?" asked Griffin.

Downs noted the almost conciliatory tone in Griffin's voice. He hesitated before answering, still unsure of the proper role for himself. "Nothing. The usual boring LP shit," he answered. Downs moved to the faucets at the front of a five hundred-gallon water bull and began to draw a helmet full of tepid water. He splashed his face from the half full helmet, feeling a layer of grit and oil dissolve beneath his grimy hands. The water ran down his neck and dribbled into the steamy green T-shirt under his camouflage blouse and flak jacket.

"Look, Downs," began Griffin, "you're gonna have to do better than that. Something here is fucked up and I want to know what it is."

"I can handle this, Sergeant Griffin. Isn't that the idea behind my promotion to corporal?"

"That's for me to decide. Now give me the breakdown on what went on out there. If I think it's better left to you, then fine, you get to handle it. If not, just remember that your team, including you, is part of my squad."

Downs continued to splash his face, feeling the stubble of beard and the clamminess of his T-shirt. The words came out with a rush, not really a conscious decision, and Downs struggled to retain an emotion-less quality to his voice. "Ferris and Smith brought a beer out on post. I heard 'em open it, but I made 'em pour it out. No big deal. You know those two, they just wanted to fuck with the boot corporal. Good ole boy shit."

"They did what?" asked an incredulous Griffin. Downs bent to cup one hand under the faucet and drank. As the water began to splash into the gritty muck below he shot a smile at Griffin and laughed, "Yeah, guess the boys from Gawgh-ah figured it was Miller time," said Downs imitating the drawl of the two cousins. "It was just the one beer."

"I'll give them fucking Miller time," said Griffin. "You go find those shit birds and tell them I said come see me. Jesus fucking Christ, Downs, what the hell was going on out there?"

"C'mon, Sergeant Griffin. You know those two. Why don't you just let me take care of this? No real harm was done. It's just their way of testing me. You know, boot corporal tryouts. I need to handle this, not you. If you do it they'll just think it's because I couldn't handle it."

"Bullshit, Downs. Both of them know this is carrying it too far. I oughta go to the platoon sergeant with this. Goddamn it! He'd bust both of them back to private and he'd be right. You just go tell those two to come see me, and you make sure you're with them. Got that?"

"Yeah, I got it, but I still don't think it's the right decision." Downs slapped his helmet liner into the steel helmet and filled a canteen, debating whether or not to pursue the question further with Griffin, but still not looking at him. He didn't know Griffin well enough to decide if he was really angry or just doing what he saw as the right thing. Downs turned to go back toward the squad's tent and find Ferris and Smith, almost colliding with the company first sergeant. A feeling of liquid electricity moved through Downs's stomach as the first sergeant stood glaring at him, hands on his hips, "Corporal Downs, collect your fireteam and be in my office in five minutes. You can expect to go up on charges, mister."

Downs returned the contemptuous stare of the first sergeant, not trying to mask his own anger and said evenly, "Aye, aye, First Sergeant." Without further comment the first sergeant spun on one highly polished boot heel and strode off, his back ramrod straight in a freshly starched set of camouflage utilities. As Griffin nudged past Downs he said under his breath, "Air wing motherfucker." Downs almost smiled.

CHAPTER

3

S hit, Steve, I knew the Rock Man wouldn't do us in. Me and Jimmy been in the company since before he was. Anyway, he knew we was just havin' a little fun out there.'' Downs shot an exasperated glance at Smith, who continued to shovel sand into the mouth of the bag being held open by Ferris. "Yeah, ol' Captain Ward was gonna let us go with just the loss of pay if it wasn't for the first shirt. He's the one seen to it we got all this extra duty. Rock Man knows we can't spend any money out here anyway. Shit, Jimmy, you remember the first shirt's face? He was so mad he almost spit on the Rock Man!''

At this both cousins chuckled and Ferris screwed his face into a grimace and imitated the first sergeant, "Captain, I insist these men be given extra duty at my discretion!'' Ferris and Smith burst into uncontrolled laughter and Downs tried not to smile before adding, "He did look just a bit disappointed, didn't he?'' All three of them again laughed and Downs wondered silently at the ability of the other two to find humor in an incident he could only view as humiliating.

They returned to filling the bag as Mac ambled up, smiling broadly. "You boys sure are one happy-extra-duty-sandbag-filling work party. I'd like to help, but I'm not sure the first sergeant would appreciate my efforts.''

"Aw, c'mon on over and lend a hand, Mac,'' drawled Ferris. "We're all just one big happy family. First sergeant knows that.''

Ferris grinned at Smith, who winked and added, "Yeah, ain't there something on our Band of Brothers cards about always rendering assistance to fellow Marines? I bet the first shirt would understand. Hell, he might even help us himself if ol' Corporal Downs was to explain it to him that way. You know, us being a Band of Brothers and all."

"Yeah, I just bet he would," answered Downs as he took the canteen proffered by Mac, passing the other to Smith. As he drank, Downs thought about the Band of Brothers card jokingly referred to by Smith. The card listed a code of honor for all Marines, printed on a small yellow wallet size card and emblazoned back and front with the Marine Corps emblem. The cards, and slogan, had suddenly appeared around the division when Downs was a private, undoubtedly the brainchild of some public affairs officer. Both had been heartily embraced by the division commander, an old Marine risen from the ranks who sought some means of closing the gap between his young troops and his too often arrogant officers. He had quickly issued an order making the card a uniform item, requiring individual Marines to carry it on their person at all times. The first sergeant was fond of stopping Marines in the company and ordering them to produce their cards. He had even gone so far as to have the company clerks laminate one card for every man in the unit, thus assuring the cards unmarred survival in the wallets of the Marines. Downs snorted and mumbled to himself, "Sort of like a Marine Corps Ten Commandments."

"What's that, Steve?" asked Mac.

"I was just saying those Band of Brothers cards are just like a Marine Corps version of the Ten Commandments."

"Oh. I guess so," smiled Mac, not really knowing if Downs was being sarcastic. "Anyway, I came over to tell you there is a company formation at sixteen-hundred this afternoon. And the first shirt, or Moses if you prefer, has specifically requested your presence."

"I'd be delighted, Mac," said Downs. "You tell him I said that." Mac shook his head and said, "Formation in fifteen minutes. I wouldn't be late if I was you guys. Some people might not understand, you know?" He ambled off in the direction of the company area where men were beginning to form ranks.

As Mac took his place in the formation, he nodded to Sergeant Griffin. Griffin watched the dirty men shuffle into formation, wary looks on their faces. A gritty layer of red dust covered them from head to foot. Their camouflage uniforms showed worn spots from the constant friction of body armor and various pieces of web gear. The once-new flak jackets were faded from exposure to the summer sun and stained by the sweat from countless patrols. Scuffed and torn boots augmented the wrinkled, hand-washed uniforms. Only the weapons of the Marines carried a semblance of newness. Rifles and machine guns appeared black and well-oiled, a menacing extension of each man's arm.

As every man not then on duty slowly found his proper place in the ranks, Griffin listened to the idle remarks and comments. He had known most of these boys since their arrival in the company. Formations were usually preceded by a good deal of friendly banter between individuals and platoons. Now the Marines appeared unusually quiet, almost sullen. As Griffin stood in ranks, Staff Sergeant Whitney approached and nodded to him. Griffin nodded his hello without speaking, noting Whitney's squared away appearance. Griffin silently studied Whitney, noting his rugged features, and the slightly worn look of his uniform. Griffin almost smiled as he realized the staff sergeant deliberately hinted at disaffection by his appearance. Griffin knew that Whitney was squared away, and that he just as deliberately did things that drew the ire of the company first sergeant.

The staff sergeant turned to Griffin and said quietly, "I suppose we can expect a sermon from on high this afternoon."

"This is going to get ugly, that's for sure," said Griffin.

"Yep," said Whitney. "No time to be one of the little people. Any idea why the first sergeant had the beer and soda stacked up like that?" asked Whitney. "I don't mind it warm, Sergeant Griffin, but I don't see any reason to put it out in the sun and cook it," he said amicably.

"I don't know. No fucking telling, but it ain't a good sign," said Griffin, shifting his gaze to the large canvas covered rectangle in front of the formation. Working parties had spent half the morning moving the cases of beer and soda from the sandbagged tent that served as a makeshift enlisted club for the company to their present location. Marine Corps policy was to issue one beer or soda per day per man to troops in combat zones. At the "suggestion" of the company first sergeant the Marines had agreed to pay fifty cents per beer or soda. The idea being to use the cash raised to purchase beer and soda locally and thereby ensure a plentiful supply for the whole company. The idea had worked so well that it had been emulated by the other rifle companies as well as the headquarters units. Much to the chagrin of individual Marines, a limit of two beers per man per day had been instituted. The practice of saving beer had quickly been adopted, often resulting in weekend hooch parties in the bunkers of various squads.

Although this practice didn't escape the attention of the platoon sergeants, they realized the frustration and boredom that was rampant among their troops. Five months of unending heat and monotonous patrolling had begun to have its effect. For the duration of their deployment in Beirut the Marines had had no diversions other than each others' company and the nightly firefights between various armies and militia in the surrounding hills. Although a few men had been selected for liberty runs to Greece or Turkey, the numbers were so small as to be barely noticeable. The inevitable result had been the flaring of tempers and the occasional fistfight. The most vicious of these were often among the closest friends. All the older NCOs feared a lowering of morale and were willing to overlook the hooch parties, trusting the corporals and sergeants not to let them get out of hand. As far as Griffin knew, none of them had. The logical assumption was that the first shirt was going to make some sort of example of Downs, Smith, and Ferris.

Griffin wondered what angle the first sergeant would take with the company as he assumed a loose position of parade rest at the head of first squad. He casually studied the first sergeant who stood with one polished boot resting on the stack of beer and soda. Griffin noted the immaculately pressed camouflage, fresh haircut, and shiny boots. As he took in the polished holster slung across the first sergeant's chest Sam Browne–fashion Griffin had to repress a smirk. It was common knowledge in the battalion that the first sergeant had come from an air wing unit. Well, thought Griffin, not good, but not necessarily bad in and of itself. Only this first sergeant had something to prove. He had arrived an unknown quantity, and proven himself an inadequate troop handler. Not the air wing's fault, mused Griffin, the man is just an ass. Small, petty, and mean in every sense of the word. Now he's in charge of a company, he's got all the junior officers buffaloed into believing his way is the only way, and the staff NCOs have no choice but to go along with the program. The Rock Man will set him straight, but the company will have to pay a little bit first, he reasoned.

Griffin watched through narrowed eyes as the first sergeant drew himself up in front of the formation, hands on his hips, gazing not at them but through them. Arrogant bastard, thought Griffin, they see you for what you are, not what you want to be, and you loathe them for it. Well, these boys have had about enough of your bullshit mister, so don't push too hard. As if to confirm his thoughts Griffin heard one or two suppressed chuckles and the unmistakable sound of someone breaking wind. He exchanged a quick glance with Whitney, who seemed to be having a hard time controlling his own urge to laugh.

The first sergeant was livid. He called the formation to attention and the harsh note of the "AH-TEN-HUT" was made shrill by the outrage in his voice. "Fine girls. You think this shit is funny do you? Fine. As of this moment all liberty is secured. There will be no more drinking in the enlisted club for sergeants, corporals, or non-rates. All men not on duty will be assigned to working parties. I will personally supervise these working parties gentlemen, and you will work. Any man I find who is not on duty or on a working party will be brought up on charges for dereliction of duty. There will be no more gambling or card playing of any sort. No Marine will be in his rack or hooch during duty hours. I have been too soft on this fucking company for too long. Just because you have been ashore in Beirut for a few months and heard a few shots fired you little shits think you have the right to be salty."

The first sergeant glared at the formation of Marines who stared back in sullen silence. "Bullshit!" he screamed. "Certain officers and staff NCOs in this battalion think it is their duty to tell you what a fine job you have been doing, what good Marines you have been. How well you have handled a difficult and dangerous assignment. Well, I am here to tell you girls the truth. I was in the Marine Corps when they were in high school. That's right, while they were fucking Suzy back home in the backseat of Daddy's car I was fighting a real war. In Vietnam. And let me tell you little ladies something else, the VC would have eaten your lunch. You're lucky the only potential enemy you have is these fucked-up rag-heads. Otherwise half of you would be dead by now. You fuckers think this is all some sort of joke. You think you run this company, that you are this company. Wrong fucking answer, ladies! I run this company and I am this company! From this moment on I am going to tighten your collective shit up. A fireteam from first platoon actually had a little party the other night. That's right. They just brought a six-pack with them out on an LP and made a party of it. Well, that won't happen again. Not in my company, am I understood?"

Without waiting for any sort of acknowledgment the first sergeant tore at the oily tarp that covered the stacked cases of beer and soda. As it fell to the ground Griffin noted three axes lying on top of the cases. The first sergeant picked up an ax and swung viciously at the cans of beer, as if by attacking them he could defeat his own inadequacies. After a furious flurry of swings the first sergeant turned to face the formation again. The front of his uniform was covered by beer, and Griffin noted the spittle at the corners of his mouth as he screamed for the company clerks to come forward and finish the job. While the clerks demolished the stacked cases the first sergeant stood over them, ordering them not to leave a single can intact. He continued to glare at the formation, which remained locked in a rigid position of attention.

The last cans were smashed as Captain Rock and two of the lieutenants arrived from a briefing at battalion. As the jeep rolled to a stop the three of them got out.

Griffin noted a slight break in the rhythm of Captain Ward's stride as he marched past the formation on the way to his tent. Although Ward had not so much as looked at the formation Griffin knew he had been taken by surprise. So now the uneasy truce between the company commander and the first sergeant would be broken. And Griffin, Downs, and the remainder of Alpha Company would be caught in the middle.

As dusk turned to nightfall, Downs sat on a pile of sandbags in front of the bunker that he, Mac, Smith, and Ferris had labored most of the day to reinforce. He sat with his back to the company and watched the last rays of a setting sun play against the dark green of the Lebanese mountains, which rose dramatically before him some five kilometers to the east. As the sun reflected in the windows of the houses tucked against the mountains, and the dark began to settle upon him like a protective mantle, Downs allowed the pent-up tension and anger to fall away. Each word spoken by the first sergeant had hit him like a hammer blow. He had felt humiliated, deliberately and maliciously humiliated, during the length of the first sergeant's tirade. Downs was able to concentrate on the scene before him only briefly. Always his mind brought him back to the first sergeant. He longed for the darkness to close around him, as if it were a physical barrier that would separate him from the company. Then he would think. He would decide what his reaction to the first sergeant should be.

Downs's mind raced ahead to her. A pang of emotion struck him at the mere thought of her. At least she hadn't witnessed this day and his humiliation. He struggled to push her from his thoughts. He wanted to clear his mind of the first sergeant and Lebanon before he thought of her. Downs knew he needed the quiet and the solitude to recover his dignity. Then he would think of her and somehow things would seem better. He fingered his watch and wondered what time of day it was back home, what she would be doing right now. He wondered if she ever did the same and the thought that she had forgotten him crept into his mind and he felt a familiar tightening in his throat.

His hand slipped into his cargo pocket and he touched her last letter. Before he could pull it out and read it in the fading light he heard the familiar footsteps of Mac. From the far side of the bunker he heard him ask, "Steve?"

"Yeah," he answered.

"How goes it, man?" said Mac.

"It goes, Mac, it goes," he said.

"Fucked-up day, man," Mac said, lowering himself to the ground next to Downs. Mac stared at the sandbag between his feet without looking at his friend. Downs continued to stare ahead, as if transfixed by some unseen drama on a faraway stage. Mac gathered loose pebbles into a pile and followed Downs's gaze toward the mountains. "Steve?" he began.

"Let's just sit for awhile, Mac. Okay? You know, man. No talking. Just enjoy the scene." He silently replaced her letter in his pocket. "God, this place can be so beautiful at times." As the details of the city before them faded into the darkness, lights from houses began to shine, emulating the smaller, purer light of the stars that now appeared above the ridge line. Soon the mountains dissolved into dark, formless shapes, sprinkled with light from the houses. The sounds of the Marines in the company came to them, softened by the twilight. They could make out the occasional word, but the voices were just an indistinct murmur. In the distance they could hear a tank or amtrac turn its engine over, and the metallic clinking of the treads was audible to them as the huge machine moved out of earshot.

Downs let out a long sigh as his friend strained to see him through the darkness. "You know, Steve, this place is beautiful. I never saw mountains like this before I came here. I wonder why these people have to fight all the time?"

"Maybe they fight because it is so beautiful. Who knows why anyone fights anyone else?" said Downs. "Maybe they want something somebody else has." As Downs spoke a long burst of machine-gun fire floated across the mountainside in front of them. The red tracers bunched together before striking their target and splintering off in a hundred directions. From somewhere down the Marine line Downs and Mac heard laughter and faint applause.

"Time for the evening show, man," said Mac. As if on cue an answering burst of tracer made its way across the mountain in the opposite direction. Faintly, the heavy thumping of the gun's report came to them, and was joined by the pop of small arms fire. A dozen glowing lights rose over the ridge line in front of the Marines, then sputtered out.

"Rockets," mumbled Mac. Almost instantly a dozen explosions appeared as ugly yellow flashes of flame against the mountainside, each briefly illuminating the area it struck. As the reports rolled down the hillside the small arms fire steadily increased, as did the cheering and catcalls of the young Marines. From the southern end of the airport came the heavy rumbling of tanks and armored personnel carriers. "Sound as if the LAF is going to join the fight," said Mac.

"Well, I'm not so sure, they usually stay clear of this stuff," remarked Downs. He had been aware of movement in the Lebanese Army encampment south of the Marine position, but had discounted their active participation in any conflict. Now he could make out the shouting of the Arab soldiers, and though the words were indistinct and foreign, Downs had been a Marine long enough to recognize commands given in any language. He climbed to the roof of the bunker, hoping the added few inches of height would enable him to see what was taking place in the LAF camp.

Griffin approached from Downs's rear, and seeing the corporal standing atop the bunker he said, "Why don't you just paint a fuckin' bull's-eye on the back of that flak jacket, Corporal Downs?"

"Yeah, right, Sergeant Griffin. I will tomorrow. What's up with our friends in the LAF?" Downs stepped off the roof of the bunker and turned toward Griffin, his face flushed with embarrassment at having foolishly exposed himself to enemy fire in front of the big sergeant.

"Nobody's sure, but word has it that they have a company of Rangers in some little village up on the ridge line that has been cut off for a couple of days and is about to be overrun. The going theory is that these guys down at the Khaldeh camp are going up in force to get them out."

"No shit, huh?" asked Downs. "Think they can pull it off?"

Griffin cast a quick glance in the direction of the Lebanese. "Well, that's anybody's guess, there isn't any way to tell if they're even really serious about trying, is there?'' As the two spoke the far end of the airport was brilliantly illuminated by the spotlight from an LAF tank. The light swung wildly about the lower reaches of the hillside as the Lebanese column inched out of its camp. Young Marines along the length of the line began to shout their encouragement, holding their weapons aloft and signaling to the Lebanese soldiers, most of whom appeared somewhat sheepish to Downs.

"There they go,'' said Mac. The column made its way up the hillside, the Marines marking its progress by the searchlight of the point tank, and the occasional fire from nervous gunners. Houses that lay along the road chosen by the tank commander extinguished their lights long before the first vehicles had them in view.

Down shook his head and swore, "Jesus, I hope they have enough sense to put infantry out in front of those tanks.''

"I don't think so,'' said Griffin, "the whole column is moving too fast. Maybe they know the area and it's friendly, or maybe they just think the other guys will take a look at the column and decide to back down.''

"You mean discretion being the better part of valor?'' asked Downs smiling.

"Yeah, Downs, you fucking professor. That's what I meant,'' said Griffin, shaking his head and laughing to himself.

"We'll see shortly I guess,'' Downs laughed back.

Mac glanced toward the sea, and noting the two warships maneuvering closer to shore he said to no one in particular, "What do you suppose they want?''

Griffin and Downs both looked to see the ships turn in unison and parallel the Lebanese coast barely two thousand yards from the beach. Before either of them could speak the ship in the lead began firing from its forward gun mount. Seconds later the second ship also began firing, the sound of the shells arcing through the air clearly audible to the Marines ashore.

For a few moments none of the Marines spoke, then the sound of the Marines yelling their encouragement could be heard. Bored by days of endless patrolling and ceaseless watches stood at all hours, the Marines welcomed any relief from their routine. Griffin shook his head and said, "Well, this is just about the dumbest thing the navy could have done.''

"Why is that, Sergeant Griffin?'' asked Mac. "We can't just stand by and let those guys from the LAF take it in the shorts, not when we've got all this firepower."

"Why not, MacCallum? Who the hell are we anyway? These people been killing each other for a long time before we got here. What's a few more either way matter to us?"

Downs faced the big sergeant then said, "We came here for a reason, Sergeant Griffin."

Before he could finish Griffin cut him off, "No, Downs. Not for this. Don't you see? Now we're taking sides. Once the navy shells targets for the LAF or anybody else we've chosen a side. And whether or not we like it we're going to be a part of this. You don't have to be a genius to understand how a fight works. Jesus, any idiot on the street in New York can tell you to stay out of someone else's fight. We've got nothing to gain here and everything to lose."

"I don't think we came ashore just to sit and watch," said Downs. "There has to be more to it than that."

"Well, Downs," said Griffin as he turned to go. "You can bet the guys on the receiving end of those shells think there's more to it than that now." Griffin shook his head in obvious disgust. "We're not bystanders anymore. You can mark my words on that."

CHAPTER 4

G riffin descended the three sandbagged steps and knocked on a piece of ammo crate that shored up one side of the entrance to the bunker.

"Yeah?"

"It's Sergeant Griffin, Staff Sergeant Whitney. Got a minute?"

"Come on in, Sergeant Griffin," said Whitney from inside the bunker.

Griffin entered and nodded to the other occupants of the bunker. Sensing that Griffin wanted to speak privately with his platoon sergeant they edged past him and moved out of the bunker. "What can I do for you today, Sergeant?"

Griffin drew a long breath, "About the first shirt, Staff Sergeant. It's been two weeks now and this bullshit is just getting worse. My people aren't just tired, they're pissed. He's gone too far. He expects them to work sixteen hours a day, then pull watches at night. That's garrison bullshit. We've got more problems than just unpolished boots and wrinkled utilities. Maybe he hasn't noticed, but we've been rocketed almost every night since the navy started shelling hostile areas. Most nights we get some sort of H&I fire and its starting to wear people down. The platoon and the company are demoralized. They feel like the staff NCOs or the platoon commanders ought to say something. They expect something. The first sergeant demoralizes us

50

at every formation. All he ever says is what a bunch of douche bags we are.''

Before Griffin could continue Whitney held up a hand to stop him. ''Sergeant Griffin, how long have you been in the Marine Corps?''

''Seven years and some change, Staff Sergeant.''

''Well, I've been in almost fourteen. If there is one thing I've learned it's that all first sergeants can be assholes at times. Don't worry. The company will come out of this. Is that the real problem, or is something else bothering you?'

''A lot of shit is bothering me. I'm not as ready to dismiss the first shirt as quick as you seem to be. The man is demoralizing my squad and my platoon. You tell me what the fuck I'm supposed to do and I'll do it.''

''Look, Sergeant Griffin. We know there's a problem. Okay? But put yourself in our place. Short of a mutiny, what do you want us to do? You know the system. Everything revolves around chain of command, and the first shirt is at the top of the chain in this company as far as the enlisted personnel are concerned. The best shot we have is the company gunny, and he has already talked to the first shirt, and right now the man just isn't going to listen. Give it a little more time and it will pass.''

Griffin ran a finger through his close-cropped hair. He wasn't really satisfied with the staff sergeant's answers, but he knew better than to press the issue. ''Okay, Staff Sergeant Whitney. I see your point. But there is something else on my mind.''

''Shoot,'' said the older man.

''Well, it's the way we're running our patrols. Last time we got hit we were lucky. Whoever it was that threw that grenade was an amateur. A scared amateur. He didn't even stick around to see the damage. But it's different now. They're getting serious about hurting us. Everybody talks shit about lousy rag-head cannon cockers, but they killed the corporal of the guard in Bravo Company the other night. And that fucking village is a nightmare. Half the time I can't see the whole squad, and the other half my comm with the company is out. And what's all this bullshit about 'creating a presence?' I write that on every patrol report, but what the fuck does that mean? Does anybody know what the hell we are supposed to be trying to accomplish here? Jesus Christ, Staff Sergeant, they don't even want us to load our fucking rifles on patrol.''

The staff sergeant chuckled. "Well, I haven't noticed first squad going out unloaded of late."

"You're damn right you haven't," snapped Griffin. "Let 'em come along and check weapons for themselves if they're worried about the fucking Rules of Engagement. I'm not going out there unloaded. It's stupid, and you know it."

Whitney rose from his cot and edged past Griffin in the narrow bunker. "Grab a seat, and try to calm down a little. It's too early in the morning to get so pissed off," he said. He went to his olive drab Val pack and rummaged around inside it. With his back to Griffin he tried to think of something to say. He had come to the platoon some thirteen months before, and since that time Griffin had never spoken to him in this manner. Griffin was an old school Marine. Keep your mouth shut, follow orders, accomplish the mission. For him to speak like this meant there were serious morale problems. Not just with Griffin's squad, but with Griffin himself, and probably the other squad leaders. Griffin was liked and respected by the platoon. He would have to be careful what he said. Whatever tone Griffin set would be adopted by most of the others, and Griffin's attitude would be affected by what he was about to say.

"Ah, there it is now," he said to Griffin, extracting a half-empty bottle of bourbon from the depths of his Val pack. "All of us southern boys damned near cried when they started issuing those plastic canteens. Fucking plastic melts, or holds the smell of the goods. Damn risky carrying a bottle, too. Glass breaks, and you're shit out of luck. It's enough to break a man's heart, seeing good bourbon go to waste. Well, war is hell they say." He turned in time to see a faint smile from Griffin, and his apprehension eased a bit. He poured a couple of shots into two canteen cups and passed one to Griffin who grimaced as he swallowed a mouthful of the warm liquid. The staff sergeant studied Griffin over the lip of his canteen cup before speaking.

Fourteen years in the Corps, he thought, and this part of it never gets any easier. He had asked the same questions of an older Marine a decade before. The frustrations and anger were the same, only the battlefield was different. And he was different this time around. He had changed in the dozen or so years since he had left Vietnam for the last time. He was less emotional now, less caring about some things, more understanding toward others. He had come away from Vietnam with scars, on his body and in his mind. Those scars had marked the boy and shaped the man. His concept of duty had been altered, and he had lost any semblance of innocence. Now he had begun to realize what mattered in life. It was nothing he could put into words, it was less tangible than even an idea. The Marine Corps mattered to him. The whole of it, with its myriad of regulations and its crushing weight of conformity. But what really mattered were the traditions, and the thought of the others who had gone before him. The ones who had made the legends at places whose names were now an inseparable part of the lore of the Corps. Tripoli, Belleau Wood, Tarawa.

He had known it would come to this since he was a boy. He had readied himself his entire life for the physical challenges, the long marches, the endless cycles of training. He had endured it all, the abuse, the harassment, the discipline. He had naively clung to the belief that somehow the system could really prepare a man for the shock of combat.

Those first few seconds in a nameless firefight in Vietnam had served to erase those beliefs forever. Now he realized that nothing readies a man for war. The overwhelming terror that seizes a boy during his first battle. Or the stark, haunting realization that you aren't any different from the others and that when your turn comes you will die. It didn't matter that he had run the mile faster than any boy in the county his junior year in high school, or that a girl back home loved him. One moment in an otherwise ordinary day and his life would be reduced to the memories of a few people who had known him and a name carved into a piece of stone.

He had decided to remain because of some inner calling, an indefinable desire to be a part of something bigger than himself, and to share the company of others with that same sense of duty to the Corps. He had spent his entire adult life in service to the Corps. He had never really known anything else.

It hadn't come without its price. Two daughters that he barely knew who were now back home with their mother in Kentucky. And a letter in his pocket from a lawyer telling him that his wife wanted a divorce.

Ten years ago he would have thrown the letter away and gotten drunk. He would have had more emotion for her then, more to give, and more to lose. Now she mattered less somehow, and both of them knew it. It was less of a surprise than he might have once imagined. He couldn't even blame her really. He had been a real bastard, first with the drinking, then with the other women, and now with the months-long deployments.

He had stayed in the Corps even after her father had offered him a job back home. A job with a decent salary. Enough to buy a piece of the mountains they both loved. A chance to raise their girls with family, put down roots in a place they both knew as home. She had tolerated it all. She had done what she could while he destroyed their marriage, first by drinking, then by his silence. He had never been able to tell her about Vietnam, or about the boys he had lost there.

One boy really. One young lieutenant who had died on a nameless battlefield on an otherwise unremarkable day. A battlefield without any particular distinction or glory, except perhaps the distinction of being the place where one more Marine died.

Even now he was unsure why this one death had affected him so deeply. He only knew that it had, and afterward he had known he could never leave the Marine Corps. He had thought about that lieutenant often in the years since Vietnam. He had been a sergeant then, on his second tour. He was acting platoon sergeant and the lieutenant had become his friend over the months spent in the bush. He had shaped the boy, even though he was little more than a boy himself. He had taken a great deal of pride in the fact that he was acting in the tradition of Marine NCOs by helping to form the character of one of the Corps' young officers.

When they had put him on the medevac bird the lieutenant had pulled him close and said over the noise of the helicopter that he should write his family, and that he hoped he had earned the respect of his Marines. And he had said "Thank you." He could have forgotten the boy had it not been for the thank you. Not forgotten exactly, just pushed him back into the crevices of his memory where you put the things that are too painful to think of very often.

Griffin reminded him of that lieutenant in an odd sort of way. Maybe it was because he had done what he could to shape both of them. Or maybe it was because they were both so determined to be good Marines. There was some quality they both shared that he could never put a name to. Something fierce and unyielding in their character that had destined them both to be Marines. Good Marines.

And now, a decade later, it was happening all over again. Soon enough the dying would start. He recognized all the signs that he had been too young to know the first time. He glanced at Griffin and wondered if he was getting old, becoming maudlin. Trying to sound as much like a father as he could he plunged ahead, "Look, Sergeant Griffin, we're Marines. Nobody in Washington, D.C., gives one single flying fuck about us. The only thing that matters back there is votes. Dead Marines, at least lots of dead Marines, means less votes for the guy in office at election time and shitty stories in all the newspapers. Other than that, they're not real worried about us. So don't waste a lot of your time worrying about crap like 'creating a presence.' That's just a line of bullshit for them to feed to the press. Your mission, and mine, is to get back home with this platoon in one piece. If we're lucky we'll pull it off. So let's concentrate on that for now."

He shook his head and continued, "As far as the first sergeant, well, fuck me if I know what kind of rock got stuck in his shorts. If it will make you feel any better, I'll have a talk with the company gunny and see what he thinks."

The staff sergeant paused and looked at Griffin for a moment, wondering if he was striking the right chord. "But you remember this. We're Marines, you and me. Neither of us is some wet behind the ears private on his first pump. Both of us have been around. So when you're out there in Indian country, you run your squad the way you see fit, boy. And you let the politicians in Washington worry about counting votes. Now it's time for formation, so let's go out there and get our collective ass chewed like the true professionals we are." The staff sergeant smiled and slapped Griffin on the shoulder as he left the bunker.

CHAPTER

5

Griffin's low whistle broke the morning stillness as the squad rose like long dead specters from the waist-high grass. A torn gray mist hung over the ground as the Marines stood and began walking out of the grass toward the village. The only sound was the creaking of their equipment as they moved past the first few houses. Downs, walking point, noted that the village dogs had not even bothered to bark at them, and he was conscious of the gritty sound of his own footsteps as he moved along a stretch of dirty pavement between a row of houses. Downs glanced at Mac on the opposite side of the road. Mac was looking toward Downs and said in a whisper, "Something ain't right, Steve."

Downs nodded and kept moving forward. Rounding a corner he locked eyes with an old woman wearing a cheap cotton print dress and thin scarf. She was washing clothes under a faucet and did not look up again as the patrol moved quietly past.

Downs's eyes swept each door and window ahead of him as the patrol moved cautiously down the narrow street. His stomach tightened as he walked past a stone wall, and he fought the instinct to walk faster and clear the blinding obstacle. He quickly glanced over his right shoulder to check Mac's position. Mac's eyes locked with his and he gave a slight nod forward, indicating the direction of the squad's movement. Downs glanced toward the center of the squad and saw Griffin, Samson, and

Tiger striding along on opposite sides of the road. Tiger caught his eye and patted his machine gun with a smile.

Downs rounded another corner as the village gave way to open fields planted with a dark green vine. His eyes searched the fields, but detected nothing. He looked up the road and saw the mosque, its minaret scarred from past battles and the morning mist clinging to its dome. Two men stood on the steps of the mosque, and Downs knew instinctively that they had seen him first and were studying him. They continued to stare at him as they unhurriedly descended the steps and drove away. He shot a glance at Mac and asked, "What the fuck was that?"

"I don't know. Morning prayers maybe," Mac shrugged.

Downs forced himself to continue searching the fields as each step brought him closer to the mosque. His eyes strained to see detail, but the gray walls of the mosque melted into the ground in the uncertain light. Twice Downs held up a fist to halt the patrol, his instinct telling him that somehow this morning was different from the others.

He again moved toward the mosque as his eyes locked on the fuzzy shapes at the base of the steps. He fought the urge to run, knowing that the squad would immediately mimic any action he made. Already he could feel their tension pushing him forward. "Do you see it, Mac?" he asked.

"Yeah, but I can't tell what it is," shrugged Mac.

Downs inadvertently slowed his pace. "Keep your eyes on it." He and Mac advanced toward the mosque with the squad strung out behind them. Downs froze in mid-stride as his eye detected movement in the shapeless brown mass. Without waiting Mac yelled "Cover!" and the squad threw itself into the shallow drainage ditches on either side of the road.

"Ambush front! Ambush front!" screamed Downs. "At the base of the steps!"

From his position Griffin gave a series of commands that moved the squad on a new line perpendicular to the road. Marines crawled over the low rows of vegetation, forming a skirmish line with Tiger's machine gun roughly in the center of the squad. All eyes strained to pick out a target as each man struggled to press himself into the damp soil. Griffin scrambled up the ditch, stopping about one yard behind Downs. "What you got, Corporal Downs?" he asked.

"Movement to the front. Something at the base of the steps, but I can't make it out," said Downs.

Griffin rolled onto his side and pulled the binoculars over his head, his helmet hitting the dirt with a dull thud. He grunted, "Jesus! It looks like two or three men. But it ain't no ambush, Downs. Those guys look pretty fucked-up." Griffin tossed the binoculars to Downs, who caught them by the strap and brought them quickly to his eyes.

"Jesus, Sergeant Griffin, they look like they're covered in blood. What the fuck is going on?"

"I don't know. But we're going to have to check it out. What the fuck were those rag-heads in the van doing before they drove off, Downs?"

"Nothing," said Downs shaking his head, "watching us."

Griffin peered again at the mosque, squinting his eyes into the binoculars. "We just get all the fucking breaks lately," he muttered. He rolled onto his side and looked at the squad, noting the position of each man. He turned to the radioman and said, "Inform company we got three locals down in front of the mosque. Give 'em the grid and tell 'em to stand by while we check it out. You got that?"

"Yeah, Sergeant Griffin. We're up," replied the radioman.

"Good, do it. Doc!" Griffin looked at the corpsman, obviously making a decision. "Doc, you fucking stand by to treat these guys, but don't waste a lot of our shit on them. You understand?"

The corpsman nodded and Griffin again turned impatiently to Downs, "You see any movement in that mosque?"

Downs swept the mosque with the binoculars, trying to peer into the darkness of the arched doorways. The right side of the mosque was in ruins, the roof and sections of the wall having collapsed during some forgotten shelling. The minaret rose on the left side, its walls pierced by long windows all the way to the narrow circular walk at the top. Downs was unable to detect any movement. "I don't see anything, but it's too dark." Downs paused. "It's gotta be time for morning prayers, Sergeant Griffin. Somebody has to be in the fucking place now, or it just isn't right. These fuckers might be setting us up."

Griffin nodded absently, not really listening to Downs. He hesitated, then came to a decision. "Okay, Downs, check it out. Take your fireteam forward and do it. The squad will stay here and provide a base of fire. Take your team into the mosque and watch your ass. We're not in any hurry. I'll move the squad up on your command. Got it?"

Downs nodded his assent and turned to his fireteam. "Mac, are you, Smith, and Ferris ready?" Mac looked at the other two, both of whom checked their rifles and nodded their heads.

"Yeah, we're ready," said Smith. Ferris muttered a low, incredulous "shit" and looked at Smith who just shrugged.

Downs rose to one knee as the other three got to their feet and looked down the line of Marines. The squad adjusted themselves on their weapons and sighted in on what they thought would be likely places of concealment for an enemy squad. Samson caught Downs's eye and smiled tightly, giving the thumbs up signal. Downs tried to return his smile, but his mouth was dry as he gained his feet and moved forward in a low crouch. The fireteam advanced a few steps before Downs raised his fist and dropped to one knee, putting the binoculars to his eyes. As the other three lay on the ground, Downs scanned the mosque for signs of movement. Seeing nothing he again moved toward the mosque.

The four cautiously approached the building as the groans of the wounded men reached them. Downs glanced briefly at them, forcing himself to continue searching the mosque for any movement or sign of an ambush. His quick look at the men had erased any doubt he had that their wounds might not be legitimate. One man lay on his back, a knee cocked in the air, his clothing torn and his hair matted with blood. Flies buzzed around all three of them, and as Downs stole another glance at them he had to fight the urge to vomit. Each of them had been mutilated in some way, and Downs was immediately certain it had been from some form of torture. The thought occurred to him that none of the men were soldiers. He could see gray in their hair, and each one appeared overweight and middle-aged. The one man laying on his back looked at Downs and began to sob, muttering something unintelligible in Arabic. His shirt was ripped and his stomach lay exposed and obscene, streaked with blood. As he watched Downs with one eye he began to make a high pitched whine.

Downs peered into the inner court of the mosque. He became aware of the sound of water bubbling from a fountain, and waved the fireteam forward. The Marines moved past the wounded men, unconsciously walking around them as the man's whining intensified. Downs mounted the steps of the mosque and flattened himself against one of the arched doorways. Inside he could see the center court, with its fountain and small garden. He signaled Smith and Ferris to stay and watch the flanks as he and Mac moved forward.

Easing through the arches Downs was unable to observe any movement. The mosque appeared deserted and gray in the early morning light. As he and Mac moved slowly around the inner arches Downs became aware of someone in the far end of the courtyard. The two Marines froze at the same moment, bringing their rifles to their shoulders. Downs didn't bother to sight his rifle, knowing at this range he could instinctively put the rounds into any target.

Across the court he saw movement behind another column. The pair moved to the right, weapons fixed to their shoulders, angling their steps to have a clear field of fire when the target emerged from the other side of the column.

The seconds passed as both men tensed, knowing the man should have reappeared. Downs felt his stomach muscles tighten, anticipating a burst of fire from across the courtyard. He stepped back behind the covering column, his eye darting to the base of the enemy column, looking for the small black eye of an enemy rifle. Downs and Mac stood transfixed, staring across the courtyard, willing the man to show himself.

To their rear the crying of the wounded man had grown faint. Downs suddenly became aware of a low humming from across the courtyard. Someone was humming a tune in the low, heavy tones of a man, but the tune was broken, as though the man were drunk. Downs looked at Mac, who caught Downs's glance in his peripheral vision, shot a glance at him and made a puzzled expression that Downs knew meant "what the fuck?" He nodded for Mac to follow, and quickly moved to the next column as Mac covered. They moved around the court in this fashion, leapfrogging their movements until Downs had reached the corner column.

Downs peered around the corner and saw the back of a heavyset man, kneeling on the stone floor, his bare feet tucked under his buttocks. The man was carefully straightening his prayer rug, smoothing the cloth over the stones of the floor. Downs watched for a few seconds, noting the man's awkward, heavy movements. As he moved behind his column, out of sight of the man, he looked at Mac and mouthed the word "one," then shrugged his shoulders. Downs again leaned around the edge of the column as the man scooted to the other end of his prayer rug and began to straighten it, repeating the motion for perhaps one minute as Downs looked on. He noted the man's dirty robe and unshaven face, estimating him to be somewhere between forty and fifty years old. The Arab continued humming happily to himself. He reached behind the column and Downs quickly brought his rifle to his shoulder, leveling the muzzle at the man and taking up the initial slack on the trigger. The Arab locked eyes with Downs and half stood, a second prayer rug in his hand. Mac moved up to cover Downs as the man made a noise that was half sob and half scream. He quickly turned his back on the two Marines and shuffled off down the arched corridor, obviously frightened by the sight of the two. As Downs and Mac looked on he disappeared through a dark doorway, blubbering noises echoing behind him in the stone hallway.

The two Marines continued to stare down the arched corridor before Mac broke the silence by asking, "What the fuck was that?"

"Who knows?" shrugged Downs, "but something ain't right."

"That guy looked retarded or something. The whole thing isn't right, Steve. Did you see the way he was working on that rug? And he almost fucking cried when he saw us. Call Sergeant Griffin, man. Give him the scoop, and let him bring up the rest of the squad. This situation is fucked. We're too far from the squad, and we're out of sight of Smith and Ferris. Let's just ease out of here."

"Too late, Mac. We've got company." Downs nodded down the corridor, indicating the approach of a dignified older Lebanese in a flowing white robe. His beard was neatly trimmed and his head was wrapped in the traditional headdress of a mullah. A few paces behind him the first man followed, obviously too frightened to stay behind by himself, but hesitant to approach the Marines, even with the mullah present.

The mullah slowed his gait as he drew closer, his hands open, his face friendly. "Welcome, young gentlemen," he said easily in English. "My name is Ibrahim, and I am the keeper of the mosque. This is my brother, Zouhair, whom you have already met. Please forgive him. He is feebleminded and I am afraid that you frightened him." At the mention of his name Zouhair bobbed his head and emitted a strangled sob, confirming that this was indeed his name. He remained a few cautious steps behind his brother, wringing his hands, his back firmly against the stone wall of the courtyard.

"May I ask what brings you into our mosque? I do not wish to give offense, young gentleman, but the mosque is only for believers of the true faith. Of Islam."

Downs nodded and asked, "Where are all the men who usually say their prayers here?"

"Ah, this morning I am afraid there has been some trouble. Young ruffians frightened the faithful who usually come to pray. These are difficult times, as you know. Most of the worshipers here are old, and easily frightened. They wish only to come and go quietly. In Lebanon, in these times, that is often asking too much," said the mullah.

"Is anyone else in the mosque?" asked Downs curtly.

"No, just my brother and myself. We are alone."

Downs looked at Mac, who shrugged. "Who are the guys out front, on the steps?" asked Downs.

"I do not know. I was preparing for morning prayers when my brother told me you were here. I know of no one else." Downs took the small radio from his flak jacket pocket, depressed the transmit button and said, "Sergeant Griffin, this is Downs. Over."

"Go, Downs," came back Griffin's voice sounding metallic and far away.

"The place is empty except for the mullah and his brother. He says there was some trouble in the ville last night and everyone is afraid to come to morning prayers. Says he doesn't know about the wounded guys out front. We haven't searched the place, but I think it will be okay to bring the squad up. How do you copy?"

"We're comin' up. You sit tight and hold onto the Arabs, Downs. Out."

"Roger," answered Downs, noting Ibrahim's quick glance toward the front of the mosque at the mention of the wounded men, and his genuine look of surprise. Downs decided that he believed what the mullah said, and felt a pang of conscience over his unwelcome entry into the mosque courtyard. As Downs replaced the radio in his pocket he noticed that Ibrahim seemed agitated for the first time, his calm demeanor shaken. "Please, sir, if there are men hurt in my mosque I must see to them. It is my duty. I am the mullah and must extend the hospitality of the mosque to them. May I go to them?"

Downs hesitated, then looking around at the stone walls of the mosque, he answered, "Yeah, sure. Let's go see about them."

Downs led the way as the two brothers fell in behind, Mac bringing up the rear. Downs felt the impatience of Ibrahim, who walked quickly toward the front of the mosque. He noted Smith and Ferris, and Downs saw a look of surprise cross the mullah's face as they left the inner court and saw the squad moving steadily toward them in a skirmish line. Downs felt a wild surge of pride as he looked at his squad moving menacingly across the open field. Griffin had kept them in a skirmish line so as to have maximum firepower to the front if an ambush were set in the mosque.

Downs stood at the top of the steps and noted the confident stride of the Marines, and their dark, ominous appearance. The image of his comrades moving across that field would remain with him the rest of his life, and in later years would evoke a bittersweet sense of pride and loss.

Ibrahim gasped as one of the wounded men moaned. He quickly descended the steps and knelt over the man, whispering under his breath in Arabic. The only word Downs understood was "Allah."

"So who do you think did up those dudes in front of the mosque this morning, Steve?"

"I don't know, Mac, but whoever it was meant business. Those guys were pretty messed up." Downs absently stirred his can of beans and franks as it cooked over the low flame of a heat tab. "This stuff burns okay, but whatever you heat with it smells like fucking gasoline," he observed.

Mac grunted and stirred his own lukewarm concoction. "Do you ever wonder what the hell we're doing here? I mean, at first it was okay. We walked patrol and everybody was pretty friendly. Now it's different, man. I can just feel it. It's not just that they don't like us anymore, now they're afraid of us. You know what I mean?" he asked.

"Yeah, I know, but there's nothing we can do about it. Just sit tight and hope for the best." Downs and Mac ate in silence, each absorbed by his own thoughts.

"You ever think about going home, Steve?"

"You mean Camp LeJeune?" asked Downs. "Yeah, once in a while I guess. You?"

"No, man, not LeJeune. Home, man," said Mac. "Real home. Do you think about that?"

Downs stared into his C-rat can for a long moment before answering, "No, not really." Downs knew that Mac understood he was lying, but he trusted his friend to brush over the topic.

"I do. I'm going to get out, Steve. I mean, I'm proud of being a Marine, but it just isn't what I thought it would be. The only guys who stay in are the losers like the first shirt who couldn't make it on the outside anyway. They get promoted 'cause everybody else gets out, then they wind up being in charge and screw with whoever comes in. I'm doing my four years and then I'm going back home, find some babe, get a job, and do the suburban routine."

"Are you going to make a down payment on the station wagon with the money you save up over here?" chided Downs.

"I'm being serious. Look at this company. Some of the staff NCOs are okay, but most of them are just doing their twenty years and no more. They're just marking time."

"Yeah, maybe so, but some of them are all right. There's some professionals in the company. Look at Staff Sergeant Whitney. He's the real thing, and Sergeant Griffin knows what he's doing. Captain Ward, too. They're not all losers, man. It's just the fucking bad ones are so miserable they make the rest of us suffer. Just 'cause they're lifers doesn't make them pricks, Mac."

"Yeah, but those three are the exceptions, not the rule. You know I'm right. Shit, Steve, we'll both hit our discharge within a couple of days of each other. Let's get out together and hit the road for a month or so. We'll stop in New Jersey and see Anderson. Remember him, man? He wrote me a couple of months ago. He's working with his old man, doing construction. He got out and he's making it. You and me can do the same, but we can do it together," said Mac. "Look, Steve, I know you don't like to talk about it, and that's cool. But I guess you don't have much of a family to go back home to. That's okay, man. You can just come home with me. My family is okay. They already know all about you from my letters, and everybody wants to meet you. We can crash in my house while we look for work, then get a place together. It can work, man. What do you think?"

Downs looked away from his friend, Mac's words having found a deep, private pain. He felt exposed, naked. He struggled for the right thing to say, something witty or funny that would turn the conversation back to the friendly banter he was used to. "Look, Mac, it's not like that for me. Maybe a lot of losers do hang on in the Corps and fuck things up, but I'm not denying that. Hell, even they admit there's ten percent of 'em that shouldn't be here. But I belong here. For the first time in my life everybody accepts me because I'm earning my own way. No more, no less. I appreciate what you're saying about your family, but they're just that, your family. No matter how great they are they can't be my family. Do you understand, Mac? I'm going to stay in because I don't have any other place to go, and because these guys are my family, no questions asked. No matter how fucked up I am, or they are, I belong here. And it doesn't matter that guys come and go. I still have a place here." Neither of them said anything as they continued stirring their rations. Downs was unwilling to continue the conversation, and Mac was unsure of how to proceed.

The two finished eating in silence as Griffin approached. "Corporal Downs, I need to see you in my hooch when you're finished eating," he said.

"I'm finished now, what do you need?" asked Downs, making no move to rise from the wooden ammo crate that served as his chair.

"C'mon," said Griffin. As the two strode off for Griffin's bunker Downs tried to think of what Griffin might possibly want to discuss. Platoon or squad matters were routinely passed in a communal fashion, with all of the squad and fireteam leaders present. Since Griffin had singled him out for personal attention, it must be something involving Downs or one of the Marines in his fireteam. He tried to think what infraction of the Marine Corps' plethora of rules and regulations he might have infringed upon. Unable to think of anything specific he concluded that he was about to answer for the actions of Smith and Ferris.

Griffin descended into the bunker he shared with the other squad leaders. Downs had been inside only rarely and he glanced about, trying to pick up details that would reveal some facet of Griffin's personality. Even in the Spartan confines of the bunker the other two sergeants had put up a photo of a wife or girlfriend, or a centerfold. Griffin's area above his cot was unadorned, nothing showing but the sandbagged wall or the red clay of Lebanon. All business, thought Downs, all the time.

Griffin motioned for Downs to sit on one of the empty cots and dug into the pocket of his pack. He withdrew a small green memo book from his pack and tossed it to Downs. "Okay, Corporal Downs, now you get to learn about mail call. All my corporals do this because I expect it of them. So before you start giving me the thousand-questions routine, shut up and listen. When the platoon gets mail the individual pieces are given to squad leaders to tally before the staff sergeant passes it out. I'm sure you've noticed second and third platoon get their mail before we do. The reason why is the squad leaders tally how much mail each guy gets every time there's a mail call. We do it so that if one guy quits gettin' mail all of a sudden we know about it. The reason for this whole procedure is that morale depends on news from home. The only thing worse than bad news is no news. So I like to know who is getting their mail and who isn't. Are you following me?" Downs nodded and Griffin continued, "Good. That little book is so you can keep track of your fireteam's mail. Here's this week's mail call, so start with these letters and mark it down by date. Got it?" Downs marked each piece as Griffin called it out to him. When they had finished Griffin put the mail back into his cargo pocket.

"Okay, Downs, now I'll take all of this back to Staff Sergeant Whitney. If you or I notice one of your Marines isn't getting any mail we'll pull him aside and have a talk with him. Sometimes they aren't writing home, or sometimes they get dumped by their girlfriends or wives.

"It happens, Corporal Downs," said Griffin, noting the look of disbelief on Downs's face. "And when it does, guys get crazy. Especially out here. So take this shit serious. It's part of being an NCO. There's more to it than just wearing the extra stripes."

Downs contemplated Griffin, then asked, "Is that all, Sergeant Griffin?"

Exasperated, Griffin ran a hand through his hair and said, "Corporal Downs, are you still writing to that girl back home?"

Turning away from Griffin, Downs mumbled "no," attempting to make his voice sound casual and unemotional. "It was no great romance, Sergeant Griffin. So you don't have to worry about me. I'm fine."

"I didn't think that I did, Downs. You're a damn good Marine, and you're going to be a good squad leader one day. Just relax and let it happen. All you need is some more experience."

Downs turned to face Griffin, "Okay. Thanks, Sergeant Griffin," he said.

"Hey, Corporal Downs. Sometime if you want to drop by and discuss broken hearts, let me know. I've got a story or two to tell you," said Griffin.

Downs smiled. Feeling uncomfortable, he turned and left the bunker. Just the mention of her by Griffin had been enough to reawaken his memories. As he absently made his way back toward his bunker Downs was lost in thoughts of her. Amid the noise and confusion of the battalion he heard her playing the piano on a long-ago summer evening. Downs was able to see the curve of her neck as she bent over the keyboard during a difficult passage, and hear her laughter as she missed a note.

Downs felt her near, the warmth of her touch, the smell of her hair, as they sat in the twilight on some anonymous evening. Slowly making his way back to his bunker, Downs's reverie was broken by a shouted command, and she was lost to him again.

He wondered how much Griffin actually knew. Without understanding why, he knew he wanted to keep her from Griffin and the others, to prevent them from knowing of her. Downs knew that he never wanted her to be touched by the Marine Corps, or by Lebanon.

He can't know that much, Downs reasoned. Just her name and the city where her letters were postmarked. He surmised that Griffin's tallying of the squad's mail was just another method of controlling them, being constantly in command of them. Even as the thought occurred to him Downs knew he was being too hard on Griffin. The plain fact was that Griffin was genuinely concerned, and he had gone about letting Downs know of his concern in the least awkward manner possible. The thought struck him that Griffin was not merely a hard-as-nails professional with no personal life.

He began to think of Griffin outside the context of a Marine sergeant. He pictured him with a family. Even Griffin had to have some sort of family, a mother at least. Downs drew a mental picture of Griffin as a small boy, sitting at a table blowing out candles on a huge birthday cake. The incongruity of the image hit him, and Downs laughed out loud. Not Griffin. He had never been a small boy, and undoubtedly was an orphan. Probably abandoned at birth by his mother.

Downs was still chuckling to himself as he walked up to Mac, whom he cuffed on the back of the head and said, "You wimp, figures you're going to get out of the Corps before your thirty years are up."

CHAPTER

Downs, Griffin, and most of the platoon watched as the bunker was constructed two hundred yards from the Marine perimeter. A bulldozer, American made, but painted with the green cedar symbol of the Lebanese government, had arrived and began pushing dirt into a barricade that straddled the street and tied into the houses on either side. The Marines stood by as the bulldozer scraped earth from nearby empty lots and piled it well over six feet high. From their vantage point they could see men with shovels working on the far side, doubtlessly hollowing out the rear of the bunker to accommodate a gun emplacement. As the afternoon progressed a truck arrived, loaded with flat, brown sacks. The puzzled Marines watched as the sacks were laboriously hauled to the top of the bunker, split open, and the contents spread over the sides of the bunker.

After this was done water was thrown on the bunker, and men began working it into the gray powder that had spilled from the sacks. Griffin had been the first to deduce that the powder was actually concrete mix, and that the afternoon sun would harden the mixture in a matter of hours. Silently he had risen from his position and walked off in the direction of the company command post. He had returned a short time later and ordered the platoon to fill sandbags and reinforce their own bunkers. The Marines had angrily gone about their task, then watched

68

incredulously as the tripod for a heavy machine gun was brought up the street by two smiling young men wearing the distinctive black and white kaffiyehs of the PLO. Before entering the bunker they waved to the watching Marines. This was followed by a steady stream of young men entering the bunker carrying boxes wrapped in heavy paper. They would appear from around the corner of the building, in groups of three or four, walking heavily under their burdens. Griffin had concluded that the boxes were ammunition and that it was being ferried to the location by the young men in their own cars.

As the fifth delivery was made one of the Arabs turned and blew a kiss to the Marines. Within seconds a shot from one of the Marine bunkers shattered the masonry beside the group of Arabs. They quickly scurried around a corner and the deliveries stopped for a period of about an hour. A woman dressed in the traditional black flowing robes of the Shiites appeared and walked toward the bunker. In her arms she carried one of the boxes, wrapped in the same brown paper. The woman walked purposefully to the bunker, never glancing at the Marines. She disappeared into the bunker and emerged again, seconds later, minus the bundle. After she slipped around the corner of the building two more women appeared, both obviously nervous as they walked quickly to the bunker.

Within minutes two young Arabs approached, warily looking in the direction of the Marine lines. As the first man went in the second climbed onto the face of the bunker, laid his tools at his feet, and smoked a cigarette as he sat calmly watching the Marines. After finishing his smoke he picked up a hammer and chisel and began chopping a small window into the face of the structure. Griffin watched carefully, trying to gauge the thickness of the concrete by the difficulty the man had in piercing it. As he chipped at the concrete Griffin guessed it was probably an inch thick, possibly two. The man enlarged the hole until it was big enough to accommodate the muzzle of a machine gun. He had no real idea of how much dirt was behind the concrete, but he knew no round fired from an M-16, or an M-60 machine gun, was going to penetrate it. And those were the only weapons available to the squad under the Rules of Engagement specified by higher headquarters. The Rules of Engagement required that they fire only after being fired upon, and that they use only the minimum amount of force necessary to accomplish any mission. The platoon had LAAW rockets available, and 40mm grenade launchers, but technically they were not to be used unless they received fire from like weapons first. Even then, Griffin knew, only a solid hit upon the firing port punched out by the man would do any real damage. The chance of such a hit at this range while taking fire from a heavy machine gun was slight at best.

While Griffin continued to study the man Staff Sergeant Whitney approached and squatted down beside him. "Sergeant Griffin, how are things looking today?" he asked.

Griffin grunted, and passed the older man the binoculars. "Okay for now. But this is going to get ugly later on, Staff Sergeant."

Whitney took the binoculars and raised them to his eyes. "Yes, sir, that looks like the recipe for trouble." Whitney looked down the Marine lines, and said, "Maybe we'll get a little help."

Griffin looked at the other Marine without amusement then said, "How do you figure, Staff Sergeant?" he said. "There's no way battalion headquarters will approve a request for any artillery missions."

The staff sergeant inclined his head down the line of Marine bunkers. Fifty meters away, kneeling in a shallow depression, were two Marines. Griffin watched as they approached, catlike, staying under the line of sight of the Arab, who continued sitting smugly on his newly constructed bunker. The two Marines paused, then moved cautiously forward. Griffin noted their approach, but did not recognize their faces. The first man carried his M-16, the other had his weapon slung over his back. Griffin took in the slung rifle and thought, not good. You'll never get it off your shoulder in time to use it. As he continued to study the two he saw the long fiberglass case the man was carrying. He looked at Whitney as comprehension dawned on his face. Under his breath he said one word, "Snipers."

Whitney chuckled and said, "More than one way to skin a cat, Sergeant Griffin."

The snipers approached the rear of Downs's bunker and dropped to a crawling position, moving slowly to the rear of the sandbagged emplacement. Downs, sitting atop the roof, turned to see why the two were making such a cautious approach. Other Marines in the vicinity took little notice of them, their attention focused on the Arabs. As the first sniper reached the rear of Downs's position he sat up and looked at Downs. "Just stay where you are, Corporal," he said. "If they know we're here they'll get spooked."

"Okay," replied Downs.

"Are we about even with that bunker they're building?" he asked.

"Yeah," said Downs flatly. "About dead even I'd say. You two planning to do something about it?"

"Yeah," the sniper answered as his partner gained the rear of the position and nodded hello to Downs. "I guess we can make it hot for them. Do us a favor and stay where you are. We're going to set up inside your hooch. Let us know if they bring that gun up. And if you see an airliner lining up to land or take off on the east runway let us know."

"Why, you waiting for a flight home?" quipped Downs with a smile. The two snipers grinned mischievously at each other, then entered the bunker. Once inside they arranged sandbags to block two thirds of the existing firing port.

Mac, Smith, and Ferris continued with their game of spades as the two snipers fashioned a rest for their heavy rifle. They then laid the rifle into its bed, the muzzle of the weapon some six inches inside the sandbagged outer wall of the bunker. They removed the rifle from its position and lined the sandbags surrounding it with towels they had brought with them.

"What are you going to do? Give it a bath?" asked Ferris sarcastically. The snipers turned to face Ferris and laughed. "No, but these towels are pretty clean, and they reduce the amount of dust kicked up by the rifle. Once that gunner realizes it's us firing at him he is going to suppress us with his fire. It's kind of hard to concentrate on getting a clean shot with those big slugs coming at you. If we can get a shot through his firing port it's probably going to be hard for them to find another gunner willing to step into that position."

Smith looked at Ferris and said, "Yeah, any asshole but you would've known what the towels were for. Sometimes you embarrass the shit out of me. It's a wonder you even graduated from high school." Ferris laughed as the sniper continued, "We'll lay a couple more towels just in front of the firing port on the ground. That way we shouldn't get much of a dust signature. I guess we ought to tell you that we're going to draw a lot of fire when this starts. You might want to go to another bunker."

Mac looked at the other two, then said, "Fuck those assholes. I'm stayin' here."

The sniper shrugged and stepped outside. His partner walked up to the firing port, laid the rifle in its rest, and took a pencil and paper from his pocket. Looking through the rifle scope he used the scale on the lens and a mathematical equation to determine distance to the enemy bunker. After completing this he replaced the paper in his pocket and dialed windage and elevation onto the telescopic sight. Having completed that he rechecked his computations and returned to the rifle case. He removed a box of specially loaded 7.62mm cartridges, and after careful examination, loaded one into the breech of the weapon and rolled the bolt forward with a metallic click. Just as he sat down on an empty cot his partner dropped into the bunker and said, "Plane!" The sniper snapped forward, then asked, "Our runway?"

"I don't know. All I can see are his approach lights. He's five minutes away at least and it's hard to tell which runway he's going to use. Are you all set up?"

"Yeah, but recheck me. And check the dope I put on the rifle. Set up the spotting scope where you can get a good view so we can make any changes. Did you talk to the corporal outside about being a lookout?"

"Uh-uh. You'll have to do it." The sniper exited the bunker, a pair of powerful binoculars around his neck. He looked directly behind the bunker and gauged the distance to the runway. Maybe 150 yards, 175 tops, he thought. He noticed the heat radiating directly off the surface of the concrete and smiled when the thought came to him that there was no wind this afternoon. He looked in the opposite direction, toward the bunker. An open field stretched some three hundred yards from him to the Arab now chipping away at the concrete on the face of the bunker. Well, he thought, 330 yards to be precise. And precision is what this is all about.

He brought the binoculars to his eyes and searched the field in front of him. After a few seconds looking he found the small bush he was searching for. Two months previous he and his partner had spent most of one night tying small pieces of cloth to bushes and shrubs in front of the Marine lines. These pieces of cloth were small and inconspicuous, and moved by the slightest rustle of wind.

He had learned the trick from a gunnery sergeant at sniper school, who had learned it in Vietnam from a VC sniper. The pieces of cloth aided snipers in gauging wind direction and speed. He had made sure to use cloth that blended well with the terrain. He grimaced inwardly at the recollection of the gunny's story. The Vietnamese had given away his position by his use of the homemade range flag. It had taken the gunny only one shot to end the man's career.

He moved the binoculars onto the bunker. The man was smoking again, his tools lying on the sloping face of the concrete. He noticed the sniper watching him and waved. From the top of the bunker Downs waved and said, "Hi, asshole." A green flag bearing the symbol of the Amal, the Shiite militia, now floated above one of the houses. It hung limply by the staff. All that work for nothing, the sniper silently thought. These amateurs supply their own range flags. He looked at his watch, then at the sky. The plane floated to the north of the runway, at least two minutes from touchdown. The sniper looked at Downs. "Hey, Corporal, do me a favor?"

Downs looked at the man. He had seen him around the battalion but had never before spoken to him. "Yeah, what do you need?" he asked.

"If you see an officer or a staff NCO coming before that plane gets here, jump into the bunker and let me know."

"All right," said Downs unsure. "What's the big deal about the plane?"

"Camouflage," answered the sniper with a malicious grin as he shared a conspiratorial wink with his partner. Downs smiled and said, "Good luck."

"Yep. You get your ass in the bunker after the plane rolls past us." Downs nodded as the sniper descended into the bunker and positioned himself behind the rifle. "Did you figure range?" he asked his partner.

"Yeah. I get three hundred twenty yards," the other Marine answered.

"Okay, that's good. I make it three-thirty, so we'll just split the difference." He made a minute adjustment on the fine-tune elevation knob of the rifle scope. He set the windage adjustment for "zero" as the Amal flag still hung limply on its staff.

"No wind," said his partner, then asked Downs, "where's that plane, Corporal?" Downs looked to the north. The big MEA airliner was approaching the runway, nearly at stall speed. He could already make out each wheel on the landing gear, they were no longer fused into a single indistinguishable black blur.

"Not long now, maybe a minute or two," said Downs from outside the bunker. The sniper looked at his partner, who grunted to acknowledge Downs. He peered through the telescopic sight and told himself to breathe evenly. He moved the crosshairs into the middle of the man's chest, then relaxed and closed his eyes. When he opened them again a few seconds later the crosshairs still rested at the same spot on the man's chest. Good, he thought, my position is nice and tight. Now all I have to do is wait for the plane.

The sniper knew that the noise from the plane's engines would obliterate the report from his rifle. So long as no officer or over zealous staff NCO was looking directly at the bunker when he fired, the shot would go unheard and unnoticed.

He and his partner had used this trick before when the Lebanese, or the Palestinians, had been bold enough to challenge the Marine position. He didn't relish the act of killing in this manner. Somewhere in his mind the idea existed that it was cowardly to shoot a man in this fashion. At such close range he could pick any area of the man's body and hit it with virtual certainty. The thought occurred to him that he should deliberately wound the man. Aim high into the right shoulder, or maybe at a leg. It would be easy enough to do, and no one would question him. Maybe the guy was just a carpenter or masonry worker who the militia had persuaded to do their work for them.

The sniper heard the high-pitched whine of the plane's engines and knew he would kill the man. At least I'll do it cleanly, he thought, with one shot through the heart and lungs. As the huge plane settled onto the runway the pilot reversed the engines and the air itself vibrated. A sudden fury rose in the mind of the sniper, alone behind his weapon, his finger on the trigger. The rifle flung itself into his shoulder, and he had a quick vision of blue sky through the scope before it settled back down onto its bed of sandbags. Through the sight he again saw the man, sprawled across the front of the bunker, his legs kicking spasmodically as he convulsed in death.

A large red stain spread across the Arab's chest as Downs lowered himself into the bunker. He looked at Mac who had watched it all with Smith and Ferris from another firing port. The four exchanged silent glances. "Jesus Christ," said Downs, then he sat on his cot at the rear of the bunker.

"Jesus Christ," he repeated. Smith, Mac, and Ferris remained at the firing ports. All the Lebanese disappeared off the street. From somewhere down the line of Marine bunkers rifle fire pierced the afternoon air as the noise from the plane fell to a low rumble. The Marines yelled wildly as the first shots rang out and the firefight began.

The sniper backed away from his weapon. He could smell his own nervous sweat as he rose to leave the bunker. He avoided the faces of Downs and the others. As he stepped past his partner the other Marine laid a hand on his friend's shoulder. "It's a war, man. Remember that," he said.

CHAPTER

7

Awaad awoke in the early morning, before the sun rose, and washed. The stones of the floor were cool and refreshing on his feet as he shuffled to the basin and ran water from the tap. He allowed it to run until it became clear. He splashed his hands in the pool of water, then onto his face. The water was cold and washed away the sleep from his face. He felt the beginning of a mustache and whiskers on his chin. When this day is done he thought, anything I ask will be mine. My name will be praised by generations and I shall be a great martyr. He thought of the photos taken of him by the Brotherhood. He had sat upon a beautiful green chair, the kaffiyeh of the Brotherhood wrapped around his head, an AK-47 rifle clasped defiantly across his chest and the flag with the emblem of the Brotherhood draped behind him. They had taken many photographs of him, and after his death he knew that these would be made into posters and nailed to every house, wall, and communal building in his village and many others. Beautiful girls would gaze at his photograph and be saddened that they would not know him. He smiled to himself at the image of a beautiful dark-eyed girl standing in front of his poster, her heart made heavy by the loss of one so young, and so committed to the purity of Islam. The thought warmed him as he sat on his small bed and began to dress. He would not take food this morning. On this day, of all days, he wished his body, and his mind, to be pure.

He thought often of the girl standing in front of his poster. Perhaps she would have a younger sister or brother with her. She would tell the child of Awaad's exploits, and his great victory, and say that the child should strive to be like Awaad. The girl herself would be young, perhaps sixteen or seventeen years old. She would be innocent. Not like the woman they had brought for him in Damascus. She had not been young, or innocent, or even beautiful. She had not been pure in her thoughts, and the Syrian officer who had brought her to him had laughed when he refused to lay with her.

He had never liked the Syrian officer. He did not trust the man. The Syrian was perhaps forty years old, with a muscular build that belied his age. Awaad had noticed that he rarely wore his uniform, but his bearing identified him as a military man. Awaad had seen the Syrian alter his clothing as well as his demeanor when the situation demanded it. He knew that behind the Syrian's calm demeanor and smooth manners lurked a repressed fury that casual observers missed.

The others members of the Brotherhood respected him and said that he had great influence in Damascus, and was a great warrior. Awaad and two others had been selected by this man only one month ago. He had taken them to Damascus for training. There was no talk of the holy *Koran,* or the Prophet in the Syrian training center. His days had been devoted to the study of electrical apparatus, learning to fire the AK-47 and Tokarov pistol, and to driving various-size vehicles. Awaad and the two others, Salem and Rifat, were poor village boys. They did not understand mechanical devices, and only Rifat had any experience driving a car. Awaad had done poorly with the driving and electrical and explosive studies, but he had been the best shot with both the pistol and the rifle. These were the matters he felt were most important. A warrior must know how to handle his weapons.

Two days before they were to complete their training Salem had wrecked the small truck he had been given to drive that day. Although he was not hurt badly the truck was demolished, and the Syrian officer had been furious. After he learned of the incident he had slapped Salem across the face, then hit him with a leather belt. That night, after swearing revenge, Salem had slipped out of the barracks. When his absence was discovered the next morning, the Syrian had berated Awaad and Rifat, saying that all Lebanese were weak, and this was why the Israelis and the Palestinians were able to invade Lebanon and make its people do their bidding. He had not hit Awaad, or Rifat, but that evening, after the day's training was completed, they had been moved to a small room with one narrow window, and locked in for the night. From that moment at least one of their Syrian instructors was always with them.

Within a few days other members of the Brotherhood had arrived from Beirut. They came to celebrate the completion of Rifat's and Awaad's training. There had been a lot of talk of great victories, courageous deeds, and devotion to Islam and the Prophet. Rifat and Awaad were treated with a new respect by the members of the Brotherhood.

After a day of rest Awaad, his brothers Marwan and Ahmud, and the Syrian officer had driven to Beirut. Once there they had gone to a house Awaad had never seen before. Each day the Syrian had taken him for endless hours of aimless driving. He could now drive the two paths to the U.S. Embassy from memory, and he could recognize the building without fail from any angle.

Each day of driving had built his confidence and sharpened his skills. Yesterday he had told the Syrian that he was ready and they had driven past the embassy. The Syrian had taken the wheel in order that Awaad might take a better look at the entrance. Later, they had parked the vehicle and strolled down the corniche, stopping in front of the embassy long enough to buy pastries and fresh almonds from a street vendor.

As they looked at the photos the Syrian had told Awaad that he would be close by, saying that he would take photographs of Awaad's moment of triumph. The Syrian had stressed, over and over again, that Awaad could make only one pass. He must not drive by the embassy, then return to it. The security guards would suspect a trick and possibly prevent Awaad from entering the embassy compound. Awaad knew why the Syrian would be close by, and why he insisted that Awaad make only the single pass. He thinks that I might not have the courage to do it. If he sees me go past the embassy he will use his radio device to detonate the bomb, and I will die anyway. Awaad smiled to himself, I won't fail, he thought.

After he finished washing Awaad prayed. He knew that he was capable of the task before him, and asked only that Allah smile on him and grant him that many Americans might be in the building when he reached it. He heard the Syrian approach from down the hall and rose from the floor. As the Syrian unlocked the door Awaad smiled again. Today is my day he thought, and mine alone. He looked into the impassive face of the Syrian, who asked, "Will you take breakfast with me?"

"No. I am ready now," he answered.

"It is too early. We must wait until nine-thirty or ten o'clock so that the staff will be in their places working. Everything must be perfect. You may wait here until I call for you." As the Syrian began to close the door Awaad asked, "Why do you lock the door? I am not Salem."

The Syrian regarded him briefly, then shrugged. "As you wish," he replied. Awaad knew that he would be just down the hall, sitting at his desk, facing the only door that led out of the small house. Still he did not like the Syrian and even so small a point as this, once conceded by the Syrian, was a point of pride for Awaad.

Awaad looked on as a shining black Chevrolet Blazer pulled into the walled courtyard below him. The Syrian officer went outside and spoke to the driver. The two men spent about one hour finishing the wiring of the explosives. The Syrian checked each connection that led to the various packages of explosives concealed throughout the small truck's interior. Side panels had been removed, as had the box for the tools, even the spare tire had been packed full of explosives. Each package of explosives was wired separately to the switch that acted as a trigger. Ideally, the explosives would all detonate simultaneously, producing an enormously destructive explosion.

The Syrian officer knew from experience that the jolting of the vehicle could loosen even the best connections, or in other ways disturb the wiring harness. He had therefore installed three independent firing mechanisms. The secondary wiring harness was color coded black, and paralleled that of the first. It was virtually identical to the primary system, with one important exception. Built into the system was a pressure sensitive switch under the driver's seat. This feature was activated by a toggle switch mounted in the rear of the vehicle. Once the driver was seated, and the toggle switch was thrown, the circuit was complete. Should the driver take his weight off the seat after the circuit had been completed and the system armed, the switch would detonate the explosives, killing the driver and whoever else happened to be in the vicinity. He would personally fasten the driver's safety belt, which once locked, could not be unlocked by the driver.

The third system was also a precaution against a last minute change of heart by the driver. Buried within each pack of plastic explosives was an electric blasting cap attached to a thin receiver. A small wire ran from each blasting cap to the vehicle's aerial. Should a driver fail to detonate the car bomb at the most opportune moment, the Syrian would be close by with a handheld radio transmitter and he would send a signal on a preset frequency that would detonate the explosives.

He was rather proud of his wiring arrangement. He had perfected it over the course of some months by the trial and error method. Until now he had not failed to do at least substantial damage to a target. Only rarely did the driver have an opportunity to actually detonate his own bomb, and thus bring about his own death. He had found that they tended to either not detonate it at all, or to do it too late to take full advantage of the explosives' potential.

He had made something of a reputation for himself among his fellow officers. He was known as a man who did not fail. He was proud of his reputation, and he guarded his techniques and procedures closely.

He had refused all orders to return to Damascus and become an instructor for other officers. He had no desire to share his knowledge, and he knew it was a measure of the esteem in which he was held that he was not forced back to Damascus. No one questions success, he reasoned.

He again checked the trigger assembly, and the connections to the wiring harness. This was his most important mission and he had no desire to see it ruined by mechanical failure. The vehicle had been prepared during the previous week in Damascus by technicians skilled in such matters, and the preparations had been supervised by his most trusted sergeant, Farouck. The men who had prepared it had been held at a barracks outside of Damascus while the project was in progress and would remain at this barracks until the completion of the mission.

He insisted on such precautions to prevent even the slightest hint of his preparations leaking to a foreign agent. More than one Arab operation had been met by Israeli commandos just as they hit the beach in some secluded part of Israel. He was convinced that the Mossad had thoroughly penetrated the Syrian government and armed forces, and this belief, combined with his knowledge of other types of electronic and satellite surveillance, was enough to make him go to any lengths to protect his operations.

After the vehicle had been wired and the system checked and rechecked by Farouck and the technicians, it had been held in a warehouse outside of Damascus until he had called for it. Once he had contacted Farouck and instructed him where to bring the vehicle in Beirut it had simply been a matter of waiting and watching the boy for signs that he might not have the nerve to go through with the operation. Farouck had driven the truck from Damascus with an escort of two security vehicles. They had left during the early evening hours so as to avoid any aerial surveillance and, to anyone who might have cared to watch, appeared as no more than casual traffic headed for the Lebanese capital. They had arrived some three hours after departing Damascus and returned to Syria the next day after their crews spent the night in a comfortable hotel in the city.

As soon as the security men were out of sight, he and Farouck had driven to the house where the boy was being held. No one knew the location of this house, not his controllers in Syria, not the boy's fellow militiamen, or even Farouck prior to his arrival. He did not communicate with his superiors from this location, and he had even taken the precaution of removing the telephone so as to ensure the boy could not make any calls from the house.

He had rented the house almost one year earlier from a Lebanese who was known for his discretion and who was an absentee landlord, choosing to spend most of his time in Paris since the advent of the violence in his native Beirut. The house was located in a modest but peaceful part of the city and had a small courtyard and large garage. A stone wall fronted the street and an iron gate was the only way to enter. The Lebanese landlord believed him to be a merchant who had relocated to Beirut to take advantage of the panic atmosphere in the city in order to make huge profits by importing foodstuffs from Syria and the Bekka Valley. The man had understood when he explained that he did not want to buy property, even at greatly reduced prices, in a city with so uncertain a future as Beirut. The Lebanese had offered to rent him this house, which he explained while modest, was comfortable and offered privacy and peace. He had agreed to the rental and paid six months' rent at their next meeting. The Syrian had signed an option to rent for another six months using false identification papers he had acquired without the help of his superiors. At the end of the first six-month period he had simply mailed a cashier's check to his landlord with a note explaining that he might want another six-month option and would the man be so kind as to forward him the paperwork. His Lebanese host had done so, the paperwork arriving promptly one week later.

During the previous six months he had used the house sporadically, but never in connection with a mission and he had never taken anyone to it. He had spent time there on occasion so as to give it the appearance of being occupied. He had also installed a timing device, purchased from a hardware store in Paris, that turned the lights of the house on and off in a logical and random manner. Although he had not met any of his neighbors he was confident that had they been asked by someone about the occupants of the house they would have answered that he seemed to be a good neighbor, quiet and never any trouble.

He had also taken care whenever approaching the house to clean himself of any possible surveillance. This he did by walking or driving a circuitous route that allowed him to detect anyone who might be following him. Often he would spend hours doing this to ensure that no team of agents, enemy or his own, was behind him. Although he had never detected surveillance in Beirut, he always checked for it, and now felt secure in bringing Farouck and the boy to the house.

After his inspection he was confident that the wiring had survived the trip from Damascus intact, and that the job had been done properly. The thought crossed his mind that this mission, while not his most difficult, was his most daring. He had not told Farouck what the target was, and he was not certain he would. Although he trusted Farouck and knew him to be reliable, there was no real reason to tell him.

He would ask Farouck to talk to the boy. He was interested in Farouck's evaluation of him. He had not been able to find any common ground with the boy and that thought nagged him. Everything depended on him. He must get close enough to the embassy for the explosive to do real damage. If he drove by and the detonation took place on the street only minor damage would be done to the building and perhaps a few people would be injured or killed. He wanted a stunning event that would draw the international news media and shock the world community.

He sighed. All the mechanics were in place. He had done everything he could to ensure the mission achieved the maximum effect and success. The rest was up to the boy. He had been selected with care, chosen over the other because he was a bit more naive and had the light of a true believer in his eyes. It was a shame to waste him on this when the real test would not come for some months. But success today was critical, and he was more certain of Awaad than Rifat at this point.

Two hours later he strolled casually along the sidewalk, glancing at the sea as it shimmered in the morning light. The day was slightly overcast, and a chill hung in the air. He had driven by the location at least half of a dozen times in the past two weeks. No hotel was close enough to serve his purpose, so he had finally decided on a different course of action. Before he had always taken a room within sight of his target. Preferably a room on the higher floors, to eliminate any object that might interfere with the radio signal. He preferred to strike early in the morning. Men who have stood a long midnight shift are at their worst in the hours before dawn, and just before they are relieved. Weekends were also good. So were Mondays and holidays if the target were a Westerner. Like a lion he would wait in his lair for the pride to do his bidding. He would not eat until it had been done.

The first time he had expected the driver to detonate it himself, and this expectation had almost ruined the whole operation. The man had driven his vehicle onto the sidewalk in front of the target, then sprung from the vehicle and run. Automatically his hand had gone to the radio detonator and nothing had happened. He had looked on in horror as guards emerged from the building. Reflexively he had hit the radio detonator again. A split second later the target, and the bomber, had been ripped apart by the explosion.

Afterward he had been sick. Not at the idea of what he had done, but because of the fear of a near failure. The target had actually survived the blast, a fact that caused him more than a little worry.

He had spent a nervous few hours listening to local news reports and hoping for the man to succumb. While his prey clung to life he had debated his next move. Should the man live another attempt would have to be made while the security forces were at their highest state of alert. If he did not finish the job, and do so in short order, he would face almost certain reprisals in Damascus. To allow the man to live after a bungled attempt was unthinkable. The president of Syria had publicly declared him a personal enemy. To the rest of the Arab world that meant the man was marked for death. For an attempt to be made unsuccessfully was a loss of face for the president among his fellow Arabs. While the president seethed he would be made to pay for his mistakes. Better a chance of success fighting the security forces of his target than a certain slow death in some cell in Damascus. Mercifully, the man had died in his hospital bed within hours of the bungled attempt.

Since then he had worked constantly to refine his plan of attack. The key was that each target held its own unique set of circumstances, and these dictated variations on the general theme. He had also found that the older bombers were not the best for the job. Nor were those with even limited education. With men such as these it was always necessary to trigger the detonation himself. He surmised that they knew enough about life to treasure it, even if they came to the realization when it was too late.

He had found that younger boys made the best bombers. Especially those boys who were from the small villages. Perhaps because they knew so little of life, or that their lives were so without pleasure, they were willing to give them up. Again, each boy was different. Each one a puzzle to be studied, and shaped into a weapon. A mechanism really. He was the weapon, they were simply one of the components that allowed it to function.

The Syrian realized that this boy was perhaps a little different from the others. This boy was simple, but not without intelligence. The Syrian knew the boy disliked him, but also realized that he must do his bidding in order to accomplish their mutual goal. Long ago he had dismissed his own faith, but this boy had a real belief. Not fanaticism exactly, just a very strong, very basic faith. He thinks he is the one who is using me, thought the Syrian. He feels unclean associating with me.

Offering him the woman had been a mistake. He was not sure why, but it had been. He had almost lost him then. He had compounded his error by laughing in front of the boy's brothers and the other members of the Brotherhood. But he was certain of this boy, he would detonate the bomb himself. That was rare.

Allowing him to train with the weapons was the master stroke. He saw the light in the boy's eyes, and he knew then that he had struck this boy's center and that when his moment came he would not fail. He smiled to himself. Presenting the boy with the pistol this morning had been another inspired idea. He had toyed with the idea of presenting it in the name of the president of Syria, but decided against it. That would have meant nothing to this boy who had his own reasons and motivations. The Syrian knew, without understanding, that this boy paid homage to a higher figure than Assad.

He took a seat at a table on the sidewalk, two hundred meters from the embassy. It wasn't an ideal position but he was well within range of the transmitter and he had a good line of sight to the front of the building. As he ordered coffee he patted the transmitter in his jacket pocket.

He fretted momentarily as a large truck drove by, blocking his view of the target. Such a truck would also block the signal from the transmitter. He scouted the street for a secondary location, and seeing none he decided to move across the street and stand on the sidewalk. He almost rose from the chair, then settled back down to wait for his coffee. An odd thought occurred to him, that it added excitement to the game if he waited where he was. He was equally sure the boy would detonate the device as planned, still, he enjoyed the thrill of the possibility of something going wrong. The stakes he was playing for added to his excitement, and the enjoyment of seeing his plan unfold.

His hotel was only a few blocks away. He had ordered a huge meal to be sent to his room, and champagne. French champagne, and turtle eggs. He was always ravenous afterward, something about the undercurrent of fear that accompanied any operation. Usually he liked to sit in his room and eat as he watched the confusion in the streets below him. It was not possible this time, but this would be a great victory.

His eye caught the vehicle as it rounded the corner, the boy driving smoothly in the right lane. He smiled. The street was clear, no trucks to block the signal or his view, even if he did need to use the detonator. He clenched his teeth, wondering if the boy would do it, fighting the urge to move his hand to his pocket and grasp the detonator.

As the black Blazer swung into the embassy compound a guard shouted. The vehicle jumped the curb and smashed through the plate glass doors of the lobby. A huge explosion ripped the air as an orange ball of flame leapt up the face of the building. Glass, paper, and rubble shot into the air appearing to hover on an invisible fulcrum high above the street before descending on the pedestrians below. As the rubble showered those on the ground and the sound of the explosion died away, a symmetric rumbling rose above the shouts of the people on the street.

Huge sections of the embassy broke away from their shattered supports and tumbled to the ground below. A thick cloud of black smoke arose from the center wing of the building as ruptured gas mains ignited and set fire to anything combustible. Vehicles that had been parked in front of the building were instantly ignited and spewed oily black smoke into the morning sky.

Rubble blown into the air above the embassy fell back to earth as a layer of dust and grit covered everything in the vicinity of the embassy. Papers floated back to earth at a leisurely pace or were carried away by the breeze from the sea. Chunks of concrete smashed to the ground as terrified embassy personnel descended the remaining stairs and ran from the dying building. In the first few minutes after the explosion the area around the embassy was a scene of utter chaos and disorganization.

Within minutes Lebanese civilians in the area recovered from their shock and began to search for survivors amid the wreckage. Vehicles driving along the corniche were stopped and injured from the embassy were unceremoniously thrown inside, the driver having been instructed to take them to the nearest hospital. Rescue workers appeared shortly thereafter and began to scour the rubble for survivors buried beneath tons of concrete.

The boy had placed the truck perfectly. The building was built in three wings facing the broad boulevard and the ocean. The two outside wings faced slightly inward, as if attempting to embrace the lawn and half moon drive leading to the center section of the building. He watched in satisfaction as the center wing of the embassy disintegrated before his eyes. The rumbling he had heard was the successive collapse of the eight floors of the embassy toward the foyer, where the boy had detonated his truck full of explosives. The building had been gutted and large chunks of concrete hung from steel reinforcing rods. In several places the face of the building had been ripped away by the force of the explosion and the collapse of upper stories. Offices now lay visible to people on the street in front of the burning structure.

The thought occurred to him that it was a bit like looking in a neighbor's window, except the people inside were not visible. He realized as he reached for his coffee that his hand was on the detonator. As the first sirens began to wail in the distance he settled the bill and headed for the hotel.

CHAPTER

Griffin walked away from the platoon sergeant, unsure of the task that lay before him. The platoon was to pull out of the line, be loaded on trucks, and driven to the U.S. Embassy somewhere north of the airport, in the heart of Muslim west Beirut. All the lieutenant and the staff sergeant could tell him was that some sort of bomb had hit the embassy. First reports indicated that part of the building had collapsed, and there would be civilian casualties.

Griffin passed the word to his corporals as a squad from Bravo Company came up to relieve them. They sat in the grass, resting on their packs while first platoon packed its gear, drew rations and ammunition, then loaded onto six-bys. Two jeeps, each having a .50 caliber heavy machine gun mounted in its rear well, rolled into place at the front and rear of the small column. The squad sat in the trucks, laughing and joking among themselves.

Griffin sat down with Downs and his squad and pulled a laminated map from his pocket. The map showed the entire city, with major routes and buildings clearly marked. He spread it over his knees and began searching for the American Embassy. Street names appeared in Arabic, but, mercifully, the glossary and corresponding numbered buildings were marked in English. "It's around here," said Downs, looking over Griffin's shoulder and stabbing the map with a dirty finger.

"You sure?" asked Griffin.

"Pretty sure. What does the glossary say?"

"Fuck me, who can read this rag-head shit anyway," said Griffin annoyed. Samson lifted a corner of the map. Looking toward Downs he asked, "Do you know where it is, Corporal Downs?"

"Yeah, up north, on the coast. The locals call it the Corniche, or something like that. I think it's even numbered, maybe one fifty-three. I'm not sure."

"Son of a bitch, he's right. It's right here. Look," said Samson. All three bent to take a closer look at the map, then automatically checked the distance between their position and that of the embassy. "It's a long way, Sergeant Griffin," continued Samson. "How long do you think it will take us to get there?"

Griffin looked at Samson, then shrugged, "Who knows? Downs, you got any idea?"

"Not really. An hour maybe. Give or take a few minutes." The driver of the heavy truck came around to the rear of the vehicle and slammed the gate into place. He looked at Griffin and said, "Five minutes, Sergeant."

"Okay," nodded Griffin absently. "You people lift that canvas up so you can see out," he ordered the squad. "I want every man facing outboard. Tiger, you put your gun up front, over the cab. We're gonna be the last vehicle in line so the jeep with the fifty cal will cover our ass. I want a rifleman and a grenadier at the rear of the vehicle. Corporal Downs, you sit up front with the driver and help navigate. Don't let him get separated from the rest of the convoy.

"Is comm up?" he asked the radioman.

"Yeah, Sergeant Griffin. We're up," replied the radioman.

The truck lurched forward as the convoy turned north out of the Marine perimeter. The Marines stared at the traffic in the street. Lebanese drivers honked their horns and waved gaily. Occasionally a Marine would lift a hand and return the gesture. The convoy moved north on the coast road, traffic moving out of the way as the vehicles gained speed.

Griffin noted the battle-damaged buildings, periodically consulting his map for references to determine the position of the convoy. As they moved past a series of rocks off the coast Griffin jabbed the map and said, "We're here."

Samson looked over his shoulder and grumbled, "We're a long

fucking way from home. How much farther do you make it to the embassy?''

"We're about halfway. Maybe another twenty minutes if we keep up the pace." As the vehicles turned east along a wide boulevard they slowed in traffic. Ahead they could see a black column of smoke billowing into the sky. Traffic choked the street and the lead vehicles moved onto the median, crawling ahead. Griffin noted that very few of the buildings now visible had any battle damage. The convoy ground to a stop and the troops began to dismount and form up. One squad was left behind as security for the vehicles as the platoon moved off, the sea on their left some twenty yards away.

Lebanese civilians lined the sidewalk and looked out of windows of houses fronting the street. Griffin nodded occasionally, not understanding what they said. He decided their tone was friendly, if somewhat confusing. He noticed a line of vehicles with red lights and red and white markings on their sides. As the squad drew abreast of the last vehicle he decided that they were ambulances, lining up in order to pick up the wounded.

Crowds of curious Lebanese were pushed aside as the platoon drew even with the embassy. French military vehicles were parked on the boulevard in front of the building and at least a dozen charred cars were tossed haphazardly on the street and drive in front of the embassy. Oily smoke rose from the center wing of the eight-story building, obscuring most of it, but Griffin could see that it had borne the brunt of the blast. The floors of the center section had collapsed, leaving a huge pyramid shaped mound of rubble covering what was once the entry to the embassy. Flames leapt from the rubble and periodically chunks of concrete and other debris would fall, scattering the myriad of rescue workers moving in and out of the ruined building.

The squad moved to form a perimeter in front of the embassy grounds. French Marines acknowledged their presence with curt nods. Griffin noted that French medics were treating a number of casualties on the sidewalk across the street. Other casualties were brought to the first ambulance in line, which would then speed off, sirens wailing. Griffin even saw two bleeding people placed in the back of a station wagon which appeared to have been commandeered for the occasion. He heard staff sergeant Whitney shout "Sergeant Griffin!" and turned to face the platoon sergeant.

"Yeah, Staff Sergeant," he answered.

"We are going to have to clear people out of our perimeter. I want you to anchor your squad on the far end of the building and tie it in with the second squad somewhere near the center of this yard in front of the embassy. When we've done that we will limit the number of people moving in and out of our area. All of this paperwork blowing around here belongs to the embassy, and most of it is probably classified. As soon as possible we'll assign a detail to start picking it up. The French are going to put up roadblocks on the boulevard in front of us and on that street leading up the hill, away from the embassy. They will also provide security for the rear of the building. There's some sort of parking lot back there and they are going to set up behind the retaining wall."

"How soon will third squad be up?" Griffin asked.

"I don't know. Soon I hope," answered Whitney. "When they get here we'll pull the vehicles in front of the embassy fence. That will give us some cover and block the view of the curious. We'll put a jeep on each flank to cover traffic from either direction on that boulevard."

Griffin surveyed the wreckage in the embassy compound, then looked at the tall buildings lining the street. "How is our comm, Staff Sergeant?"

"Not good. The radios are blocked by all these office buildings. There's a captain around here someplace though. He's assigned to the French as liaison officer and he's trying to work through their net to get comm with the battalion or with MAU."

Griffin grunted then said, "Okay, Staff Sergeant. I get the picture." He walked away frowning and got the squad on line, the last man a few paces from the first man in the second squad. Anyone not helping the rescue effort was moved back, away from the crumbling building. As the squad moved farther away, the distance between each man increased. When they were almost ten yards apart Griffin halted them, and each man took cover behind whatever was available. Most just stood, stealing glances back at the embassy, whose center section continued to burn unabated. The ground around the drive was littered with broken glass, fragments of masonry, and other bits of debris. As the wind shifted the smell of tear gas hit the Marines. Griffin approached Downs. "You smell gas, Corporal Downs?" he asked.

"Yeah. You?" came the reply.

"Yep. Our fucking masks are on the trucks with our packs, too. Great," said Griffin sarcastically.

"Where do you think the gas is coming from?" asked Downs.

Griffin glanced back at the embassy. Flames leapt from the pile of rubble. "Well, I'm not sure," he shrugged. "Probably it was in the armory that the Marine detachment kept. Maybe the heat from the fire is cooking it off."

"Well, if that's the case then some of their ammo might start cooking off. Wouldn't that be great."

Griffin rubbed his chin, thinking, "It could happen. What a kick in the ass. First they bomb our fucking embassy, then we get shot in the ass by our own ammo. Serves us right. They should'a shut this place down months ago. It's nothin' but a pain in the neck anyway."

Downs cast a quick look at Griffin. "How could we do that? Closing down our embassy here is like saying we give up on them as a country. If we did that they wouldn't have any faith in us."

Griffin raised an eyebrow and looked quizzically at Downs. "Tell me something, Corporal Downs. What fucking planet do you come from? Do you think we came here to save the world? Didn't you even notice that we are holding the airport as well as several kilometers worth of the Israeli supply route for their troops on the other side of those mountains over there? Shit, we're just here helping out our good buddies in the IDF. Helpin' to make sure that if their MSR is cut off at some point they can use good ol' Beirut International to keep the boys stocked up on beer, chips, and ammo." Griffin nodded at the smoking embassy, "This ain't nothin' more than a sideshow, Downs. Somebody's way of making a point. And the point is, watch your ass."

"Ah, I don't know, Sergeant Griffin. I think a lot of these people, Muslim and Christian, really want our help."

"Yeah," Griffin said in agreement, "sure they do. But we took sides, Downs. Did you really think nobody would get pissed about all those shells the navy threw up into those hills the other day? Or had you forgotten about that?"

"Maybe, but it only takes a few individuals with some explosives or a TOW to do something like this. Then everybody at home focuses on this and not the bigger picture. When that happens the guys who blew up the embassy accomplish what they set out to do."

Griffin shook his head and continued, "I don't know, Downs, but I'll tell you what I see. I see my platoon, and a French platoon, in a city of two million people. We're an hour from any real help, they won't give us supporting arms even if comm were up to ask for it. We're standing around while what's left of the American Embassy slowly collapses and burns. This is not what I consider an ideal tactical situation. So until help gets here let's make sure we watch our collective ass."

Downs grinned, "Sure, no problem, Sergeant Griffin. We can handle this." Griffin shook his head and walked away as Downs moved off to speak with Mac who stood nearby.

Mac shifted his weight to the other foot for the thousandth time and nodded toward the crowd on the sidewalk, "What do you suppose they want, Steve?"

"I don't know. Some of them are just curious no doubt. Like people who follow fire trucks to a fire just to watch the building burn. Probably some of them had relatives working in the embassy. I saw some Lebanese being carried out on stretchers. I guess the embassy might have some Lebanese employees. I don't know. Maybe the embassy is only in part of this building and the rest is office space for companies."

"No, I'm pretty sure the whole thing belongs to us," said Mac. "Jesus, look at it. This whole place is just all fucked up. Ferris stepped on somebody's hand awhile ago. Just a hand. Nothing attached to it. God, Steve, what the fuck is going on here?"

Downs shook his head. "I don't know, but Sergeant Griffin says this is just payback for the navy shelling that ridgeline and those Lebanese villages the other day."

"That what you think?" asked Mac.

"Who knows," shrugged Downs.

"Did you see that girl they brought out of here this afternoon? The one in red skirt that the Doc was working on over by the trucks?"

"No," Downs lied.

"Well, I did," continued Mac. "She was American. I don't think she had been here too long. Christ, Steve. She died right there on the sidewalk. What sense does that make? You tell me. If they're pissed at the navy and they want to fuck with us, fine. But Jesus, why this fucking place?"

"I don't know, Mac. They're not like us I guess. Not in a fight anyway." Downs turned away and looked again toward the sea. Images of the girl played across his mind's eye. He had watched as she was lifted from beneath the rubble and brought to the aid station. Downs saw again the first trickle of blood slip from the corner of her mouth. He felt again the terrible sinking sadness in his chest. He had known the girl would die. He heard her ask for someone to talk to, but he couldn't go to her. While he watched Griffin had knelt next to the girl and spoken with her. Although Downs couldn't hear their conversation he saw Griffin take her hand, and he heard the girl's sobs. Downs had looked on as the girl's face was covered with a dirty piece of cloth. The corpsman had moved off to the next casualty, but Griffin continued to kneel by her. The battalion chaplain had arrived and tried to comfort the girl. Downs had watched as the chaplain pulled the white chasuble from a small case he carried and draped the cloth over his shoulders. The girl's red skirt peeked out from beneath the cloth used to cover her as the priest made the sign of the cross. Downs had watched numbly as the priest administered the last rites.

He had felt like an intruder, someone who accidentally looks into a house while passing by and sees some private moment of the family inside. He was unable to turn away until the priest broke the spell by mumbling something to Griffin, who nodded his head. Downs turned and fought to control his emotions. He was horrified as he realized the people around him were oblivious to the girl's death. Everywhere rescue workers moved about, searching for the wounded, dodging falling rubble, loading the injured into ambulances. Downs noticed two French soldiers standing at the far end of the building, sharing a cigarette. He could not comprehend the girl's death.

The bombing of the embassy, the death of nameless people who happened to be inside at the time, that was real enough to him as long as he wasn't personally involved in it. News accounts of the event read in the paper over breakfast, his mother remarking what a tragedy it was. That would be more real to him than the scenes that had passed before his eyes.

An oily cloud of smoke had drifted by and the heavy stench of burning rubber forced him to turn. He saw Griffin, still kneeling next to the girl, run a dirty hand through his hair. From the liner of his helmet Griffin took a handkerchief, wet it, and cleaned the girl's face. Then he had pulled the cover over her and walked away.

CHAPTER

Griffin looked at the squad as they shuffled toward the six-bys. They seemed tired, dispirited. There was none of the usual banter and horseplay. Well, it's been a tough couple of weeks, that's for sure. No fucking way to train for this kind of shit, it just happens, he thought.

"Well, what do you think, Sergeant Griffin? Will they make it?" Griffin turned to face Staff Sergeant Whitney. He looks like a new fucking penny, thought Griffin. How the hell does he manage that all the time?

Griffin shook his head and smiled, "Yeah, they'll make it, Staff Sergeant. But they look like shit. I've never seen 'em look this bad. Not even after a desert warfare exercise at Twenty-nine Palms."

Whitney chuckled. "Nobody gets killed when we go play war in California. 'Course, this really ain't much of a war. It's kind of chickenshit to bomb an embassy. Most secretaries and ambassadors aren't gonna put up much of a fight."

Griffin cocked an eye at the staff sergeant, who held up a hand and said, "Oh, I know, I know. I'm not taking anything away from them, son. They've had one hell of a sorry week. Picking up dead bodies and classified rubble ain't anybody's idea of a good time. Still, it ain't exactly Iwo Jima either. And I don't reckon these people are quite ready to call it even, if you know what I mean."

"Yeah, I know what you mean. The question is what are we going to do about it?"

The staff sergeant rubbed his chin and said, "I don't know. Right now we are going to get our asses a hot meal, a hot shower, and a good night's sleep in our own bunkers back at the company. Never knew I could miss that old cot so much, but just the thought of it gives me a hard-on. I can live without the other two, but I'm damn tired of sleeping on this fucking concrete."

Griffin grinned. "I didn't think it got to you, Staff Sergeant."

"Well, Sergeant Griffin, it does. Everybody bitches and moans, but you have to be careful who hears you when you do it. The troops are going to give credit to anything you say. Do you see what I mean?" Griffin nodded dutifully. "Well, this has been a shitty week, that's for sure. There's not much worse than picking up dead civilians. I don't much care for it. I don't imagine they do either," he said, nodding to indicate the platoon.

"So what happens now, Staff Sergeant Whitney? Do we just go back, dig in, hold on, and wait for the next attack?"

"Probably. Look son, this isn't a war. Not yet. Somebody at home has decided that the United States needs to make a statement to these people, or more likely to the Syrian government. We're just here to prove to them that they have to take Washington's bullshit a little bit more serious than usual. Somebody had to know this was going to happen. Hell, they evacuated all the diplomatic dependents months ago. After what happened in Iran the State Department knows damn well that embassies aren't sacred any longer. Look at this place. It's a mess. And what do they do about it? They move in with our buddies the British two hundred meters down the street. Nobody ever seriously considered shutting down the embassy. Business as usual, with a platoon of Marines outside to fill sandbags and guard the front door." Whitney shook his head and chuckled. "How's that for a sermon from the mount?"

Griffin grinned again, pleased that Whitney was confiding in him. It was unusual for the staff sergeant to offer his opinion. "Well, it'll have to do I guess," he said.

"C'mon, let's get our ass back to the house," said Whitney. He slapped Griffin on the back good-naturedly as he strode off.

Griffin took his place on the truck as the driver revved the engine and pulled into traffic. He looked over the squad. They seemed tired, but wary. The adventure part of it is over, he thought.

He unwrapped a chocolate disc and began to eat it. He looked again at the squad sitting shoulder to shoulder on the hard wooden benches in the back of the truck as the convoy picked up speed and headed south for the battalion headquarters. Downs sat across from him, his rifle held lightly in both hands, warily watching the buildings lining either side of the street. God, I'm tired of all this, he realized. The staff sergeant is right, a good night's sleep will feel great. He thought not of his cot back at the airport, but of the squadbay at Camp LeJeune. Griffin saw the rows of beds, equipment, and footlockers all precisely on line and scrubbed clean. He could almost feel the starchy stiffness of the clean sheets and hear the breathing of the platoon as they slept. His mind's eye pictured the uniforms neatly hung within his locker, and the gleaming shower stalls. A shower would feel good. A hot, steaming shower. So hot that it left your skin red.

As the truck bounced along Griffin recalled when he had first checked into the platoon, straight out of infantry training regiment at Camp Geiger. He had arrived in the steaming North Carolina summer sweating profusely into his class "A" uniform as he struggled to carry two seabags and a hanging bag with his dress uniforms. Most of the day had been spent going from regimental headquarters, to battalion headquarters, to the company headquarters, where he was finally assigned to a platoon. After a short lecture from the company commander regarding the numerous ways he might run afoul of the regulations and incur the full wrath and fury of the Uniform Code of Military Justice, he had been directed to a squadbay by a skinny redheaded company clerk. The clerk had shown him the way but had not offered to help carry the heavy seabags. Griffin arrived late in the afternoon on a day when the platoon was in the field. A lone Marine was in the squadbay standing fire-watch. He had introduced himself to Griffin and shown him an empty rack and wall locker that he could use. At first Griffin had been grateful for the sight of a friendly face. But after the guard repeatedly referred to Griffin as a "boot" he had decided he disliked the boy.

For two days the platoon had been out in the field and the squadbay was quiet. Griffin became acquainted with the four Marines who had been left behind to stand watch. He checked into the company, disbursing, and battalion offices. He drew his combat gear, went to chow, jogged, and lifted weights. Each morning he would stand in formation in front of the company office with the clerks who were not required to go to the field, then be assigned some menial chore by the company gunnery sergeant. No one spoke to Griffin except to give him instructions, and the tone then was usually condescending.

The squadbay was cool and quiet. The concrete floors had been worn smooth by the passage of thousands of boots over some forty-odd years. Each rack was neatly made, a six-inch wide white facing of sheet turned down on each one, and the black US printed on the blanket arranged squarely in the center of each rack. The head's white tiles gleamed, and painted on the vertical portion of each step leading to the second deck were words such as "honor," "integrity," and "camaraderie." The buildings themselves were of sturdy red brick, and neatly aligned on broad green lawns. From the window by his rack Griffin could see the salt estuary called New River, and a line of oak trees guarded the road running between the buildings that housed the other regiments. Griffin had found a certain comfort in the order and neatness of everything about him. For the first time in five months he was able to unpack his things without worrying when he would be leaving next, or without a sergeant instructor screaming in his ear.

The return of the platoon had been a shock to him. They had marched in from across New River Sound, hot, tired, and smelling of sweat and the field. He had seen them coming from the second-story window where he was sweeping a passageway. First the two lone "headlights" out in front of the formation, then the solid dark green snake of men dotted by the scarlet and gold guidons. He had heard their vulgar bawling as the squadbays came into their view and they knew this exercise was over. They had formed up in orderly ranks on the lawn in front of the barracks. Griffin could see that their uniforms and even their boots had salt stains on them. As the command was given to fall out none of them ran for the barracks. They picked up their gear and walked into the squadbay.

Once inside the platoon exploded with noise. Lines of men formed at the lavatories to drink and splash water on their faces. Those at the back cursed those in front. Others threw their gear onto their racks and lay on the deck. Boots were taken off and the stench of sweaty feet permeated the air. Some walked into the showers and turned the nozzles on themselves, still fully clothed. None of them acknowledged Griffin.

A huge staff sergeant entered the squadbay and gave orders for the weapons to be cleaned and returned to the armory prior to anyone taking a shower. NCOs shouted for them to get out of the heads and begin cleaning weapons. Mud from boots covered everything. Griffin had felt like an intruder. He stood by the entrance to the squadbay where he had been sweeping and tried to appear busy.

The squadbay now seemed an alien, hostile place. The noise was overpowering and seemed to increase every moment. Radios were taken from wall-lockers and blared at full volume, the noise bouncing off the concrete walls.

Within a few minutes of their arrival a sergeant had introduced himself to Griffin as his new squad leader. He asked if Griffin had a place to sleep. When Griffin pointed to his rack the sergeant told him to move his things. He explained that, even when they slept, the Marines were arranged by fireteam and squad. Griffin was out of order.

For the next few evenings, after the platoon had been secured from duty, Griffin would eat alone in the mess hall. The other Marines in his fireteam referred to him as "new guy" or "the boot," and Griffin had no desire to spend any extra time with them. After chow he would walk the mile to the base theater and watch a film. It wasn't important to him what was playing. As soon as the lights dimmed the audience would quiet down and he had time to think. It was often the only real rest he got. He would return to the squadbay minutes before the 2200 lights-out, polish his boots, and lay his uniform out for the next day. He thought the one step, with the word CAMARADERIE emblazoned boldly across its riser was a mockery. He glared at it in silent disgust each time he entered the squadbay.

Griffin quickly found out that only NCOs were allowed to enter the squadbay from the doors placed conveniently at the ends of the squadbays. Non-rates were required to enter from the central passage-ways that ran between the two wings of the building and then enter the squadbay through the double doors at its center, thus avoiding the areas at either end of the squadbay reserved for the NCOs.

Griffin had unknowingly used the entrance once, the evening the platoon had returned from the field. A corporal named Mackenzie, bone thin, had berated him while he stood at attention in front of the rest of the platoon. Griffin had been furious. His squad leader had returned from chow in the middle of Mackenzie's tirade and ordered Griffin at ease, then told him to exit the way he came. Griffin had felt the hair rise on the back of his neck as he walked past Mackenzie, who lounged on his rack, a smirk on his face as Griffin walked past glaring.

A week after the incident one of the lance corporals in his squad had suggested Griffin challenge Mackenzie at the Friday "smokers."

Griffin had asked the lance corporal to explain what "smokers" were and the lance corporal had burst out laughing. He had said that the company commander was a former Golden Gloves champion and still relished the sport. One Friday a month he would set aside an afternoon for boxing. Anyone below the rank of sergeant could be challenged, and though acceptance wasn't mandatory, no one had the courage not to accept. The bouts were no more than three, three-minute rounds, and each man used heavy sixteen-ounce gloves. Several of the larger non-rates had scored knockouts against smaller NCOs.

That afternoon Griffin had gone to the company bulletin board and penciled his name in under the "challenger" list, and Mackenzie's name under "challenged." For the rest of the week he was careful to avoid the squadbay between the evening meal and lights out. He knew he was bucking the system. He was too new to challenge anyone, but he was tired of being called "the boot," and frustrated over the public humiliation he had suffered from Mackenzie's dressing-down.

When Friday arrived Griffin sat alone and ate his breakfast. The platoon spent the morning cleaning weapons, then the platoon sergeant marched them to chow. Griffin ate a light lunch and drank extra glasses of water. He cast a quick glance at Mackenzie, who sat laughing with the other corporals and eating a normal meal. Before the boxing match the platoon sergeant took the whole platoon on a long run, finishing with a punishing sprint back to the company area.

Griffin struggled to remain quiet through the other bouts. He had to mentally will himself to sit still. Just before his bout he walked to the squadbay and took a short sip of water from the fountain, casting a sidelong glance at the CAMARADERIE on the step. As he turned to go out his squad leader stepped through the door. Without saying a word he had laced the heavy gloves onto Griffin's hands.

Griffin stood in silence, aware that the sergeant wanted to say something, but unwilling to initiate any conversation and thereby risk humiliation. Finally the sergeant had spoken, telling Griffin that, while Mackenzie might deserve any beating he could give him, Griffin would have to exercise good judgment. The whole purpose of the matches, from the sergeant's perspective, was to allow the settling of such grudges without destroying the credibility and authority of the NCOs. It also served to limit the excesses of the more zealous corporals. Griffin had cynically waited for the sergeant to tell him Mackenzie was really a good guy, and that Griffin had just caught him on a bad day. The sergeant stopped short of that. Griffin had asked what was expected of him, and the sergeant replied that anytime he fought he expected Griffin to win, plain and simple.

As he walked toward the ring he expected to hear catcalls, or worse, silence. Here and there he heard a word of encouragement for Mackenzie. A lance corporal from another platoon stood in Griffin's corner, loosely holding a towel. He winked at Griffin as he climbed through the ropes of the makeshift ring. Griffin defiantly wore the scarlet gym shorts issued to every Marine in infantry training regiment and scorned by those same Marines as an emblem of inexperience after they joined the fleet forces.

The staff sergeant who was refereeing the fight brought them together in the center of the ring and explained the rules. He then checked to see that each man wore a mouthpiece. He did not require that they shake hands.

The bell rung and Griffin felt the familiar tingling in his arms. He danced lightly toward the center of the ring and circled his opponent. He allowed Mackenzie to throw the first punches, in order to gauge his skill. He easily warded off the blows and decided that Mackenzie was a street fighter, and probably not very effective if he failed to land the first punch.

Mackenzie threw a flurry of wild punches and Griffin stepped inside his guard and landed a jab squarely on the nose. He knew that Mackenzie's eyes would water as the rush of pain hit him. Griffin correctly guessed that Mackenzie's next move would be to blindly charge him. He stepped to one side and landed a quick flurry of punches to Mackenzie's head.

Griffin knew that he could finish him, but instead he drew back, allowing Mackenzie the chance to clear his head. He looked at the corporal as his eyes cleared and knew that Mackenzie realized he was outclassed. The platoon was on its feet and chanting, not for Mackenzie, but for Griffin.

The corporal approached as Griffin got a quick glance of his squad leader, standing outside the ring, arms folded impassively across his chest. Griffin threw a quick series of punches to Mackenzie's head that broke his nose and knocked him to the mat. He noted with satisfaction the blood from Mackenzie's shattered nose staining the canvas. Automatically, he went to a neutral corner. He had watched as the Marines screamed their delight, and the staff sergeant counted Mackenzie out.

After being declared the winner Griffin had offered his hand to Mackenzie, who refused it.

That had been nearly seven years ago, and he had never again
entered the squadbay through the NCO hatches. As the truck full of
Marines wove its way through the city, Griffin glanced at Downs, his
fine features masked by a fuzz of beard and the dirt from a week without
a shower. I know you, Downs, he thought, because I know myself. It's
a cruel system unless you take it to heart. You have to surrender a part
of yourself to it, or it will cast you aside and make you bitter. The hardest
part is finding a graceful way to surrender to the system outwardly and
still retain the inward dignity your conscience requires. It's not so easy,
is it Downs? It takes everything from you with only the promise of
something better, and it's not kind or gentle, or even likable most of
the time. Every son of a bitch in the place screams at you, beats you,
and humiliates you in any way he can think of. And the only thing you
get in return is the right to call yourself a Marine and a couple more
years of guaranteed misery if you make it through the training.

Griffin looked at the boys sitting in the back of the truck as it jarred
along. He had known some of them since boot camp, others since they
came to the battalion. All of them were his friends to some degree. The
thought occurred to him that even his friends didn't know him any
longer. In order to survive in the Marine Corps he had changed himself,
at least outwardly. He had become harder, less friendly. Friends he had
known since becoming a Marine showed a certain coolness to him since
he had become a sergeant. That was the system. No fraternization
between the ranks. He was proud of having been promoted to sergeant.
It was a difficult rank to achieve, especially in a peacetime Marine Corps.
Still, it hadn't come without a price.

He looked again at Downs. He sensed that Downs had some inner
difficulty, some reason for escaping from home. Maybe he had gotten
into some trouble, or gotten a girl pregnant. Whatever the reason he
was here now, and he was Griffin's responsibility. Downs was different
from the rest, that was for sure, and Griffin had been unable to hit on
the proper means of reaching him. Well, Downs, he thought, along with
all the misery it gives to you the Marine Corps can give you something
else. It can give you a home for as long as you need one.

The trucks pulled into the compound that served as the battalion
headquarters. A massive four-story concrete structure once used by
the Lebanese Aviation Safety Bureau now housed the various units of

Marines. While some of the troops were combat units, most of them were support troops, and their tents ringed the retaining wall which surrounded the courtyard of the building on three sides. To the south, the face of the building looked toward the terminal across a broad flat expanse of macadam. The building itself was heavily battle-damaged and pieces of plastic and tent canvas hung in many of the building's ruined windows.

The troops began to jump out of the trucks and form up. Marines from the headquarters unit hung back. A pickup basketball game being played on a makeshift court in front of the building came to an abrupt end. Griffin jumped down and looked at the building. Officers strode in and out of it. Headquarters units had lots of officers and Griffin tried to avoid them whenever possible.

The staff sergeant approached Griffin and said, "The H&S company commander is going to have the engineers turn the showers on for us. They're in those tents over there. Leave two men to watch the gear, designate reliefs, and then turn 'em loose. The shower ought to be up in about twenty minutes. Hot water, no less. If we make it last long enough we can even get a hot meal from the H&S company mess."

Griffin laughed. "Aye, aye, Staff Sergeant," he said and turned to face the troops. Helmets, packs, and web gear began to hit the deck at regular intervals as the platoon shed its clothing and gear in place. Towels and shaving kits emerged from grimy packs, and the Marines filed into the shower tents. Inside the tents were clammy and humid from months of use. Pipes ran along the length of the tents, pierced at regular intervals by holes that served as shower heads. The pipes were encrusted with mineral deposits and supported by a network of moldy wooden framing. Cheers erupted as the shower heads nearest the reservoir sputtered to life, followed by cursing as the icy water hit the platoon. Amid catcalls a grimy engineer in coveralls stuck his head inside the tent and said the water wouldn't be hot for ten minutes.

Griffin worked to create a lather of soap under the chilling spray. The soap refused to lather and he decided it was due to the dirty water as much as anything else. He felt better as the grime washed off. His hands were hopeless, though. He scrubbed them with a toothbrush, but the grime refused to leave all the crevices in his skin. He toweled off then put on the same uniform he had worn for the past week. He noticed Downs putting on a clean one and smiled to himself. Better save that one, Downs, he thought. The trucks will leave before we've eaten, if they even let us eat, and then we'll have to hump back to the company. That nice clean uniform will be full of sweat before we're halfway there. He started to say something, then stopped. No need to rush it, there's plenty of time to bring him along, he realized.

Griffin left the showers and walked over to the staff sergeant, "Well, how does it look for the hot chow?" he asked.

"Pretty good," said Whitney. "Once they get showered up let's move 'em up by the MAU headquarters at the top of the hill there. I don't want 'em milling around down here. Better with the out of sight, out of mind approach," said the older Marine.

Griffin laughed. "Okay, Staff Sergeant. I'll form 'em up as soon as everybody's done. Is it okay if I let 'em go into the little store? All these headquarters troops are moving in and out of it."

"Yeah, go ahead, but let 'em go in threes and fours. We don't want to gum up the works if you know what I mean." Whitney paused, then said, "Sergeant Griffin, I'll be taking second and third squad back to the company tonight. Sometime after dark we'll hump back. You and first squad are going to be trucked out to a position near the U.S. ambassador's residence. The operations people have the details, and you and I will go up and get the scoop later. From what I gather it's some sort of uncompleted mansion sitting on the top of a hill deep in Indian country. The brass put a fancy radar rig up there, and left a squad of dragon gunners to guard it. For whatever reason they've decided to abandon it now. You and first squad will be trucked up with the fifty cal jeeps, then load up the gear and troops there, and come back to the BLT headquarters. It is only supposed to take one day, so you should be back at the company sometime late tomorrow evening or early the next morning."

Griffin digested the outline of the operation. Until this moment he hadn't been aware that any such isolated position existed. He had noted the cautious note in Whintey's voice, and he didn't relish the prospect of being trucked through a hostile city again, no matter what hour of the night or day. The trucks provided no protection from hostile fire, little cover, and forced the squad to bunch up. Griffin almost winced as he remembered what the grenade had done to the squad just a month ago when they were on foot and properly dispersed.

The trip back would be worse. With another squad in the same number of trucks they would be packed in and traveling through the city in the late afternoon or early evening. If they were ambushed it would be a disaster. He looked into the face of the staff sergeant, who had been watching him. "I don't like being trucked all over the place, Staff Sergeant Whitney. Can't they just evac these guys by helo?"

"Yeah. I asked that, too. The answer was no. Probably the pilots have been getting some infrared warnings and they're gettin' jumpy. Or maybe they have some equipment up there they want brought out that's too heavy for the birds. Anyway, we got the call 'cause we're here, and we're available."

"Jesus, we're gonna end up hauling out the ambassador's bedroom set. I can see it now," said Griffin.

Whitney laughed. "Well, it wouldn't really surprise me, but I don't think so this time."

"What do you think?" asked Griffin.

"I guess I think it's going to get a whole lot worse before it gets even a little bit better, so let's watch our ass. No sightseeing, no provoking the locals. Just get in and get out." The staff sergeant jerked a thumb toward the battalion headquarters building, "Somebody up there has figured out these people are playing for keeps and is bringing the boys in before the shit hits the fan. I'm going to give you another M-60 team. That way you'll have four machine guns all together, and two of those will be fifty cals. Make sure the gunners draw extra ammo from the armory. They won't have to hump it, just stack it on the trucks. If you end up staying there for the night, have them take the extra ammo in and set it up with their guns. Are we clear on that?"

"Yeah," nodded Griffin, "but do you think I'm going to need the extra gun?"

The staff sergeant winked at Griffin, "Better safe than sorry, Sergeant Griffin. Besides, I'm an old machine gunner and I don't think there's any such thing as too much firepower. Now let's go get some hot chow. We'll brief your squad later. I hear they even show movies against one of the hanger walls up by the MAU headquarters." The staff sergeant smiled broadly at Griffin, "What do you think. Feel like a movie tonight, son?"

CHAPTER

10

Downs settled down next to Mac on the sloped cement of the driveway. The concrete was still warm from the day's sun, and he and Mac arranged their packs to form a backrest. Downs leaned back and looked at his friend, who offered him a warm can of Pepsi. He laughed and took it. "God, I feel like a new man after that shower, Mac. It's like being born again, you know?"

"Felt good, that's for sure. Chow wasn't too bad either. Beats C-rats or an MRE."

Ferris and Smith sauntered up and dropped their packs with a thud. "Hey, Steve, y'all want some pogey-bait? Me and Wayne came prepared to watch this movie in style." Ferris offered a huge bag of M&Ms to Downs and Mac, who each took a handful. "Wayne, offer Corporal Downs a beer. He's looking a mite parched." Downs shot a look at Ferris, who grinned wildly, then withdrew a twelve-ounce Miller from his cargo pocket. "All perfectly legal, Corporal Downs. You know me and Wayne have the utmost respect for Marine Corps regulations. Ain't that right, Wayne?" grinned Ferris.

"Yep, that's a fact," said Smith, as he took a beer from each pocket and offered them to Downs and Mac, then located another in his pack for himself. "You know, at fifty cents a can a man could grow to like this place. Gotta do something about a 'frigerator, though. I can't get used to warm beer. It ain't civilized. That's how you can tell we're in a third world country, no cold beer," concluded Smith.

"Hey, Mac, do y'all know what time the movie starts?" asked Ferris.

"Well, Jimmy, they'll probably wait for it to get dark before they show it," answered Downs.

Ferris looked at Downs. "Yeah, I hope we're in the right place. Sergeant Griffin said this is it. And they got a part of that wall there painted white. We pretty much got front row seats if this is it."

Downs settled back against his pack and looked at the sky. Here and there a star appeared in the pale blue backdrop. Other members of the platoon wandered up and settled around them, automatically arranging themselves in neat rows. Word had filtered down from battalion operations section that first squad was to be sent out again before returning to the company area, while the other two squads would return the following day. Downs realized he was too tired to give it much thought. Instead he turned to Mac and asked, "What are you thinking about, Mac?"

"Aw, I don't know. This ain't too bad, Steve. You know? I'm glad we drew that run up to get those dragon gunners. Sort of breaks the routine. I didn't really want to go back to our holes at the company. Guess I'm bored with the same old shit all the time. At least this way we get to see a little of the city. Know what I mean?"

"Yeah, I think so. I'm sick of standing watch and walking patrol, that's for sure."

"Maybe we'll get liberty in the Med on the way home. Do you think we might?"

"I don't know. Maybe." Downs knew Mac was thinking of Athens. He had met a girl there. A small dark-eyed girl who spoke broken English and wrote him frequently. He knew because he recorded the number of letters Mac received. He felt it was an intrusion of Mac's privacy, but he did it because Griffin had ordered him to do it.

As if on cue Mac asked, "Think we might go to Athens again, Steve? That'd be cool, man. I could see Marina. It's been eight months since I saw her."

"I don't know, Mac. We've always gone to Athens on all of our other Med cruises, but it might be different now because of Beirut. You know, usually we float around the Med for six months and hit all the ports. But now, with Beirut, we might only go to one or two, or maybe just Spain to clean our gear."

Mac frowned. "Yeah, I was kind of thinking the same thing. Leave it to the Marine Corps to screw up everything. She said she would fly to anyplace around here we got liberty, as long as it's in the Med." Mac paused, then looked at Downs. "She wants to fly here," he said, obviously concerned.

"To Beirut?"

"Yeah, can you imagine that? Her comin' here to see me."

Downs looked at Mac, then laughed, "Something tells me the first shirt wouldn't exactly lay out the red carpet for her, you know?"

"Yeah, but she doesn't understand why I can't just take a few days vacation. Her life is so different."

"Yeah, I guess it is." Downs looked away from his friend, at the platoon sprawled around him. Helmets and weapons lay across bulky packs, and extra ammunition was strapped to each man's gear. Every man wore his heavy flak jacket with the attached web gear, and carried bandoleers of ammunition for his M-16. She wouldn't understand this, thought Downs.

She has no way to comprehend my life now. The thought struck him like a physical blow, and he turned farther away from Mac, ending their conversation. He wished it would hurry and become dark. He wanted to think of her, to lose himself in the daydream of her. Someone laughed and Downs inadvertently turned to face him. He was at odds with the person he was now, and the person she knew. Even if he left, it would never be the same. He could never explain this to her, or his desire to be a part of it.

Griffin walked by and nodded to him without speaking. He wondered what she would think of Griffin. Downs relished the thought that she would dislike him, but instinctively knew that he was wrong. She would see Griffin as an integral part of something she herself could never like or understand. But she would also view Griffin as a natural part of all this. He was in his element she would say, while you, Steven Downs, are an impostor. She would tell him that he didn't belong here, that he should be somewhere else, pursuing other things.

Downs thought of a summer day, they were both in high school, and she had come to watch him play baseball. He always walked to the games alone, knowing she would be there later to watch and to drive him home. Downs was in the habit of arriving early for the games, before any of his teammates arrived. He would enter the huge wooden grandstand with its tin roof and wire netting to shield the spectators from foul balls and sit alone. Halfway up the bleachers, amid the peeling green paint, he would sit. It was one of his favorite places. Alone in the silent stands he would absorb the sights and smells of the place as it slowly came to life before the game.

The ballpark had been built for a minor league club in the early 1920s when baseball was America's favorite pastime. The old club was long since defunct, and the diamond relegated to the games of various high schools and summer-league teams, but the stadium retained all its grandeur and recalled a time when a baseball game was a special event. Downs would stare out over the field, absorbing its colors, feeling as though he owned the place.

Just behind the old ballpark, beyond the left field wall, was a small zoo belonging to the city. Animals from various parts of the world paced their cages while high school boys played baseball. The big cats were located just behind the center field wall and often enough the cheering of the crowd would be answered by a roar from the old lion who lived out his life in a cage just out of range of home run balls.

Downs had been going there, sitting alone in the bleachers, since he was a small boy. He had watched two older brothers and a collection of neighborhood boys play on that field. He had waited, patiently, to play his own games there. And now that he was playing there the feeling was even better than he had imagined, and he wanted to relish every second of it. After his senior season he would once again be reduced to the role of a spectator, no longer a player on the field.

He hated himself for being aware that it would all end too soon. He tried not to let himself think of the day when he would play his last game here, and he envied his friends who enjoyed themselves blissfully unaware that it would all end far too quickly.

During the games she would be there, waiting to catch his eye and share a conspiratorial smile. She had once told him that she loved baseball because it was a gentle sport that required a combination of strength and grace. She had watched Downs play football only once, and they had argued afterward.

When he had told her he was joining the Marine Corps it was just a quick, barely audible phrase, mumbled the day before he left for Parris Island. That night he had played his last game at the old ball field, and a terrible melancholy had overtaken them. They were sitting on the hood of her car, a half moon low over the lake. She hadn't said anything to him. He had looked straight ahead, knowing that he was at the end of the most extraordinary summer of his life, and knowing that he would lose her.

Downs knew better than to try and make promises of writing, of coming home to her. They had driven home in silence, and said a quick good-bye in front of his house. As Downs walked up the drive he had heard her say, "I love you, Steven, but I won't when you come home. I'll love someone else."

He had almost turned. His step had faltered, and his eyes had watered. He had left the next day for boot camp. When he returned four months later she was away at college and they had exchanged letters only twice. He knew that his letters had been stiff, too formal.

He was at a loss for a way to bridge the distance between them, and her words had hurt him deeply. It wasn't so much his joining that had hurt her, it was that he had this hidden part of himself that wanted to do it. It was a solitary act, an act of independence, both from the boy he was and the person he was with her. He knew that he had hurt her, he just didn't know how to explain something to her that he didn't fully understand himself.

While he was home on leave he had gone to the old ballpark and sat alone in the bleachers. The weather was turning from autumn to winter and he had felt a sadness descend over him as he sat there. It was the first time he had felt the absence of others in the old stadium.

He wasn't able to drop the rigidity forced upon him at Parris Island. He had sat there for over an hour, realizing that he would always be too complex to be just a Marine, and that after Parris Island he was not able to return home. He wasn't a part of it any longer. He waited for the feeling to come to him, knowing that he had lost it forever because he had changed.

He had left the old ballpark and walked through the zoo that day. Eventually finding himself in front of the lion's cage. The old cat sat gnawing contentedly on a mangled baseball. Downs had wondered if someone had finally hit a homer long enough to reach the cage. He noticed that the lion was getting old, its coat had lost its shine, and his eyes were black holes sunk in swollen lids. Downs felt sorry for the lion, sorry that the animal would never know the freedom of the grasslands, that he would spend his whole life in the cage where he had been born. He had left the zoo then and gone home, glad that he was leaving that afternoon for his regiment.

On the ride to the airport his father had driven past the ballpark, recounting the exploits of his sons on the old diamond. Downs had stared out the window in the opposite direction, not wishing to see the old stadium fade from sight.

He realized then that he had paid a terrible price to become a Marine. He had lost a part of himself. He wasn't able to fully give himself to the Marine Corps, and without such an embrace of the system, he could never fully belong to it. The Marine Corps had taken something from him. It had taken a part of his innocence. Downs thought of the day the sniper had shot the man on the bunker. He felt a part of the incident, soiled by his participation, no matter how peripheral. He knew that he could never again sit in the bleachers and feel the old feeling. He had known it all before, long before the killing at the bunker. He had known it when he left Parris Island. He glanced at Mac, thinking of his girl in Athens, then said, "Don't ever let her see you here, Mac. Not as we are now, not a part of this. She won't be able to understand this. Nobody should have to understand this."

CHAPTER

11

The squad stood idly by as the bulk of the platoon moved off to resume their position in the line. A few Marines joked with their buddies in first squad as they moved past. Griffin nodded to Whitney, who winked as he led the way in the morning darkness. Griffin watched as the two squads swung around a corner and disappeared from sight. He had discussed the mission with his three corporals, and looked again and again at the route the little convoy would take through the city. A lieutenant from the battalion operations center had explained to Griffin and the staff sergeant that, although the assigned route was longer, and more difficult than necessary, it would make its way around areas judged hostile by battalion intelligence. The staff sergeant had said, half jokingly, that he thought all of Beirut was hostile since the embassy had gone down.

Griffin moved the squad onto the waiting trucks, three dark behemoths guarded at each end by a jeep mounted with a .50 caliber machine gun. He would ride in the first jeep, the map balanced on his lap. Griffin had no real confidence in the map. He knew from experience that it was practically worthless. It had almost no detail, and many of the roads marked on it were now impassable due to the fighting. He had gratefully noted that the route made its way past several prominent landmarks that were well marked. This would allow him to judge the progress of the convoy and hopefully stay on course. Maybe someone at battalion knew what was going on after all, he thought gratefully.

The convoy moved out of the perimeter in the predawn darkness. As each vehicle passed the checkpoint at the entrance to the Marine compound, bolts went home on weapons and the Marines shifted their rifles to point outboard. A quarter of a mile north the convoy passed a Lebanese Army checkpoint, the sleepy soldier inside waving as the convoy gained speed and roared past. Griffin held his rifle awkwardly across his lap, one finger on the spot on the map that he judged to be the approximate position of the convoy.

The jeep topped a small rise and Griffin could see the concrete shanties and dirty trees of what he knew was Shatilla Wood. To the west was the Sabra refugee camp. No lights showed from either area as they passed quickly by. The driver looked at him and made a motion as if wiping his brow. The corporal manning the gun in the rear of the jeep said, "Drive, Watson. Forget about being funny."

As they passed through a small traffic circle and entered a broad boulevard the gunner said, "That's the French headquarters, behind that stone wall. I know this area. We make a right up here, Sergeant." Griffin nodded and shifted his weight to maintain his seat as the little jeep rounded the corner. He turned and checked the rest of the convoy. It was still dark but he could make out all the vehicles, which ran with just their blackout lights showing. All of them were in place, maintaining the proper spacing. The driver moved his jeep into the center lane and slowed as they approached a French checkpoint. Before they came to a halt a French soldier stepped from behind his sandbagged wall and waved them through. Griffin nodded to him, noting the man's weapon tracked them until they were past.

The jeep moved under a darkened overpass and the gunner said, "Indian country from here on in, Sergeant." Griffin looked at the eastern sky and noticed the first gray hints of dawn. Multistoried apartment buildings blocked his view of the mountains. He noted that few lights were visible in the buildings, all of which bore the scars of fighting. The roadway was clear of vehicles, and Griffin was suddenly aware that they had not passed a single vehicle since leaving the Marine compound. He quickly glanced at his watch. He checked the map and knew that they should soon be making a series of turns. He had the driver slow down. His apprehension built as he failed to locate his landmark. Without warning he realized they were at the intersection marked on his map.

He looked down at the map, checking the reference point, noting the configuration of the roads, the odd angles at which they met, then said, "Okay, right up here. Go south here." Before the vehicle turned Griffin spun around in his seat, memorizing the buildings from the perspective he would see them on his return trip. He had worried half the night about this turn, for it was only an intersection with no real landmarks. Even had he been able to read Arabic, no street signs existed to guide him. He had gauged the distance between landmarks, and by calculating the speed of the convoy had gotten a rough estimate of how long it would take them to reach this intersection. When the convoy reached the more rural areas he would use terrain features to fix his position.

Griffin ordered another turn and the convoy resumed its eastward trek. The broad boulevard wound uphill past more houses, spacious châteaus with high stone walls. Clusters of smaller homes, and multilevel apartment buildings were grouped near the intersections. Griffin noted the occasional light showing in a window and glanced down at his watch. Half past six and most of the people were still asleep. Not like the City he thought. Any time of the night or day someone was moving in New York.

He thought back quickly to his own neighborhood in the Bronx. The summer after his graduation from high school he had worked nights on the docks, rising early to load produce trucks that carried fresh vegetables to every corner of the city. He had worked long hours loading and unloading the big trucks as most of the city slept. Huge reefers kept the produce cold, and he and the others had worn jackets to stay warm even though it was the middle of summer. Not wanting to ruin his own winter coat Griffin had taken his father's old field jacket. The left breast pocket was still emblazoned with the black eagle, globe and anchor and the USMC below the emblem was clearly legible. The other men on the docks, mostly older Italians from the surrounding neighborhood, had chided him about the field jacket. They had asked him when he was going to join up, and not just sport the emblem. Griffin was seventeen, and had already asked his father to sign enlistment papers for him, allowing him to join the Marines. He had caused a terrible fight between his parents. His mother had openly defied his father, something Griffin had never before seen. In the end his father had told him to wait until the end of the summer and join when he turned eighteen, if he still wanted to then. So Griffin had found himself spending the odd months on the docks.

Midway through the long hot summer a new man had hired on. He was the son of one of the foreman. He had been friendly to Griffin initially, then turned sullen. Griffin had been puzzled until the man told him he was a veteran, and had served in Vietnam. Griffin could still remember the words, but not the name of the man. "It's not you, kid. It's the emblem. You ain't earned it. You wanna wear it, go earn it. Then you can wear it. Understand?"

Griffin had understood. At the end of the summer, the day before he left for Parris Island, the dockworkers had taken him to a corner bar. It had been his eighteenth birthday, and everyone had crowded around to buy him drinks. Before he left the veteran had walked up to him with a shot glass full of warm whiskey and said, "Here, you dumb bastard. I'll buy you another one when you get back. Look me up, tiger. I'll be around." Griffin smiled at the memory. Well, he thought, now I really do understand.

"Okay, Sergeant, here it is. Don't worry, this road isn't marked on your map but it winds around this hill, and up at the top is a little gate and then you're there. I know 'cause I brought these guys up here and I usually come up with supplies and shit. Another five minutes and we're home."

Griffin grunted his assent and automatically turned to check the position of the convoy. All of the vehicles were clearly visible in the morning haze. "This road is pretty narrow, will the six-bys make it through?" he asked, looking to the corporal for an answer.

"Yeah, it's tight, and they usually scrape in places, but they can make it if the driver has any balls."

"Great," said Griffin. "What the fuck happens if we need to get out of here in a hurry?" The driver geared down and the jeep ground up the hillside. Griffin reflexively pulled his weapon in closer. He could have reached out and touched the side of the hill. He noted the steep slopes, the loose rock and sand. Cedar trees clung precariously to the sides of the hill.

Griffin looked up but could not catch a view of the house, or any Marines. The air was scented with the pungent odor of cedar, belying the closeness of the city. He looked to his left, where the hill fell away sharply. The city now lay below them, and Griffin noted that the area they had driven through was coming to life. A few vehicles moved in the streets, and lights were visible in most of the houses. Below them the tops of trees testified to the steep angle of the hill. Griffin rose in the seat to get a better view, but couldn't catch a glimpse of the ground, only shrubs and trees.

"It's pretty steep, Sergeant Griffin. No place to hang a wheel over the shoulder," said the driver. Griffin looked behind him at the truck inching its way around a tight turn. The bumper constantly gouged the side of the hill as the driver hugged the road. At some points the tandem wheels on the rear axles actually had the outer tires freewheeling as the hill fell away from the narrow road.

"Yeah, I see what you mean about the driver's needing a set of big brass ones. This ain't much of a road," he said. The corporal grinned widely. "Maybe so, but at least we know the Lesbos can't come up here with any tanks to get us."

Griffin looked forward instinctively as the driver slowed his vehicle. The lance corporal shot a glance at him and said, "When we round this next curve we'll be in front of the gatehouse. They have an M-60 set up in there, and a fireteam with it. We'll also be in sight of the house, from the roof they'll have a good view of everything, and also from the second-story windows." The driver hit the horn twice, a prearranged signal, then rounded the corner.

Griffin took in the small stone gatehouse with its one sandbagged window. The black muzzle of a machine gun barrel peered at them from its interior. He noted the pockmarks from small arms fire on the structure before lifting his gaze beyond the gate and into the courtyard. The house was a solid looking three-story stucco affair with a large flat roof. It reminded Griffin of something out of an old Western, right down to the large windows with no glass in them. A Marine stood on the roof behind a waist-high wall of masonry and observed the entry of the convoy into the court. A slender sentry stepped out of the gatehouse and waved them forward. He threw a heavy bar to the ground and opened the wrought iron gate that blocked the road. As the jeep inched past he grinned and said, "Welcome to the Alamo." Griffin noted that he quickly crossed the road back to the gatehouse before the first six-by could pass. Clever bastard, thought Griffin, if the truck rolls over the side he can just watch instead of being crushed.

The convoy pulled into a sizable courtyard paved with large stones. Griffin noted the unfinished look of the large house, as if construction had stopped once the walls and roof had been completed. The top of the hill had been leveled and the house rose from the far side, the hill falling away to give the occupants a spectacular view of the city. A low stone wall ran in an unbroken circle around the top of the hill, enclosing the courtyard. Cedar trees rose above it all, leaving Griffin with the impression that whoever had built the place had a desire for privacy and enough money to afford it. As the squad jumped from the trucks Griffin walked to the wall and leaned over. Below, he glimpsed part of the road, perhaps fifty meters beneath him. The steep sides of the hill were covered with small wiry cedar trees and juniper bushes. He stood on top of the stone wall, perhaps two feet wide, and walked its length, moving toward the house. Nowhere was the slope of the hill angled to allow an advance that would be anything less than heroic under fire. The house itself appeared to rise from the bedrock of the hill. Griffin leaned out over the wall, attempting to see if the house had any windows on the lower floors.

"Well, are you gonna buy it or what?" a voice asked in a heavy southern drawl.

Griffin spun to see who had spoken. "I'll be damned," he said. "Figures you would get the cushiest billet 'ole mother green has to offer. How are you, Bobby?" he said.

Griffin jumped from the wall, offered his hand to the other Marine, and added, "You fucking boot."

"Boot!" said the other Marine with an air of dismay. "Boot?" he repeated. "Is that what you said? Shit! I got more air time jumpin' out of the back of six-bys than you got in the Corps. I'll give you a boot. A boot right in the ass!" The boy shook his head good-naturedly and asked, "How are you, Dave? Long time, man. Where's that fucking no-good Samson? I didn't see his fat butt fall off that truck y'all rode in on."

Griffin smiled and shook the hand of his friend. "Shit, Slocum. Samson is probably in your hooch right now, eating your chow and looking through your mail."

Slocum grinned wildly. "Aw, he ain't nothin' but another muscle-bound hoodlum from New York, Dave. Figures the two of you are still hangin' around together," said Slocum. Slapping Griffin on the back, Slocum continued, "Hey, how's Downs doing? I bet you and he are big pals now that he's a corporal. He get his PhD yet?" asked Slocum sacrastically. "I hear you can get 'em through the mail now."

Griffin smiled at his friend. "Bobby, it's reassuring to know that some things never change. You being a smart-ass and the first shirt being a jerk are real constants in my life." Griffin looked at Slocum, then asked, "How's the pride of North Carolina anyway? Anybody ever teach you how to box yet?"

Slocum laughed, "Hey now, boy. I'm a hundred and seventy pounds of fighting wildcat. Never you mind all that fancy-ass city-boy boxin' you're so fond of. So just don't you go abusin' my hospitality and all or I'll have to teach you some proper manners." Slocum smiled broadly and asked, "No shit, they sent you up to help out little ole me?"

"Yeah, they sure did," answered Griffin. "The reason I'm up here is to escort you and your squad out."

"Oh yeah. Somebody did mention it to me. I guess you're right for once." Slocum turned to look at the house. "Sure will hate to leave though. This is one grade-A piece of real estate, Dave. Good living. Away from the battalion and all the Zeros. I hate to leave, that's for sure."

"Yeah, I can understand that. Nice view from up here. Not to mention not having to deal with the command. How did you swing it?"

"Just lucky, I guess. They figured nobody in Lebanon knew how to drive a tank anymore, so the dragon platoon didn't really have much of a mission. We ran mobile patrols up through the city for a while. You know, drive the jeeps around, wave at the girls, don't spit on the sidewalk bullshit. The usual 'Create a Presence' crap on the patrol reports."

"Beats walking," said Griffin.

"Sure does," grinned Slocum. "Anyway, this place was going to be the U.S. ambassador's residence if they ever got it finished. Guess he was getting tired of the old mansion. Who knows? They sent us up here with a few guys from a radio unit. There's four of them and about fifty tons of their gear that we lugged up to the roof and sandbagged in place." Slocum nodded, indicating the roof. "Guess the officers will want us to bring all that shit back with us, right?"

"Yeah, they're funny like that, Bobby. They usually want us to hold onto the crap they give us."

"Umm, well, I guess we can drag it back down in the morning. Right now we got other problems."

"Like what?"

"Well some fucker named Ahmud, or somethin' like that, was up here yesterday afternoon. Gave me a bunch of shit about how this land belonged to Lebanon. The people, you know. I couldn't understand him very well, but the gist of it was he wants us off his fucking hill."

"Yeah, so what did you tell him?" asked Griffin.

"Well, what do you think I told him? I told him the great white father in Washington bought and paid for this place fair and square and he sent me here to mind the store. Jesus, what the fuck was I supposed to tell him? I ain't no real estate agent. Anyway, our twenty-four hours ain't up until sixteen-hundred this afternoon, so if we hurry we can be gone by the time he gets back."

Griffin stiffened and stared at his friend. "Fuck you, mister. I ain't leaving this damned hill until I'm good and fucking ready."

Slocum laughed. "Yeah, that's what I told him. Figures a nosy bastard like yourself would want to know though."

Griffin relaxed. "Well, what do we do now?"

"Ah, who cares? Ol' Ahmud won't be back until sixteen-hundred or so. He'll come trotting up the road there with his little white flag and that big-ass pistol strapped on his hip like he's John Wayne or some shit. You talk to the fucker this time. I cain't understand him, except about every fifth word anyway. Besides, he smells like he's been bathing in goat piss. And his breath could kill elephants. It would take a regiment to get us off this hill if we decide to stay. You looked at the place, what do you think?"

"It's good ground, no doubt about that. Really only one way in, and that's right through the gate," said Griffin nodding toward the iron gate. "I brought two fifty cals and an extra M-60 with me, plus plenty of ammo. The house covers the approaches up the hill and I assume there's some sort of view of the entrance from the road?"

"Yep. I got a gun on it now. We saw you come in, you asshole."

Griffin ignored his friend's jibe and continued, "Good. The road's too narrow for armor, except maybe the light stuff, but I've seen plenty of that around here. Panhards mostly, maybe a British Ferret. Can you handle something like that?"

"What kind of jerk-off do you think I am? We'd nail him with a dragon before he could even start up the hill. We got a few LAAWs laying around that might come in handy. We strung a line of claymores around the hill, as well as trip wires for our flares and about a half million dollars worth of concertina wire. Any more questions?"

Griffin smiled. "Well, not really. Staff Sergeant Whitney had me bring a lot of extra ammo, which leads me to believe battalion may have already gotten word of this somehow. You said anything to them?"

"Not me," said Slocum innocently, "I'm forbidden to fraternize with the officers, staff NCOs, and the locals. Regulations and all, you know. Besides, our comm is down."

Griffin shot an alarmed glance at Slocum. "You're shittin' me. Right?"

"Not exactly. The other night we took some fire. Small arms, no big deal. So I called it in. Later they started mortaring us. One of my guys spotted the tube that afternoon, so we knew where it was comin' from. I radioed battalion for permission to use our 60mm mortar." Slocum paused and looked at Griffin. "Did I mention we had one of those laying around?"

"No, it must have slipped your mind," answered Griffin in a knowing tone.

"Yeah, ol' Ahmud and his boys were a little surprised to find out we had one, too."

"So what about comm, do you have it up now or not?"

"Well, yes and no. I asked battalion for permission to use our 60mm. They didn't think it was a good idea, so we sort of lost comm for a while." Slocum studied Griffin, trying to gauge his reaction to what he had said.

"Anybody get hurt, Bobby?"

"Well, nobody you and me know. Ahmud's a little pissed about the whole thing though. That's when this 'get off my hill' shit started. Up till then we never heard a peep out of anybody. Funny how a little woolie pete can fuck up a whole relationship. Some people are just petty I suppose."

Griffin shook his head and said, "Yeah, I guess so. How are you fixed for ammo on the 60mm?"

"Okay. We've got about forty rounds left. They're pretty stingy with that stuff back at battalion. We only used a few rounds the other night."

Griffin stared at his friend, trying to figure out just how much of the truth was in what Slocum was telling him. It was obvious to him that Slocum and his squad had engaged the Arabs after suffering through various forms of harassment and interdiction fire. Griffin had known Slocum since his arrival in the battalion. He trusted Slocum's judgment, and he knew by Slocum's joking manner that the situation must have been pretty serious. At any rate it had been serious enough for Slocum to expend precious rounds of 60mm ammunition. And for Slocum to defy battalion orders and fire on the attackers. "What do you think their next move will be?" he asked.

"I'm not sure. Ahmud will be back probably. Maybe a few more mortar rounds today. They'd have to be crazy to try and come up this hill and take this place. I've been all over it and the only real approach is the road. You've seen it. Would you try it?"

"Yeah, the road is it," agreed Griffin. "Even without the wire and the claymores the hill is suicide. The trees would give 'em some cover but there'd be no way for 'em to advance in any order. Even if they could, they'd be so busy climbing they wouldn't have a free hand to fire with. It has to be the road, if anything. If they're smart they'll wait for us to move. We'll be vulnerable as shit coming down that hill in vehicles."

"Fuck 'em then. We'll just wait here for Ahmud and company to come get us. I'm in no hurry to leave." Griffin took a few steps toward the courtyard where the squad stood beside the trucks. "That may be our best bet. How is this house for cover? It looks solid, but is it?"

"Just like the Rock of Gibraltar. The inside isn't finished but it's all concrete and stone. It's got a good deep basement. Most of our ammo is down there. We took the liberty of punching out a few extra firing ports at ground level." Slocum knelt beside the wall and pulled back a piece of canvas to expose a small hole bored through the wall at ground level. He looked up at Griffin who asked, "How many of those do you have?"

"Four."

"That's it? Just four?"

Slocum grinned. "No asshole. Four on each side of the house."

Griffin laughed. "Bobby, you're a man after my own heart."

"Yeah, maybe so, but I'm not real big on Ahmud's Christmas list. Wait till he hears about this shit. Us puttin' holes in the wall of his house." Slocum shook his head from side to side. "Man, he's gonna be pissed all over again." He rose and walked with Griffin in the direction of the squad. "Let's get your guys inside and give 'em some breakfast."

Griffin spent the rest of the morning supervising the placing of the two .50 caliber machine guns and assigning positions to his fireteams. Extra ammunition was off-loaded and placed in close proximity to the guns. Fields of fire were assigned to each gunner and fireteams placed so as to lend support to the heavy guns. He discussed tactics with Slocum and both agreed that the gate should be wired shut and claymores rigged so as to sweep the entryway. Griffin also placed flares in the trees overhead, with trip wires running back to the house. This would allow them to illuminate the principal approach at will, without shedding any light on themselves. Griffin also placed claymores in the trees overhead. Before returning to the house to sleep he walked down the hill with Slocum, stopping every fifty meters to gaze back up the narrow road. "You mind telling me what you're looking for," asked Slocum, "or is it top secret?"

"Look, Bobby. We can handle just about whatever they throw at us when we're on the top of that hill. But sooner or later we have to leave. If we pick the best spots to place an ambush and set a few claymores in the trees above those spots we can detonate them as we come out. That way we clear our own path before we ever get close to their kill zone. Even if we don't get all of them we'll know there's an ambush by the wounded screaming. At worst we lose a few claymores."

Slocum considered Griffin's suggestion then added, "Or they find our claymores on the way up and use them against us on our way down."

"That's a chance we'll have to take. Just to hedge our bet though we'll send a fireteam out this morning to set them in place. No detonators, just put 'em in place and string the wire back along the road, but far enough away from the road so it's not too obvious. Follow me?"

"Yeah, I get the idea. You're a mean bastard though."

Griffin grinned. "I know. They pay me extra for it."

"I expect they ought to. So what's bothering you? The hill?" asked Slocum.

"How to get off this hill in one piece. That bothers me. We're gonna be vulnerable on the way down." Griffin thought for a moment. "How tough do you think these guys are?" he asked. "Straight up? No bullshit."

Slocum stopped. They were almost at the bottom of the hill, one of Slocum's fireteams nearby. Griffin had pointed out the likely ambush positions and the corporal had noted them, assuring Griffin he could find them again and would properly place the claymores. Slocum squatted and picked up a small rock from the road. He tossed the rock, skipping it down the road, and looked up at Griffin. "I'll tell you, Dave. I think they're gonna try us. I don't know if it will be tonight or not, but they'll try it. If one of them knows what the fuck he's doing they'll wait for us to leave and hammer us on the way out. The claymores are a good idea, but it's still going to be nasty, no doubt about that."

Slocum paused and turned to look out into the village that bordered the road leading away from the hill. "I know they spend a lot of time observing us. Every now and again we catch a reflection of sunlight off glass from the ville over there, and that's got to be somebody with binoculars checking us out." Griffin grunted his acknowledgment and said, "Go on."

"Well, you're right about the hill. It's fucked if they wait for us on the way down. Even if we send a fireteam down first, they'll just let them pass and then hit the main body. We're still no better off." Slocum stood and looked at the fireteam. He gave a slight nod and took a couple of steps down the hill. Griffin followed.

"The way I've got it figured, Dave, is that they'll think you're just the regular resupply convoy. Just a couple of extra trucks. That's no big deal. If you don't leave this afternoon they'll probably think we've been reinforced 'cause of Ahmud's visit. He'll come back this afternoon. He's no dummy. Even if they missed you on the way in Ahmud will see the six-bys and figure it out. Hopefully his boys didn't see the fifty cals come in this morning. Anyway, that'll be enough to throw a kink in his plans. He won't know what to do. Dave, I think the stupid fucker means to rush the hill. Maybe the extra trucks will put him off and we can get out without a scrape, but I doubt it. We could have everybody man the rails. Show of force shit, you know. Try and intimidate him, but that will only make him rethink his plans, and that's no good to us."

"So what's your point, Bobby?"

Slocum lowered his voice. "Let's wait 'em out. They got more balls than brains. I say we stick to the top of this hill like white on rice and wait for 'em to come to us. They'll try it, but not tonight. Ahmud will want to think about this, but he's already shot his mouth off in front of his buddies. If he doesn't move on us they'll think he's chickenshit. He's got to make his move, and soon. If we wait a day or two we force his hand, and all to our advantage."

"Battalion wants us out of here at zero-dark-thirty tomorrow," said Griffin.

"Yeah, well then let 'em come up here and get us. That's fucking suicide and you know it. Look, Dave, we hurt those rag-heads the other night and they're looking for some payback. A couple of our flares were triggered last night and I don't think it was fucking rabbits crawlin' around the side of this hill."

"You take any fire?" asked Griffin.

"When did you fucking go blind? Did you get a look at that gatehouse on the way in? Those holes weren't drilled by woodpeckers."

"So what do you suggest I tell battalion operations? After all, they did send me up here for the express purpose of getting you and your people out of here," said Griffin.

"Tell 'em to get fucked. Who gives a shit what you tell 'em? It's our ass that's on the line. What difference does a day or two make to them anyway?" said Slocum angrily.

Griffin looked at his friend, then said, "Well, go on. Seems you've got this all thought out."

Slocum smiled tightly. "It ain't pretty no matter how I look at it. I say we keep this between the two of us. In the morning we rig one of the six-bys so it won't start and radio battalion we got a breakdown. There's no way they'll tell us to leave any equipment here. You said it yourself. They'll tell us to sit tight and try and fix it. That'll buy us another day, at least. By then maybe Ahmud will have made his move." Slocum paused, then said, "I'll tell you something, Dave. I want to kick their fucking asses. They're a bunch of assholes. The only way they'll ever get this hill is if we give it to 'em. I don't care for the idea of leaving the day after Ahmud tells me to get off. We're fucking Marines, man. Who the fuck are they?"

Griffin shrugged. "Well, I agree with you for what it's worth. Let's try the mechanical failure bit and see what happens. We've had it if they tell us to leave it in place though." Griffin started back up the hill. "I think you're right, Bobby. He'll be back this afternoon and he'll scope us out. Then he'll go home and think about what the extra vehicles mean, especially after we don't leave like the resupply. We want him to hit us while we're in place. I don't even like to think of an ambush on the way down this road. But one thing is for certain, a lot is riding on what he makes of us this afternoon."

"Yeah, I guess so. But you know something, Dave? I was happier than a pig in shit to see it was you and not some boot lieutenant in charge of this convoy. I was shitting bricks wondering what I was going to do if I didn't know the convoy commander."

"Lucky me," said Griffin sarcastically as he continued striding back up the hill. "I feel like a regular prince charming riding to the rescue of a damsel in distress."

Slocum laughed, "Hey, Dave, I'm sorry about all this. You know? Nobody tells me shit about anything. They just stick me out here and drop off the C-rats every couple of weeks."

"Ah, fuck it. Shit happens, Bobby," said Griffin with a shrug.

"Yeah, I guess. Well, anyway, why don't you get some sleep? I'll wake you up when Ahmud gets here. I'm sure the two of you will have lots to chat about."

"Yeah, fuck you very much, Slocum." Griffin walked up the hill in silence. Slocum fell behind a few paces, pointing out likely ambush spots to his fireteam leader. When they reached the top of the hill Griffin turned to Slocum and said, "I'll be inside. When you see Ahmud at the bottom of the hill wake me up, but don't you go out to talk with him. Just have him stand at the gate and wait for us. And instruct the fireteam leader at the gate he's not to open it. Let Ahmud wait outside until we show up. Got all that?"

"Un-huh," replied Slocum lazily. "But I feel it is my duty to warn you that Ahmud is not going to consider this a friendly welcome. He might even be a little pissed."

Griffin let out an exasperated sigh. "Just do it like I told you, and remember to wake me up when he's at the bottom of the hill."

"Okay," said Slocum. "You got it."

Griffin walked into the house and descended a flight of concrete steps into the basement. Light from the firing ports, punched into the wall at ground level, poured in, stabbing the darkness. Griffin shone his flashlight into the corners of the room. The squad was sprawled out, asleep on the concrete floor. Here and there someone shifted in his sleep. Griffin noted with satisfaction that weapons were neatly stacked and they had taken the time to remove their boots, although they slept fully clothed otherwise.

He went out and climbed the flight of steps to the second story. A window there commanded a view of the courtyard and entrance. The gate, perhaps seventy meters away, was in plain view. The window was heavily sandbagged, and a .50 caliber machine gun was placed well inside the room in its own protective nest of sandbags. Griffin directed the crew to line the heavy stone walls with sandbags as high as was possible. When the gun crew shot a questioning glance at him Griffin explained, "Look, these walls are made of stone. You're going to draw a lot of fire. Any round that comes through that window and enters here is going to ricochet off all this stone. Got it?" The crew chief nodded. Griffin then instructed him to rig a shelter half as a sort of curtain in front of the window. When the crew chief complained that the window was the only source of light Griffin suppressed an urge to scream at him and again explained, "For right now leave it down, but have it rigged and ready to pull shut. That way nobody outside has a view of your position in here. If you need the light, adjust it so light can come in over the top but the canvas still hides the gun. Follow me?" The Marine nodded. "Good. Now have Sergeant Slocum rig the rest of the windows the same way."

Griffin walked around the third story with the same commanding view of the courtyard and front gate. All of the rooms here had views of the courtyard, although the window openings were much smaller. He entered a smaller room that he assumed was a bedroom. Two lance corporals stood by a sandbagged window. They moved aside as Griffin walked to the window and peered out. Looking below Griffin had a clear view of the hillside as it fell away from the house. There were no tall trees on this side, although he could see a few stumps. "Who cut the trees down?" he asked. The lance corporals looked at each other, then back at Griffin, and shrugged.

"I don't know, Sergeant. Probably whoever was building this place, so they wouldn't spoil the view," said one of them noncommittally. Griffin followed his gaze out the window. The city sprawled before him, the Mediterranean a blue haze on the horizon. The morning sun blazed in a gray sky as Griffin squinted into it. Rooftops stretched away toward the water, the skyline broken by taller, more modern apartment buildings. From this distance he was unable to see the effects of the war on the city. He stared for a few seconds then dropped his gaze down the hill. "Did you see us down there this morning?"

The lance corporals laughed, "Yeah, Sergeant. You can see everything from up here. The entrance off the road is just out of sight to the left, but everything going up or down passes by, and they are in our view for a few seconds."

Griffin grunted and leaned farther out the window to get a clear view. The roadbed was visible below, a short expanse of gray ribbon two hundred meters down the side of the hill. Griffin estimated he could see half the roadbed when he stood in the well of the sandbagged window. "Get your corporal up here now," he said to the one lance corporal. Griffin looked at the ceiling, judging it to be ten feet high. He looked at the other lance corporal. "Any furniture in this place?"

"Not that I know about," answered the Marine.

Slocum entered the room just in time to catch Griffin's last question and said, "Jesus, Dave, are you really thinking about buying this place? Or are you just trying to be the biggest possible pain in my ass? Next you'll want to know if we have air conditioning, for Christ's sake."

"Come here, Bobby. And shut up for a minute." Griffin pulled Slocum to the window and pointed down the hill. "Look, if we build some sort of step, maybe two feet high, here next to the window, we increase the field of view out of this window. An M-60 gunner has a clear field of fire to that part of the road, only standing on our stoop he can see all of the road, not just part of it. Follow me so far?"

"Yeah, I think I get the drift. And I can tell you Ahmud ain't gonna give a shit for this idea either. He won't even get up the fuckin' hill before you start makin' Hamburger Helper out of his boys, and he is bound to feel unwelcome."

Griffin's eyes shone. "He'll feel welcome alright," he said.

Slocum looked at Griffin, then raised himself on the balls of his feet and again looked out the window. "No, he won't, Dave. His shit will be over before it gets started." Slocum stepped away from the window. "Guess I fucked up not seeing a chance to improve this position," he said, embarrassed. "But there ain't no way he'll get past a gun firing down on him like you got planned."

"Yes he will, Bobby, because we won't fire on him on the way up."

Slocum glanced over at Griffin, rubbing his chin. "You're a mean son of a bitch today. Next thing you'll probably want a couple of claymores strung down there with enough wire to detonate them from here."

"That's right, and see if you can rig some flares down there, too. We might as well see what we're shooting at."

"Okay, what else?" asked Slocum.

"Have your people rig shelter halves across all the windows. I don't want him to have any idea of our numbers, or of where our guns are. If he does it right he'll bring an RPG with him and it will be a duel. We don't want to give him any help. Also, let's keep everybody out of sight. When he gets here you and me will go out and talk to him. Leave a fireteam at the gatehouse for now with the M-60. After he leaves we'll wire it shut with concertina, rig some claymores, and pull the gun and the fireteam back here. That way when the shit hits the fan we can fire away without having to worry about hitting any of our own people. Any questions?"

"No, not really. I guess you mean to break their assault at the gate then?" Slocum continued without waiting for Griffin to respond, "That means they'll be pretty close. You sure you don't want to just hose 'em down right here with one of the fifty-cals? No assault is going to advance under that kind of fire at this range." Slocum paused again and looked down the hillside. "It's a helluva opportunity to hurt 'em bad without really exposing ourselves to any fire."

"Yeah, I thought about that. If it weren't for this house I would probably do it your way," said Griffin.

"What's the house got to do with it?" asked Slocum.

"Jesus, Bobby. This fuckin' place is built like a castle. These walls are stone, man. Not brick, stone. Rock, with mortar. Nothing they bring up, short of a tank, is going to do any real damage. The firing ports in the basement are perfect. The gunners won't even have to worry about grenades, even less about return fire. They can just rake the place with fire. Even if we get jams we've got plenty of firepower." Slocum studied Griffin as he went on outlining his plan. "The assault will stall at the gate. It's designed to open from the inside only. He'll look at it this afternoon and he'll think we'll leave the gun team there. He'll think we won't be able to lock the gate 'cause that would lock out our fireteam in the gatehouse. They'll shoot up the gatehouse like they did the other night. Then they'll storm it. When they get there it'll be their only shelter. We'll rig it so they have to expose themselves to cut the wire off the gate and free it before it can be opened. Some claymores and flares will break their assault, if they even get that far. Until they do though, we'll just rake the dumb bastards with small arms and machine gun fire. Even if they shelter behind the gatehouse or around the hill the grenadiers and your 60mm mortar will take care of that. That road is only wide enough for five or six of them at a time. The fifties will mow them down."

Slocum raised his eyebrows. "It'll be a slaughter if it happens like you said." He looked out the window at the exposed portion of road. Without turning his gaze from the window he said, "You mean to break their assault at the gate, then use the mortar to force them off the hill. When they get here," said Slocum, indicating the road below, "you'll finish it with machine gun fire on them as they withdraw?"

"Not quite that easy. I want to have strict fire discipline on the guns when they are at the gate. Let them think for a while that they can pull it off. I'm betting they are a bunch of amateurs. Heavy fire will scare them off. I want to encourage a frontal assault, a rush on the gate.

They'll think they scared your fireteam out of the gatehouse. That should encourage them. They'll rush the gate. If it's done right they won't be able to open it. Probably they'll try grenades, blow it open, that sort of shit."

Griffin paused, then explained, "If they try to bring up any sort of vehicle we'll hit 'em with a LAAW from here. No vehicles get to the gate. Not even a jeep. After we break them at the gate they'll retreat down the hill using the road. Since they didn't take any fire on the way up, and since you haven't had a gun in this window before, they won't expect any fire on the way down. When they get there," Griffin indicated the road below with a finger, "we hit 'em again. Just to make a point."

"Pretty strong point you're making, I'd say." Slocum sighed. "You aim to really fuck them up, don't you? I mean, this shit is more than just a firefight, isn't it?"

Griffin shrugged and turned away from the window. "Fuck 'em, Bobby. They fight like animals. You weren't at the embassy, man. We spent a week scraping civilians off the sidewalk." Griffin looked at his friend. "Besides, who the fuck are they to order us off this hill, or any place else? I'm going to teach these motherfuckers a lesson."

Slocum nodded his assent. "Yeah, I'd say you are. Well, you know what they say, payback is a medevac. I hope battalion buys our story about a truck being down."

"They'll buy it. The real trick is going to be making sure Ahmud attacks tonight. We can only use that bullshit about a breakdown to stall for so long. If they don't come at us in the next day or two, we're fucked. They'll wait for us to leave and hit us on the way out, and we both know how that will turn out." Griffin dug into his cargo pocket. "Here, take this and fly it instead of the colors from your flagpole on the roof."

Slocum unfolded the scarlet flag bearing the emblem of the Marine Corps. "Damn, I didn't know you were so fucking gungy you deployed with the regimental colors in your cammy pockets. Where did you get this anyway? Back at Camp LeJeune?"

"No," said Griffin as he left the room, "I dug it out of the rubble at the embassy. It must've belonged to the Marine detachment."

Slocum followed him out of the room. "Hey, Dave," said Slocum. Griffin turned, "last room on the left has my gear in it. Go ahead and get some sleep, my cot is against the wall, under the window."

Griffin hesitated, then said, "Thanks. But I'll just go down and rack out with the squad."

While Griffin slept Slocum prepared the defenses as he had been instructed. By early afternoon the claymores had been placed, shelter halves hung in all the windows, and sandbags had been laid in front of the tires of the vehicles. Slocum had hauled down the small American flag flying from the homemade flagpole on the roof and replaced it with the scarlet colors of the Marines. He stood on the roof watching two Arabs walk toward the entrance. The village below appeared normal, people moved about, and traffic circulated. As Slocum brought the binoculars to his eyes he heard Griffin ask, "What ya got?"

"Don't you ever sleep?" Slocum asked, feigning annoyance.

"All the time when I'm not following after boot NCOs and unfucking their defenses," said Griffin.

"Yeah, thanks for the help. And fuck you very much. By the way, I think our buddy Ahmud is on the way," answered Slocum.

Griffin rubbed his face. "Let me guess. He's gonna be pissed, right?"

Slocum suppressed a grin and looked at Griffin in wide-eyed innocence. "Not at me. I'm not the asshole that added all those nasty claymores and those machine guns." Slocum shook his head and put the glasses back to his eyes. "He looks pretty serious, too. Got his hat on and everything. I hope you're up to this, Dave," Slocum said in mock seriousness.

"I'll manage, I'm sure. What do you plan on doing during all of this?"

"Me?" asked Slocum. "Me?" he repeated. "I'm not doing anything. Ol' Ahmud and me are buddies. You're the one screwing everything up."

"Yeah, thanks for your help. Let's go downstairs and wait for him. Let your corporal at the gatehouse know he's on his way up. Tell him to radio us when Ahmud gets to the gate." Griffin turned and walked across the flat roof heading for the stairs. "Bobby, did you radio battalion?"

"Yep. Comm was sort of broken up, but they got the message. They're standing by with spare parts for our down vehicle if we need it."

Griffin paused, thinking, then muttered, "Great. Do you think they bought it?"

Slocum shrugged. "Maybe. But they sent a bird out here to check on us. A Huey. He made a couple of flybys then split. Who knows? Probably sent a couple of Zeros up with the bird and told them to look and see if we were actually working on one of our vehicles." Slocum followed Griffin down the steps and added, "Fuck 'em anyway. I don't see any of them out here."

Griffin searched his mind for an answer to their dilemma. To attempt a withdrawal down the hill as ordered and perhaps lead his men right into an ambush would be suicide. The simple facts of the matter were that the best solution was for the Marines to remain on the defense and hope for an attack by the militia. Before he had come up with any firm plan he heard Slocum's PRC-68 crackle to life. "Roger," said Slocum. "We'll be out to your pos in two minutes." Slocum cast a questioning glance toward Griffin. "You ready?" he asked.

"Let's leave Ahmud standing at the gate for a few minutes. Just the one guy with him?"

"Yeah, that's it. Both of them are packed though. Forty-fives on their belts, no rifles."

Griffin chuckled. "Fucking John Wayne, eh?" Slocum grinned and followed Griffin to a window. Griffin was concealed behind the heavy canvas of the shelter half. He pulled it away from the side of the window and peered out. Slocum did the same from the other side. "Which one is Ahmud?" he asked.

Slocum glanced at his friend out of the corner of his eye and answered, "He's the mean one."

"Okay, asshole, is he on our right or left?" asked Griffin.

"Uh, our right," answered Slocum. Griffin watched as the slender Lebanese pulled a pack of cigarettes from his pocket. He offered one to his companion, then to the Marine corporal, who shook his head. Ahmud wore the olive drab uniform of the Lebanese Armed Forces, but Griffin could not see any rank or unit insignia. He noted that his boots were highly polished, but improperly bloused. His .45 caliber pistol hung heavily from his belt and Griffin took in the two canvas magazine pouches next to the holster. He's no soldier, thought Griffin, or his magazine pouches would be on the other side so he could feed them with his left hand as he dropped the empty from his pistol. Griffin shook his head and said, "Fucking amateurs" under his breath.

He shifted his gaze to the other Lebanese. The boy stood across the narrow road behind Ahmud. Griffin watched as he puffed furiously on his cigarette. He was obviously having a hard time deciding where to position himself, and he continually searched for something to do with his free hand, shifting his cigarette from one hand to the other. Griffin noted that the Marine corporal stood across the road, rifle held loosely waist high, covering the two Arabs. Well, thought Griffin, at least somebody out there knows why he's here.

He turned to Slocum and said curtly, "Amateurs. Let's go. Bring your M-16 and cover Ahmud's slack man. I'll handle Ahmud. I'm going to open the gate and let him come in a couple of steps." Griffin pulled his own .45 from its holster, checking to see that a cartridge was in the chamber, then pulled on his leather field gloves. "Okay, Bobby, let's do it."

"Promise me you'll be gentle. He's the sensitive type," said Slocum sarcastically. Griffin grunted and walked out of the house, striding purposefully across the courtyard. He caught the eye of the corporal at the gate and gave a slight nod of his head indicating the gate should be opened. The corporal opened it, then stepped back inside the stone gatehouse. Griffin noted the muzzle of his weapon, visible just outside the gatehouse doorway, still more or less pointed at the Arabs.

Ahmud took a tentative step through the gate as Griffin approached. When Griffin closed to within four steps of Ahmud he saw the Arab's arm rise hesitantly, as if to shake hands with him. Griffin could feel Slocum tense and the corporal stepped half out of the gatehouse, clearly ready to cover Griffin and Slocum. He silently hoped that neither of them would do anything to interrupt the next few moments when he confronted Ahmud.

"You speak English?" Griffin snarled. The hand dropped reflexively as Ahmud stopped walking, his feet coming together heel to heel. Trying not to smile Griffin saw Ahmud stop himself halfway through a formal bow. Griffin knew this was the customary greeting of enlisted soldiers for their superiors in the Lebanese Armed Forces.

"Yes, I speak English." Griffin closed the distance between himself and Ahmud, stepping well within Ahmud's guard.

"You're on my hill, mister. What do you want?" The menacing tone in Griffin's voice left no doubt as to his intent. He noted with satisfaction that Ahmud wavered, then took a step backward.

"It is you who are on my hill. I am afraid."

Griffin laughed, then looked at Ahmud as if he were inspecting a recruit. Ahmud tensed and Griffin saw resentment in his eyes. "Well, I'm not afraid. So state your business. Then get the hell off my hill. And take your friend there with you." Griffin leaned forward as he spoke, forcing the smaller man to take a half step backward. Griffin was a head taller than the Lebanese and as he leaned forward he compelled him to bow his back or literally touch noses. Griffin had learned the technique at Parris Island when he had been on the receiving end of it. "Well?" he asked in an impatient tone.

"This is not yours, your hill." Griffin noted with satisfaction that Ahmud was obviously angry and was searching for the foreign words. "You will leave today, or you will die. All of you."

Griffin snorted, then shook his head. "Now you listen to me. We're not leaving until we're ready. Got that? You understand?"

"This hill, this house, do not belong to America. This is Lebanon. You will leave this place," said Ahmud.

"You're right about one thing. This hill don't belong to America. See that," Griffin pointed to the Marine flag that floated lazily above one corner of the building, "That means this hill belongs to the Marine Corps. And it belongs to us until we decide we don't want it anymore." Griffin again leaned forward poking Ahmud's chest with his forefinger to punctuate his comments, and noting the lack of any guarding movement by Ahmud's hands. "Get your ass off my hill, mister. Now!"

Ahmud took a half step back, glancing over his shoulder at his companion. He straightened up and spat. "I spit on your flag, and your country . . ." Griffin's right fist caught him full in the face with a bruising roundhouse. Ahmud crumpled and would have gone down but was caught by an uppercut by Griffin's left. Slocum and the corporal leveled their rifles at Ahmud's second, who meekly raised his hands. Another quick combination to Ahmud's head and the young Arab was prostrate on the cobblestones, his nose bleeding profusely. Griffin stepped over him and lifted him by his pistol belt. Ahmud moaned and cradled his face in his hands as Griffin rolled him onto his back and removed his pistol belt. He tossed the belt into the gatehouse and stepped toward the other Lebanese, who took an instinctive step backward and tried to cover his face with his arms.

Griffin looked at Slocum and his corporal and said, "Lower your weapons. These assholes didn't come to fight, they came to talk." Slocum covered Ahmud as Griffin removed the other man's pistol belt.

"You speak any English?" Griffin asked the boy, who nodded.

"Yes or no, asshole. I haven't got all day."

"Yes."

"Good," said Griffin. "Now you take this other asshole and get off my hill. And tell him next time I see him up here I'll shoot his stupid ass. And pass that along to whoever you work for. Got that?" The boy said nothing. "Do you understand what I'm telling you or not?" asked Griffin.

"Yes," replied the Lebanese.

"Move," said Griffin. "Now." He and Slocum watched as the Arab helped Ahmud to his feet and the two limped out of the courtyard. Without waiting for them to disappear around the curve in the road Griffin turned and began walking back toward the house.

"Well, I think that went pretty well," quipped Slocum. "I mean, speaking as an ambassador in green, I think we had some meaningful communication here today," drawled Slocum.

Griffin cast a murderous glance at Slocum, then said, "Bobby, is everybody where you come from a smart-ass?"

Slocum hesitated for a moment, apparently to consider his answer, then said, "No. Most folks are fairly straightforward. It's a talent I've refined over the years. Part of my acquired charm, you might say."

"Just my fucking luck I got to meet you," said Griffin tightly.

"Well," said Slocum genuinely, "some folks are luckier than others, Dave. Now take ol' Ahmud there. He probably ain't feeling real good about havin' made your acquaintance today. But you and me both know there's a bright side to it."

"Yeah?" said Griffin.

"Yeah," answered Slocum. "Hell, all of us had to leave the homes we love, our families, our friends, and travel great distances to benefit from the training offered by the good ol' USMC. But, thanks to you, our friend Ahmud has received some of that same training for free, with no obligation to spend long years in service to the Corps. What more could a man ask of a complete stranger who just happens to be in his own backyard?"

"Don't you have something you could be doing?" asked Griffin as the two entered the house. "Maybe seeing about your troops, or cleaning a weapon or something? Away from me?"

"Now, Dave. You know I live to serve. And to learn from my senior NCOs. No, sir. I think this is too important an opportunity to waste. Why, the masterful way you handled that difficult and dangerous situation is an example to us all," said Slocum with no trace of a smile as Griffin disappeared down a flight of stairs and into the basement.

CHAPTER

12

The Syrian smoked his cigarette slowly, the remains of his lunch on the table before him. He was aware that Ahmud had returned, but had instructed the sergeant not to disturb him while he ate. He had finished eating while Ahmud fumed in the room below. Then Ahmud had told the story of his treatment by the Americans. His face was bruised and swollen, the nose obviously broken. The Syrian noted that Walid, his friend, was untouched.

"And what of you? You do not seem to be harmed? Did you not fight?" he asked.

"I had no chance, there were many of them, and they had many weapons."

"I see." He sighed and rose from the table, crossing the room to stare out the window. He carelessly flicked his cigarette butt out the window, watching as it arced to the street below. "And why have you come to me, today?" he asked, placing emphasis on the last word to indicate his annoyance.

"The Brotherhood will kill all the American invaders. We will do this. They will die for their insult to me. No one may insult the Brotherhood." Without acknowledging Ahmud's statement, he again looked out the window, his back to the two young Lebanese.

He sighed again, then said. "Yes, I understand. But what do you ask of me? May I assume this is not merely a social visit?"

Ahmud glanced at his friend, who shrugged. He plunged ahead. "We need your help," he said tightly.

"Ah, I see," answered the Syrian. "What do you propose?"

"That the Syrian Army shell the hill occupied by the invaders. It is important. They are very strong. Artillery can destroy them, then the Brotherhood will attack the hill and reclaim it for the people of Lebanon and Islam."

The Syrian turned to face Ahmud, then shook his head sadly. His gestures and mannerisms were those of a father talking to a recalcitrant child. Sensing his answer, Ahmud spoke, "You must help us. The Brotherhood has been generous to you, and to our Syrian allies. Did I not supply my own brother as a holy warrior and provide you with the means of our great victory against the American Embassy? The Americans are as nothing. We will sweep them from the hill as we swept them from their embassy. But we must act together to insure victory and to cement our friendship."

The Syrian sat behind the table, and gestured for Ahmud to sit. "Sit Ahmud. Sit Walid," he said. He regarded both of them, stalling for a moment, choosing his words carefully. His plans were completely formed, his equipment in place. All of his people were trained and ready to move. But he was not ready to move yet. He needed more time to study his prey. He continued to search for the elusive details that would insure victory. The small, almost trivial knowledge of an enemy that allowed him to succeed where others failed. He was not ready, not yet. And until he was ready he would require the hospitality of Ahmud and the Brotherhood. He didn't have the time to select another militia leader and develop a friendship that would allow him the support required. He let out a long breath, another month and he would be done with this strutting schoolboy who gave away his brother as one would trade a rare coin in a gold souk for something of greater value. He looked into Ahmud's face. "You must not attack the Americans tonight. Not now. Wait a little. Give me time to talk to my superiors. We will develop a suitable plan of attack for you. Supply you with adequate weaponry, training, and other necessities. You shall have your revenge, in time. Remember the proverb, Ahmud, revenge is a dish best eaten cold."

Ahmud blanched and said, "I will not wait. We will attack. Without your help if the Syrian Army is afraid of a few American Marines."

Walid opened his mouth to speak, but the Syrian raised a hand and stopped him. "Ahmud, do not rush into this. You are hurt, and angry. Use this to your advantage. I counsel patience, cunning, shrewdness. Let us not sink to petty insults. We are allies. Together we can overcome the Americans."

"I will not wait. The Brotherhood shall destroy the Americans. They violate our land, and the memory of my brother," spat Ahmud in anger.

"Ahmud, maybe he is right. Let us listen to him," counseled Walid.

Ahmud turned on his friend and said, "No, he is not right. All he wants is talk. Talk of friendship, talk of training, talk of great victories. It is time for us to act. We will have our victory. And we will have the blood of the Americans."

The Syrian took a cigarette from the pack on the table. He lit it, blowing a stream of smoke into the air. "You have seen the American position?"

"Yes," answered Ahmud.

"Their defenses?" he continued.

"Yes."

"Good, tell me what their defenses are. I will need to know this."

"Then you will help us? You will have artillery shell the hilltop?"

The Syrian shrugged noncommittally and flicked an ash into his dinner plate. *Mumpkin*, he said, the Arabic word for maybe. "Tell me, what is their defensive layout?"

Ahmud looked to Walid, then spoke, "They have taken the usual precautions. The house is of stone. Some jeeps are in the courtyard. Some of them are always in the small house at the gate."

"Ahh," noted the Syrian, "and how many of them are there?"

"Not many. Fifty perhaps," answered Ahmud.

"And how many vehicles?" he asked.

"Five, perhaps six."

"How many machine guns do they have?"

"I do not know. They have one in the little house at the gate. We attacked it last week."

"How will you get to the top of the hill? What route will you take?" asked the Syrian.

"We will wait for your shelling to cease, then we shall go up the road. We have a truck, it shall lead the assault. The truck shall ram the gate and destroy it. Once we are in the courtyard we shall destroy them. We will not spare them. The Brotherhood has no mercy for infidel invaders who do not heed our warnings."

"Can you not approach up the side of the hill, utilizing the trees for cover?" asked the Syrian. "Then spring upon them in surprise?" The Syrian noticed that Ahmud was becoming increasingly annoyed at the questions. He is losing his patience with me, thought the Syrian. I shall not be able to control him unless I allow this attack to take place.

Ahmud rose and paced in front of the table, then turned to face the Syrian and spoke, "It is not for you to question me. I am not your pupil. I am the leader of the Brotherhood's holy warriors. We shall attack tonight, and we will slaughter them."

The Syrian calmly regarded Ahmud. He said nothing, but looked to Walid, who seemed slightly embarrassed. "Walid, what is your position? You are the Brotherhood's deputy commander. Can the Americans be taken? Are they so weak as Ahmud believes?"

Walid shrugged. "I do not know. There are many of them. But I follow Ahmud. He has been in the army. He knows if they are weak."

"The army, Ahmud?" The Syrian cocked an eyebrow in mock surprise. "I didn't realize that you had formal military training. You have not been fair with me. You should have told me. I could have relied on your experience in the past." Ahmud straightened before the Syrian as if to support Walid's assertion of his military service. The Syrian nodded approvingly and Ahmud again took his seat. "Ahmud, how many men do you have presently?"

"Perhaps one hundred. Some from the village will come to us when they learn of our plan to attack the Americans."

"Yes, that is good." The Syrian leaned back in his chair as if planning a strategy. He did not look at Ahmud, but at Walid, who quickly averted his eyes. This one knows it cannot be done, he silently realized. The Syrian had scouted the American position only once. He had walked by it one afternoon and seen the narrow road that served as a driveway. He saw the sentinel on the roof and noted the steep sides of the hill. Although he could see only a portion of the house he could tell it was well built of native stone. He was unable to tell how many men were inside, but he knew from bitter experience that positions such as these required few defenders. He had never considered it as a target since that day.

He knew now what he would do. The plan took shape quickly in his mind. He leaned across the table, moving the china out of his way. Looking directly into Ahmud's eyes, he spoke in his commander's voice, "Since you have decided that you must attack, I will, of course, assist you as far as is within my power. But I must warn you, none of my superiors must know of my assistance to you or the Brotherhood. I extend you a personal favor, Ahmud. I consider this a debt of honor, as you are my personal ally here in Beirut. Do you understand?"

Ahmud raised himself in his chair and answered, "Yes, of course."

"Good. It is not possible for me to arrange artillery for you. My orders for my operations here in Lebanon specifically forbid me to engage the Americans in any type of direct armed confrontation. That means that I cannot ask higher headquarters for artillery fire on a known American position. However, I may still be of some assistance to you. If you would like to listen I think I may have a plan."

Ahmud nodded and the Syrian continued, "I agree with you that the assault must come tonight. However, I have a means to support your attack. Do you wish to carry out your attack as you have said, using the road as your avenue of approach?"

"Yes. I have seen this road, it will serve our purpose."

"Fine. However, I must use your truck. If you want some sort of artillery support I will require the truck."

Ahmud seemed unaffected by the request for the truck, "It is of no consequence. We shall find other vehicles. What do you propose?"

"You say you have one hundred men. That is more than enough. Give me twenty of them to crew the mortars. Walid can be the leader of these men. We will prepare the mortars and shell the Americans. Then you can make your assault. After the hill is taken we will join you. Does that suit you?" asked the Syrian.

Ahmud glanced at Walid. "Yes" he said.

"Walid will also command a small force to remain at the bottom of the hill and capture any Americans who escape. They will attempt to retreat down the hill, and this measure will ensure a complete victory."

The Syrian studied Ahmud, who was now leaning forward listening as he explained his plan. The fool, he thought, he will believe all of it. He suppressed an urge to smile, as a cat smiles before pouncing on its unsuspecting prey. Now for the final touch. "Ahmud, I will require of you and your men a special task. You must capture at least one of the Americans alive. I want to question him regarding some of their outposts."

"It will not be difficult. We will do as you have asked," replied Ahmud. "But why?"

"They have other outposts. If the man knows their locations and their strengths it will make our task much easier in the future."

Ahmud leaned back in his chair and smiled slightly. "It will be done as you have asked."

The Syrian continued, "Farouck, my sergeant, will accompany you and the assault team to the gate. Also, one of my men with some demolition gear. The gate will not be a problem with such equipment. You will not miss the truck." He looked to Walid. "Does this suit you my friend?"

"Yes, I will do as you and Ahmud ask," answered the boy.

"Fine. The assault shall take place tonight then. I will require twenty of your men. Walid and I shall speak later of the details. He stood and walked to the window. Ahmud and Walid rose to go. Ahmud extended a hand, which the Syrian dutifully shook. "We shall have another great victory tonight, Ahmud. Remember, I need one of them alive. Then it will truly be a great victory."

"Inshallah," said Ahmud.

The Syrian nodded almost imperceptibly and said, *"Inshallah."* As they left the room he stared out the window at the village. How many times each day did he hear this simple phrase "If God wills it?" Every Arab eventually left matters in the hands of Allah.

A story came to him, from his childhood. A story his father had told him as a young boy. His family had been in Syria for hundreds of years, but during the crusades his village had been captured by the Christian crusaders and forcibly converted to Christianity. At some point after the expulsion of the crusaders most of the villagers had reverted to Islam, but his family had not. His father had told him the story of the crusaders' expulsion from the village.

A small force of Christian knights had held the town for months against superior Moslem forces. Eventually, the Moslem army had breached the wall and slaughtered the garrison and the inhabitants. But a handful of knights had retreated to the Christian church. Inside the church the families of the knights had taken shelter. The only approach to the church was down a narrow street, and the knights had mounted their chargers and barred the way of the Moslem army. As the knights stood between the Moslem force and the church, the Arab commander mounted the roof of a nearby building to signal the assault that would annihilate the knights and destroy the last vestige of Christian resistance in the town. Before he could give the signal one of the knights stood in his stirrups and cried out *"Deus Vult!"* in his foreign tongue. The knights charged headlong down the narrow street, crying *"Deus Vult!"* as they flung themselves into the Moslem lines. Their heavy mounts crashed into the Moslem infantry and the force of the charge broke the line, the sounds of the battle ringing above the cobblestones of the street. The courageous knights were soon overcome but the Arab commander had been so impressed with their daring that he ordered their families spared. He had asked one of the women what their war cry had meant. The woman had replied that it was Latin for "God wills it."

The Syrian had never forgotten the story, or that he was the descendant of one of those knights. He realized that something of the essential difference between the Eastern mind and the Western mind was reflected in the war cry of the knights and the phrase "Inshallah." For the Westerner, God's will was a command to be carried out dutifully no matter what the cost. The Arab accepted events passively and acknowledged the consequences as the will of God.

Behind him the door opened and Farouck entered. He did not allow Farouck to sit. He was, after all, a sergeant. Farouck had been with him for years. He was tough, and perhaps more important, he was cunning. He faced the big sergeant and said, "I have a mission for you. Tonight the Brotherhood will attack the Americans who are in the house on the hill. You and one of the men familiar with demolition work will accompany them. Ahmud will lead the assault after the entrance gate is opened with explosives. Ahmud plans to storm the house and kill any Americans he finds there."

He studied Farouck's face. It was impassive, reflecting nothing of his thoughts. He knows this is suicide, and he is wondering how to question my motives. Or already planning his desertion, thought the Syrian.

"Do you have someone you can trust to handle the explosives?" he asked.

"Yes, sir. Of course. But I could do it myself if you prefer, Excellency."

Ah, there it is, he thought. If he goes alone it will be easier to desert. Perhaps feign his death, then slip away once the battle is in progress. "No, Farouck. I have an assignment for you tonight that will require all your attention." He chose his words carefully, stealing a glance at Farouck as he spoke to catch any reaction he might have. "As you know, I am sure, this attack will fail. The Americans have a strong position, and they have reinforced it within the past few hours." Farouck remained impassive. "However, Ahmud is determined to attack and annihilate the Americans. He has asked me to provide an artillery barrage prior to his assault. I shall arrange some mortars to pacify him. He will try to force an entry through the gate. I suspect that the attack will fail there, and I do not anticipate any real pursuit by the Americans." He paused. "Ahmud has reached the limit of his usefulness. I wish now to concentrate on Walid, his deputy. You will ensure that Ahmud does not return after the assault to further complicate my task here."

"I understand," said Farouck. His demeanor reflected no emotion, no opinion about the mission assigned to him. The Syrian again walked to the window and looked out. He smiled slightly to himself. He had done well to choose Farouck. The man had played it perfectly. He had done nothing to hint that he might not be willing to carry out such a foolhardy attack with a group of untrained boys, but had listened impassively while the entire plan was explained to him. If he had questioned me, the best he could have hoped for was a transfer back to a line unit where he would die an ignominious death fighting the Israelis. Now I must reward him, as one rewards an obedient child. "You will take no chances with your own safety tonight, Farouck. I have too few good sergeants. Am I understood?"

"Yes, sir. Of course, sir."

"Fine, Farouck. You are dismissed." He heard the muted click of Farouck's heels coming together, then the door shut behind him. He lit another cigarette, the smoke hot and acrid in his throat. It will work perfectly. Ahmud will die tonight in the assault and Walid will take control of what is left of the militia. He must ensure that Walid comes to no harm tonight. Well, he thought, that isn't very likely as long as he has the good sense not to go with Ahmud out of some twisted sense of loyalty. He thought again of the knights and their hopeless charge. How stupid men can be. They will sacrifice themselves for what they perceive is honor, or duty, losing their lives for an idea they are incapable of expressing. He sighed. Ahmud's insistence upon satisfying his honor had almost cost him months of careful planning and meticulous work. There had been a few close moments, but all should be right now. His plan would go forward without delay, only some of the minor players would be changed.

CHAPTER

13

Griffin nodded to Slocum, "So it's gonna be tonight? Ahmud has more balls than I thought. Give me the radio." Slocum handed the small radio to Griffin, who keyed the handset. "Downs, how many of 'em are there?" he asked.

A burst of static was followed by Downs's voice. "I'm not sure. At least thirty, and they're still coming. It's a steady file. They're not spaced apart or anything. Just walking up the road, close to one side. Over."

"Stand by, Downs. Let me know if any vehicles or heavy weapons come up. Especially any RPGs. Got that?" asked Griffin.

"Roger."

Griffin looked at Slocum. "All your troops in place and ready to go?"

"Yep," he casually answered. "Everybody is one hundred percent. All the guns are up and ready."

"Good. Remember what I said about fire control. I don't want to break their assault too quickly. Let them think they're gonna get through. We'll hammer 'em when I say."

"Got it. I'll supervise the guns," said Slocum.

"All right." Griffin put the radio into his flak jacket pocket and leaned forward, moving the canvas aside in order to see out the window. He peered into the darkness, the iron gate barely discernible. He ran down his mental checklist for the hundredth time. He had spent the afternoon walking the ground, gauging avenues of approach, calculating the most effective fields of fire, supervising the placement of the claymores and the flares. His most experienced corporals were in the most critical places on the line, and Slocum would see that the machine gunners covered their assigned fields of fire. He had put Downs in the rear of the building, his fireteam virtually eliminated from the expected action. Surprisingly, Downs had not questioned his decision, and no resentment had shown in his eyes. He had accepted the positioning of his fireteam without question. When Griffin had briefed the squad as to his design to break the assault at the gate, then ambush the retreating survivors as they left the hill, he had noted a questioning look from Downs. After the briefing he pulled Downs aside, mustering his self-control in anticipation of Downs's comments. Instead Downs had accepted his instructions calmly, nodding and asking the occasional question. Griffin had gone so far as to point out to Downs that he had been selected to man this post as he was the only fireteam leader whose primary MOS had been a machine gunner. Griffin was surprised when Downs said, "I understand, Sergeant Griffin. I won't let you down."

That had been several hours ago, and now everything was in place. Ahmud was bringing his men up the hill. It couldn't have worked better if he had given a schedule to Ahmud that afternoon. As Griffin looked out the window the night was ripped by the force of two quick explosions, the machine gunners behind him chuckled, and one of them muttered, "Claymores." As the sound of the explosion rolled away the screams of a wounded man could be heard. The screaming continued for about five minutes then stopped abruptly. Griffin wondered if they had corpsmen with them, guessing that they did not. They probably just gagged the poor bastard, or he bled to death while they tried to apply a tourniquet, he thought.

A flare arced into the sky, electric-white against the black of the night. Griffin knew that they were now fifty yards from the gate, reasoning that the attack would begin soon. He was somewhat amused that their advance even continued. He glanced down at the detonators for the claymores. Well, he said to himself, getting there is the easy part, my friend, getting home won't be so easy. He didn't move the safety levers, judging that things would develop slowly now that they had taken at least one casualty.

A few shots from rifles echoed through the night. Griffin guessed that their point men had spotted the gatehouse and were now taking it under fire. That will hold them another couple of minutes. They'll figure out it's empty eventually. A bullet snapped loudly overhead, then whined off into the night. The gunner behind him shifted restlessly.

"Sergeant Griffin," came Downs's voice over the radio.

Griffin keyed the handset. "Go Downs."

"We just saw two troopers go up the hill with the type of backpacks that carry RPG rounds. We didn't see a launcher though. Over."

"Roger. Sit tight. Let me know if you see anything. Vehicles, launchers, whatever. You know the drill. Over."

"Affirmative. Out," said Downs.

Griffin leaned forward and picked up one of the claymore detonators. A loud *whoosh* was followed almost instantly by an equally loud explosion. He grimaced and said, "Fuck!" looking at Slocum, who laughed under his breath.

"Maybe these guys mean business, Dave. That RPG must've hit the gatehouse," said Slocum.

Griffin grunted, concentrating on the spot in the darkness where the gate would appear. Minutes passed in silence before the first faint clanging of metal on metal could be heard from the direction of the gate. Without warning a flare lit and sputtered to life in the branches of a tree over the gate. For a brief instant an electric-white image of two young Arabs replete in kaffiyehs, kneeling at the gate with a crowbar twisted into the chains that secured it at its center, burnt into the eyes of the waiting Marines. Before the flare could fully ignite Griffin had given the detonator the required two squeezes.

The claymore sent its dozens of deadly balls directly into the bodies of the two Arabs, the force of the blast blowing them away from the gate. The two bodies lay in the roadway, smoke from the explosion hanging in the air, the whole scene lit by the brilliant light from the still-burning flare. As Griffin looked on, another Arab moved into the roadway and knelt, bringing an RPG to his shoulder. Half a dozen shots rang out from the Marines as the rocket arced wildly into the night sky, the gunner now sprawled in the middle of the road.

The flare began to sputter and Griffin knew the Marines would not hold their fire much longer. Those who had fired had been selected earlier in the day. Griffin guessed that the next rush on the gate would be met by every weapon the Marines could bring to bear. He noted that the tree where the flare had been placed was now on fire, providing some illumination of the area adjacent to the gate. A few shots came from the direction of the gate, and he could plainly hear commands being given in Arabic. Griffin picked up another detonator, knowing he had two mines left outside the gate, one left inside. He selected the detonator that would trigger the claymore by the gatehouse.

Slocum said, "Hit it, Dave. The dumb fuckers are sheltering behind the gatehouse."

"Yep. Here goes," answered Griffin. He again squeezed the detonator twice, quickly. Another tremendous explosion was followed by more screaming. Slocum and the machine gunners laughed. From below Griffin heard whoops and the triumphant yelling of the Marines. Someone was calling to the Arabs, taunting them, calling them various vulgar names. Griffin could hear some of the others laughing. "I'll go shut 'em up, Dave. God forbid somebody's enjoying themselves while you're around," said Slocum. He was halfway across the room when Griffin called him back.

"Let 'em scream all they want. I want to piss this guy off so he comes after us. I just hope that second claymore didn't get him. I'm not too sure how willing his friends are to rush us if he's not around to make them."

From the darkness another *whoosh* came as an RPG round struck the gate, the warhead splintering against one of the iron bars, then ricocheting wildly through the compound. A chorus of shots rang out from the Marine position, quickly answered by the Arabs. Griffin looked at Slocum. "Here we go. Watch your ass." The firefight quickly escalated into a general exchange of rifle fire. Griffin could not detect the fire of an opposing machine gun, and so far none of his gunners had fired. The burning tree provided enough light to illuminate the gate, making it unnecessary for Griffin to trigger a second flare.

"Sergeant Griffin," the radio in his pocket crackled to life.

"Go, Downs."

"We got mortar tubes down in the ville. Ferris just saw the flashes from the tubes." Before Griffin could answer the rounds impacted on the hill.

"Can you take it under fire, Downs?"

"No way. They're out of range. Maybe with a fifty cal. Over." After a pause Downs said, "Stand by. Three more shots out." Automatically Griffin began to count the hang time of the mortars, trying to get a rough estimate of their range. He noticed that the rifle fire had died away. Three quick explosions, all overshooting the hill, echoed in the distance. Another three rounds impacted, no closer than the second salvo. He debated the wisdom of notifying battalion headquarters of the mortars. To do so would be correct procedure. He had already notified them, via the squad radio, that he was in contact, but had deliberately downplayed the seriousness of the attacking force.

"Three more." Downs's voice came over the radio speaker, flat and disembodied. Griffin silently counted, hearing the crunch of the explosions. The gunners had shifted their aim, but were no closer than before to the Marine position. He made the decision not to notify battalion. Griffin looked at the radioman, who mutely extended the radio handset. Griffin shook his head negatively. At this point he didn't want the battalion operations officer breathing down his neck. The mortars were no threat unless the gunners improved a great deal. He reasoned that their forward observer was probably pinned down behind the gatehouse, or that his radio had failed. Otherwise their fire would have been more accurate. Their problem, thought Griffin, not mine. He stared again at the gate as three more rounds impacted. The attack should come soon. His heart sank momentarily as the thought came to him that the Arabs might be retreating down the hill without assaulting the gate. He pressed the transmit button on the PRC-68. "Downs, is anybody trying to move off his hill? Over."

"Negative. Just a few stragglers going up the hill. Over."

"Roger. Advise me if anybody goes down the hill. You copy? Over."

"Roger. I copy. Over."

As Griffin stared at the gate by the light of the flames, a tremendous explosion echoed across the compound. The shock wave hit the building as Griffin felt the heat from the blast on his face. He returned his gaze to the gate which was partially open, canting drunkenly on its hinges. "Shit, those bastards must've used a satchel charge." Griffin searched the darkness for Slocum. "Bobby!"

"Yeah, Dave."

"Make ready with the guns. They'll try it in a minute or two. Let 'em get in the gate, then let 'em have it all."

"You got it," said Slocum flatly. "We're ready."

Griffin picked up the detonator with his left hand, holding it and bracing his M-16 against the small sandbagged firing port. Without taking his eyes off the gate he hollered at the .50 cal gunners, "Wait for the claymore. When the smoke clears, if you see anybody standing, fire them up. Got that?" A chorus of screams rang out from the gunners who had held their fire as instructed by Griffin earlier. Griffin knew their frustration had been building as the riflemen fired at the Arabs and they sat by their guns waiting for his command.

Without prelude three Arabs broke from the darkness and ran toward the gate entering the circle of light thrown by the burning tree. A dozen shots rang out and two of the men fell. The third reached the gate as all the Marines began firing. His body slumped against the heavy iron bars. Seconds later Griffin saw another satchel charge flung toward the gate, followed by another terrific explosion. Instinctively he ducked as a second shock wave rocked the building, echoing off the heavy stone walls. As he looked up Griffin saw them coming. Four young Arabs in various bits of military garb, firing wildly from the hip as they ran toward the gate. Behind them other figures emerged hesitantly and began advancing. From the darkness he heard Slocum say, "Jesus, those motherfuckers got balls."

"No, Bobby," said Griffin, "they're just fucking stupid." He hit the plunger twice and the claymore detonated with terrific force, spraying the roadway with shrapnel. The .50 cal erupted almost simultaneously with the claymore. Griffin could see bursts of tracer sweeping the roadway. The noise inside the house grew to a crescendo as all the Marines fired. None of the Arabs were moving in the roadway. Within a few seconds the firing died and Griffin cursed as he heard the sound of M-16 magazines hitting the floor. "Fire discipline, Goddamn it! Aimed fire! Aimed fire!" He swore again, "Son of a bitch, those dumb shits never learn." Slocum chuckled softly as Griffin again screamed, "Aimed fire!" at the top of his lungs to no one in particular. "And take those weapons off auto or I'll have all your asses."

"Aye, aye, Sergeant Griffin," he heard Slocum say.

Griffin ignored the sarcasm as he turned and asked, "Casualty count, Bobby."

"You're shittin' me, right? Casualty count? Those assholes haven't even hit the building yet."

"Downs?" he asked, speaking into the small radio.

"Nothing. No movement even. Over."

"Roger. Everybody sit tight. They may try again." Griffin saw the flash of another RPG as it exited the launcher from beyond the gate. Instantly machine guns fired, the red lines of tracers converging in the darkness beyond the burning tree. The round impacted the front of the building as the Marines laid a deadly barrage of small arms fire on the gate. A grenadier fired his weapon, its distinctive *bloop* audible during a pause in the firing.

From beyond the gatehouse came the explosion of the 40mm grenade followed by screams from the wounded. Griffin screamed, "Cease fire" just as a half dozen Arabs emerged from the shadows. The fire again commenced with an incredible roar, the Arabs appearing to dance obscenely as the machine gunners found them and held them in a deadly raking fire. The gunners continued to fire long after the Arabs had gone down. Griffin sensed that this would be their last assault on the gate. At least ten bodies were visible in the roadway. He ordered the grenadiers to stand by, then ordered illumination. As the flares lit, several young Arabs froze in the electric-white light. The front of the building again exploded with fire from the Marines, their yelling audible above the din of the weapons. The grenadiers fired fragmentation rounds as fast as they were able, lobbing the rounds over the side of the hill where the Arabs were assembled on the roadway. The noise of the weapons, combined with the wild, exuberant screams of the Marines, built toward a climax. Griffin ceased to fire his own weapon as the two squads expended five months of frustration in a two-minute orgy of firing at a half seen enemy. The noise from the .50 caliber machine gun was deafening, its report echoing off the stone wall.

Griffin knew the squad was out of control, lost in its own desire for vengeance. They were unable to stop, desiring only to find another target. Griffin had heard Whitney refer to similar situations as being "lost in the flood." Unable to control itself, the squad became a single entity whose only purpose was to kill anything before it. Griffin knew he was powerless to stop it. It would stop only when they emptied their magazines and machine guns became overheated and unable to fire. Even then they might take it upon themselves to charge the gate. He would stop that. He had already cautioned Slocum and the corporals to be aware of the possibility of such a charge.

Incredibly, the firing stopped almost simultaneously. Griffin heard the metallic ringing of a link from a machine gun belt as it bounced across the floor, the gun itself empty. Before the link could stop bouncing the squad had recovered and was screaming at the top of its lungs. Primeval screams without words or language. Screams that had echoed across countless centuries and countless battlefields, and Griffin, having removed himself from participation, acted as the conductor of this barbaric opera. He felt no part of it, no remorse, no satisfaction, no emotion.

He surveyed the gate by the light of the burning tree. The bodies lay crumpled on the ground, limbs twisted at odd, impossible angles. Already the smell of burnt powder was being replaced by the putrid smell of death. Griffin was faintly surprised that he felt no sense of accomplishment, of satisfaction. He realized, oddly, that for the first time he felt separated from the squad. Always before he had been an integral part of it. Now he was watching but not participating in the squad's emotion. They were slapping each other on the back, triumphant, exuberant. He was an outsider. The squad was an extension of his will, but he wasn't joined to it by emotion.

From the back of the house came the rattle of a machine gun. "Downs!" Griffin said it out loud, realizing he had been lost in reverie. He told Slocum to take over, then took the stairs two at a time. He entered the pitch-black hallway as the machine gun continued to fire in short, controlled bursts punctuated by the thump of a grenade launcher. He felt his way along the wall in total darkness until Downs fired again, the muzzle flashes of the gun lighting his way. As he stood in the doorway he watched Downs fire on the Arabs from his narrow perch. He moved from side to side on the sandbags, three feet above the floor, Mac circling and feeding the gun ammunition while avoiding Downs's rhythmic shifting as he searched out new targets. The flashes from the gun muzzle lit the otherwise pitch-black room, giving the impression that Downs was firing in freeze frame action, the gun slamming heavily into his shoulder. Smith and Ferris worked as a team from a second firing port. As Smith fired and broke open his grenade launcher Ferris immediately loaded another round from a pile of grenades on the floor. The four Marines continued to fire, not noticing Griffin behind them. Griffin stepped back into the darkened hallway as the gun continued to hammer away.

As he stood watching Downs, his shoulders hunched to absorb the recoil of the gun, the muzzle moving from side to side as he searched out his targets, Griffin realized he had doubted Downs. The decision to place Downs here was purely tactical, had one of the other machine gunners been available, or one of the other corporals a better gunner, Griffin would have assigned that man here. He had never really thought that Downs wouldn't fire at all, he had just subconsciously assumed he wouldn't be as aggressive as Griffin wanted him to be. Looking at Downs now, Griffin knew he had been wrong. Downs was a good machine gunner, and he was laying down a deadly fire on whomever was in his view below.

Griffin took another step back into the darkened hallway. He realized that he didn't want Downs to know he was here, checking on him. He's come around, thought Griffin. He'll always be Downs, always a fucking question or that slightly defiant look in his eyes. But now he understands.

Alone in the darkness, Griffin smiled. I won, Downs. It's in your blood. No matter that you'll leave the Corps eventually. You're a part of it now because of what you are, in spite of yourself. Griffin looked again at the fireteam. Downs quit firing and peered down the hill. The other three leaned out the window and did the same. As they looked into the darkness Downs turned and stared directly at Griffin, who stood perfectly still, knowing he couldn't be seen in the inky blackness of the building's interior.

Mac turned and followed Downs's stare. "What are you looking at, Steve? I can't see shit."

"Nothing," said Downs. He turned and gazed out the window, surveying the damage below. "Jesus, Mac. Look at all of 'em."

Ferris laughed, "Guess we really fucked up their health record."

"No shit," said Smith, "they are just all fucked up, man. There must be two dozen of them down there." The four Marines stared again at the carnage below, visible in the glow from the flare. "Well," concluded Smith, "they were assholes to even try and take us in this place."

CHAPTER

14

Downs fingered the safety on his rifle and peered toward the gate and the scene of last night's battle. The squad was ready to move, waiting only for a signal from Griffin. As was customary Downs would be the point man, taking the squad down the twisting road and off the hill. Today's patrol would be different than usual. Downs and his fireteam would lead off while the rest of the squad, Slocum's dragon gunners, and the vehicles, remained atop the hill. Griffin's plan was to leapfrog Downs's fireteam down the hill, blowing the claymores along the way in case any force lay in ambush. The claymores were placed in what Griffin thought were the most likely ambush sites and Downs knew the locations of the detonators.

In effect, what Griffin was doing was dangling Downs and his fireteam out in front of the main body as bait. An attacking force would have to be extremely well concealed for Downs to miss them as he went by, forcing them to fire on the smaller force and warn the main body of their location. Griffin was counting on the claymores to break up any such ambush.

A nod from Griffin and Downs was on his feet and moving toward the gate, which hung from one hinge, paint chips scattered about it on the cobblestones. Initially, Downs had considered the possibility that some of the bodies on the ground near the gate might still be alive and capable of firing at him, but a few seconds' observation through his binoculars had served to convince him that they were in fact all very dead. As he approached the gate he cast a quick glance at the faces of the dead men. Already their features were distorted by death, appearing to melt into the rest of their faces, their uniforms stretched tight by bloating.

"Jesus, what a fucking stench," cursed Mac. Downs grunted and continued peering ahead. Several bodies lay in the roadway, dark pools of blood by each one. Griffin had instructed him to shelter behind the stone gatehouse and blow the first claymore. Downs made it to the wall of the gatehouse and signaled for Mac to come up. Mac ran across the cobbled courtyard in a crouch, his M-16 cradled to his chest, and stopped beside his friend. "What a sight, Steve. Did you see all those dead fuckers?" he asked.

"Yeah. Keep an eye out while I look for the lead wires and connect them to the detonators." Downs brushed away the loose soil from the wall at the foot of the gatehouse and uncovered the two wires. He quickly hooked them to the detonator then reached for the radio to let Griffin know he was ready to blow the first claymore. As he keyed the handset he signaled for Smith and Ferris to come up. They crossed the courtyard five yards apart and stopped a few feet short of the gatehouse, sheltering in the lee of a small retaining wall. Downs leaned out and peered around the corner of the small building, and looked directly into a pair of brown eyes.

The man blinked but otherwise did not move. Downs took in the ugly blood stain that covered the man from his stomach down to his crotch. He sat with both hands folded over his abdomen, his back resting against a large cedar tree. The man opened his mouth as if to speak, but only a froth of blood issued forth. He coughed once and Downs noted with horror a bright crimson wave spread from beneath the man's hands. The eyes closed and Downs thought for a moment that the man had died, but then his breathing became apparent. Downs keyed the handset and spoke, "Sergeant Griffin."

"Go, Downs."

"I've got a problem. There's a wounded guy here, just forward of the gatehouse. He's out of your line of sight. If I blow the claymore he'll take the blast full in the face. Over."

"Roger, I copy. How bad is he hurt?" asked Griffin.

"Pretty bad. It's an open stomach wound," said Downs.

"Sit tight, Downs. I'm comin' up."

"Roger." Downs took another look at the man as Griffin ran across the courtyard and past Ferris and Smith. Griffin put his hand on Downs's shoulder, and without looking at Downs asked, "Where is he?"

"About fifteen meters forward, left side of the road, leaning against the base of a tree."

"Anybody else out there moving?" asked Griffin.

"Not that I've seen. We haven't been forward of the gatehouse though." Griffin took a quick look around the corner of the small structure. He waited a few seconds and repeated the gesture. Downs and the rest of the fireteam held their positions.

"Okay, Downs. This is what I want. First, hook up that detonator. Let Smith handle that. You and the other two move forward, beyond our friend at the tree. At the first sign of trouble you and your people get the hell back here. I'll move up with you and check out the Arab. Before anybody moves, let's radio back to the platoon and let them know what's going on. If we do get into trouble tell Smith to blow the claymore as soon as we're on this side of the gatehouse. The claymore is forward of there and we won't have to worry about it at that point. And have the squad send the Doc up, we're gonna need him if nothing goes wrong. Got that?"

"Yeah," answered Downs.

"Downs, did you notice anything strange about the wounded guy?" asked Griffin. Downs peered around the corner, taking a long look at the wounded man, who stared vacantly back at him.

"I'm not sure what's different, but something is. What do you think?" he asked.

"It's the uniform, Downs. Look at the guy. He's the only one wearing a real uniform. The rest of them are just wearing bits and pieces of gear. That guy must be some sort of advisor, or a deserter from the LAF or some shit. In any case he's not an amateur like the rest of them, or that knucklehead that was up here yesterday."

As the corpsman arrived and took his position along the wall behind Griffin the fireteam prepared to move forward. Downs explained the situation to them as Griffin briefed the corpsman, who began readying sticks of morphine. "Okay, Downs. Let's go," he said. The four Marines stepped around the corner in single file, Griffin and Downs going to the opposite side of the road where the wounded man remained sitting under the tree. Griffin knelt beside the Arab, quickly removing his pistol and checking for any sign of a booby trap, as Downs took up a position just forward to confront anyone coming up the road. Mac and Ferris positioned themselves likewise. Griffin turned and waved the corpsman forward.

"Okay, Doc," he said. "Give it your best shot, and be fast about it. I ain't got all day." The corpsman gingerly pried the man's hands away from the wound in his stomach. Purple clots of blood clung wetly to his shirt, and portions of his intestines bulged through the fabric where it had been torn apart. Griffin, Downs, and the corpsman exchanged glances. The wounded man remained motionless as the corpsman took the plastic cap off one syringe of morphine and injected the thigh with the clear yellowish liquid. Downs looked on as the corpsman removed a roll of gauze from his hospital bag and wet it with water from his canteen. He looked into the man's eyes and said, "This is still gonna hurt some mister, morphine can't do everything."

"Doc, is there any way in hell that this guy is gonna make it?" asked Griffin. The corpsman continued to wet the gauze and began tenderly applying it to the man's stomach. The big Arab made a few painful noises as the gauze contacted the tender flesh, and the corpsman looked into his face. The man nodded and the corpsman continued working.

"Not really, Sergeant Griffin," he answered at last. "I gave him a stick of morphine to try and ease the pain, but he's lost all sorts of blood and his stomach has just been laid open by the claymores. No doubt his intestines are perforated in a dozen places and bile has been leaking into his bloodstream half the night. I don't know how he made it this far. He must be strong as an ox."

"The morphine do him any good?" asked Griffin.

The corpsman shrugged. "A little maybe. Not much."

"How long will he last?" asked Griffin.

The corpsman looked at Griffin and shook his head. "It's hard to say, but he's a goner one way or the other. Even if we med-evac him we'd probably kill him trying to get him on the stretcher. His guts would just come spillin' out as soon as we tried to move him." The man groaned and Griffin looked into his face.

Griffin hesitated a moment, then asked, "How much morphine to put him out of his misery?" Both Downs and the corpsman looked at the big sergeant. The corpsman shrugged again and said, "Maybe another two sticks. He's pretty far gone."

Griffin turned and looked back toward the building. Nothing moved in the empty courtyard. The large stone house was framed against a blue sky and the wind moved through the trees overhead, belying the death and agony below. He looked again at the wounded man, obviously considering his decision. "Doc, give me three sticks of morphine, then get your ass back to the house," he said.

The corpsman dutifully went into his bag and produced the three syringes. As he ran back toward the house Griffin looked at Downs, who dropped his gaze. Griffin moved back toward the wounded man and uncapped the three syringes, laying them in a neat line on the ground. He picked them up and squeezed a drop of the drug from each one, insuring no air remained in the needle. Griffin looked at the man who seemed to be in somewhat less pain. He held up one of the syringes and mimed the action of inserting it into the man's thigh and injecting the drug. Then he pointed to the other two syringes which still lay on the ground. Griffin held up three fingers and pointed to the syringes, then to the man, then drew a finger slowly across his own neck. After a brief hesitation the man seemed to understand and nodded his assent. Griffin noticed that Downs was looking on as he inserted the first of the three needles into the man's leg. The Arab remained motionless, not reacting to the prick of the needles as Griffin inexpertly inserted them into his leg. When Griffin was done with the last dosage of morphine he knelt back on his heel and picked up his rifle. "Okay, mister, you ought to be feelin' no pain in about ten seconds. Good luck, you look like the only soldier here." The man's head rolled lazily to one side and he struggled to speak. Griffin leaned forward to hear the man.

"What's he saying, Downs? Can you understand any of it?"

"He said 'shook run,' Sergeant Griffin. It means thank you."

"No shit, huh?" said Griffin. He looked at the man one last time before turning to Downs. "Well, we still gotta get off this hill before his friends come back. No point in blowing that first claymore now, I'll have somebody pull it down as we go by. Okay, the next set of lead wires are behind a rock, right-hand side of the road. Don't miss any of them, and don't get in a hurry. Form up and get your people moving, we've been screwing around up here long enough."

Downs ordered the other three back onto the road and resumed his position at the head of the little column. He looked at the road and knew that the next few steps would take him out of line of sight of the main body. Ahead lay the narrow descending roadway, flanked on each side by the steep slopes of the hill and cedar trees. He cast a glance back over his shoulder to ensure that his team was in place before stepping off. Mac, Smith, and Ferris all looked nervously forward. Griffin remained kneeling by the dying Arab.

The road as he rounded the curve was empty of bodies, but Downs noted several large blotches of dried blood. He stopped frequently to observe the trees, rocks, and crevices that might hide an attacking force. As instructed by Griffin he detonated the claymores at the appropriate spots. The hill, except for the Marines and the dead, was deserted as far as he could determine. He was struck by the utter stillness of the morning. No birds sang in the trees overhead, and no sound came from the sleeping village below. Downs reminded himself to concentrate on the business at hand. The farther he descended, the fewer pieces of cast-off gear and blood trails he encountered.

Rounding another curve in the road he spotted a perfectly green cedar branch lying in the center of the pavement. Downs raised a clenched fist, signaling Mac and the others to stop.

An electric current of fear raced through Downs as he sank to his knees, his eyes searching the hillside before him for any sign of movement. He stared again at the branch, obviously newly cut and dropped or placed in the roadway. His brain frantically searched for a plausible explanation as to how the branch might have come to be there. The only explanation was that it had been placed there by someone. He slowly moved forward, his heart racing, his mind expecting the ambush at any second. Downs took up the slack on the trigger of his weapon, bracing himself for the impact of the bullets. He crouched, now even with the fallen bough, and examined it for any sign of an ambush or trip wire. Seeing none he felt no relief. As he again moved forward he heard the rasping of Mac's boots as he followed a few paces behind.

Coming around the next curve Downs saw more fallen branches, the white of the cut end plain on all of them. Looking up the hill he was able to discern a path of fallen branches reaching up to the summit. He signaled for Mac to close up and asked, "What do you make of all the branches? They all look as though they've been cut. Can you figure it out?"

Mac looked up the hill and studied the path of the fallen branches, then shrugged. Downs again resumed the forward movement, the three others following. Within seconds Downs spotted the first of the fallen Arabs. The man was sprawled across the road, face down. Another of the Arabs lay in a pool of his own blood a yard from the first man. Downs looked up the hill and saw through the trees the window that had served the night before as his firing position. It gaped above him, a black square in the stone face of the house, the fallen branches an arrow pointing accusingly to it. He realized that the rounds from his machine gun would have acted like a saw, cutting any branches before them as he sprayed the roadway. He resumed his inevitable descent, each step revealing new horrors from his attack the night before. Downs automatically looked at each body, realizing that he was hoping to find at least one of them still alive. A dozen bodies sprawled before him, none moving. Weapons were strewn about the road and flies buzzed around the dead men. Blood covered large parts of the road surface, dried black where it had not been absorbed by the soil.

Downs fought the urge to vomit, kneeling to regain his composure. His face was wet with his own sweat, cold and smelling metallically of fear. He noticed one body in particular. The man had obviously crawled to the side of the road nearest the hill and taken shelter behind a large rock. The blood stain on the front of his shirt and the dried black puddle at his feet were all the evidence needed to conclude that the man had bled to death. Noticing the .45 holster slung across his chest Sam Browne–style, Downs knew it was the militia leader he had watched Griffin beat the day before. He noted absently that the holster was empty.

He glanced back at Mac, who was staring in horrid fascination at the scene before them. Mac shook his head from side to side, as if to deny what he saw. "Let's go, Steve. We're holding up the rest of the squad. Let's get the fuck out of here."

Downs picked his way through the bodies, careful not to step in any dried blood. He keyed the handset and spoke, "Sergeant Griffin."

"Go Downs."

"We got some more bodies down here. Maybe a dozen. None of them are moving, they're all KIA. Over."

"Roger, Downs. I copy. How far are you from being to the bottom of the hill? Over?"

"Not far. Fifty meters maybe."

"Roger. When you can see the road, stop. I'm coming down with the main body. You copy?"

"Roger," answered Downs, "Over."

CHAPTER

15

The Syrian leaned back in his chair and studied the boy before him. He noted that Walid's hands shook, his uniform was filthy, and he had not lifted his gaze from the floor since entering the room. The attack last night upon the American position had been a traumatic and stunning defeat for the militia. The only surprise for the Syrian was that they had stayed on the hill after their first futile attempt upon the gate.

The American commander had played it perfectly. He had drawn Ahmud into an attack that could not possibly succeed and crippled his force. The Syrian wondered if the Americans had even suffered any casualties. The attack had cost him the loss of Farouck, his best sergeant. The explosives technician could be replaced, he was merely a mechanic. Finding someone suitable to replace Farouck would be more difficult. For the time being, and probably until his mission in Beirut was completed, he would have to see to the details personally. An annoyance, but nothing that would even remotely jeopardize the mission.

He watched the boy through narrowed eyes. He guessed him to be not more than twenty-two or twenty-three years old. No real experience to speak of, certainly nothing that would have prepared him for last night. The boy was practically in shock. He and a few of the lucky others had been selected the night before to help the Syrian crew the mortars. They had worked hard, hauling ammunition, digging gun emplacements, sandbagging the tubes in place, and firing relentlessly as the Syrian adjusted the elevation and charges. All of it had been futile. He had not been so careless as to actually fire on the militia, but none of the hundred or so rounds they had fired had done more than cause the occasional worried glance among the Marines.

"So, Walid. It seems we have suffered a setback," offered the Syrian. "The Brotherhood has lost many and has gained little."

Walid nodded, then mumbled a barely audible reply, "We have lost much and gained nothing."

The Syrian paused, nodding in agreement, then said, "The Americans are not to be taken lightly in matters of arms. The Marines are noted for their prowess." He waited for a reply and when it became apparent that the boy meant to say nothing he continued, "We are not strong enough, you and I, to take them by force. We must find other ways to defeat them."

The boy lifted his gaze from the floor, if only for a moment, and the Syrian continued, "Even the mightiest army can be defeated, Walid. The difficult thing is to find their weakness, and all armies have weaknesses. It is an inherent characteristic, but one must look for it, and one must be wise as well as courageous. Simple courage is not enough." The Syrian was pleased to see the boy cross to the window and slump into a chair.

After some moments of silence, Walid asked, "But what now? The Marines have beaten us. We can not hope to drive them from the hill."

The Syrian waved his hand in a gesture of dismissal. "And what of this hill? Suppose that we had driven them from it last night? What then? They would send another group of Marines and they would occupy a different hill. And then would we fight them again? For what, yet another hill? And all of these hills would be in Lebanon, would they not?"

The boy nodded, seeming to agree with the older man. "Our task is to drive them from Lebanon. Return the country to its people." The Syrian paused, then continued, "Wouldn't you agree?"

"Yes, of course," answered Walid.

The Syrian leaned back in his chair and rested one foot on the open drawer of his desk. "I have been a soldier a long time, Walid. And I have seen many nights like the one you and your friends witnessed last night."

"What do you mean?" asked the boy, staring contemptuously at the Syrian's business suit and expensive Italian loafers.

The Syrian noted the boy's glance, correctly guessing what he was thinking. "I have seen battles with the Israelis, most of which we lost because we foolishly challenged a stronger army."

The Syrian repressed a smile as the boy looked at him expectantly, waiting for him to explain. He removed a battered photograph from his wallet showing a younger version of himself standing before a burning Israeli tank.

"The Golan," he said, "during the seventy-three war." He paused, "Do you remember it?"

The boy shook his head. "No," he said softly, "but I have heard of it. Your army won a great victory."

The Syrian again fought the urge to laugh, then said quietly, "No, Walid. My army suffered a humiliating defeat. But we tell ourselves it was a victory because, for a day, we fought well." He noted the boy's puzzled expression, then continued, "I was in charge of a section of tanks. We advanced rapidly the first day, taking and even passing our objectives. That first evening we found ourselves on high ground, in a virtually impregnable position. We had advanced quickly, isolating and destroying numerous Israeli vehicles and tanks. We had advanced so rapidly that we outdistanced our supply convoys. That night we watched the Syrian Air Force battle the Israelis for the sky, and when we slept we thought we would wake victorious the next morning."

"And did you not?" asked Walid.

The Syrian shook his head slowly, smiling at the boy's childlike questioning. "No, we did not. The next morning we woke to the sound of advancing Israeli armor."

"But you held the better position, the heights," protested the boy.

"It made little difference to the Israeli pilots who destroyed our air force the night before. They rapidly set about destroying our tanks, including the ones I commanded." The Syrian said nothing for a moment, remembering the sounds of his command being destroyed as the Israeli aircraft thundered in on their strafing runs. "Do you know, Walid, that I walked back to Syria from the Golan?" The boy looked at him with a quizzical expression, as he continued, speaking in a quiet voice, "It was quite a feat, really. I moved only in the dark, always wary that I might be killed by patrols from either side. I eventually made my way to the remnants of a supply unit that ferried me back to Damascus."

"And what became of you then?" asked Walid.

The Syrian thought for a moment before answering, "I was given a medal," he said, a smile again overtaking his features. "A medal, although all my tanks had been destroyed, and most of my men killed or captured. It seems that by holding our position we had held open a corridor allowing other units to retreat back to Syria."

"You were a hero," said the boy. "The Israelis had the advantage."

"I was no hero, Walid. My tanks were without fuel, we had no choice but to stand."

The boy shook his head, saying in anguish, "Why do you tell me this? So that I will know that what seems an Arab victory is not?"

"No, Walid. I tell you this for two reasons. The first is that you should learn that we lost because we attacked the Israelis on terms favorable to them. We allowed them to fight on grounds that favored their strengths. Although we initially won, their superior weapons, the tanks and aircraft, were invariably to make the difference between victory and defeat for us."

"And the other reason?" asked Walid.

"So you will realize that even the most vigilant enemy is vulnerable at certain times, and in certain circumstances, even if only for a short time. Learn to avoid their strengths, and to attack their weaknesses and you will begin to sense what it takes to be the victor, instead of the vanquished."

"I can not learn these things in one night, after seeing my friends die. I am not you."

"I do not ask that you learn them in one night. No man can pretend to gain the wisdom of a lifetime in a single night," said the Syrian, sensing his moment was at hand.

"What then," asked the boy, obviously confused, the despair evident in his voice. "What should I do?"

The Syrian said nothing. He glanced at the boy, knowing that he was nearly distraught. "You must listen to my counsel, Walid," he said in a soft voice. "You must avoid more foolish adventures against an enemy you can not defeat by conventional methods. Otherwise you will have no hope of victory." The Syrian paused, knowing that he had won. "Are we agreed on this?" he asked.

Walid shook his head. "Yes," he said, his voice full of resignation.

The Syrian regarded him with silent amusement. It might have been worse my young friend, he thought, I might have permitted you to accompany Ahmud. He rose and crossed to the window. Touching Walid lightly on the shoulder he said, "Come, we have work to do if we are to avenge the deaths of our brothers."

Without hesitation Walid followed him out of the room, down the stairs, and into the courtyard. The Syrian smiled, thinking that he had at last found the proper man to lead the Brotherhood.

CHAPTER

16

Griffin nudged Slocum with his shoulder and said, "There it is, home sweet home." Slocum gave a nod to Griffin but didn't say anything as the trucks carrying both squads approached the checkpoint in front of the battalion headquarters. The guard waved them through after a couple of words with the driver and the massive trucks swung into the entrance and stopped in front of the four-story structure that housed the headquarters and service company. Marines on the top of the building leaned over the concrete guardrail and watched the squads as they got off the trucks and formed up in a ragged line. News of the firefight the previous night had spread rapidly through the battalion and now Marines who were acquainted with the various members of Griffin's and Slocum's squads began to approach and ask questions about the fighting. Already the story had taken on a life of its own and Griffin knew the facts would soon be lost as each Marine remembered and told his own version of the events. Griffin noted with a sense of dread that the battalion operations officer was standing in the lobby of the headquarters building, a scowl on his face. He looked at Slocum, who followed his gaze and shrugged, then said, "What did you expect, pretty girls and firecrackers?"

"Well, let's just say as little as possible about all this for now. No sense giving these guys a chance to fuck with us if we don't have to. I imagine they'll have all sorts of questions anyway without us giving them anything more to think about.''

"Fine with me. Just remember, you're the one who came up with that bullshit story about a vehicle being down,'' said Slocum casually.

Griffin looked at Slocum, then gave a wry smile. "Yeah, no shit. Let's get out of here before they figure out they want to talk to us.'' He shook Slocum's hand and gave the order for the squad to form up and make ready to march back to the platoon area. Griffin debated the wisdom of delaying the squad's departure by a couple of hours so as to allow the squad a chance to get a hot meal at the battalion chow hall, but then decided against it. The longer they hung around the battalion the more people they would talk to and sooner or later it would come out that he had hit the local militia leader and forced the whole confrontation. He dreaded the thought of trying to explain that to one of the battalion officers.

Griffin ordered the squad to move out and they began the journey back to their bunkers on the line. The squad skirted the north end of the runway before turning south and paralleling the runway for about one kilometer. Upon arrival at the company position, there were loud catcalls by the other Marines who were aware of the firefight of the previous evening. Griffin dismissed the squad and they headed for their respective bunkers to change into clean uniforms and get something to eat. Although he would have liked to have slept for at least a couple of hours he made for the platoon sergeant's bunker. Whitney was standing in front of the bunker, no hint of his disposition betrayed by his manner or expression. Griffin walked toward him and nodded. "Hello, Staff Sergeant Whitney. How goes it?'' To his relief the staff sergeant smiled and said, "Welcome back, boy. Come on in and let's have a talk.'' The two men stepped down into the bunker and the staff sergeant indicated that Griffin should sit on one of the cots. "Can I get you something to drink, Sergeant Griffin?''

"No thanks,'' said Griffin with a smile.

The older man sat across from Griffin and rubbed his face with his hands. "Okay, Sergeant Griffin. Now tell me what happened out there. And don't give me any bullshit. This has yours and Slocum's signature all over it. Just tell me what happened and why. We'll worry about the details later.''

Griffin quickly relayed the basics of the night's events, including his fight with the militia leader and his plan to delay leaving the area in order to force a confrontation on his own terms. The staff sergeant listened quietly, nodding occasionally but not making any real comment. When Griffin finished he took a deep breath and looked him in the eye. "Well, we're probably gonna have some problems over all this. You realize that, don't you?"

"I figured as much. Anything so far?" asked Griffin.

"Well, our first sergeant has already been down here asking questions. I imagine he'll want to talk to you as soon as he gets back this afternoon. He's gone out on ship for some reason. My suggestion is for you to have some answers ready for him. My personal advice is for you to say as little as possible, and to avoid giving any details if at all possible."

Griffin took a deep breath, slowly releasing it and feeling extremely tired as he did. "I didn't have any choice, Staff Sergeant. That's the bottom line. Maybe we could have avoided a fight, but as long as we fought from the house we had all the advantages. Shit, we didn't even have anybody hurt."

"You were lucky, boy. I haven't seen that house, but judging from what you've told me you are just plain lucky nobody got hurt. If somebody had, you could just about kiss your sergeant's stripes good-bye. As it is they are going to raise one hell of a shit storm. You may still be looking at some sort of court-martial for insubordination or disobedience of a direct order if they are able to get the real story from some of the troops."

"I told 'em to keep their mouths shut about the incident at the gate, and none of 'em know the real deal about the vehicle being down. They think we really did delay leaving because we needed time to work on that truck. Besides, they are more afraid of me than they are of the Zeros at headquarters."

"What about the truck driver? And Slocum's squad? Are you sure nobody will say anything if the officers start coming around asking questions?"

"I guess I really can't be sure, Staff Sergeant. But it was a chance I had to take."

Griffin looked at the staff sergeant who nodded his head affirmatively. "Yeah, Sergeant Griffin, I understand, but I'm not the one you have to convince," he said.

Griffin smiled and said, "No shit."

The staff sergeant crossed to the doorway of the crowded bunker and stood looking across the company area to the battalion headquarters building that loomed in the distance. "It wasn't always like this. Used to be they expected us to be full of piss and vinegar. Shit, I can remember when I joined we used to go out into town every Friday night and leave bail money with the sergeant of the guard. Everybody just assumed we would go into town, get drunk, and tear some place apart until the police and the shore patrol got there. Then the officer of the day and the sergeant of the guard would come and get us after we slept it off in jail for a few hours. Nobody ever lost a stripe over having a good time on liberty." The staff sergeant passed a hand through the stubble of hair that covered the top of his head then turned toward Griffin and said, "Times have changed, Sergeant Griffin. Nowadays all they worry about is how we are going to look in the press, or what some pansy-ass congressman is going to say. A good combat record used to mean something when you got your ass in a sling. I'm not so sure it does anymore."

As he walked back into the bunker and sat on the rack opposite Griffin he chuckled softly to himself. "If you can't answer the questions they are going to ask you are going to be facing a familiar situation as far as I can see."

"What's that?" asked Griffin.

"Well, Sergeant Griffin, you are going to find yourself having been shot at and missed, and shit at and hit, as they used to say when I was a young Marine," said the staff sergeant with a wink.

Griffin attempted to laugh at the staff sergeant's humor, but found his throat going dry. He dreaded the thought of being questioned by the battalion officers. He knew that it would be a simple matter for them to determine that the vehicle had not really had mechanical trouble, and once that was done it could only be a matter of time for him and Slocum. "So you think they are going to come after us?" he asked the staff sergeant.

"Yeah, boy, I do. Let me tell you why. If we had a good first shirt, and a strong sergeant major, I don't think you would have any problem. But that just isn't the way it is. The sergeant major is new to the battalion, just been with us for this deployment, no more than a few months. He doesn't know you or me, or anybody else to speak of. The only people he can really associate with, being the battalion sergeant major, are the company first sergeants. The rest of us he has to get to know from our performance and what he hears and sees around the battalion." The staff sergeant glanced at Griffin, who was leaning forward, listening intently. "See, the only reason the sergeant major has heard your name in the past few weeks is because of the first shirt making a circus out of Downs's fireteam having that damn beer out on post. Now the first shirt is going to see him about this firefight last night and make it sound as if you and your squad are just a bunch of independent shit birds that do as you please. The next thing is the CO is going to ask the sergeant major what the hell happened out there. Now, the sergeant major may or may not tell him what the first shirt passed to him. You following all this?"

"Yeah, and it sure isn't looking too good. I should have broken the first sergeant's nose as well as that fucking Arab's," said Griffin.

"Yeah. I know how you feel, Sergeant Griffin. I guess I should tell you that a few years ago I got into a fight out in town with a gunnery sergeant and I wound up losing a stripe and doing a little brig time."

"That doesn't surprise me, Staff Sergeant. Shit happens all the time."

The staff sergeant smiled broadly at Griffin and added, "Well it might surprise you to know that that particular gunnery sergeant was promoted and is now our company first sergeant."

Griffin looked the staff sergeant in the eye and said, "You're shitting me. Right?"

The staff sergeant laughed and shook his head. "No, I sure as hell am not. Wish I was though. It would probably go a long way toward solving this whole mess." He rubbed his chin and added, "Sorry, boy."

The two men sat in good-natured silence for a few minutes. Griffin liked the staff sergeant. He was a good Marine and a good platoon sergeant. He was a veteran of the Vietnam War and was well liked and respected by his troops and peers. Everything about him said "Old Corps," from his slight disrespect for junior officers to his cavalier approach to garrison life with its myriad of rules and regulations.

The story about the staff sergeant's experiences in Vietnam were legend in the regiment. He was one of the last of the old-timers who had won their stripes in Vietnam and since not been promoted to the higher ranks, which would have removed them from direct daily contact with the grunts that formed the backbone of the Corps. Griffin and the others had seen the rows of ribbons on his dress uniforms at inspection and also the scars that ran the length of his back. Although Griffin had never heard first hand the story of how they were earned, the Navy Cross and Purple Heart with its small stars pinned on each side spoke for themselves. There had been speculation as to why he had not been promoted to the rank of gunnery sergeant, and now Griffin knew the answer. He let out a long sigh and said, "Well, fuck me. What a kick in the ass this has turned out to be."

"Well it isn't the end of the world. What's the worst they can do? Take some pay and maybe a stripe. You'll get it back. You're a good Marine, Sergeant Griffin. And unless I miss my guess you did what you believed was the right thing. And more important, you didn't lose any of your people." The staff sergeant paused, then spoke again before Griffin could say anything, "Look, son, what else could you have done? If you and Sergeant Slocum really believed that they were going to ambush you on the way down that hill then you didn't have any choice. When push comes to shove you're responsible for the Marines in your squad, not the first sergeant or some shavetail lieutenant at battalion operations."

The older man looked Griffin in the eye and continued, "Let them second-guess you all they want to. As long as you're satisfied you did the right thing, then your conscience is clean. Am I making any sense to you?"

"I understand, Staff Sergeant. I know I did the right thing. I didn't have any choice anyway. But sergeant's stripes are hard to come by."

"So is a man's self-respect. Maybe you ought to think about that. Or maybe you ought to think about what might have happened if you had stuck with the operations officer's plan and led your squad down that hill and into an ambush. How would you feel then?" The staff sergeant's face relaxed and he gave a slight laugh. "You know, now that I think about it, it wouldn't have made any difference to battalion if you had. They would just haul your ass up there and question you as to why you didn't stay on the hill in a good defensive position and let the enemy attack you." As he completed the thought he laughed aloud and slapped Griffin on the shoulder. "Shit, Sergeant Griffin, there just wasn't any way you were going to come out of this one without losing a few feathers."

Griffin attempted a smile and said, "A regular catch-twenty-two," under his breath.

"What's that?" asked the staff sergeant.

"Nothing," he answered. "Just thinking out loud."

"Well, in your position that's about the one thing I wouldn't do out loud for the next few days. When you go back to your squad area you have a good heart-to-heart with your corporals and make it understood that all hands are to keep their mouths shut. God only knows what the first shirt will be asking them. But you can bet it isn't anything you'll want 'em to answer." The staff sergeant paused for a moment, then asked, "Is there anybody in your squad who might not understand what's going on? Anybody you can't trust?"

Griffin paused. He had wondered silently on the ride back about how Downs might react. They hadn't spoken much in the last week, but he had noticed a subtle change in Downs. It wasn't anything he could define, but it was there. He realized that he was feeling guilty for even thinking a member of his squad might choose to dump on him to the first sergeant. It was the most inviolable of all the unspoken rules of the Marine infantryman that no one ever gives up another Marine to the higher ranks for punishment. They might ostracize him, ridicule him, or even beat him, but justice was dealt out from within the squad or the platoon without interference from the company hierarchy.

Before he could answer the staff sergeant asked, "Is Downs bothering you?"

Griffin looked at the Staff Sergeant and said, "No. I thought of him. He's been a real pain in the ass at times, but after the embassy bombing I think he changed. He sure as hell was quiet up on that hill." Griffin paused, trying to gather his thoughts. "I'm not sure what it is, Staff Sergeant. Downs is different, you know? But I can't see him ratting on me to the first shirt or anybody else, anymore than I can see him not doing his duty. He's just fucking different, and even he knows it."

The staff sergeant nodded and said, "He is that now. I'm damned if I can figure him. But you're right, I can't really see Downs answering anything the first sergeant asks with anything more than one of his smart-ass 'yes sirs.'" The staff sergeant chuckled, "God knows the first shirt can't stand the sight of him anyway. If I were the first sergeant I would be damn sure I knew where Downs was at any given moment. Be just like Downs to frag his air wing ass on a dark night and have his coffee and eggs the next mornin' like nothin' ever happened."

Griffin smiled and said, "Doesn't sound so bad to me right now."

"Well, just don't go gettin' any ideas in your head. This ain't that big of a deal. Anyway, if there is more shootin' in the next few days they'll forget all about this up at battalion."

"You think they'll attack us? Here? At the battalion?"

The staff sergeant shrugged. "Who knows? These people are funny as hell. One minute they're giving you flowers and candy and the next they're blowin' the shit out of the embassy. But if you hurt them as bad as you say you did last night then there is no way they are going to just walk away from this. What would you do in their place? Think about that."

Griffin cocked an eyebrow and answered, "Yeah, I see your point." He paused for a moment then asked, "So what do Slocum and I tell them when they start asking questions? The officers, I mean."

"Well, I suppose you have to tell them the truth as far as possible. But I wouldn't volunteer any information. And you should remember that you know all the facts, they're only guessin' at what happened based on what they think they know. You following me?"

"I guess so. Do you think it'll be a board of inquiry or a court-martial?"

"I'm not really sure. If they can prove you didn't actually have a down vehicle they'll convene a court-martial." The staff sergeant rubbed his chin in a familiar gesture that Griffin knew meant he was thinking, then said, "Let's not worry about this too much right now, Sergeant Griffin. Why don't you go to your hooch and get some rest. I'll see what I can find out in the meantime. Maybe you don't have a thing to worry about."

Griffin rose to go and as he did he extended his hand to the staff sergeant, an odd gesture among Marines who commonly greeted each other with salutes, or good-natured banter. As he shook the staff sergeant's hand he said, "Thanks," then strode out of the bunker and went to find his cot.

CHAPTER

17

The Syrian looked through his binoculars at the Americans walking around the outside of the building that sat squarely in the cross formed by the intersection of the two runways. He noted the absence of barriers and fencing that would allow approach by a vehicle to within perhaps fifty meters before a sentry could effectively challenge the driver. He observed the sentry and machine gunners standing atop the building. Sweeping the binoculars over the roof he assured himself that no antitank weapons were in view. Another building, smaller than the first, was just north of the one he had been looking at and also occupied by the Marines.

He knew the buildings fairly well. They had formerly served as the headquarters of one of the various Palestinian factions that occupied the city prior to the Israeli invasion. Both structures were made of reinforced concrete and of fairly modern design. He was certain that the larger, a four-story structure formerly the Lebanese Aviation Safety Bureau, was now the headquarters of the Marines. He searched his memory for details concerning the structure. He remembered a large atrium that rose through the center of the building and was crowned by a series of triangular skylights. He had been in the building only a few times and therefore checked the roof for evidence of the skylights. Through the binoculars he observed the center of the roof and saw the neat symmetrical rows of skylights, confirming that his memory was accurate.

As he continued to look at the building details of the interior returned to him. The structure was a rectangle whose interior was hollow and whose sides were ringed by offices. The long sides of the rectangle faced north and south and it was the south face that he now studied. The offices in the building were accessed by means of broad stairways located at the east and west ends of the interior. He could not recall if the building had an elevator or a basement. The building was supported by a series of Y-shaped concrete pillars, and through the pillars he was able to discern the Marines entering and leaving the building from the south portal. He was certain that it also had a large plaza on the ground level that in former times had been a welcome center occupying almost the entire lobby area.

The structure had obviously suffered during the Israeli invasion. The south face was pocked by shell holes and ugly black stains climbed the concrete walls, evidence of a large fire in the interior. He scanned the windows, noting that many of them had been blown out and were now covered by the ponchos of the Marines who lived within. At ground level, ringing the exterior of the building, were a series of improvised shelters and tents set up by the Marines to house their troops. Here he could see that the specialized troops had been barracked. On several jeeps he saw the cylindrical fiberglass tubes that he knew only too well as the launchers for the TOW antitank missile favored by the Marines and the Israelis. On the far side of the building he could observe a column of perhaps twenty men gathering before four or five of the small jeeps the Americans used to move about the city. He watched as they mounted their vehicles and slowly left the compound by a road leading to a gate north of the compound. He saw two of the huge amphibious vehicles used by the Marines parked just west of the building, their hatches open and the crews wandering around outside their vehicles.

Immediately to the south of the structure, which he was now sure was the headquarters of the Marines, was a large parking lot that served the airport terminal. Across the center of this lot stretched a strand of razor wire and two outposts constructed of sandbags. By patient observation he was able to determine that the posts were manned by individual Marines who were lightly armed. He broadened his search and saw that the whole compound was ringed by a series of such sandbagged outposts. Punctually, on the hour, a Marine would emerge from the south side of the headquarters building and walk the entire perimeter, stopping at each post. He smiled to himself. All armies are the same in some respects. Guard duty, poor food, and miserable living conditions were common to all soldiers no matter the side they fought for or where or when they fought. He noted that the sentries appeared to be generally alert and the sergeant who checked them was prompt. He was certain that the guard posts were linked by radio to the sergeant who no doubt would have a post somewhere in the center of the building.

To the east of the headquarters he observed a large gravel lot that was obviously the vehicle repair and maintenance facility for the Marines. Several vehicles of various descriptions were parked neatly in this lot and mechanics worked on others. His eye ran over several large inflatable rubber fuel bladders that he found tempting targets. Further observation convinced him that the fuel had wisely been placed far enough from anything else so that even if he were to cause its detonation, it would achieve very little in the way of casualties or destruction. He dismissed the vehicle park as a likely target for any number of reasons. It was in the center of the Marine compound, and even though it was lightly defended, it simply did not offer the type of target he wanted. The American public would hardly notice the destruction of a few jeeps or trucks.

Immediately north of the vehicle park he was able to discern a series of large tents housing what appeared to be more troops. He noted that Marines from these tents did not move back and forth between this area and either of the two large buildings. They seemed to be primarily concerned with the large hangar that serviced the eastern runway of the airport. A few more minutes' study of this area and he was certain that these men were the ground crews of the helicopters that flew regularly between the Marine base ashore and the fleet anchored a few kilometers off the coast. He contemplated the wisdom of attacking this area. Again, it was lightly defended and therefore vulnerable. But just like the vehicle park it did not offer the type of target he was looking for. So far, he was certain, the large headquarters building offered him the greatest opportunity, and also the greatest challenge.

Moving the glasses farther north he saw the tent city created by the 42nd Brigade of the Lebanese Army. The Lebanese soldiers wandered about their camp with no apparent goal. Rows of tents sagged along dirt streets and soldiers stood around and smoked or chatted. He noted that the Lebanese were separated by a dirt road from their American allies, who appeared only marginally concerned with them. Several armored personnel carriers were parked in the Lebanese compound, as were a few jeeps and heavy trucks. A few guards appeared at the corners of the Lebanese camp, but they seemed to be generally inattentive. He examined the road that led between the Marines and the Lebanese. Any access it may have once offered was now denied by the fencing placed across the intersections. Although a heavy vehicle would have no trouble simply running through the fence, by doing so it would lose all possibility of surprise. At this point no plan was formulated, but he preferred to have the element of surprise if at all possible. He quickly decided to dismiss the Lebanese as a means of defense of this area of the Marine perimeter. They were not an army so much as an well-armed mob. They would do little for either side in this struggle. He brought the glasses south for another look at the hangar area. A sentry walked his post around a parked helicopter gunship, perhaps two hundred meters south of the Lebanese. An easy entry to a very tempting target. He doubted if the Marines had any effective communications with the Lebanese, and he was sure he could have his attacker through the LAF compound and on his target before the alarm could be raised.

He brought his gaze west of the hangar area and again observed the smaller building occupied by the Marines. A constant line of men moved between this building and the larger one to the south. He decided that this building probably served as billeting space for the officers and the men moving between the two buildings who were carrying messages or returning to their quarters after their duty shift was over. The traffic in and around the two buildings seemed to support this theory as well as his own experience in the Syrian army. He also was able to see another still smaller building behind the billeting building, and this he took to be more barracks. Access to this area would be by foot traffic only. He could not specifically recall ever having been in either of the two buildings. He observed the low one-story structures for another few minutes and satisfied himself that his analysis was correct. These two buildings were the type of "soft" target he was looking for, but they would be difficult for his bomber to reach, perhaps impossible given the depth of the defenses.

To the immediate north of these two buildings was a heavily defended gate accessing the compound. A broad boulevard leading to the airport terminal ran just west of the gate and paralleled the western perimeter of the Marine compound. Civilian traffic moved constantly along the boulevard, just yards in front of the Marine sentries. A few hundred yards north of the headquarters building, sitting astride the boulevard, was a Lebanese Army checkpoint.

He smoked another cigarette and watched as the Lebanese guards at the checkpoint stopped traffic and conducted cursory checks of the cars and trucks that approached. No vehicle remained longer than a minute or two at the checkpoint, and in thirty minutes of careful observation he did not see a single vehicle pulled aside for a secondary search of its occupants or cargo. A steady stream of construction vehicles moved through the checkpoint and into the terminal area where repairs were being made along the eastern runway.

He followed the traffic as it moved south past the Marine headquarters and into the terminal area. Most of the cars stopped in the immediate vicinity of the terminal, obviously delivering or picking up passengers. The trucks of the construction company, however, moved past the terminal, swung east, then followed a dirt road south of the parking lot with the Marine sentries and into the construction site. Here they took on loads of dirt from the excavation, then reversed their route and exited the terminal area. At their closest point they were no more than one hundred meters from the Marine sentries.

He waited another half hour for a truck marked OGER LIBAN to pass through the checkpoint and into the terminal. He noted the time on his watch as the truck entered the compound and recorded it in a small notebook. As the truck swept past the sentry post the Marine and the driver exchanged a friendly wave. It took the truck fifty-seven minutes to take on a load of dirt and rubble before exiting the area. He noted again the attitude of the Marine sentries as the truck left. They did not seem alarmed or to be recording any information regarding the entry and exit of the vehicles. He smiled. The trucks had a plausible reason to be there and the Marines therefore had no reason to question their arrival or departure. The fact that the construction had probably been going on for some time would also help him. By now the guards would have become conditioned to seeing the arrival and departure of the trucks marked with the logo of the Lebanese construction company. Their appearance was so regular and expected that it caused no alarm in the sentries. The exchange of greetings between the driver and the Marine was evidence of that.

A rough plan began to take shape as he sipped scalding coffee and smoked, sitting on the balcony with his feet propped comfortably on the low stone wall in front of him. This would be a difficult enterprise, but the rewards would be tremendous if he could bring it off. The planning would take several days, perhaps a week. Already he knew that he would have to spend days observing the movements of the construction vehicles in and out of the area to determine their schedules and normal working hours and procedures. But the basic idea was sound and he found no immediate flaws to discredit it.

He swept the glasses over the airport. From his vantage point he could see the entire airport and the sea beyond where the American vessels floated. Helicopters circled above the ships like bees around their hive, then angled for shore with their cargoes of supplies and men. Below him the Marines went about their routines in the warm summer air. Their lines were laid out in a neat arc around the eastern runway, the troops dug in and well positioned. Bunkers were linked by trenches and supported by tanks and artillery. The helicopter gunships and naval batteries were capable of delivering massive and accurate fire within minutes directly onto the formations of an attacking enemy. Somewhere over the horizon, out of sight, lurked an even more deadly foe, an American aircraft carrier with its complement of jet aircraft. In the gray haze of the horizon he was able to discern the battleship *New Jersey*. With her sixteen-inch naval rifles and batteries of five-inch guns, she was a not so distant threat.

The Marines themselves he could see quite plainly, and it was obvious to him that they were well-trained and disciplined soldiers. The battle for the house atop the hill had proven to him that they were capable and able to maximize the situation at hand. They had fought well despite their youth and lack of experience.

He had great respect for them as soldiers, just as he had great respect for their Israeli allies. And yet, he was confident on the day he chose to attack them, all their training, experience, and firepower would count for nothing. He had not wasted his time in idle observation. He knew that the Marines would withstand any attack the Brotherhood or any other militia could mount against them. Just as he had counseled Ahmud not to attack them directly he would not attack them in such a manner. The result would be obvious.

To harass them by sniper fire and the killing of the occasional sentry would not accomplish his objective. Neither would random ambushes of the patrols the Marines ran through the villages adjacent to the airport. They would simply tighten their security and thereby reduce his possibilities to hit at them effectively. He also reasoned that the American government would not be convinced to leave Lebanon unless it was confronted by a really dramatic event.

He was certain that a bomber could reach the compound used by the Marines for their headquarters. Initially, he had planned to attack them at the building he reasoned to be the barracks housing their officers. Not only would this have provided a target offering the maximum number of casualties, the men who would die as a result of the attack would be the sons of middle-class American families. They would not be the lower-class men who served in the ranks and had no family and no real choice as to whether or not to enter the military.

After observing the compound every morning for a week he was able to begin the detailed planning for his attack. He had drawn a small map of the compound in his notebook, carefully recording each building used by the Marines and the various routes that gave access to these structures. At the approximate position of each barrier he drew in an "X," noting the number of men posted there and any weapons they might routinely have with them. To his consternation he noted that the men manning the key posts all had small antitank rockets. A carefully aimed LAAW would end his attack before it had any chance of success. He therefore resolved to avoid entering the compound through one of its fixed entrance points if at all possible.

To each building he assigned a numeric value between one and five, with the higher number representing the maximum level of difficulty for an attack. He also assigned a second value to each building, this time using the first five characters of the alphabet, and corresponding to the desirability of the structure as a target, with the latter characters denoting the least desirable targets. Using this system a building having a value of 1-A would be the most desirable target, being rated the lowest defensive posture and the highest desirability as a target. He assigned similar values to all three entrances to the compound, but erased them as he decided the boulevard offered the best means of entrance for the type of attack he planned.

By week's end he had decided that the four-story structure that served as the headquarters and operations center of the Marine battalion was to be his target. He was reasonably certain that a large number of troops were housed there, and virtually positive that the Marines' command center was located somewhere in its interior.

He had been puzzled by the constant foot traffic between this building and the two buildings to its immediate north. Both buildings had all the hallmarks of a military headquarters, the constant arrival and departure of officers, antennae arrays, communication gear, troops moving about, and around-the-clock activity. His detailed knowledge of the structure of a U.S. Marine infantry battalion was not sufficient to explain why, or if, the battalion would have two separate command posts. And he was unable to find a logical reason why two such redundant command centers would be placed side by side. As he had no desire to contact Damascus for any reason, and by asking questions about the organization of Marine Corps units he might give away his intended target, he was left to his own devices to solve the mystery.

It did not take him long to hit upon a solution. He became an avid reader of the daily papers and weekly news magazines that had reappeared in the Lebanese capital as soon as the situation began stabilizing. He was particularly interested in acquiring and reading the Christian papers. As the Christians perceived themselves as the natural allies of the French and American forces in the city, their papers wrote constantly of the multinational force. Judging from the articles that he read, their journalists had frequent contact with the military commanders of the multinational force units.

By reading these articles and studying the photos that accompanied them he was able not only to learn the names of the individual men who commanded the various multinational force units, but which buildings they used as their headquarters. In one week he had collected the photographs of the commanders of the American, French, and Italian battalions deployed in Beirut. He had also begun a collection of published photos of these men and their subordinates standing in front of various structures in and around Beirut and the airport. By carefully studying these and comparing them with the facades of the buildings he observed through his binoculars he was able to determine the purpose of most of the buildings in the Marine compound. He considered the possibility that the journalists were being fed false information, but the activity around the buildings in question did much to allay his suspicions.

After he was certain of the purpose of the target buildings he began a careful, close-in surveillance of the Marine compound. To his surprise it was accomplished with much less risk than he had anticipated. He began by taking a taxi to the airport terminal in order to purchase a ticket to Athens. Actually, the destination had been unimportant, he was merely using the purchase as a ruse to enter the terminal area.

He had dressed neatly and brought with him a small briefcase containing documentation that identified him as a resident of one of the Sunni districts of Beirut. After taking a taxi from his residence in another part of the city he left his cab in the busy Hamra district and melted into the throng on the street. He walked his habitual route to determine if he was being followed or surveilled, then stopped in a café where he had never before been and ordered breakfast. A young boy selling newspapers stopped at his table and he caught himself with a smile about to order one of the French-language dailies. Without giving any indication of changing his preference he took one of the Arabic papers, noticing it had a large article and photograph of the Marines on the front page.

After a leisurely breakfast during which he was careful to scan the sidewalks and other diners for anyone who might be following him, or whom he had seen before, he left the café and resumed his walk through the busy shopping district. Following half an hour of brisk walking, he crossed a wide boulevard then reversed himself in the middle of the intersection, as though he had mistakenly gone in the wrong direction. Although he was careful to look he did not notice anyone adjusting to his sudden change of direction in order to maintain surveillance.

Within another few blocks, the time now being almost noon, he hailed a taxi and told the driver to take him to the airport. With a flourish the driver pulled into traffic and began a leisurely drive west toward the wide boulevard that paralleled the coast and ran almost directly to the terminal at the airport. The Syrian feigned only occasional interest as the driver pointed out former tourist attractions or spots where the fighting had been particularly intense.

The driver pulled into the line of cars waiting to be cleared at the checkpoint in front of the airport while the Syrian sat calmly in the rear of the taxi. His demeanor gave no indication of nervousness or apprehension. As he exchanged the occasional comment with the driver he made mental notes of the Marine compound, the northern extremities of which were just to his left. He noted that most of the Marine positions were sandbagged in place, the sentries warily eyeing the passing vehicles.

The entrances to the compound continued to intrigue him. They lacked any heavy barricades, and the soldiers standing in front of them were not supported by armor of any kind. As the driver was waved forward into the inspection area of the checkpoint the Syrian nonchalantly removed his Lebanese passport from his vest pocket and handed it to the young Lebanese soldier who took it politely and stared at him as he sat in the rear seat of the taxi. He was not worried about his documentation, as the passport was an original he had taken from the offices of the Lebanese government some months before with the help of his friends in the PLO.

He suppressed a smile as he noted the young Lebanese was holding the passport upside down. As the boy flipped through the small book he found the page with the Syrian's photograph and, with an embarrassed look, turned the book right side up in order to examine the photo. The driver had dropped the car into gear and was about to leave as an older man in uniform exited the small guard shack and held up his hand, indicating the car should pull into a small area reserved for more detailed searches.

The Syrian replaced his passport in his pocket and quickly examined his memory for any reason why the guard might detain him. He could think of nothing in his documentation that might alert them other than the fact that it was stolen. He dismissed this as the Lebanese government was in far too much disorder to possibly have disseminated a list of stolen passports to its army. Besides, he reasoned, any such list would contain thousands of numbers, and the sergeant who had waved them over hadn't even seen his passport.

As the sergeant approached he again withdrew his documents and handed them through the window without saying anything. The sergeant, he noted, spun the passport right side up and thumbed quickly through to the page displaying his photo. He thought of the worst that might happen under the circumstances. If the sergeant questioned him as to why he was going to the airport he could supply a perfectly adequate reason. All of his documentation would support the fact that he was a Lebanese businessman, and that he had legitimate reasons to travel outside of the country.

If his person were searched the situation might become more complicated, but not impossible. The small pistol tucked into his belt would be awkward to explain, but even that was not unusual in Beirut these days. He would simply tell the man that he often carried cash and the pistol was for his own protection. He could feel himself beginning to tense as the man continued to look at his paperwork, glancing at him over the edge of the small passport booklet.

Trying to seem adequately concerned he glanced at the driver, catching his eye in the car's rearview mirror. The middle-aged man shook his head slightly from side to side, then raising his hand almost imperceptibly so that the Syrian could see it above the seat, he rubbed two fingers against his thumb. The driver then adjusted his hat without ever making an unnatural motion.

The Syrian understood immediately that the man was indicating he should bribe the sergeant. Bribery. It was the pension plan of every policeman and customs official in the Arab world. He had been so thoroughly absorbed by his study of the Marine compound that he had forgotten. The only problem was that now the sergeant had his paperwork and he had no way of gracefully giving the man the money.

He cursed himself under his breath and peeled two large bills from the roll in his pocket. When he had handed the guard his passport lacking any money, he had signaled his sergeant who stepped out of the guardhouse and waved their car over. The sergeant had quickly sized him up, noting the Western style business suit and the small attaché on the seat beside him. The man had given him every opportunity to correct the situation, even now he was standing expectantly by the door of the taxi. He had no desire to search the cab, but neither could the Syrian simply hand him the money in full view of the boy or anyone else who might happen to see. He looked again toward the driver, who understood and reached over the seat and quickly took the two bills.

The driver exited the cab and opened the trunk as the Syrian sat tensely looking straight ahead. It was just such ignorance of small details that resulted in the failure of whole missions. He cursed again. If it hadn't been for Ahmud he would have had Farouck to attend to details such as this, while he did the planning and coordinated other arrangements.

The driver got heavily into the cab and the car pulled away, the man looking discreetly ahead. The Syrian concluded that the driver must be puzzled as to how he could be so stupid as to not know enough to give the guard something with his passport.

As the cab pulled into the semicircular drive in front of the terminal and stopped the man fairly leapt from the car and opened the rear door before the Syrian could do it for himself. Feeling like a schoolboy he deftly took the man's hand, careful to place the bill in his palm. Without glancing back he strode past the guards and into the terminal not allowing the man a chance to ask if he should wait for him to return. He fumed for a quarter of an hour at his oversight at the checkpoint before he was able to regain his concentration.

He approached the counter of the Mediterranean Eastern Airlines and spoke with one of the ticketing agents regarding a flight to Athens. As the man juggled the dates and times the Syrian had given him, he decided that he would not purchase a ticket. It had originally been his plan to take a flight to Athens and return in a day or two. By doing so it would facilitate his return to the airport on legitimate business and perhaps give him the opportunity to view the Marine compound from the air.

The events of the morning had convinced him that this precaution was unnecessary. He was certain that he had not been followed. In fact, he was certain that the Lebanese were incapable of fielding a viable police force, and certainly not a competent intelligence service. The Israelis did not appear to be aware of his operation, and since he had not specifically targeted them, and Damascus was unaware of his location or intentions, he had no reason to think he might be known to them. The Americans appeared unconcerned as to most of the activity around them, which left him with the French. He was cautious where the French were concerned, but he believed his cover was intact and that they knew nothing of his operations with the Brotherhood. He had been wise to confine himself to the Shiite sections of the city. The accommodations had not been as comfortable, but he had enjoyed a greater level of security.

For the past months, since returning from Damascus with his general orders outlining how he was to proceed and whom he was to target, he had ignored the biweekly radio contacts with headquarters in Damascus. The radio receiver and transmitter were buried in the garden of one of his rented villas. He smiled at the thought of his superiors in Damascus trying to explain why they could not make radio contact with him nor could they send a messenger to him in Beirut.

He bought another newspaper and took a seat in the small café in a corner of the terminal building. An ancient waiter brought him scalding coffee and shuffled off without speaking. As he read the paper he glanced out the window to the boulevard that led into the terminal drive. To the casual observer he appeared to be no more than a middle-class business-man waiting for the arrival of a flight. Through the window he was able to see that an access road led east from the boulevard and into the hangar and runway area. This was the same road he had observed the Oger Liban construction vehicles using the week before from his perch in the foothills. The entrance to the road was guarded by a couple of Lebanese soldiers who stood by a simple weighted lever gate that had been painted red and white and topped by a stop sign.

Traffic on the boulevard moved past the road after discharging or picking up passengers at the terminal. No one seemed to pay much attention to the terminal area although a few Lebanese soldiers in the khaki uniforms and red berets of the Internal Security Forces stood on the sidewalk in front of the building. As he sipped his coffee a jeep flying the American flag pulled into the drive in front of the terminal and two Marines carrying their M-16 rifles jumped from the rear of the vehicle and entered the lobby. He watched as they crossed the floor and knocked on a gray door at the far end of the terminal. An older Lebanese opened the door from the inside and the Syrian had a brief glimpse of a tiled stairway that he surmised must lead to the tower. The two Marines entered and disappeared from his sight as the old man drew the door closed.

Not five minutes later two different Marines exited the door and walked across the lobby and got into the waiting jeep. The driver and guard exchanged greetings with them as they jumped into the rear seats and the jeep headed north toward the entrance to the Marine compound. The Syrian reasoned that he had just witnessed some sort of changing of a guard mount. He looked nonchalantly at his watch. The time was ten minutes after two o'clock. From his detailed observation of the Marines the week before he knew they changed guard shifts at eight o'clock, four in the afternoon, and midnight. Why two o'clock for these men in the tower?

He quickly decided that they must be the air traffic controllers for the Marine aircraft that constantly circled the airport. That would explain the odd shift hours. He knew that air traffic controllers often worked short or odd shifts to compensate for the stress of their occupations. He made a mental note to add the tower to his map of the airport as an area that would almost certainly have some sort of guard post.

Returning his gaze to the building that he had judged to be the Marine headquarters, he saw that his memory had indeed been correct. The building was the same four-story structure that he remembered. A broad paved parking lot was between the terminal and the building, which sat squarely in its own yard just east of the boulevard leading to the terminal.

He began to mentally map the details of the approach to the building. By entering the terminal area and taking a left-hand turn onto the access road the driver would be directly south of the headquarters building at a distance of approximately three hundred meters. Another left-hand turn would bring him north across the lot in front of the building. The first obstacle he would encounter would be a thin strand of concertina wire placed across the parking lot.

Between the wire, at intervals of about one hundred meters, were two sandbagged guardhouses. These were the same posts he had watched the sergeant of the guard check promptly on the hour for a whole week.

Beyond the line of wire and the guard posts was an iron fence that surrounded the building on three sides. The fence was set in a low stone base and directly in the center on the south side that he now scanned was a large double gate. The gate was an integral part of the landscaping of the building and had never been intended as more than a device to limit access to the parking spaces directly adjacent to the building. He was pleased to see that it seemed to be in poor repair, with a decided inward cant at its center. He made a mental note to check it carefully when leaving the terminal.

He now turned his attention to the building itself. Although it displayed a heavy black smoke stain on the south side it appeared to be reasonably sound. Its construction was of heavy concrete with broad expanses of glass, the style favored by modern designers. As the waiter filled his now empty cup he lit another cigarette and counted the upright columns that ringed the building at regular intervals. There were exactly ten on the south side with the heaviest smoke damage visible between the second and fourth uprights on the western end. To his disappointment it did not appear possible for a bomber, utilizing surprise and speed to gain the target, to direct his vehicle toward the portion of the building that had obviously received the heaviest fire damage.

The first floor of the building was supported by large concrete yokes that thinned into the slender uprights that ran the height of the building. By rough calculation he reckoned them to be at least five meters high at ground level. Such calculations would become an integral part of his planning with regard to the height of the vehicle that would deliver the bomb and the point of placement on the building.

The plan began to take shape in his mind as he rose to leave the terminal. Glancing at his watch he realized he had been in the terminal over an hour, more than enough time to draw the attention of a conscientious guard. He left a few Lebanese lire on the small round table and walked out the glass door and stood on the broad sidewalk in front of the terminal. Internal Security Force troopers sat on their heavy American-made motorcycles and smoked as he waited for a cab to appear. He noted them with some trepidation. Of all the Lebanese uniform services, only the ISF had retained its former authority and continued to police the streets of the Lebanese capital.

He had been standing in front of the terminal for over five minutes without even seeing a taxi when he was approached by a sergeant from the ISF. He regarded the man casually as he approached, cautioning himself to adopt the demeanor appropriate for the businessman he was supposed to be. The man spoke courteously to him without asking him for identification. He sensed the sergeant wanted something, but was puzzled as to why he didn't just state his business.

Finally the man asked if he was waiting for a friend to arrive or if he needed a taxi. When the Syrian said that he was waiting for a taxi the man smiled and offered his assistance. Without missing a beat the sergeant motioned to another trooper who picked up a radio and spoke into it. From around the corner of the terminal building a cab materialized. The Syrian nodded gratefully and slipped the man a couple of notes. The sergeant ambled off, no doubt to extort a percentage of the fare from the driver, thought the Syrian.

The cab passed the access road heading north as the Syrian took a long look at the gate being manned by the Lebanese soldiers. One glance was enough to assure him that the soldiers at the gate were young conscripts who would not pose a threat to his plan. As the cab drew abreast of the Marine headquarters he noted that the Marines had barracked troops under the eaves of the building as well as others in tents that were pitched on the broad courtyard surrounding the building. Vehicles were parked on all sides of the structure and troops moved in and out of both sides of the building through broad doors.

The doors held particular interest for him. He noted that they were constructed of aluminum frames and were placed side by side directly underneath the center of the building. Although he was unable to see the east side of the structure he had a good view of the west face and it did not appear to have any entrance. He noted that the ground rose slightly as they continued north past the building and the far side of the courtyard wall was actually dug into the side of the hill to a depth of about seven feet in places, with steps located in it at the center to facilitate access to the buildings just to the north of the headquarters.

The driver slowed near the checkpoint and the Syrian saw the entrance to the group of smaller buildings. A row of shade trees lined the small road and at its intersection with the boulevard was a checkpoint manned by Marines and soldiers of the Lebanese Army. A red and yellow sign with Roman and Arabic lettering announced that this was the headquarters of the 24th Marine Amphibious Unit and the 42nd Brigade of the Lebanese Armed Forces. Looking east along the road past the checkpoint he noted that a bomber would have to make a ninety-degree turn approximately one hundred meters past the checkpoint followed by another ninety-degree turn to gain access to these buildings. The trees lining the road would prevent his leaving the road earlier and would also serve to limit the height of the attacking vehicle.

If the bomber were to take the northern branch of this road he would immediately be stopped by a heavy gate manned solely by Marines. Behind it, some fifty meters to the rear, was a low one-story building. In the yard surrounding the building were various vehicles of the Marines and troops who appeared to be repairing them. He surmised that this was a vehicle-maintenance facility and that mechanics were housed in the structure.

The car picked up speed heading north and he noticed that the ground rose steadily to a series of small hills. These hills had obviously been occupied by the Marines, and hidden from the view of anyone approaching from the opposite direction was another small road leading east past the entrance to this compound. Traffic from the village of Al Laylakah moved along the road and past the heavily defended entrance to the Marine position. He dismissed immediately any idea of attacking this location. It was obviously well defended and the bomber would have the added disadvantage of attacking uphill against a force of infantrymen who were well dug in and dispersed.

The remainder of the ride back to the busy center of the city he spent in thought of what he had seen that morning. He was already convinced that the four-story headquarters building was the obvious choice as his primary target. It offered the highest chance of success for a variety of reasons.

It could be fairly easily approached from the south by using the parking lot as a means of access, even though the bomber would lose speed by turning at a right angle into the lot. This would be offset by the distance between the access road and the broad expanse of parking lot just south of the building. The driver could use this virtually unobstructed approach to gain speed, crash the gate, and ram his vehicle into the center of the building.

The smoke damage on the outside of the building lent credibility to his theory that the building had suffered significant damage during the invasion, but his observation of it that morning had convinced him that it was structurally sound. Its modern construction would not have been severely damaged by fire, and its structural members appeared to be intact and undamaged. Although he would have preferred to have the bomber direct his vehicle at the fire damaged portion of the building he had concluded that the loss of speed from doing so would limit the penetration of the vehicle into the atrium of the building and lessen the effect of the explosion on its structural components.

The heavy concrete construction and modern design also worried him. All of his successful attacks to date had been against less substantial buildings. Only the attack upon the American Embassy had been anywhere near the dimensions and scale of this attack. Even though he had achieved virtual ideal placement of the explosive at the embassy, he had failed to bring the whole building down, a fact that had gnawed at him since. He had returned to the building after the bombing and studied it. The center wing had collapsed up to the highest floor, but the two outer wings had remained upright and apparently received only minor damage. He had eventually concluded that his bomb had not had sufficient explosive power to bring down such a large structure without the explosives being deliberately placed near key load-bearing members of the building's frame.

Since he would obviously not be able to gain entrance to the Marine headquarters and study it from the interior and thereby assess its structural weaknesses he was forced to assume that he would need a somewhat larger charge than had been used against the American Embassy. Acquiring the explosives would be a logistical headache, but an effective vehicle for delivering them would be the real problem. He would obviously need a much greater charge than had been used at the embassy, and this would logically require a correspondingly larger vehicle. However, if the vehicle were too large it would be unable to force itself under the heavy concrete eaves of the building and penetrate to a sufficient depth to cause the maximum damage upon detonation. An explosion occurring outside the building, not under the building itself, stood much less chance of effecting enough damage to collapse the major portion of the structure.

There were also other factors to be considered in selecting a vehicle. Height would be a prime consideration. Too low and the vehicle would pass under the eaves, through the doors, and into the atrium where he would be forced to detonate it once it was out of his sight. If the vehicle were too high it would become jammed under the eaves and the greatest portion of the blast would be directed outside of the building with equally poor results.

He was also concerned over the design of the building. Because the building had a large atrium its center was, in reality, hollow, with the offices being wrapped around the inner rectangle. This presented a problem regarding the direction of the blast once the detonation took place. If the bomber were to run his vehicle through the doors and into the atrium before detonating the explosives it was conceivable that the blast would be directed up the concrete interior of the building blowing off the roof while doing little damage to the sturdy sides of the structure.

Such an explosion might have the desired effect in regards to creating casualties, but it would not dramatically destroy the building as he wished to do. He would have to design a bomb vehicle such as he had never before created. As successful as the embassy bombing had been, it had not been without flaws. One immediate problem he faced was the fact that his training had emphasized placing a small charge in close proximity to the intended target, and the target had always been somewhat fragile. He had studied placement and explosive charge requirements necessary to effect the assassination of a person in a crowded room or to bring down a commercial airliner, but never anything dealing with the destruction of an entire four-story building.

His previous missions had required much smaller explosive charges and he had been devastatingly effective due in no small part to careful placement of the bomb. Now, due to the sheer size of the target, he would be forced to confront problems that he never anticipated and for which he had no real training.

The taxi ground to a stop in front of the hotel he had given as his address. He paid the man quickly and entered the lobby as though he were a registered guest. He watched through a window as the taxi entered traffic then exited the hotel and disappeared among the pedestrians on the street.

CHAPTER

18

Downs poured another helmet full of water into the galvanized tub and stood back as Mac, Ferris, and Smith scrubbed their utilities. The three others worked at washing their uniforms as Downs went for another helmet of water. Most of the Marines in the infantry companies had long ago resorted to washing their own clothing instead of sending it to the support ships where it would be laundered by working parties and returned to them by helicopter. Too frequently they received the wrong clothing in return, or none at all. As he walked back toward the washtub he heard the other three discussing Griffin.

"Well," said Ferris. "The first shirt is nothing but hot air anyway. Nobody believes anything he says, so it's no big deal if he gives the sergeant major a bunch of bullshit about what happened up at the hill fight. Who's gonna believe him?"

"I don't know," said Mac. "The staff sergeant and Sergeant Griffin seem plenty worried. And anyway, since when do they need a reason to conduct a witch-hunt for somebody they don't like."

"Yeah, no shit, Jimmy. Remember what they did to Sergeant Hall before we deployed last year?" asked Smith.

Downs joined the group and added, "Yeah, he was late for formation and they busted him. Took a stripe for nothing but bullshit like that. It just goes to show you they give out whatever punishment they want to whoever they want to give it to."

The other three shook their heads and there was silence before Smith added, "Hall was a good NCO, but that didn't count for shit when the system got him in its sights. I heard after they sent him to Third Battalion he got busted again on another bullshit charge."

"So what do you think they'll do to Sergeant Griffin and Sergeant Slocum, Steve? Have you heard anything?"

Downs shook his head. "Not really. But the staff sergeant called me in to his hooch and asked me about what went on up at the hill. Mainly he just wanted to know the straight scoop. He really didn't say much, you know."

"Well, word in the battalion is that the first shirt is pushing for a court-martial of Griffin and Slocum for disobedience of a direct order."

Downs looked at Smith and asked, "Where did you hear that?"

"From a guy in radio platoon. He has to go back to the battalion CP every couple of weeks on a supply run and one of the other radio operators told him. I guess he got it from somebody at the head shed."

"Nothin' would surprise me anymore in this chickenshit outfit. We're turnin' into a bunch of queers. What the fuck do they want from us?" Ferris looked at the other three angrily and Downs sensed that he was seeing a rare moment when the two cousins were troubled about something enough that it penetrated their sense of good humor. "Jesus, have you seen what they have the sergeants write on the patrol reports after we get back from the ville?" The other three exchanged looks and shrugged as Ferris continued, "Well, I have. They write some bullshit about 'Create a Presence' in the block where it asks for purpose of patrol. What the fuck does that mean? I'd like to know the answer to that one. That just doesn't make any sense to me. I thought our mission was to locate the fucking enemy and kill their ass. That's why me and Wayne joined up. Not any of this peace keeping bullshit where nobody knows who the fucking enemy is or even why we're here."

"Yeah, Ferris," said Downs. "That's okay under normal circumstances, but this is hardly normal. We're not at war with anybody here. We're just caught between all the fighting groups and our job is to try and keep them separated."

"What a load of bullshit, Steve! If we're not at war with anybody then why did they bomb our embassy? And who the fuck was the navy shootin' at up in the mountains? Hell, damn near every night now they shell the shit out of those mountains, and as soon as they're done the fucking Lebanese shell us. Maybe that doesn't sound like a war to you, but it pretty much does to me."

"He's right, Steve," said Mac, "almost every night now we get some sort of shelling. Jesus, I haven't slept the night through since we got back from the hill. We always get at least H&I fire from those mountains at night."

Before Downs could answer Ferris continued, "And what the fuck is the big deal about what happened up on the hill anyway? So what if we had a firefight with the fuckin' rag-heads? It isn't like they didn't attack us first. So we handed them their ass and killed a few of them, that's what the fuck they get for attackin' us. Maybe they learned a lesson. If not they know where to find us. They can try it again if they like. I'm sick and tired of the command actin' like we have to walk on eggs in this fucking country."

Ferris looked at Downs as if expecting a reply before continuing, "And I don't see what the big deal is about Sergeant Griffin punchin' out some rag-head in front of the building. Fuck 'em anyway. If they want to ask me about it I'm not sayin' anything. I didn't see any of our glorious leaders out there with Sergeant Griffin when a decision had to be made. I'm not gonna help them second-guess him so they can bust him just because the first shirt has a hard-on for the guy. And anybody who does give them any ammunition to hang him with is fucked up. I don't care what kind of oath they want to make me swear. I believe in God and all, but I'll lie for the guy with my hand on the Bible if it will keep them from being able to bust him for just doing his job." Ferris looked at the others, obviously uncomfortable after having spoken so angrily.

For a few awkward moments the silence continued. Downs concentrated on washing his uniform and not looking into the eyes of the others. As the silence continued he made up his mind to speak. "Hey, look. I've got something to say, but it has to stay just between us. Just in our fireteam." He looked at the others and asked, "Does everybody agree? No rank or anything. Just us." The other three nodded their assent.

"Okay, then. Here it is. I think Jimmy is right. They're gonna try and hang Sergeant Griffin and Slocum. And if we tell them anything they'll use whatever we say against them. You can bet the first sergeant is going to push for some sort of official inquiry, and the deck is going to be stacked against Griffin and Slocum." Downs looked into the faces of the other three, who stared back expectantly. "What I say we do is agree here and now that none of the four of us give them anything to use against them. I mean nothing. If they ask, we just say we didn't see anything and when the Arabs attacked all we did was respond within the limits of the Rules of Engagement. Does anybody have a problem with that?"

The other three exchanged glances, then nodded their assent. "What did the staff sergeant really say to you, Steve? Straight up, no bullshit?' asked Ferris.

Downs hesitated, then answered, "He said the first sergeant is pushing for a court-martial up at battalion and it looks as though he will get it. Once the court-martial starts they'll call all of us as witnesses to testify as to what really happened. The idea is to prove that Griffin provoked the Arabs into a fight and disobeyed orders by not bringing us off the hill when he was supposed to."

Ferris looked at his cousin and said, "I was afraid of something like that. They're out to hang him and Sergeant Slocum." For a minute none of the four spoke, then Ferris asked, "Steve, do you think it will do any good if we don't say anything about what really happened? I mean, it's not like Sergeant Griffin really did anything wrong. They sent us up there to escort the dragon gunners out, so they must have been expecting trouble of some sort or else why send us?"

"Yeah, all he did was arrange the defense. They're the ones who attacked us, we just defended ourselves," said Mac. "How can they hang them for that?"

"Well, according to the staff sergeant there are some things we don't know about. I've got some ideas, but I didn't see any more than any of you did, so it's really just guesswork on my part. The staff sergeant didn't spell it out. I guess he's worried about saying something to us and then having to testify before the court himself."

"So what else is the problem? If you know, Steve, you ought to tell us because we don't want to say something we're not supposed to. If we do have to talk to the officers about all of this it's gonna be better if we all know what's going on."

Downs hesitated, thinking over the conversation he had had with Staff Sergeant Whitney. He was certain that the staff sergeant had been giving him a not too subtle message to have just this talk with his fireteam. He had even tried to think of a suitable way to raise the topic before this conversation had started. "Well, according to Staff Sergeant

Whitney, they think that Griffin and Slocum faked the story about the vehicle being down and us not being able to leave for that reason. I guess that's enough right there to get them both for disobedience of a direct and lawful order.''

"They also know that some Arab came up to the gate and that Griffin beat the hell out of him.'' Downs was unable to suppress a smile at the thought of it, and the other three chuckled and made comments at the thought of Griffin using his fists on some Arab with the audacity to give him an ultimatum.

"So what's the crime in that?'' asked Smith. "What are they gonna do, bust a sergeant for fighting? I kind of thought that was our job.''

The other three laughed as Downs continued, "Yeah, I know what you mean, but there's a problem. Apparently the story has gotten back to the CO that Slocum and Griffin deliberately provoked the Arab into making an attack. The word is that the guy Griffin punched out was a local militia leader and that Griffin knew that when he did it. He and Slocum had it all planned, if you can believe what the staff sergeant says.''

"Wait a minute, Steve. How could Griffin have had it all planned? He didn't even know we were going to the hill before we got back to battalion after the embassy bombing. There's no way he could have planned anything. The shit just happened and Griffin took care of it. What's their beef with that?''

"I guess there's been enough talk around the battalion that the officers have heard differently. The story they have is that we were offered safe conduct off the hill by the Arabs and that Griffin and Slocum cooked up the downed vehicle in order to stay on the hill and provoke a fight with the Arabs. At least that's the way the staff sergeant explained it to me, and I'm sure he got it from the first shirt.''

Ferris shook his head in disgust and spoke, "The long and short of it is that the first shirt is out to get a piece of ass from Griffin and Slocum and make an example of them in front of the company and the battalion. He wants to make sure that the troops and the officers know what a hard charger he is so he can be sure of a good fitness report.''

"Did you get all this from Staff Sergeant Whitney?'' asked Mac.

"Most of it,'' answered Downs. "Some of it I've heard around the company or the battalion. You've got to remember that we weren't the only ones on the hill that day. All those dragon gunners were up there and they've all talked to their friends at battalion. They're billeted at the Battalion Landing Team building, so whatever they said to their friends back there is going to get back to the officers quick enough.''

"What a bunch of idiots,'' said Smith. "Why didn't they just keep their mouths shut? The damn BLT building is crawling with officers. Nothin' would've been said then.''

"Aw, that's bullshit,'' said Ferris. "We all talked about it with everybody. Sooner or later they were going to hear about it somehow. There's just no way to keep something like this a secret very long. Besides, why the hell should it be a secret? Nobody did anything wrong. So Griffin beat up some Arab. So what? Griffin has beat the shit out of half the company and you don't see any of us cryin' about it and asking for him to be court-martialed. That's life in the big city. I still say the whole problem is the first sergeant is trying to kiss up to the officers. We oughta just do that motherfucker and be done with it. Right, Wayne?''

"Hey, you got my vote, Jimmy,'' answered his cousin. Smith laughed conspiratorially and added, "Shit, we owe him one anyway. That asshole took away our beer. That's enough for me, never mind all this crap with Sergeant Griffin.''

Downs looked warily at the two cousins and said, "Well, not that I'm totally against the idea, but don't get any wild ideas. I hear the jerk already sleeps with a .45 automatic in his sleeping bag.''

"As big an asshole as he is, he ought to,'' said Mac.

"Won't make any difference if he's got a howitzer in his rack when I get ready to come for him. Ain't that right, Jimmy?'' said Smith.

Without missing a beat his cousin replied, "Aw, shut up, even a good-size girl scout could kick your ass, you homo.''

Without preemption Smith tackled his cousin and the two began rolling in the mud around the base of the wash bucket as Mac and Downs stepped out of the way, carefully moving the tub full of clean uniforms. Amid curses and punches Smith took his revenge on his cousin, all the while calling him "first shirt'' and flailing away at any exposed portion of his body.

Downs looked at Mac, who laughed and asked, "Think they'd really do it?''

"The first shirt you mean?'' said Downs.

"Yeah.''

Downs regarded the two cousins as they rolled on the muddy ground, locked in an apparent death struggle, cursing and punching each other. "Not a doubt in my mind,'' he said.

CHAPTER

19

Downs walked toward the company area with his armful of wet uniforms. A noise registered in his subconscious and he reflexively threw himself to the ground seconds before the first round impacted in the hard-baked clay. Automatically his hands went to his head to hold his helmet in place. He pressed his body to the ground and stole a glance at the bunker some fifty meters ahead of him. Two more mortar rounds impacted and Downs saw Marines running and crawling for shelter.

He began to crawl forward, his knees and elbows scraping the ground, his face pressed into the dirt. He heard his own breathing coming hard out of his chest. He knew he was panicking, but was not able to stop himself. Downs stole another glance at the bunker ahead, then cursed as he realized he had crawled slightly off course. Someone ran past him, laughing as another series of explosions detonated nearby. Downs smelled the acrid smoke as it drifted over him.

He crawled faster, afraid to lift himself off the ground and run. He lunged forward, bruising his knees, his mouth sucking in gritty sand and blades of dry grass. He focused again on the bunker. He heard Ferris and Smith laugh from the shelter of the bunker just ahead and cursed them for their good fortune. Another round impacted nearby and Downs felt a hot stinging pain along his right wrist. He tucked himself into a fetal position, expecting more shrapnel. Downs covered his wrist with his other hand, the warm blood soaking his uniform sleeve and seeping through his fingers. He stood and ran the last few yards to the bunker, then flung himself in the entryway. Ferris and Smith howled with laughter as he landed heavily and rolled down the sandbagged steps leading into the bunker.

"Hey, Corporal Downs. Glad you could make it! Did you see the first shirt, Jimmy? That fucker ain't moved that fast in ten years!" The two convulsed in laughter, oblivious to everything but their delight at seeing the first sergeant run for cover. "Did you see it, Steve?" asked Ferris. "The first shirt was shaggin' ass for the nearest bunker. He was almost there, when, blam! Ole Wayne hits him with a flying tackle that would've stopped a freight train. Shit, he never even saw it coming, man!" The two again howled with delight, as Downs sat in the entryway gently trying to unbutton his uniform sleeve.

"Wayne caught him perfect, man. Laid his fat ass out cold. Shit, just like when we played the Fulton Falcons. Remember that, Wayne? You blasted that big-ass fullback they had that made All-Georgia our senior year."

"Hey, Steve. You okay, man? What happened?" asked Ferris.

"I'm all right," said Downs. "I think I got some shrapnel in my arm. It doesn't even hurt though."

"Well, let's look at it." Smith walked over and peered at Downs's arm in the dim light of the bunker. He struggled to unbutton Downs's cuff, then said, "You're bleeding some, but I can't see much. I'm gonna cut your sleeve. Okay?"

"Yeah, go ahead. My cammy top is ruined anyway," said Downs.

Ferris gave a low whistle as the material came away and exposed the arm. "You're lucky, Steve. It looks like it sort of just ran up your arm longways without really going in anyplace. Could've been a lot worse. Let's rinse if off with some water, get all the dirt and shit out of it. What do you think, Wayne?

"Sounds good to me," said Smith amicably. "Let's get a flashlight so we can get a good look at it."

Downs looked at his arm, bloody and pale where the sleeve was cut away. A red trough ran the length of his arm, from the back of his hand almost to the elbow. The water stung as Smith poured it over the wound.

"Jesus! That's gonna leave one ugly scar. Impress the shit out of the poon-tang with that, man! No shit, you're a regular war hero now,'' said Smith.

"Yeah, but where the fuck is he gonna put his tattoo now?'' asked Ferris. "Oh his fucking left arm? That'll make it twice as hard to show off. Too bad it didn't get your left arm. Then you could put your tattoo on the right and have the scar on your left. That'd be boss man! Wear a short sleeve shirt and the babes would just have to notice that shit!''

"Jimmy, I swear, sometimes you're so fuckin' stupid it hurts me to admit we're kin. Man, this is perfect. He'll just get his tattoo up high, on his bicep. Steve, it'll be too cool. Just where the scar stops you can get an eagle, globe, and anchor with USMC blocked out underneath it in green letters. Maybe some color in the eagle. That'd be all right. You don't want to overdo it. Just let them work together and speak for themselves. You'll be gettin' laid anytime you want to. It'll be great.''

Downs smiled as Smith wrapped his forearm in gauze. What a pair, he thought. In the middle of a mortar attack they tackle the first sergeant, then all they can think about as they dress my arm is where am I going to put my tattoo now? Downs wondered silently at the conversational possibilities an amputated leg or other major limb might inspire.

Looking at the newly wrapped arm Downs watched curiously as the gauze slowly turned red. His head swam as Smith completed his work, then turned to his cousin, "What do you think, Jimmy? Is this a number one job or what?'' he asked. "Maybe when I get out I'll be a nurse or something.''

His cousin laughed and said, "Maybe you should go see how the first shirt is doing, Wayne. I bet he could use a little TLC right now.'' The cousins broke into loud guffaws as three more mortar rounds burst nearby, the dirt thrown up by the explosions showering the roof of the bunker like a light rain.

As the explosions rolled away Griffin rushed into the bunker. "Corporal Downs, I need a head count. Are all your people here?'' Griffin crouched in the narrow entry squinting into the dark interior, his eyes not able to adjust to the dimness of the bunker.

Downs snapped alert and automatically answered, "We're all here, and we're all okay.''

"No, we ain't, Corporal Downs,'' said Ferris. "Me and Wayne ain't seen Mac. Maybe he made it to one of the other bunkers, but he didn't come in here. We were all together just when the shelling started though, Sergeant Griffin."

Griffin glanced at Downs, who answered, "I thought he ran past me after those first few rounds," said Downs. "I thought he was here all this time."

"Where was the last place you saw him, Corporal Downs?" asked Griffin.

"I'm not sure now. I thought that was him that ran past me. The last place I saw him for sure was down by the water bull. We were down there drawing our water ration and washing our clothes."

"How about you, Ferris?"

"Same place. When we heard those rounds come in all of us made for the bunkers. I just assumed he went to one of the other ones. Wouldn't be the first time. Some of the other bunkers are closer anyway. Me and Wayne just like to spend our time in our own house, so we came here," answered Ferris, winking at his cousin.

"Yeah, you're probably right. I still have two holes to check. What happened to your arm, Corporal Downs?"

"I got caught out there between salvos. A piece of shrapnel sliced up my forearm. I'm okay."

"It really ain't bad, Sergeant Griffin," added Smith, "but it looks pretty fucked up."

"Okay. Have the Doc look at it ASAP. I'm going to check those other bunkers. If I don't find MacCallum I'll be back. All of you sit tight." Griffin rose and sprinted to the next bunker, timing his movement so that he arrived just before the explosion of the following salvo.

Downs fought to control his emotions. Why would Mac go to another bunker? This bunker was just as close as any other, and his natural instinct would be to run for his own bunker. Downs stood and walked to the entry. He waited for the other two mortar rounds to impact, remembering the warning of the instructor at infantry school that mortar sections always work in threes, and sometimes space shot intervals so as to deceive their enemy.

"Tell Sergeant Griffin I went to check the water bull," said Downs. He flung himself out of the bunker and raced for the sandbagged water bull. Halfway there he heard the two late rounds whistling toward the Marine lines. He dropped to the ground and prayed as the rounds impacted somewhere in front of him and to the rear of the Marine lines.

The thought occurred to him that Griffin would have his ass if he got wounded now after being told to stay put. He raised himself to his knees and saw the circle of sandbags protecting the water bull. A set of boots protruded from the open end of the low circular wall of sandbags.

Downs grinned as he realized that Mac had simply gone to the nearest available cover. All the others had run through a mortar barrage to gain the safety of the bunkers. Mac had gone thirty feet to relative safety behind the wall of sandbags built to protect the metal water bull from just such attacks.

"Hey, Mac. What the fuck are you doing? Griffin is looking for you, man," said Downs. "We have to get back to our hooch for a head count." Downs noticed the throbbing in his arm for the first time as he used it to help him scuttle toward Mac. A warning sensation shot through Downs at Mac's lack of an answer. He rounded the corner of the sand-bagged wall on all fours and slapped Mac's boot. "Hey, asshole. This ain't funny. I risked my ass to come out here and see what you're doing. Now quit fucking around and let's go."

He noticed the odd angle of Mac's legs and Downs realized that his friend was wounded, and fairly seriously. "Corpsman up!" he yelled automatically. Downs heard Ferris and Smith echo his scream, then others down the line. "Jesus, Mac. Are you okay, man? What the fuck happened?" He felt Mac's neck and detected a good pulse, then rolled him onto his side. Mac made a liquid coughing noise as Downs eased him onto his back and began to look for the wound.

Mac coughed again and blinked as if awakening from a deep sleep, then said, "Steve, I'm hurt."

"It's okay, Mac. You're not hurt bad. I don't even see any blood. You're okay, man. Just try to relax."

"I don't think so, Steve. It doesn't hurt, but I don't think so."

"Okay, okay. Don't move," said Downs. "I'll do everything." Downs ran his hands over his friend's legs, looking for blood, or an entry wound. Finding nothing he loosened the Velcro strap running the length of Mac's flak jacket and ran his hand inside, trying to detect blood. He felt nothing. He opened Mac's camouflage blouse and put his hands underneath Mac's T-shirt. "Jesus, Mac. I can't fucking find it. Where does it hurt, man?"

Mac tried to answer, but managed only another liquid cough. Mac locked eyes with his friend and Downs saw panic flash across his face.

As Mac grabbed his friend's arm Downs screamed "Corpsman!" at the top of his lungs.

"It's okay, Mac. You're okay. Just don't panic, all right?"

Mac shook his head "no" and struggled to suppress a sob as tears began to roll down his face. "I don't want to die, Steve. I don't hate anybody. God, Steve, I'm scared."

"You're okay, man." Downs located the wound on Mac's side, high, just under the armpit. He began to work at exposing the wound, trying not to move Mac anymore than necessary.

"Downs!"

"By the water bull, Sergeant Griffin!" he answered.

Downs felt Mac tighten his grip on his forearm. "Don't let them see me crying, Steve. I wanna do this like a man. Don't let Sergeant Griffin see me cry. Okay?"

"Okay," said Downs, leaning over his friend and wet his hands from the faucet above Mac's head. Downs quickly smeared the tears on Mac's face with his hands. Three more rounds whistled overhead and exploded as Griffin and a radioman slid around the corner of the sandbagged wall.

"Where's the Doc?" asked Downs. "He needs the fucking Doc!" Downs furiously screamed "Corpsman up!" as Griffin leaned over Mac.

"Okay, MacCallum, help is on the way. Just hang on. The Doc is on his way and a medevac bird is coming for some second platoon casualties. We'll probably just throw you on it." Mac nodded, struggling to repress his tears. Griffin grabbed Downs by his shoulder harness and spun him around, opening his first aid kit. Jerking out the plastic wrapped pressure bandage he handed it to Downs and looked into Downs's eyes, ignoring Mac. "Treat him with this, Corporal Downs. You know how to do it. Make sure you get a tight seal. Do it now," said Griffin, roughly shoving the bandage into Downs's chest. Griffin turned to the radioman and asked, "Are we up with that bird?"

"Yeah, Sergeant Griffin. He's Tango One," said the man, handing Griffin the handset.

"Tango One, Tango One, this is Charlie Bravo Four. Do you copy?"

"Roger, Charlie Bravo Four. Give me a sit rep. Over," came the voice of the pilot.

"Tango One, I have a man down who needs immediate, I repeat, immediate, medevac. Can you assist. Over."

"That's affirmative, Bravo Four. Are you taking hostile fire?"

Griffin hesitated as two more mortar rounds impacted and scanned the sky for signs of the helicopter. He glanced at Downs and said, "Get it on there tight, Downs. Hold it on if you have to, but it's got to be tight."

Downs increased his pressure on the bandage while Griffin keyed the handset and said, "Negative, Tango One. We are not receiving hostile fire and request immediate medevac. I will mark my position with green smoke. Do you copy? Over."

"Roger, Charlie Bravo," came the voice of the pilot, "I copy green smoke marks your pos. Throw it when you hear my engines, Charlie Bravo. I'm the only bird in the air. Do you copy? Over."

"Roger," answered Griffin as he reached for the smoke canister in his flak jacket pocket. Looking at Downs he said, "As soon as we hear the bird I'll throw the smoke. He's got to be close. Hang in there, MacCallum. Everything is okay."

The corpsman ran up and shoved Downs out of the way. Kneeling over Mac he examined the bandage without comment. Looking at Downs he said, "Hold it tight to his side and don't let off of the pressure even if you hurt him, got that?" Downs nodded as the corpsman removed a syringe of morphine from his bag and held it upright between two dirty fingers. He flicked it firmly with a fingernail as a drop of the oily liquid dripped from the needle.

"Okay, Mac," said the corpsman in a bantering tone, "the doctor is here and this little jewel is about to make it all better. Just lay chilly man, 'cause the doctor will make everything cool." He bent over Mac's arm, deftly exposing a vein and injecting the drug in one movement. "How does that feel, Mac?"

Mac attempted a smile, but managed only a sidelong grin at Downs. "C'mon Mac. I can hear the bird. You're on the way, man," said the corpsman. As Griffin prepared to throw the smoke Mac began to convulse. His coughing overcame him and a bloody froth covered his lips. His legs quivered uncontrollably.

"Shit!" cursed the corpsman. "He ain't gonna make it by himself. Downs, you and Sergeant Griffin hold him down for me!" As the corpsman attempted to resuscitate him, Downs felt his friend's grip tighten, then loosen on his arm. The corpsman eventually straightened up, sat on his heels, and looked at Griffin while his fingers went to Mac's neck searching for a pulse. "I'm sorry, Sergeant Griffin. I'm really sorry.

He didn't have a chance. Even if the bird had gotten here I don't think he had a chance. It must've pierced both his lungs, or maybe his heart. I'm really sorry, Corporal Downs. There just isn't a lot I could do for him." The corpsman idly threw his gear into his green canvas bag and said to no one in particular, "God, I hate this fucking place."

"Charlie Bravo Four, Charlie Bravo Four, this is Tango One. Throw your smoke, son. I need to see that smoke now. Over."

Griffin keyed the handset. "Tango One, this is Charlie Bravo Four. My casualty is no longer a priority. I repeat, my casualty is no longer a priority medevac. Do you copy? Over."

As Downs looked into his friend's face he heard the tinny voice of the pilot, "Roger, Charlie Bravo. I copy that you do not, repeat, do not, require assistance. Can you confirm?"

"Affirmative," said Griffin, "Charlie Bravo Four. Out."

CHAPTER

20

G riffin looked out the window through the fog of plastic the previous occupants of the room had used to replace the glass. He angrily ripped the tape aside and threw the plastic back, giving himself a clear view of the battalion positions around the perimeter of the airport. The cool morning air felt good on his face, and he had just taken his first hot shower in two weeks, but he felt no peace. He and Slocum had been ordered back to the battalion headquarters and told to report to the H&S company commander at 0900 this morning. In the parlance of the Marine Corps, Griffin knew that meant he and Slocum had been accused by the first sergeant. From experience he knew that it mattered little if he was actually guilty, or if he had good reasons for taking actions not sanctioned by the command. What mattered was that the first sergeant wanted to see him punished and that the officers of the battalion would side with the first shirt whether they believed him and Slocum or not.

The issue of guilt or innocence would be lost in the greater issue of maintaining discipline in the battalion. The first sergeant would by now have talked privately with the various officers responsible for their fates, and he would have given them the impression that Griffin and Slocum were a pair of misfits who had no respect for authority and should have never been promoted to the rank of sergeant.

Slocum entered the room and Griffin said, "Morning, Bobby." Slocum toweled his short hair and walked to the window and stood by Griffin who continued to gaze out over the airport.

"Where did you get off to so early this morning? You must have been up a couple of hours before daylight," said Slocum.

"Yeah, I couldn't sleep so I went up on the roof and talked to the guys on the OP there."

"No shit, huh? What are you so worried about? It's not like they're going to shave our heads and send us to Parris Island," said Slocum. "For Christ's sake, all we did was kick the shit out of a few rag-heads. Fuck 'em if they can't take a joke."

Griffin shook his head and said, "I don't think it's going to be that easy, Bobby. The first shirt is out for our ass, and to be honest, I think he's got us. The bottom line is we disobeyed orders. And that means they have all they need to hammer us."

"Aw, fuck him," said Slocum casually. "What's he gonna look like standing in front of the Zeros whining about how these two big bad sergeants went out and kicked ass. That's our job. What are they gonna convict us of, winning a firefight?"

"How about disobedience of a direct and lawful order. That ought to be good for a stripe or two," said Griffin morosely.

"Well, I know you're a lifer and all, but they can have my fucking stripes. I'm sick of all their bullshit anyway. I EAS almost the day we're due back in the States and my young ass is headed back home to North Carolina just as fast as I can get there. If they want to bust me back down to private, its okay by me. It just means to me that I don't have to be responsible for anything or anybody anymore. And that's fine with me. I never much cared for it anyway."

"Great," said Griffin, "ambition in reverse."

Slocum laughed. "Don't worry so much. You're takin' all this way too serious. Just relax. Fuck 'em anyway."

"Yeah. Right, Bobby. I'll just stroll into my court-martial and pick my teeth while they crucify me and ruin my career. It'll be great. I can hardly wait. Hope you enjoy the show."

"Well, if we don't tell them anything they won't know anything. And I personally don't have a lot to say to any of those assholes. They can't make us say anything that is going to incriminate ourselves, and I just ain't going to say anything at all. Since none of those assholes were anywhere near the actual fighting, and I'm including our much-loved first sergeant, how the hell do they know what really went on?"

"All they have to do," countered Griffin, "is put us in separate rooms and tell us to give them our account of events. If we try to lie they'll see the differences in our stories and they'll know we're lying."

"Are you stupid or what? Why would you answer any of their questions? If they want to know what goes on at the front then they ought to be up there when it happens. I'm not going to answer any of their questions. Hell, if they ask me I'm going to tell them I can't even remember if I saw you there."

Griffin burst out laughing. "Well, maybe so, but you're going to look awful stupid."

Slocum laughed and replied, "Probably so. I'll come visit you in the brig, professor. Since lookin' smart is so important to you."

Griffin let out a long breath and said, "I just don't think it's going to be that easy. Even if they don't make us talk to them they can still go to every Marine who was there and ask him what went on. Sooner or later they'll piece together what really happened, and then they'll have us."

"And who do you think is going to tell them anything? Nobody in my squad would talk to them. And everybody in your squad is afraid to talk to them for fear you'll have a flashback to your life in New York as a hoodlum, go berserk, and kill them and their families. I just don't think we have a lot to worry about as long as we stay cool." Slocum slapped Griffin on the back and said, "You just follow my lead in there and ol' Bobby will save your sorry ass one last time."

Griffin smiled at his friend and said, "I hope so. I really do. I've got a lot riding on this."

"Like what, Dave? You're one of the best infantry sergeants in the regiment. What are they going to gain by hammering you? Jesus, they're always beggin' for us to stay in for another hitch and make a career out of the Marine Corps. You're on your second cruise already. If they bust you now they have to figure that you'll just get pissed and get out at the first opportunity. Whose purpose does that serve? They would be the losers in the long run, not you. Even the Zeros ought to be able to see that."

"Well, I don't think they give a damn if they lose one more sergeant, but that wasn't what I meant."

"So what did you mean?"

"Just the whole thing, you know? I made my way up through the ranks to sergeant. My old man is proud of me for the first time in his life. He goes around the docks telling everybody how his son is gonna be a career Marine. It means something to him. It means something to me, Bobby."

Griffin paused for a moment, then continued, "I'm not like most of you guys. I always knew I wanted to be a Marine. I can't ever remember wanting to be anything else. And for as fucked up as the system is, I know I want to stay in and keep being a Marine. If I get busted again at this point in my career I'm finished. I'll never make sergeant again in time to regain the lost ground and get on the selection list for staff sergeant. They'll rift me out in another few years and I'll go home a short-haired civilian like any other shit bird who couldn't handle it."

The two stood in silence for a few minutes before Slocum began to dress in a clean camouflage uniform. From his pack Griffin removed a tin of black boot polish and began to buff his boots. As the two finished dressing they rolled their bedding and strapped it to their packs, then stacked the packs in the corner of the small room.

"You ready?" asked Griffin.

"Yep," answered Slocum. "Might as well go and get it over with."

Griffin opened the door and stepped onto the tiled corridor leading around the open atrium of the building, noting that the interior of the building was without electricity and therefore remained dim even though the sun shone brightly outside.

"Wonder what was in this place before we took over?" asked Slocum. "It's pretty big. Must've been some kind of office building." As the two proceeded down the corridor to the staircase at the east end of the building they saw Captain Ward, the Alpha company commander, climbing the stairs and coming toward them. "Hey," said Slocum slapping Griffin on the chest and nodding in the direction of the captain, "it's the Rock Man. What do you suppose he's doing here?"

"We're about to find out," answered Griffin under his breath as he nodded and said, "Good morning, sir," automatically at the captain's approach.

"Good morning, Sergeant Griffin. Sergeant Slocum. How are they treating you here at battalion headquarters?"

"Fine, sir," they replied in unison, neither showing any emotion. Griffin and Slocum instinctively locked their expressions into the emotionless mask every Marine was taught to assume when addressing an officer.

"I've spoken with Staff Sergeant Whitney about the hearing this morning, Sergeant Griffin. He seems to think that you're not going to get a fair shake." The captain paused and stared at Griffin, obviously looking for a reaction before going further. Griffin returned his gaze, but said nothing.

"Well, I don't agree with him," continued Ward. "Captain Simmons, the H&S company commander, will be heading up the inquiry. He's a friend of mine and what's more he used to be your company commander. He's knows what sort of Marines the two of you are, and I have faith in him to be fair."

Griffin and Slocum both answered with a perfunctory "Yes, sir" and the captain paused awkwardly. "It's a fair system. You have to put your trust in it and let it run its course. The officers who will sit on the board are infantrymen just like yourselves. They know how a situation can change and require some independent decision making. I urge you both to cooperate with the inquiry. If you tell them what happened then I think any formal action can be avoided. If you try to avoid answering their questions," said Ward as he looked at Slocum, "or otherwise avoid giving them the facts, it will cast you in a very unfavorable light. Both of you should bear that in mind, and be aware of the gravity of the situation."

"So what you're saying, sir," drawled Slocum, "is if we give them the facts just the way things happened, then everything will be okay?"

The captain looked warily at Slocum before answering, "Yes, Sergeant Slocum. That's exactly what I'm saying."

Slocum scratched the back of his neck and said, "Let me get this straight one more time, sir. What they're doing today is some sort of inquiry. Just a fact-finding mission. Right, sir?"

"That's correct," answered Ward.

"And if they like what we tell them, then nothing is going to be done. I mean, no court-martial or NJP?"

Sensing the trap the captain gave another reluctant "That's correct" before Slocum continued as Griffin stared at the captain's face.

"Okay, sir. But what if we tell them something they don't like? Can they court-martial us and use what we've said today against us? I mean, they'll already know the facts and then they won't need to ask us any more questions. And if they decide to court-martial us it's pretty fair to assume that something we said made them take that decision. Right, sir?"

The young captain drew a deep breath. It was unheard of for a sergeant to address a captain the way Slocum had, the sarcasm in his voice subtle but obvious. "Everything you say today will weigh in the board's decision whether or not to court-martial one or both of you. I don't think there is any reason for either of you not to say anything but the truth. From what I understand you both did your duty. In another situation you would probably be up for decorations. But this is a different matter."

Griffin sensed the captain's unease, but felt his anger rising. He had known the captain since the day he arrived in the battalion. Griffin had always thought him to be a fair and competent officer. The Rock Man, as he had come to be known by his troops, had earned Griffin's respect. Griffin knew him to be compassionate, a rare quality in junior officers trying their best to make it in an organization that demanded their individual best and culled those who failed to deliver it with merciless precision.

Griffin looked at him again, sensing Ward's discomfort. He's not much older than I am, thought Griffin. But no matter what he's saying he knows in his heart that something here isn't right. He's not like the others. He's not just some college boy who decided to join the Marines because he couldn't find a job. He belongs here, and it is bothering him to see the first shirt come after us like this.

Griffin swallowed hard and asked, "Can they use what we say against us or not, sir? That's the bottom line for Sergeant Slocum and me, and you're probably the only one in the battalion who can tell us."

The captain again looked Griffin in the eye. "Anything you say today, anything at all, Sergeant Griffin, counts. And the officers on the board are obligated to give their decision based on the facts presented to them." The captain paused again. "The bottom line is that if you answer a question today, and you incriminate yourself or Sergeant Slocum, the officers on the board are obliged to hold you accountable. For them to do less would be dereliction of duty."

Griffin and Slocum exchanged glances but said nothing. The three stood in awkward silence before Griffin finally asked, "Will that be all, sir?"

The captain hesitated for a moment, obviously wanting to say more, but unsure of himself. "That's all, Sergeant Griffin. You and Sergeant Slocum think about what I've said."

Griffin and Slocum answered "Yes, sir" in unison and stood silently while the Captain turned and walked down the dim corridor toward the battalion operations center. Slocum slapped Griffin on the chest lightly and said, "What the fuck got into him? He seemed almost human for a minute there."

"He's not so bad, Bobby. He's damn sure better than the rest of them. At least he had the balls to come and say something to us. All the others are more than willing to look the other way while the witch-hunt takes place."

Slocum shook his head slowly in an obvious air of disgust. "Are you fuckin' crazy, Dave? Were we listening to the same conversation or what? That fuckin' idiot just told us to trust the system. He has to be kidding! What system is he talkin' about?"

Slocum looked at his friend and continued, "Was he referring to the system that taught us how to use all this fancy gear and shit to kill people? Or the system that says if you break the rules you don't have any rights unless you request a general court-martial, and if you do the penalties are guaranteed to be stiffer when you're found guilty. Or was he referring to the system that says you can place your fate in the hands of the investigating officer who not only decides whether or not you're guilty or innocent, but what your punishment is going to be. After all, man, NJP stands for nonjudicial punishment. What a crock of shit!"

Slocum stopped walking and Griffin noted the anger in his voice. "If they want my stripes they can have them, but they are going to have to work for it. I'm not about to just hand them over to a bunch of college-boy officers who played soldier at ROTC meetings while I humped my shit all over the world. For the better part of four years while they were drinking beer at frat parties and screwing somebody's sister in the backseat of daddy's car I been here learning how to be a Marine."

Slocum paused and looked around the area, then spoke again, "Fuck 'em! I was in the grunts learning how to do my job from the bottom up, the way you're supposed to learn it, while they pissed away daddy's tuition money at college. You and me both spent years proving we could be NCOs. Nobody just handed us a squad or a fireteam the day we arrived at LeJeune and said, 'Okay, now that you've spent six weeks learning how to be a Marine officer you can be in charge of the platoon.' After all, you do have a college degree in business administration, and everybody knows how valuable that is on the battlefield.

"Jesus, Dave, these fucking guys start off at the top, in charge of a whole platoon, and half of them don't even know how to adjust their web gear. They're so fucking arrogant you can barely talk to them, and when you do try and unfuck them, nine times out of ten they give you a ration of shit for being out of line.

"What a collection of prima donnas. I just don't have any use for any of them anymore. I'll be glad to get out and go back home to the mountains where I belong." Slocum paused to catch his breath and looked around the empty corridor before going on. "And anyway, where the hell were they the night you came out and got us up on that hill? I don't remember seein' any of them around. For a bunch of guys who pride themselves on being leaders they sure as hell are hard to find when it comes time to do the petty, dirty shit."

Slocum's voice softened as he looked at his friend and said, "Look, man, nobody is more proud of being a Marine than I am. And I know we have some good officers. But the system is all fucked up when they punish us for doing shit that is tactically sound. And you know as well as I do that the whole point of this exercise is to find us guilty, and no matter what we say or do they'll punish us however they see fit."

"Dave, even if the Rock Man wants to help us he won't be able to. It would ruin him and his career would be finished if he bucked the system. They'd just shit can him at the first opportunity. You know it's true, we've both seen it done before."

"I think he's got some integrity, Bobby. Why else would he even have been here this morning?"

"You're right, Dave. But think about what he said to us. All that 'trust the system' garbage is for shit when you remember what he said about the officers being derelict if they didn't convene a court-martial if they know we disobeyed orders."

Griffin sighed and said, "It's a foregone conclusion that we disobeyed orders. Everybody knows we did. Hell, all they have to do is talk to the lance corporal from the motor pool and they'll know we didn't have any vehicle problems."

Slocum laughed at Griffin's comment and shook his head. "Man, sometimes you're pretty naive for a big city boy, Dave. Kind of gives you a certain charm though, I have to admit."

Griffin looked at Slocum puzzled, then asked, "Why? What the fuck are you talkin' about now?"

Slocum laughed again and explained, "Well, when we got the order to pull out from the hill and then ol' Ahmud showed up, I knew we

were in trouble. They told me over the radio that a squad was comin'
out with extra vehicles and that we were to withdraw that night and
not leave any gear behind and not to destroy the building or rig it for
booby traps or anything."

Griffin shot a glance at Slocum and said, "Somebody in battalion
ops must've known you were the one in charge out there from the
sounds of those orders."

Slocum grinned and answered, "Well, I do have a certain creative
flair. I get it from my mother's side of the family."

"Yeah," said Griffin sarcastically. "What are they, moonshiners?"

Slocum shrugged and continued, "Anyway, when I knew we were
leavin' for sure that night I started gettin' the squad ready to go, just
like a good boy. Nobody said anything about who was comin' out to
relieve us. Just that it would be one squad with some extra trucks. About
mid afternoon, after Ahmud had come up the hill the first time but
before you got there, one of my corporals tells me the natives are gettin'
restless. From the bottom of the hill you can see into the village and
his fireteam has seen them sandbaggin' some windows and draggin' in
some heavy machine guns. Anyway, things aren't startin' to look so
good for that neat orderly withdrawal we Marines are so famous for."

"So?" said Griffin.

"So I decided to take matters into my own hands. I figured it would
be a fight with them whether we stayed or left, and if we stayed we
had all the advantages. So I went over to one of the six-bys and modified
a distributor cap. Damn thing just wouldn't start when it came time to
turn the engines over that afternoon."

"Yeah, great, Bobby. I suppose you're going to tell me that nobody
saw you do that? Small as that compound is someone must've seen you
fuckin' around under the hood."

"Nope. They were all in formation on the other side of the building.
Just like I told 'em to be. After all, I had to have an all hands muster to
give them the word about us pullin' out. So nobody is the wiser, and
the only guys not in formation are members of my squad who aren't
going to say anything to any court of inquiry."

"So what was all that bullshit you gave me about the Motor-T guy
knowin' the vehicle wasn't really down?"

"Did I say that?" asked Slocum with feigned innocence.

"God, you can be a real asshole," said Griffin.

"Yeah, but anyway as far as anyone else is concerned that breakdown was legitimate. So we don't have to worry about some fucker from Motor-T saying we ordered him to rig a vehicle. We're covered as long as we stick to the story that the vehicle broke down and we couldn't leave it because we had orders to bring out all the equipment."

"Well the Motor-T guy could still smell a rat. After all, he must have seen the distributor cap after you fucked with it. How hard can it be to figure out someone deliberately screwed it up?"

Slocum shrugged noncommittally. "Who cares? They can't prove anything. That's the whole point." The pair continued to walk toward the company commander's office on the far side of the building. Outside of the office they saw the H&S company clerks standing in a tight knot. "You know what really bothers me about this whole mess, Dave?"

"What?" asked Griffin.

"That they think we are going to rat on each other so they can play God and fuck with us. These guys actually think that if they give me some bullshit story about how it's my duty to tell the truth then I'm going to rat on you and make it easy for them to hang us."

"Fuck you," said Griffin attempting to be lighthearted, "everybody knows it's all your fault. And that's just what I'm going to tell every Zero from now until the time they bust me back down to private."

"Well, it is my fault mostly, I guess." Slocum paused and Griffin stood beside him, the two of them well away from the clerks who stood near the office door. "Look, Dave. I'm sorry, man. I'm sorry I got you mixed up in all of this. I never thought it would come to this," said Slocum.

"Don't worry about it, Bobby. We both did what we had to do. Shit happens."

"Well, maybe so, but I'm going to tell them it's my fault. If they can burn one of us they'll be happy. All you have to do is keep your mouth shut and everything will be fine."

Griffin looked at his friend and shook his head. "Look, shit for brains, that won't work. Not this time. This is personal. The first shirt is out to prove a point. If it's not this then he'll just dream up somethin' else. And if we both beat him on this he'll still dream up somethin' else to fry us for, so don't go tryin' to be heroic or some shit. Just do like you said and try not to say anything. If it's like you said and nobody but us knows about the vehicle then we've at least got a chance."

"Yeah. Thanks, Dave," said Slocum. "You know, I'm proud of being a Marine, too. I don't think I ever meant to stay past my four years, but this is the proudest thing I've ever done in my life. And now this. I sort of wanted to go home a sergeant. My mom and dad sure would've been proud of me."

Griffin looked at his friend and traced a circle on the dusty floor with his boot. "Yeah, I know what you mean." He paused, remembering Parris Island and the pride he had felt when he had worn the Marine Corps emblem on his uniform for the first time. "Well, we'll still be Marines, Bobby. Nobody can take that away from us. Let's just make sure we don't let them take our self respect along with our stripes."

The door to the company office swung open and the first sergeant stepped out as Griffin nodded to indicate the waiting room and said, "C'mon, it's time to go and face the music."

CHAPTER

21

Downs sat stiffly facing the seven officers who comprised the board of inquiry. The night before he had been ordered to report to the battalion headquarters with his fireteam. He had walked through the darkness with Smith and Ferris who now sat in the rear of the room waiting their turn to be questioned. None of the three had spoken during the long walk to the battalion headquarters, and Downs had risen early and eaten alone at the battalion mess.

Captain Simmons, the H&S company commander, reviewed his notes as Downs concentrated on maintaining his composure under the stare of the first sergeant and the sergeant major, both of whom stood to one side of the seated officers with their arms folded across their chests. Downs remembered his drill instructor's advice from boot camp, "Right hand, right knee, left hand, left knee when facing any kind of board." He automatically shifted his hands to their respective knees and made a mental note to keep them there.

Before entering the room he had been told by the company clerks that he would give testimony first as he was the senior member of the fireteam. Smith and Ferris would then be questioned by the board after he was finished. He was also told not to discuss his testimony with any other member of his squad, fireteam, or any of the dragon gunners who had been at the hill that night.

Downs knew that other members of the platoon who had been questioned regarding the fight that night were not allowed to return to their units. They were told to remain at the battalion command post until further notice. As his was the last fireteam to testify he was not sure what would happen after he, Smith, and Ferris had given their testimony. Downs was aware that neither Griffin nor Slocum had given their statements as of yet. The two sergeants sat impassively against the wall in the back of the room. Neither spoke to the other or to Downs as he had entered the room.

Captain Simmons finished writing and he lifted his head, speaking to Downs he said, "Good morning, Corporal Downs."

Before he could continue Downs automatically responded, "Good morning, sir," realizing as he spoke that the captain had not expected him to reply, but had planned on giving him some sort of preparatory comments. Simmons nodded and continued, "Corporal Downs, as you are now probably aware there have been some questions raised regarding the action at the American ambassador's mansion on the night of 11 October 1983. The purpose of this board is not to find fault or to establish guilt, but to clarify the actions taken by those concerned. Specifically, I am speaking about the decisions and actions of your squad leader, Sergeant David Griffin, and the squad leader of the dragon squad, Sergeant Robert Slocum. It is the belief of this board that these two Marines were responsible for the defense of the post and the safety of the Marines there." Simmons paused and looked at the other members of the board who sat studying Downs. Downs stared at the H&S company commander impassively, then realized he was expected to respond.

"I wasn't aware of the purpose of the board, sir. I was ordered to report here this morning. To you, sir. I was not given an explanation. And neither was my fireteam." Downs nodded toward the rear of the room where Smith and Ferris sat.

The captain let out an impatient sigh, then continued, "Be that as it may, Corporal Downs, the board is convened to determine the facts of the matter. Your duty is to answer the questions put to you in a clear, concise, and truthful manner. Anything less would be a serious infringement of the Uniform Code of Military of Justice. Do you understand me?"

"Yes, sir," said Downs, careful not to betray any emotion in his voice.

"Good," said the captain, "then maybe we can continue. I believe you already know the other members of the board and their assignments in the battalion." As the captain introduced the other officers Downs said "Sir" and nodded to each of the young men. None appeared sympathetic to Griffin or Slocum. Downs surmised that they were making the same effort he was, to remove any trace of emotion or opinion from their expressions or manner. As the junior officer of the board was introduced he raised his pencil, indicating that he had a question for Downs before Captain Simmons continued.

"Do you have a question, Lieutenant Walters?" asked the captain.

"Yes, sir. I do," answered the officer. The captain waved a hand at Downs, indicating the lieutenant should ask his question. "Corporal Downs, I notice only three Marines from your fireteam are present. Is there a reason why the fourth man is not present?"

Downs looked at the captain who averted his eyes then glared down the table at the lieutenant. Before the Captain could speak Downs answered the question, "Yes, sir. There is a reason the fourth member of my fireteam is not present." Downs stared at the officer, his face a mask of indifference.

"Well, Corporal Downs," said the lieutenant impatiently. "Maybe you could enlighten the board." The sergeant major and the first sergeant shifted uncomfortably against the wall. The first sergeant went so far as to clear his throat and scowl at the lieutenant.

"Lance Corporal MacCallum was killed in action four days ago, sir. It was during a mortar attack on the Alpha company lines. We've not been given a replacement as of yet, sir," said Downs.

For a moment the silence hung in the air before one of the other officers shuffled some of his papers and the lieutenant said, "I see." After an awkward moment the lieutenant added, "That will be all, Corporal."

Realizing that the lieutenant had no authority to dismiss him Downs looked at the captain. The captain motioned for him to remain seated. To his rear Downs heard either Smith or Ferris clear his throat loudly and scrape his chair along the dusty concrete floor.

Downs stole a glance at the lieutenant. He was staring intently at some paperwork, not lifting his head from the table. Downs felt elated. In some small measure he knew he had won the opening round. He fought to control his emotions and concentrate on not saying anything that might incriminate Slocum or Griffin. The lieutenant will come after me now, thought Downs. He has to. He was trying to impress his superiors by catching me not reporting with my full fireteam and instead he stepped on his dick in front of God and everybody. Now he has to make up for lost ground or really look like an ass. Downs made a mental note to think carefully before answering any question put to him by the board, particularly the lieutenant.

Captain Simmons cleared his throat and said, "I believe we're ready to proceed now, Corporal Downs. I want to caution you again regarding answers that are anything less than the full and complete truth." Downs nodded in answer to the captain's questioning look. "Very well. Why don't you begin by telling us what your duties were that afternoon, Corporal Downs?"

"My duties, sir?" asked Downs. "What specifically does the captain want to know?" Downs heard the first sergeant shift as the captain looked directly at him.

"It's a plain question, Corporal. You do remember what your duties are, don't you?"

"Yes, sir," answered Downs. "My duties as a Marine require that I be aware of, and comply with the standing general orders of the Marine Corps. Would the captain like for me to recite my general orders, sir?"

Simmons exchanged an exasperated look with one of the other officers and Downs noted Captain Roberts, the Bravo company commander, attempting to stifle a chuckle. In an irritated voice the captain glared at Downs and said, "Corporal Downs, what were your specific orders on the night in question? I am not interested in a recital of the general orders by you or anybody else. I want to know what your orders were that night, in regard to your position on that hill and as a NCO in first squad. Have I made myself clear, Corporal?"

"Yes, sir," answered Downs without a trace of emotion. He hesitated for a long moment, obviously searching for a response.

"Well, Corporal?" asked the captain.

"My orders that night, sir," said Downs, "were to locate, close with, and destroy the enemy by fire and maneuver, or to repel the enemy assault by fire and close combat."

As Downs finished his recital of the mission of a Marine rifle squad the captain slammed his tablet onto the table and cursed. The cheap table bounced under the impact of the captain's fist and the pens, tablets, and coffee cups of the other officers leapt from the table before slamming back down in disarray. The captain closed and opened his fist several times before once again glaring directly at Downs. "Corporal Downs, perhaps you don't realize the gravity of this situation. I am not sure why you and the other Marines who have given testimony before this board seem unable to appreciate the seriousness of the situation. But I am warning you, mister. You had better answer the questions of this board in a courteous and professional manner, or I'll personally see that charges are brought against you and your rank reduced to private. Do you understand me, Corporal?''

Downs remained bolt upright in his chair and concentrated on answering "Yes, sir," with a steady voice. He returned the captain's stare without looking away and ignored the other officers. Simmons hesitated before looking at the sergeant major and first sergeant. "I am adjourning this board for ten minutes during which time I advise you, First Sergeant, to counsel Corporal Downs and the members of his fireteam on military etiquette and the severity of the UCMJ when dealing with Marines who deliberately mislead or lie to officers. Am I understood?''

The first sergeant had straightened at the mention of his name and now answered with a curt "Yes, sir" and nod of his head. The sergeant major stood by impassively, giving no indication of his opinion of the proceedings. Others in the room left after the five officers filed out. Downs, Smith, and Ferris remained in their seats. As soon as the last of the Marines had filed out of the room the first sergeant crossed to the door and slammed it shut. The sergeant major remained silent, leaning against the wall.

"Get off your fucking asses and lock your bodies!" screamed the first sergeant as Downs and the two others instantly leapt to a position of attention. The first sergeant approached to within an inch of Downs's face and began his tirade. "Who the fuck do you think you are, mister? You think you're something special? You think you can sit in front of these officers and give them your smart-ass answers and nothing is going to happen to you?" The first sergeant leaned closer to Downs and he was able to detect the odor of his after-shave and feel the heat radiating from his face. Downs concentrated on looking through the first sergeant, deliberately not focusing his eyes on the man, although their faces were almost touching.

"Well?" screamed the first sergeant. "Do you? I want an answer girls!"

"No, sir!" chorused the three.

"You fuckin' better believe you can't. Maybe you think your pals Griffin and Slocum need your help? Is that what this is, some sort of conspiracy? Well let me give you ladies a little information about Griffin and Slocum. Those two shit birds are going to the brig. And when they get there, they'll be privates. Am I understood?"

"Yes, First Sergeant!"

"That's better. Now when those officers come back in here you three are going to answer their questions in a manner I think is appropriate. No more of these half-baked answers." The first sergeant circled around behind Downs and glared at Ferris and Smith. Downs could feel his breath on the back of his neck and he fought to remain impassive to the tirade. "And don't think for a minute that this little chat we're having is going to be the end of it. I won't forget the way you shit birds embarrassed me in front of the captain and the other officers. I hope you enjoyed yourself this morning, Corporal Downs. It is going to be the last time you'll enjoy anything for a long time. I'm going to make you a personal project, boy. I'm going to instill in you the proper respect for authority that you're supposed to learn in boot camp. I'm going to be on you like stink on shit, boy."

The first sergeant again placed his face within an inch of Downs's. "And you know what, Corporal Downs?" he asked, his voice dripping with sarcasm. "I'll bet it won't be long before you're not a corporal anymore. Look at the three of you. You're a disgrace! None of you has your boots properly polished or your utilities pressed in the prescribed manner. All three of you need haircuts, and I'll bet your personal areas are as fucked up as the rest of you."

"Our weapons are clean First Sergeant and . . ." began Downs.

At Downs's comment the first sergeant leaned in closer and shoved him back toward Smith and Ferris in a fit of rage. "What did you say, boy? Did I ask you for one of your smart answers? You keep your fucking mouth shut until I give you permission to speak you little motherfucker. How dare you speak to me in that manner. You fucking piece of shit! I was in the Marine Corps before you were born and I'll be in it when they muster you out as a private, if you even get mustered out and not thrown out."

The first sergeant drew closer to Downs and said in a low menacing tone, "I own you, boy. From this day forward I'm going to be on you until you can't take it anymore. You're going to quit in front of the whole battalion and I'm going to send you home to momma and daddy a humiliated short-haired civilian with a funny haircut. Who the fuck do you think you are, boy? Who is going to help you when I come after you? Who, boy? I'll tell you, Corporal Downs," spat the first sergeant. "No fucking body. You're all alone in this. When I get through with you the rest of the company won't get within a hundred yards of you for fear I'll come after them for associating with a shit bird like you. Am I understood?"

"I understand," said Downs, deliberately failing to address the first sergeant by his rank in the proper military manner.

"Oh, that's good, Corporal Downs. You play your little games with me, boy," said the first sergeant in a harsh whisper. "You just remember that I own your little shavetail ass. Do you understand me, you little douche bag?"

"That will be all, First Sergeant! At ease Marines!" Downs and the others went to a position of parade rest, their hands folded behind their backs and their feet spread. The first sergeant spun to see Captain Simmons standing beside the sergeant major, "You're dismissed, First Sergeant. And I don't want you back in this room while these Marines are giving testimony."

The first sergeant looked to the sergeant major as if to appeal the decision of the captain but the sergeant major stood impassively with his arms folded across his chest. As the first sergeant left the room the captain looked at the sergeant major and said, "Sergeant Major, I'll speak to these Marines now. I'll notify you when we are ready to resume." The sergeant major straightened as the captain continued, "That will be all, Sergeant Major."

The sergeant major said, "Aye, aye, sir" and left the room as the captain crossed to the tables that served as a desk and sat down. He rubbed his eyes, folded his soft cover with the Marine Corps emblem on the front, and let out a long sigh. He looked up as if nothing had happened and said, "Sit down, Corporal Downs. Lance Corporal Smith, Lance Corporal Ferris," he continued, waving a hand toward the empty chairs. None of the three moved to take a seat and the captain stared at them from behind the table.

"Sit down, Marines. This isn't on the official record. I would like to talk to you for a few minutes before the board reconvenes." The three Marines sat, with Downs facing the captain as before. "Look, men. Sometimes the pressure of what we are trying to do here gets to all of us. Unfortunately, the first sergeant has used you three as a vent for his frustration. I can assure you that none of you will be the subject of a vendetta by the first sergeant or anyone else as a result of what has happened this morning."

The captain paused as the three sat stoically in their chairs. He knew from previous experience that none of them would give him anything other than perfunctory answers. "If you would like I can arrange to have all three of you transferred to other companies in the battalion for the duration of the deployment. That will ensure that the first sergeant is not in a position to harass any of you." The captain looked at Downs and asked, "Would that alleviate your worries, Corporal Downs?"

Downs hesitated, then answered, "I can't speak for Lance Corporal Smith or Ferris, sir, but I would just as soon stay in Alpha Company."

The captain nodded, and said, "I understand. What about the two of you?"

Smith and Ferris glanced at each other before Smith said, "We'll stay where we're at, sir."

"Very well. We still have the matter of the board before us. I want you Marines to know that I understand your desire to protect Sergeant Griffin and Sergeant Slocum. All the board is trying to do is establish the facts of what happened. If some sort of punitive action is taken, and I'm not saying that is going to be necessary, then the matter is out of all of our hands anyway. Both Sergeant Griffin and Sergeant Slocum would be the first to tell you that they were responsible for what went on up there as the senior Marines present."

The captain hesitated, looking at the three Marines and wondering what was in their minds. Junior enlisted men had always been something of an enigma to him. They had their own society, their own subculture within the Corps. And their own rigidly enforced code of honor. He had known from the start that Griffin and Slocum had done nothing wrong tactically. They had performed in the best traditions of an organization that prided itself on its aggressiveness and willingness to attack in the face of overwhelming odds. He had sensed from the moment he had been ordered to convene the board that it was going to be a witch-hunt organized at the whim of the Alpha Company first sergeant. When it became known around the battalion that he was searching for officers to sit on the board his peers began to avoid him. He had had a difficult time finding four other officers willing to sit on the board and had finally resorted to calling in personal favors and even ordering Lieutenant Walters to be a member of the board.

He silently thought that he could almost have predicted Downs's responses word for word. *He's sitting there thinking that he can't trust me, and he's right. If he's got any sense at all he'll just stick to the line that he doesn't know or he can't remember. In his place,* thought Simmons, *that's what I'd do.* Still, there is going to be hell to pay from the colonel if none of the facts are brought forth that might substantiate the first sergeant's accusations. Already, he knew, the sergeant major would speak to the colonel about his dismissal of the first sergeant from the proceedings. At the very least he could expect a mild-ass chewing from the Old Man. At worst he would get a poor evaluation on his annual fitness report that would effectively end his career before it had gotten started.

He realized that he had to say something to these Marines that would make them trust him and answer his questions. Nothing came to him, his heart just wasn't in it. He finally looked at Downs and said, "We'll reconvene in a couple of minutes. Let me remind all three of you that you are bound by your duty as Marines to tell the truth as you remember it. If nothing improper was done that night, then withholding information could be potentially more damaging than telling the full story. Am I making myself clear?"

The three answered "Yes, sir" simultaneously and he nodded. "Good," he said. "One other thing, and I'm sure you've all been told before. For Marines it is possible to delegate authority, but not responsibility. Sergeant Griffin and Sergeant Slocum were ultimately responsible for what occurred that night. Nothing can change that, and none of you can be punished for something they did, or something they failed to do. Understood?"

"Yes, sir," they answered.

"Fine. Lance Corporal Smith, tell the others to step inside and we'll begin."

The others filed into the small room as Downs sat expectantly in front of the officers. He was puzzled by the captain's talk, but decided that his original plan was working and that the captain had probably determined that threats from the first sergeant were not going to be effective in eliciting answers. Downs resolved to stay with his plan and not answer any of the questions put to him except in the broadest of terms. He mentally forced himself not to turn and catch Griffin's eye.

He wondered how Griffin was standing up to it. Downs knew that neither he nor Slocum had been questioned yet, although virtually everybody else at the hill that night had been. Downs reasoned that the officers had a fair idea of what had taken place, although their detailed knowledge was sketchy. The hardest part would be to answer questions in a respectful manner and at the same time deny them any real information. He had noticed Captain Roberts straining to control his laughter earlier, and combined with the talk of Captain Simmons, Downs felt that maybe their hearts weren't in it. His only chance would be if they didn't press too hard for the details. If they knew Griffin had ordered him to allow the Arabs to pass unmolested up the hill, and only to fire on them as they retreated, then Griffin would undoubtedly be subjected to a court-martial.

The captain cleared his throat and asked, "Are you ready to proceed now, Corporal?"

"Yes, sir," answered Downs.

"Very good. As you may already know it has been my policy to allow Marines before this board to relate their version of events on the night in question in their own words. I have refrained from questioning them directly when possible to avoid the appearance of a trial, which this in not. Since you seem somewhat reluctant to relate your version of events the other members of the board and myself have decided to ask you questions regarding events that night. Am I making myself clear to you, Corporal Downs?"

"Yes, sir."

"Very well. Captain Larson will ask you a few questions if you are ready."

"I'm ready, sir," replied Downs evenly.

"Good morning, Corporal Downs," said Captain Larson.

"Good morning, sir."

"Corporal, for the purposes of this board, I'm particularly interested in the position of your fireteam during the fighting. Can you tell me where you and your team were?"

"Yes, sir. My team and I were positioned in the rear of the structure on the second floor."

"And in what direction was your fire oriented?"

Downs hesitated, wondering where the captain was going with this question. Realizing that they must already know the answer to this type of question Downs answered, "Northwest, sir, if my memory serves."

"Very well. And what type of targets did you engage that night?"

"Enemy targets, sir," said Downs.

The officers shifted in their seats, but Captain Larson held up a hand, "I think it is fair to assume you and your fireteam wouldn't knowingly engage friendly targets. Wouldn't you agree, Corporal?"

"If the Captain says so, sir."

"Don't try my patience, Corporal. And that's the only warning you will get from me, Marine. Am I understood?"

"Yes, sir."

"Now, what type of targets did you and your fireteam engage that night?"

"Militia, sir. Irregular, well-armed, hostile."

"And what weapons did you and your team fire upon them with, Corporal Downs?"

"Sir?" asked Downs.

"Which weapons at your disposal did you engage this militia with, Corporal? The question is plain enough."

"All of the weapons at our disposal, sir."

"Which were?"

"The M-16, the M-60 machine gun, and the M203 grenade launcher, sir."

"And why did you engage this militia?"

"We took fire, sir. According to the seventh rule of engagement, we responded to hostile fire, directing our fire at the source of the enemy fire. No friendly snipers were present so we could not employ them, sir."

Larson hesitated, making notes on a legal pad in front of him. "Just a couple more questions, Corporal. Did you receive automatic weapons fire?"

"Yes, sir."

"And how did you respond to that fire?" continued Larson.

"I returned fire with the M-60, sir," answered Downs.

"Did you initiate automatic weapons fire on the militia force?" asked Larson.

"No, sir," Downs lied.

"Did any of the Marines under your command initiate such fire?" pressed Larson.

"No, sir."

"Were any of the Marines in your fireteam wounded that night? In this action?"

"None, sir," answered Downs.

"So none of your Marines were wounded, yet you found it necessary to bring to bear the maximum amount of firepower available to you in this engagement?" asked Larson.

"That's correct, sir," said Downs, swallowing hard.

"Why, Corporal Downs? Are you aware of the fifth rule of engagement that requires that we utilize only the minimum amount of force necessary to accomplish any mission?" asked Larson.

"I'm aware of it, sir. I felt that the amount of force employed was the minimum. We were under heavy fire from a well-armed enemy force that was attacking our position. I was concerned for the safety of my men and the security of our position. We returned fire according to the Rules of Engagement. None of my Marines were wounded. I consider that a successful completion of the mission, sir."

Larson nodded, "I'm inclined to agree with you, Corporal. However, I would like to clear up one thing. At what point did you take the enemy under fire?"

"After they had fired upon our position, sir," answered Downs.

"I understand that, Corporal Downs. What I'm driving at is whether they had already engaged the main body at the front of the house or if you engaged them prior to the assault upon the gate?" asked the captain.

"I believe it was after the main body was engaged, sir. But I couldn't be sure, I did not have line of sight to the front of the house," said Downs.

"Had you heard firing previous to firing your own weapons?" continued Larson.

"Yes, sir," said Downs.

"Was that firing outgoing or incoming?" asked Larson.

"Both, sir," replied Downs.

"Very well, Corporal. Now I would like to ask the two lance corporals in your fireteam if they agree with the story as you have related it to me and the board," said Larson.

Both Smith and Ferris stood and said "Yes, sir" in unison.

"Is there anything you Marines would like to add?" he asked.

"No, sir," answered the two cousins.

"Very well." Larson added a few notes to his paper and looked to Captain Simmons who sat in the middle of the long table. "I've got nothing further right now," he said.

"Then we'll proceed to Captain Clark."

Clark nodded and looked at Downs. "Corporal Downs, how are you?"

"Fine, sir," answered Downs.

"Corporal Downs, I've got just a few questions for you and the two lance corporals. I think I've got the gist of the matter. I just want to touch on a few points that aren't quite clear to me," said Clark.

"Yes, sir," said Downs respectfully.

"If I understand you, your fireteam was separated from the rest of your squad and placed at the rear of the building, correct?" asked Clark.

"That's correct, sir," answered Downs.

"And who ordered you to position your team there?"

"Sergeant Griffin did, sir."

"And did Sergeant Griffin give you any reason why he was placing your team there?" asked Clark.

"No, sir. He did not."

"So he just separated your fireteam from the rest of the squad and told you no reason as to why he was doing so. Am I correct?"

"The squad was going into its night defensive perimeter, sir. I did not consider it unusual that Sergeant Griffin would assign a fireteam to the squad's rear in order to provide observation and defense in that direction. If anything I expected him to assign my team to such a position."

"And why is that, Corporal?" asked Clark.

Downs realized that he had said too much. The captain had seen an opening and pursued it. He braced himself and answered, "Because I am the junior of the corporals in my squad, sir, and we were in a strong defensive position. Sergeant Griffin uses the more experienced corporals for the more difficult jobs," answered Downs.

"I see," said the captain. Downs noted that the lieutenant, sitting to the side of Captain Clark, was furiously taking notes. "Corporal Downs, am I correct that you stated you had an M-60 machine gun with your team that night," continued Clark.

"That's correct, sir."

"And is that SOP in your platoon?"

"No, sir," said Downs, "we had the extra gun because the battalion operations officer had detailed them to our squad prior to our going out to relieve the dragon gunners on the hill. Ordinarily we would not have had that M-60, sir," replied Downs.

"Very well. At what point did you order that your grenadier fire his M203 at the militia?" Before Downs could answer Clark said, "Belay that, Corporal Downs. Which one of your lance corporals is the grenadier?"

"Lance Corporal Smith, sir," said Downs.

Clark looked to Smith and asked, "Lance Corporal Smith, who ordered you to fire your grenade launcher that night?"

Smith rose to his feet slowly and looked at his cousin who sat beside him, then back to Captain Clark. He realized that his firing the grenade launcher without the order to fire being given by an officer or an NCO was a violation of the Rules of Engagement. "Nobody did, sir. I took the initiative myself," said Smith flatly.

"You realize that by firing that weapon you were in violation of the Rules of Engagement, and you therefore disobeyed a direct and lawful order, Lance Corporal," said Clark.

"Maybe so, sir, but the enemy was making use of dead space to fire on me and my team and I thought it was better to risk breaking one of the rules than have one of them get off a good shot with an RPG. Besides, as the grenadier I have the only indirect fire weapon in the fireteam and it is my responsibility to engage hostile targets making use of cover or dead space," said Smith, virtually quoting from the small unit manual for Marines.

The captain nodded, "That's correct, Lance Corporal. Corporal Downs, had you and your team taken fire from RPGs that night?"

"No, sir. But we had observed the militia with numerous men carrying spare rounds for RPGs on their backpacks so we knew they had the capability."

"Did you order Lance Corporal Smith to use his grenade launcher?" questioned Clark.

"I may have, sir. If I didn't I should have, sir, given the circumstances," said Downs.

"Very well, Corporal. I don't have any further questions at this time," said Clark.

The captain looked down the table to Simmons who then said, "Captain Roberts?"

Roberts regarded Downs for a moment and began, "Corporal Downs, I've been listening to your story and the story of the other Marines who have presented testimony before this board and I'm beginning to draw the conclusion that what took place that night was simply an attack upon your position by local militia hostile to the United States. What I don't understand is why they picked that particular time to attack, and if there was any deliberate provocation on our part that might have prompted their attack. Was there, Corporal Downs?" asked Roberts.

"None that I know of, sir," said Downs.

Roberts exchanged a glance with Simmons, who then asked, "Corporal Downs, are you aware that Sergeant Griffin struck a local militia leader in front of your position shortly before the attack took place?"

"No, sir," Downs lied.

"Well, Corporal, you must be the only Marine there that day who didn't witness it," said Simmons. "Can you offer any explanation as to why you didn't see it?"

"No, sir. I cannot."

"Was it because your team was posted at the rear of the building and you weren't physically in position to see the fight?" asked Roberts.

Downs thought for a moment, then answered, "Maybe, sir. But also the squad had been up all night during the movement to the hill and after we got there we slept in the basement for a few hours. If it took place then I wouldn't have been aware of it."

Roberts nodded his head and said, "I see. Tell me, Corporal Downs, do you think the action at the hill that night was avoidable?"

"Avoidable, sir?"

"Yes. Do you think that Sergeant Griffin or Sergeant Slocum did something that provoked the militia and induced them to attack?" asked Roberts.

"I don't think so, sir. It is my understanding that the position had been attacked previous to our arrival and the gatehouse by the entrance had evidence of previous attacks. I'm not sure that those weren't probing attacks and the end result was the militia decided to attack the night we got there."

"In your opinion, Corporal, did Sergeant Griffin or Sergeant Slocum do anything that night or that afternoon that would cause you to question their actions or motivations?"

"No, sir," said Downs, realizing that Roberts was trying to let him establish a defense for Griffin and Slocum. "They both took every precaution and measure to ensure the safety of their squads, equipment, and the integrity of the perimeter. The fact that we didn't take any friendly casualties that night while we inflicted quite a few on the attacking force speaks for itself, sir. In my opinion they are both good infantry NCOs, sir.''

"How long have you been in first platoon, Corporal Downs?'' asked Roberts.

"About three years, sir,'' said Downs.

"And do you think Sergeant Griffin is a competent squad leader?'' he continued.

"Yes, sir. I do.''

"Do you think there is anything he might have done differently that night that would have avoided an attack by the militia?''

"No, sir, not that I'm aware of,'' answered Downs flatly.

"Do you, in your opinion, believe that Sergeant Griffin and Sergeant Slocum acted within and according to the Rules of Engagement, as they are set forth?''

"Yes, sir.''

"Very well, Corporal Downs. I don't have any more questions for you at this time. I want to thank you for your candor. I believe that Lieutenant Walters has some questions for you and your fireteam now,'' said Roberts.

The lieutenant cleared his throat and shuffled his paper work. "Corporal Downs, I find a few inconsistencies in your sequence of events,'' said Walters.

"Yes, sir,'' said Downs warily.

"Why exactly did you begin firing on the militia?'' he began.

"We took fire from them, sir. Under the seventh rule of engagement we returned fire,'' answered Downs.

"And who authorized you to return fire?'' asked the lieutenant.

"I authorized my team to fire, sir. We were receiving hostile fire. As an NCO, with no officers in the perimeter, I am authorized to order my Marines to return fire.''

"And how many rounds did you fire at them that night, Corporal Downs?''

"Sir?'' asked Downs.

"I want to know how many rounds your team expended that night, Corporal.''

"Exactly, sir?'' asked Downs.

The lieutenant gave an exasperated sigh and said, "You can give me an approximate figure, Corporal.''

Downs turned to look at Smith who shrugged, then answered the lieutenant, "Sir, I really don't know."

"Well then, take a guess, Corporal."

Downs thought for a minute and said, "I'm not sure, sir. Maybe five hundred to a thousand rounds from the M-60. I couldn't even guess how many rounds the others fired. I just don't know, sir."

"Very well," said the lieutenant, obviously irritated. "Lance Corporal Smith, how many rounds did you fire from your grenade launcher? An approximate figure will do."

Smith stood and hesitated for a moment. "Maybe a half dozen, sir. I couldn't be sure either, sir. It was kind of hard to tell with the firing goin' on and all."

"I find it hard to believe that you only fired six rounds that night, Lance Corporal. Maybe you would like to reconsider and give me another number," responded Walters.

"No, sir," said Smith.

"No, sir, what?" asked the lieutenant.

"No, sir, I don't want to reconsider it. You asked me about how many rounds I fired that night and I told you about six. I don't need to guess again, sir. My first guess is as good as any. With all due respect, sir, it's a guess. I just wasn't real concerned about countin' rounds at the time and it never occurred to me afterward that somebody might be interested later, sir."

"You Marines seem to have awfully convenient lapses of memory," said Walters angrily. "Corporal Downs, maybe you remember how many casualties you inflicted?" he asked.

"It would be hard to say, sir. It was dark, and the hill is partially wooded, which prevented us from firing illumination. I don't really know, sir. A lot of them went down under fire but they were probably just taking cover in dead space and crawled out of my field of fire. I would guess five or six KIA anyway, sir," said Downs.

"And where was Sergeant Griffin during all of this, Corporal?" asked Walters.

"I don't know, sir. He's the squad leader. I would assume he was with the majority of the squad or at whatever position he thought most critical to the defense of our position. That's his job as the squad leader, sir."

"Thank you, Corporal, but I already know what Sergeant Griffin's job was that night," said Walters. "Frankly, I am beginning to find your smug attitude more than just an annoyance. You are on the verge of drawing a charge sheet from me regarding your answers, Marine. So I would advise you to carefully weigh all of your responses. Am I understood?"

"Yes, sir," said Downs, fuming. He struggled to compose himself and not let his demeanor betray him to the officers. He had known that the lieutenant would be the most difficult officer of the five, and now that was being borne out.

"Corporal Downs, when you took this militia under fire, in which direction were they traveling?" asked Walters.

Downs thought for a moment then answered, "Northwest roughly, sir."

"No, Corporal," said the lieutenant in a patronizing tone, "were they moving up the hill to attack, or were they moving down the hill?"

"They were moving up the hill, sir. And later they were moving down the hill. We fired on them both times and while they were moving in both directions," Downs lied smoothly.

"Do you two agree with that last statement?" The lieutenant directed this to Ferris and Smith.

"Yes, sir," they both answered.

"What I don't seem to understand here, Corporal, is why the militia leader would take your position under fire if he was retreating down the hill after being repulsed at the gate. Maybe you could help me and the board to better understand that point?" said the lieutenant.

"Is the lieutenant asking me why I think the militia commander fired on my position when he was retreating, sir?" asked Downs.

"That's precisely what I am asking, Corporal," said Walters.

"I wouldn't be qualified to answer, sir. With all due respect, I don't have any way of knowing what he was thinking, sir."

"Maybe he didn't fire on you at all, Corporal. Maybe you were the one who initiated the firing on the orders of Sergeant Griffin," said Walters.

"No, sir," said Downs, the anger apparent in his voice.

"Maybe he fired on us for the same reason he came up the hill that night, sir," said Smith from the rear of the room. "Or maybe he fired on us to cover his retreat off the hill. They know the area, they knew where to find us to attack us. It seems to me it follows that they would have scouted our position and known they would be visible at that particular spot on the road and that we could take them under fire there.''

"Lance Corporal, when I want you to answer a question I'll address one to you," snapped the lieutenant. "Until that time you are not to interrupt."

"I'd like to hear the lance corporal's answer, Lieutenant," said Captain Simmons. "That is, if you don't object to the interruption."

"No, sir," said the lieutenant.

Simmons looked to Smith and nodded for him to continue. "Well, sir, it's just this. They came up that hill for only one reason, and that was to attack us. They tried the gate a couple of times and found they couldn't get through, so they backed down the hill. They fired on us whenever they had the chance with whatever they had available. I just don't understand what we were supposed to do. It sounds to me as if you wanted us to take casualties before we started firing back, and that just doesn't make sense to me, sir. We acted like a squad of Marines is supposed to act when they are under fire." Smith looked around at the faces that had turned toward him as he spoke. "I guess that's about all I have to say, sir."

"That's fine, Lance Corporal. Take your seat," said Simmons. The captain looked at the others members of the board, then asked, "Lieutenant Walters, do you have anything further?"

"No, sir."

"Very well. Corporal Downs," said Simmons, "I have a few more questions for you specifically. They pertain to the movement down the hill the morning following the firefight. It is my understanding from previous testimony that you were the point man on that day. Is that correct?"

"Yes, sir. It is."

"It is also my understanding that on the movement down the hill you encountered a wounded enemy soldier, correct?"

"That's correct, sir."

"Fine. Before I ask anything further I have to admit I'm a little puzzled why a corporal would be walking point. Could you explain that?" asked Simmons.

Downs hesitated, then answered, "Sergeant Griffin assigns all the positions in the squad during movements, sir. I'm usually the point on patrols. I couldn't really say why Sergeant Griffin has me on point, sir."

The officers on the board looked at each other and Downs noted that most of them made some sort of note of his answer. He knew that his position as the point man must have been of some interest to them and braced himself for more questions about the militiaman they had given the morphine.

"So what you are stating to the board is that you routinely walk the point during your squad's patrols?" continued Simmons.

"Yes, sir. Almost always," replied Downs.

Simmons nodded his head and continued, "Fine. Corporal Downs, let's get back to the wounded militiamen you found that morning. How many were still alive when you got to them?"

"Only one that I saw, sir."

"And where did you find this individual?"

"Top of the hill, sir. Just outside the gate."

"Very well. What was his condition when you found him, Corporal?"

"He was severely wounded, sir. He had open wounds of the abdomen and stomach and he kept losing consciousness."

"Did this man offer any resistance to you or any of your Marines?" asked Simmons.

"No, sir."

"Do you think he was capable of it?"

"Probably not, sir. But we removed his sidearm and checked him for grenades or booby traps just the same."

"Is that all you did with him, Corporal?" asked Simmons.

"We also administered first aid to him, sir." Downs looked on as four heads bent toward their notepads and the officers again scribbled their notations.

"What exactly did you do, Corporal?" pursued Simmons.

"What does the Captain want to know, sir? What type of first aid was administered?"

"Precisely. Be as specific as you can, Corporal," said Simmons.

"I called up Sergeant Griffin when I determined that the man was alive. Sergeant Griffin then ordered me forward to establish security and I believe he called up the Doc, sir."

"Is that all that happened as far as you are aware?" asked Simmons.

"That's what I remember, sir. The man was wounded too badly to move. I may have discussed the possibility of calling a medevac bird with Sergeant Griffin, but I'm not sure."

"So what you're saying, in effect, Corporal Downs, is that you found this man because you were the point man and that you then called Sergeant Griffin to the scene?" asked Simmons.

"Yes, sir."

"Were you present when the man was administered medication, or dosage of medication was being discussed?" asked Simmons as he leaned over the table.

"I was in the area, sir. On the point," said Downs.

"And do you recall what was administered to the individual?" asked Simmons.

"I wouldn't be aware of that, sir."

"Answer the question, Corporal. And that's an order," said Lieutenant Walters.

Downs regarded the lieutenant, then stated, "I was on point, sir. My duty was to scout the area to the immediate front of the squad and determine the best route for movement of the squad and the possibility of contact with a hostile force. I am not qualified to state whether or not the individual in question received any medication or in what amounts, sir." Downs again looked to Captain Simmons, "That's the truth, sir. I remember the Doc coming up, but it was obvious the guy was too far gone to help."

Simmons nodded his head, then said, "Fine, Corporal. Did you encounter any more wounded on the way down the hill?"

"None, sir."

"As best as you can estimate it, how many KIA did you see on the way out, Corporal Downs?" continued Simmons.

"Maybe ten or fifteen, sir."

"Located where?"

"Near the gate at the top of the hill. And also farther down. In the area that was the kill zone for my gun and the field of fire for my team, sir," said Downs in an even tone.

"Approximately how many did you observe in your own kill zone?"

Downs thought for a minute. "Maybe five or six, sir."

"Very well, Corporal. I would like to leave the discussion of the movement off the hill and ask some questions pertaining to the briefing you received concerning your mission that night. Do you recall specifically what you were told concerning the mission prior to departing the battalion area?"

"Some of it, sir. But not word for word."

"Just do your best, Corporal Downs. A summary will be fine," said Captain Roberts.

"Yes, sir," answered Downs. "I believe our mission was to depart the battalion area at oh-three-hundred hours and proceed by convoy to the designated hill. Once there we were to relieve the dragon squad and assist them in bringing out whatever gear they had at the hill. Our orders specified that we were not to leave any gear in place that might be used by the locals."

"Do you recall at what time your squad was to depart from its position on the hill?" asked Roberts.

Downs thought for a short while. Obviously the time designated for departure would have been chosen by the battalion operations officer and would therefore be known to the board. "I'm not really sure, sir. I know we were told we could catch a few hours sleep after we got to the hill. I think we were supposed to depart the hill ASAP after the gear had been loaded."

The officers considered Downs's answer before Captain Simmons asked, "Do you recall Sergeant Griffin telling you a specific time for the squad to be prepared to move that night? After you arrived at the hill?"

Downs sensed the thrust of the questioning. The board wanted to establish that Griffin and Slocum had spent the day preparing their defenses, not loading gear as they should have done if they intended to evacuate the hill as ordered. He suppressed the urge to smile then answered, "No, sir. After our arrival at the hill Sergeant Griffin told me to have my fireteam rack out in the basement of the building for a few hours as we would have to spend the rest of the day loading gear onto the six-bys. I don't recall him giving me a specific time the movement would take place."

Downs was satisfied that his answer was a good one. It would cover Griffin and not allow the board to establish that he and Slocum had defied orders and deliberately waited for the Arabs to attack instead of preparing to abandon the position. Captain Simmons cleared his throat and asked, "After your squad got up, how did you spend the rest of the day, Corporal?"

"Sergeant Griffin had us assist the dragon squad and the radio personnel in loading gear onto the vehicles, sir."

"Is that all, Corporal?" continued Simmons.

Downs knew that the officers would know from previous testimony that the squads had also strengthened their defensive position and dismounted the .50 caliber machine guns, remounting them in the building as a defensive measure. "No, sir. We also improved the defensive posture of the perimeter. The vehicles were moved to the rear of the courtyard and the heavy machine guns brought inside the building and set up with their respective fields of fire."

"And who was responsible for this, Corporal?" asked the lieutenant.

"Sergeant Griffin was, sir. As the senior NCO present and there not being any officers in the area."

"Watch your mouth, mister!" shot back the lieutenant. "Or I'll charge you with disrespect toward an officer."

"Aye, aye, sir," said Downs, acknowledging the order.

"Corporal Downs," said Roberts, "were you aware that one of the six-bys was down due to mechanical failure and that the departure of the squads was going to be delayed?"

"I became aware of that when we started loading the vehicles and I saw the driver attempting to start it, sir."

Roberts nodded, then asked, "Do you know the nature of the problem?"

"With the vehicle, sir?"

"Yes."

"I wouldn't know, sir. I do know that our orders were to bring out all the equipment at the position and Sergeant Griffin wouldn't abandon that vehicle, sir."

"Was that particular vehicle in working order when your squad arrived at the position?" asked the captain.

"I couldn't say, sir," answered Downs.

"I see, Corporal. Do you recall at what point it became operable?" asked Roberts.

"No, sir. Not really," said Downs.

Simmons exchanged glances with Roberts, then asked, "But it did leave the position under its own power the next day?"

"As far as I know, sir."

"Very well, Corporal Downs," said Simmons. "I think that is all the questions we have for you and your fireteam at this time, unless one of the other officers has something." Simmons paused to look at the others who shook their heads negatively. He looked at his watch and continued, "Given the time we won't hear any more statements today. Corporal Downs, you will remain in the battalion headquarters with your fireteam until tomorrow at oh-nine-hundred. If we do not have any further questions by that time you will report back to your company with your team. Is that understood, Marine?''

"Yes, sir."

"Very well. You are dismissed."

Downs rose and took the required step backward and said, "Good day, gentlemen." The officers of the board nodded and Downs spun on one heel and left the room with Ferris and Smith.

CHAPTER

22

Downs ate in silence at the battalion mess and contemplated the day's events. He was not at all sure what the board of officers had been driving at during most of the questioning. Obviously they thought there was a problem with the wounded militiaman that Griffin had given the morphine.

A shiver ran down his spine as he recalled the scene, and his participation. Downs was sure that Griffin had done the right thing, the humane thing. The man was dying and he was beyond help when they had gotten to him. To have left him there without easing his pain would have been cruel, and to have moved him would have meant making his death painful. Still, the officers had asked questions that could only mean they suspected foul play.

Downs surmised that they knew the essential facts of the story and were simply fishing for the details that would allow them to make the decision to formally charge Griffin and Slocum. He picked up his plastic tray and headed out of the makeshift mess hall fashioned from pine two-by-fours and roofed by a canvas tent. The fresh smell of the pine resin from the lumber reminded him of home, and of her.

He felt a twinge of sadness. It had been days since he had thought of her. Always before he had allowed himself a few moments at the end of every day when he would think of her and of the things they

241

had done together. He had looked forward to that time each day the way other Marines looked forward to mail call. He smiled to himself remembering the old Marine Corps axiom that there are really only two times of day, the time before mail call and the time after mail call. He had stopped looking forward to mail calls a few weeks after the arrival of her last letter.

He had carried that letter in his pocket for months. There was no hint in it of another boy, or even a good-bye for him. Instead she had written of her life at college, her new friends, courses she was taking. He had read it every day for a long time, in private moments away from his friends when he was sure no one would see him reading it for the hundredth time. He had read it over and over again until the pain began to lessen with each reading.

He had tried to write to her. More than once he had started a letter only to put it in his pocket to finish tomorrow. He would take his letter out and the words wouldn't come. He would read her letter again and know he had lost her. After a while the hurt faded to a dull ache and he ceased reading the letter. He knew then that he wouldn't write to her.

Downs had fought a battle with himself to quit caring and had very nearly won. He had quit longing for mail call, knowing that no letter from her would be waiting for him. He had steeled his heart against the hurt until the pain was a dull throb he was unaware of except in the quiet moments when he lay awake in his cot and thought of her. He had grown used to the company of his friends, the camaraderie natural to all soldiers, and most intense among those who find themselves on a battlefield.

He was on his way to forgetting her. He had thought about her less and less each day. He had ceased to look forward all day to the time when he would allow himself to think of her. His rivalry with Griffin had faded as the months in Lebanon dragged on and he became sure of himself as an NCO. And then Mac had been killed. That had changed everything. He missed her again and he knew he needed to talk to her. He could even imagine the conversation, the things she would say to him. Only the words were unimportant, it was her presence he needed.

He felt as though he had lost his two best friends, and he had no hope of regaining either of them. He ran his finger along the neat cut along the back of his hand and in his mind he saw the image of Mac lying on the ground trying to mask his fear. He felt the sadness well up within him and he walked away from the other Marines in the area.

He wanted to think, to be alone. To daydream of her and of the times they had spent together. The times before the Marine Corps, and before Lebanon.

Downs walked around the courtyard of the building in the soft air of late summer. He drew a deep breath and looked at the jagged peaks of the Lebanese mountains. From above he heard the voices of Marines and realized that men were on top of the building doing the same thing he was doing, watching the sun set. He headed inside and began climbing the steps to the roof.

He ascended the stairs on the interior of the building and found the ladder leading to the roof. As he stepped out onto the roof of the building he looked past the beach to the Mediterranean where the ships of the fleet lay at anchor. From this distance they appeared toylike against the glow of the setting sun. He sat in silence on the low concrete wall that ran the length and width of the rooftop.

He tried to think of her, of the times they had spent together, but no thoughts of her would come to him. He wasn't able to block out everything and lose himself in a daydream of her. He remained in Lebanon, another Marine enjoying the sunset atop the battalion head-quarters building.

Downs looked around the roof and spotted Slocum and Griffin at the far end. They were slowly walking the perimeter of the roof, deep in conversation. He felt a sinking in the pit of his stomach as he realized how Griffin must feel. Griffin had done his best in an impossible situation, and now the system was going to make a sacrifice of him at the whim of the first sergeant.

As the two approached, Downs nodded hello. The two sergeants appeared surprised to see him, then Slocum said, "How you doin' this evening, Corporal Downs?"

"Fine, thanks," said Downs, feeling awkward at having intruded on their conversation. "How are you?"

Slocum laughed and playfully slapped Griffin on the shoulder. "Well, I'm okay. But ol' blood and guts here is a mite worried." Downs made room for the sergeants on the ledge as they drew near. "Damn fine sunset," said Slocum cheerfully.

"It's nice," agreed Downs, looking at Griffin but not saying anything to him.

"Did you have chow yet, Downs? What are we havin' this evening?" asked Slocum as if nothing had happened that afternoon. "And more important, how are the lines?"

"Not too long," said Downs, "but you better hurry if you're going to get there before they secure."

"Yeah, no shit. Ol' Dave here is making me wait until all the troops have had their share, us being senior NCOs and all. The troops probably already ate my share."

"You're not going to starve. Just relax and we'll go get chow in a minute, Bobby," said Griffin.

"Mister gung ho," said Slocum as he jerked a thumb at Griffin and smiled at Downs. "Well, anyway, it's just for a few more days. Pretty soon we'll both be at the head of the chow line with the rest of the privates." Downs looked away in embarrassment as Slocum continued, "Hey, maybe on the Marine Corps birthday we'll get the first sergeant to serve us our chow. What do you think, Dave?" said Slocum, grinning wildly.

Griffin laughed softly and said, "As long as me and you are both privates he probably wouldn't mind it too much."

Slocum laughed and said, "Probably not, that asshole. Well, anyway, I'm going down and get some chow. You coming, Dave?"

"In a minute, Bobby. I'll see you down there."

"Okay," said Slocum turning to go. Slocum turned back toward Downs and said, "Hey, Downs. Thanks for what you did today. That took balls, standin' up to the Zeros and the first shirt like that. 'Course, now they'll probably hammer you the first chance they get. But hey, you were pretty impressive up there."

"Thanks," said Downs, not knowing what he should say and aware that Griffin wanted to talk to him privately. "I hope all this shit blows over, you know?"

Slocum laughed and said, "Don't hold your breath," as he turned to go. Slocum disappeared down the ladder shaft as Griffin turned to Downs and said, "So how are you doing, Corporal Downs?"

Downs avoided his gaze and answered, "I'm okay, Sergeant Griffin. Sorry about this afternoon though."

"Don't worry about it, Downs." Griffin hesitated as both young men looked out to sea toward the gray ships floating in the Mediterranean. "I'm sorry about Mac," said Griffin unexpectedly. "That kind of thing happens. Nobody can do anything about it, Downs. Nobody. You under-stand?"

Downs looked away and shook his head before saying, "I know it happens. I'm not blaming anybody."

"It's more than just not blaming anybody, Downs. It's understanding that Mac is just like all the rest of us. He joined because whatever it was inside of him that made him want to be a Marine was stronger than his fear of dying. Nobody thinks they're going to be the one to die. We all think it's going to be somebody else."

"Yeah, I know," said Downs as he looked away toward the city where a few lights began to glow in the twilight. "I appreciate what you're trying to do. I really do."

"It's just that you think you don't need a pep talk from me or anybody else. Right, Downs?" said Griffin, trying to keep the edge out of his voice.

"Maybe. I don't know. It's not that exactly."

"Look, Downs. If that had been you that day instead of Mac, I would still be responsible. Both of you are my troops, remember?" Downs shook his head as Griffin continued, "But there are some other things we both have to remember here. The first is that no matter what the papers or the command call this or don't call this, it's getting to be one long drawn-out firefight. We can't just sit on the sidelines anymore like when we first got here and watch everybody else kill each other. Do you follow me?"

"Yeah, I understand all that," said Downs with a wry smile. "Proba-bly better than you do, Sergeant Griffin."

Griffin nodded his head and agreed, "Yeah, you probably do, Downs. But there are some other things you may not understand so well." Griffin paused and chose his words, "Downs, you're different from the rest of us. Everybody knows it. Christ, even you know it. It's not exactly a secret. Hell, Slocum and me used to think you were some kind of snitch sent from NIS to spy on us for tightening up shit birds."

Downs smiled and said, "Not quite."

"Maybe not, Downs. But you're not the run-of-the-mill Marine either. You think more than the rest of us, and you understand more about politics and shit than the rest of us." Griffin hesitated as Downs smiled again. "You could have done okay on the outside, Downs.

"Everybody sees it. Nobody knows why you came in enlisted. You look like an officer, and most of the time you talk like an officer."

Downs stood in silence and Griffin continued, "The point is, Downs, that you're smarter than the rest of us in a lot of different ways. And you worry about a lot of crap the rest of us never even think of."

Griffin looked at Downs and let out a long sigh as he plunged on, "But, this is one time you are going to have to listen to me for your own good. You can't sit here and stew over Mac's death. It isn't going to do Mac any good and it isn't going to bring him back. It happened. It happened like it happened a million times before. Sheer dumb-fucking-stupid bad luck."

Griffin rubbed his hand across his face and waited for Downs to say something. When Downs refused, Griffin continued, "He's gone, Downs. Plain and simple. And you're the type of guy that could spend the rest of his life worrying about it. I'm not telling you not to think about Mac. He was a decent guy. But when you think about him, ask yourself something. What if Mac had never been a Marine and had lived another fifty years? Do you think he would have been happy? I bet I can answer that question for you. Mac, and you, or me, would be old men in a rocking chair some place wondering what it would have been like to wear a set of dress blues and be a Marine.

"There's only one way to find out, Downs. And all of us made that choice. All of us wanted to be a Marine, and be a part of all of this. And deep down, all of us wanted to go to war. It's sort of the ultimate test, the ultimate step to becoming a real Marine and having the right to be a part of the history of the Marine Corps, isn't it? Isn't this what it's all about? Finding out just what you're made of? Whether or not you're as good as all the others that came before you and fought, and made all the legends?"

Griffin hesitated, at a loss for words, then continued, "Mac wanted to be a part of it, Downs. Why else would he become a grunt? He could have been an air winger, or been in supply or some shit, and still called himself a Marine. But it's not the same, and guys like you and me know the difference. Mac knew the difference, too. That's why he was here, and that's part of why he's dead."

For a few minutes the two stood in silence on the roof of the building. As the light faded Downs said, "I know you're right, Sergeant Griffin. I know what you mean about becoming a Marine. I'll think about what you said. I know Mac respected you."

"I'm not sure anything is worth losing your life over. I just know I would have spent the rest of my life wondering if I was good enough to be a Marine if I hadn't at least tried. And no matter how fucked up the system is, I will always be proud of being a Marine. And I'll have my self-respect."

Downs nodded his head in agreement in the darkness, "Yeah. Me, too, Sergeant Griffin. I'm not just saying that. I always wanted to be a Marine. I don't even know why. God knows my family doesn't understand it."

"They don't have to. Only you have to understand it. Or maybe you just have to feel it. I don't know. It's the same for me in a lot of ways." Griffin turned and looked out over the city and shook his head, "Well, I guess I missed chow. I think I'll go down and see if I can scrounge up a C-rat out of my pack or something." Griffin hesitated then said, "One other thing, Downs. Slocum was right. What you did today took guts. I appreciate it. Thanks."

"You're welcome, Sergeant Griffin," said Downs.

Griffin extended his hand and said, "My name is Dave."

Downs took his hand and said, "Steve."

CHAPTER

23

Griffin sat on the edge of his rack in the early morning and buffed his boots. Through the window he heard the sounds of the battalion coming to life, the noise of engines being turned over, and commands being given in the distance. As he sat, pondering his fate before the board of inquiry, the door swung open and Slocum entered. "Hey, boy," said Slocum enthusiastically, "how goes it this fine morning?"

He smiled and answered, "Okay, Bobby, how was chow?"

"Don't know. I'm lettin' you set the example and not eatin' until all the troops have had their fill."

"Yeah, right," said Griffin in an obvious tone of disbelief. "What's your angle?"

Slocum adopted a pained expression and answered, "Now, Dave, I'm hurt. Here I am doin' my best to be a good NCO and you practically accuse me of bein' a liar. Why if I didn't know you were an ignorant uneducated street urchin from the slums and ghettos of New York I might take offense."

Griffin smiled and said, "I'd guess you didn't like what was on the menu except I've never seen you miss a meal in four years. No matter what was being served. The lines must be too long. Even for you."

Slocum shook his head and said, "Naw, it ain't the lines, it's the company. I saw the first shirt go in and decided I'd rather wait and eat later."

"No shit, huh?" said Griffin. "I knew it had to be something serious to keep you away from a hot meal."

"Well, it ain't all that serious. I plan on having a breakfast fit for a king after I finish washing up a little."

"Okay," said Griffin, "I'll see you up there. Try not to worry too much in the mean time."

"No problem Dave." Slocum smiled as Griffin walked out the door, wandering the building for a few minutes before heading for the room that served as a court. He stood in the tiled passageway waiting for the members of the board to arrive. Company clerks entered and prepared to carry out the day's tasks without so much as looking at him. Slocum showed up a few minutes before the officers and stood by in silence as they entered in a group, Lieutenant Walters the last in line. "Looks like mother duck and all the little ducklings are in place. What say we go in and get this over with?" quipped Slocum.

Griffin shrugged and said, "We might as well. Good luck, Bobby."

"Good luck yourself," said Slocum as the two entered the room and sat in the chairs assigned to them. As the officers shuffled their papers a company clerk approached Slocum and told him to take the seat immediately in front of the officers. Griffin watched as Slocum walked calmly to the center of the room and sat in the lone chair where Downs had sat the day before. The sergeant major resumed his place along the wall, his expression vacant and passive as he calmly observed the others.

Captain Simmons cleared his throat and Slocum straightened in his chair. The captain fixed his gaze and addressed the young Marine, "Sergeant Slocum, how are you this morning?"

"Fine, sir," answered Slocum.

"Very well, are you ready to proceed?" asked the captain.

"Yes, sir," said Slocum, "but I'm not too sure what exactly I'm supposed to do, sir."

Simmons exchanged a glance with Captain Roberts, then returned to Slocum. "Do you mean that you have questions as to why you are here, Sergeant?"

"Yes, sir," drawled Slocum. "I'm not at all sure just exactly what's going on."

Simmons sighed and looked at Slocum as he spoke. "I believe you are aware that this is a board of inquiry convened for the purpose of establishing just exactly the course of events on the night in question. Your purpose here is to answer the questions put to you by the board and to assist the board in establishing the facts. I think that has been made amply clear in the past few days. Am I understood, Sergeant?"

"Yes, sir," answered Slocum as he sat facing the captain, "I understand what your job is, sir. It's the other stuff I'm not so clear on."

Griffin made an effort not to wince as the Captain stiffened and prepared to answer. He knew where Slocum was going with his responses and he could guess the reaction of the board.

"Just what other stuff are you referring to, Sergeant Slocum?" asked the captain as Griffin had known he would.

"Why, sir? Why question this particular action, or that particular night? It just doesn't make any sense to me, sir. Are we going to have a board of inquiry every time we walk a patrol or take enemy fire?"

Simmons stared at Slocum as he answered, "This particular action is in question because of the number of casualties sustained by the attacking force of militia and to determine the reason why the fighting took place." The captain paused and fixed Slocum with what he hoped was a withering stare. "Have I made myself perfectly clear, Sergeant?"

Griffin knew that Slocum had prepared his strategy carefully and that the captain was responding just as Slocum had expected. He shifted in his chair to get a better look at the captain's face as Slocum drawled in apparent innocence, "I'm still a little foggy on a couple of things, sir. Am I allowed to ask any more questions or do we have to go on, sir?"

"Ask your question, Sergeant," snapped the captain.

"Sir, am I being court-martialed here, or what?"

"As you well know, this is not a court-martial. It is simply a fact-finding mission." The captain paused, then finished, "You are not the subject of a court-martial."

"But could I be, sir? After y'all get done here, that is. Can you decide to court-martial me then, or Sergeant Griffin?"

The captain again looked at his fellow officers sitting beside him at the narrow table. Roberts caught Simmons's eye and shrugged slightly. "That *is* a possibility, Sergeant. Although it is not the sole purpose or mission of this board."

"But it could happen? Right, sir?" persisted Slocum.

"That's correct, Sergeant," answered Simmons.

"So based on what I say here you are going to make a decision on whether or not to court-martial me, sir?"

"That is a part of the duty of this board. Now can we get on with the business at hand, Sergeant?" said the captain in an irritated tone.

Slocum raised his hand slightly, reminding Griffin of a schoolboy who isn't sure of the answer but raises his hand anyway in an indecisive half gesture. The only difference, Griffin knew, was Slocum was playing with the officer. And now Captain Simmons had begun to see where it was going and was trying to deny Slocum the endgame. Griffin had seen his friend do this sort of thing before and he knew that Slocum would pursue his goal with a maddening tenacity.

"Yes, Sergeant?" asked the captain wearily.

"Beggin' the Captain's pardon, sir, but I'd like to ask a couple more questions if it's all right, sir." Griffin suppressed a smile. He knew Slocum would make frequent use of "sirs" now that he had them in his sights. The captain never had a chance, thought Griffin, Bobby had a plan and he's had a lot of prior experience at this. The captain's a fucking boot at this game.

"Go ahead, Sergeant. And then I'd like to get on with it."

"Thank you, sir," said Slocum, knowing he had won and beginning to relish his role. "What I'd really like to know sir, and I'm sorry but I couldn't find anything in the Guidebook for Marines regarding a board of inquiry or I'd have just looked it up myself. But anyway, sir, what I'd like to know is, if y'all do decide to court-martial me or Sergeant Griffin, can you use what we say here against us at our court-martial?"

The officers' heads came together quickly as they conferred over the answer to Slocum's question. Griffin was amazed at Slocum's ability to ask his questions with such an air of disarming inquiry. He noted that Simmons seemed to defer to Captain Roberts before answering. "That's correct, Sergeant Slocum. What you say here is admissible in any court-martial proceeding."

Slocum looked at the officers on the board who seemed to be temporarily at a loss, then asked, "Can I be ordered to answer, sir? Even if I don't want to? Is that the way it works, sir? I'm being ordered to answer your questions even if I don't want to?"

Simmons hunched his shoulders together tightly and leaned forward as he answered, "No, Sergeant. You can not be ordered to answer the questions put to you by the board. However, I must tell you that by not answering the board's questions you are going to be cast in a very unfavorable light. Am I making myself clear to you?"

"I think I've got it now, sir," said Slocum amicably. "What you're telling me is that anything I say here can be used to convict me at my court-martial, if y'all do decide to court-martial me. And if I don't answer your questions then you probably will decide to court-martial me because I'm not answering your questions. Is that right, sir?"

"I've had just about enough of your attitude, Sergeant Slocum," said the captain. "I believe you understand clearly what is taking place here and this is merely an attempt on your part to avoid answering the questions of this board. I assure you that I and the other members of the board do not see the humor in this little game. Now I am ready to proceed with the questions we have prepared for you today. Do you intend to cooperate with the board or not, Sergeant?"

Slocum looked at the members of the board for a long moment and answered, "No, sir. I'm not answering. If you want to court-martial me, sir, then you just go ahead and do what you gotta do. But I won't help you do it. You and the first sergeant will have to do it on your own, sir."

Slocum sat and faced the board in silence. The room had fallen quiet as he had spoken and Griffin braced himself for the tirade he expected Captain Simmons to deliver. Instead Simmons leaned back in his chair and said, "Fine, Sergeant Slocum. I believe you understand the implications of your refusal to answer the board's questions. I am going to give you one last opportunity to change your mind, and I assure you it will be your last. Will you answer the questions of this board?"

"No, sir," said Slocum flatly.

"Very well. You are dismissed for the time being. You are to remain in quarters here at the battalion CP until further notice. You will report to the H&S company gunnery sergeant for your duty assignments as of this afternoon at thirteen-hundred. Am I understood, Sergeant?"

"Yes, sir," answered Slocum.

"Dismissed," said the captain, looking down at his paperwork as Slocum executed his dismissal and left the room. Griffin studied Captain Simmons and the other officers as he waited to be called forward. He decided that, with the exception of Captain Roberts, they were all stamped from the same mold. Without exception they had received their commission after completing college and ROTC courses, then the officers candidate school at the Marine Corps Base in Virginia. As he sat looking at the officers Griffin tried to define what it was about the officer corps in general that he mistrusted. Some of them were better infantrymen than others, but they were almost all competent without exception. Most, he was sure, were the sons of middle-class families who, for whatever reasons of their own, had chosen to become Marine officers. Almost to a man they appeared arrogant and haughty to their men and Griffin had been told by friends who were sergeant-instructors at OCS that the arrogance was learned during training.

He had endured their superior attitudes and their patronizing lectures for the past seven years by accepting it as a necessary evil, a part of the system. He had watched as they punished his friends and his troops without remorse for doing the same things they did on liberty but were never questioned about. He had stood silently by as junior lieutenants learned the art of war at the hands of experienced staff NCOs and noncoms. He had seen them commit countless errors in training that would have meant death for them and their charges in warfare.

He had endured it all, he knew, as he sat looking at the officers. All of the condescending, humiliating, degrading lectures that they dispensed as though they were dirtying themselves by addressing him and his peers in the ranks in order to impart their knowledge. And now they don't even have the balls to court-martial me without this charade first to justify it, he silently thought.

He knew then what he would do. He wasn't Slocum. He wasn't going to play cat and mouse with them. It was a matter of principle, a question of his manhood. He had learned the lessons the system had to teach him during long field exercises and in the darkened barracks during quick, brutal beatings given to those who couldn't or wouldn't conform for the good of the whole. He had spent the past seven years with his head up and his dignity intact, and as the anger rose in him he realized it was beyond him now to sacrifice it to the group of men who sat before him in judgment.

In his anger Griffin suspected Captain Roberts knew he would answer their questions. Roberts had been with the battalion a long time, almost as long as Griffin himself. He knew most of the NCOs, either personally or by reputation. He would have known Slocum's reputation as a joker, a good NCO who didn't take himself or the Marine Corps any more seriously than was required at any given moment.

Slocum could more easily afford to dodge the questions of the board. It was common knowledge in the battalion he planned on leaving the Marines upon completion of his enlistment. Griffin understood that he was different. He was known as a professional among the officers, a career NCO who had no ambitions beyond rising through ranks as far as his talent would allow.

Even this Griffin had taken a step further. He had reenlisted and instead of taking a tour of duty on an embassy posting, where he might escape the harsh existence of the rifle companies, he had insisted on remaining in the infantry. He was known not only as a career Marine, but a career infantryman. There was a certain degree of respect afforded him because of this. The organization had difficulty finding good NCOs who wished to remain in the infantry. Griffin had never desired anything else and it was well known among the staff NCOs and officers.

He looked directly at Captain Roberts as Simmons began speaking, "Sergeant Griffin, are you prepared to answer the questions of the board?"

Griffin held Roberts's eye until the older man looked away. "Yes, sir," he answered, his voice brittle with anger, "I'll answer your questions, sir."

"Very well, Sergeant. You understand that the board is not ordering you to answer any questions it might have. That you are answering of you own free will?"

"I understand, Captain," said Griffin.

"Good. Then we'll proceed with the questions." The captain shuffled his papers into a neat stack and cleared his throat. "Sergeant Griffin, I would like to begin on the day in question with your arrival at the position held by the dragon squad. What specifically were your orders, as you understood them that day?"

"To relieve the squad in place and effect their withdrawal from the position. We were also to remove any and all gear that was in place there. Particularly radio gear and other electronics, sir."

"And your orders as far as engaging the locals?"

"I was instructed to obey and adhere to the Rules of Engagement at all times during the operation and not to draw attention to my unit or operations, sir."

"And do you feel you accomplished that task, Sergeant?" asked Simmons.

"Yes, sir. I do."

"Very good, Sergeant Griffin," said Simmons. "Now I would like to move on a bit. When you arrived at the position, at what point did you become aware that one of the vehicles was down due to mechanical failure?"

Griffin paused, trying to remember at what point Slocum had told him of the down six-by. "Maybe fifteen minutes after we were in the area, sir. Approximately."

"And who informed you of this?"

"Sergeant Slocum did, sir. As the senior NCO present and the effective six, sir."

"And did you personally inspect the down vehicle, Sergeant?"

"No, sir. I did not," answered Griffin.

"Why not, Sergeant? Didn't it occur to you to at least have a look at it?"

"It probably did, sir. But at the time I had just arrived with my squad and my primary concern was with the integrity of the defensive perimeter and the overall defensibility of the position. A down vehicle is secondary under those considerations, sir."

Simmons hesitated, Griffin's tone was respectful if a bit angry. He understood that the big sergeant had just been doing his job, but his own job was to determine exactly what had taken place on that hill. The Old Man was breathing down his neck over the whole incident and Slocum's refusal to answer questions wasn't going to make things any easier when he gave his daily report in the colonel's quarters. "That's correct, Sergeant Griffin," he said, regretting it as soon as he said it. Griffin was known as probably the best sergeant in the battalion. The last thing he wanted to do here was appear to be condescending toward him on a tactical matter. For a moment he silently wished that Griffin had elected to keep his mouth shut like Slocum. Maybe then the whole thing would just die on the vine. He might even get a night's rest without tossing until three in the morning wondering if he were doing the right thing or just playing a patsy to the Alpha Company first sergeant. "Let's continue, Sergeant. At what point were you approached by the local militia leader? Assuming that's what he was."

"Sometime that morning, sir. I'm not exactly sure when, fairly early."

"I see," said Simmons as the other members of the board leaned forward intent on the next series of questions. "And what took place between you and that militia leader?"

"He ordered us off of his hill, sir. He said something about it belonging to the people of Lebanon and the Marines being imperialist. And that he was here to get us off the hill even if he had to kill all of us."

"And what was your response, Sergeant Griffin?"

Griffin looked at the young captain as he thought what his answer should be. After only a moment's hesitation he decided that it just didn't matter any longer, it was finished. He was sick and tired of the game and he wanted no part of it. He wanted to be done with it and on with the court-martial if that was what they had in mind. "I told him to fuck off, sir."

Simmons looked again at the young sergeant. He resisted the urge to warn Griffin against showing a lack of respect, fearing the man would just get angry and refuse to answer any further questions. He paused for a few moments struggling to think of his next question, searching for the words that would elicit the answer he wanted. Finally he looked at Griffin and asked, "Sergeant Griffin, why don't you just tell the board what happened and why. Maybe that will save us all a lot of time and effort."

Griffin drew a deep breath and began, "Sir, the Arab came up the road to our position and demanded that we get off the hill. He stated that we were violating Lebanese law or some other thing like that. When I said we wouldn't leave he got smart with me and started sayin' a bunch of crap about how he would knock us off the hill. I refused to abandon my position and told him to get the hell off my hill, sir."

"Is that when you hit him, Sergeant?" asked Lieutenant Walters.

Griffin cast a wary glance at the lieutenant and said, "No, sir. I hit him when he spit on me and said he spit on the Marine Corps and everything it stood for. Including our colors that were flying from the roof of the building at the time." Griffin looked at the members of the board who seemed somewhat surprised at this latest revelation. Before continuing he looked directly at Captain Roberts again and said, "I hit him, sir. A few times I guess. And I disarmed him and his friend. I took their weapons and told them to get the hell off my hill and that the Marine Corps would be there as long as they wanted the damn hill. Nobody but me struck him, sir. I don't know if he was a Lebanese officer or what, but I was the one who hit him, and nobody else." Griffin paused and looked again at the officers on the board. None of them seemed the least bit sympathetic toward him or Slocum. He wondered in silence if they had anything in mind other than his court-martial. After a few moments' hesitation he continued, "If you're looking for somebody to punish for striking an officer, or anything else that happened up there, then I am the NCO responsible. I was in charge from the moment I arrived at the position and everything that was done was done with my approval or at my direction, sir. Sergeant Slocum modified the defensive positions at my orders and his squad was under my command during the fighting."

Roberts held up a hand to stop Griffin and said, "Sergeant Griffin, the express purpose of this board is not to find someone responsible in order to court-martial that individual. As you and the others have been told we are trying to establish exactly what happened that day and why. We are particularly interested in why fighting took place and who initiated it, but we don't have any preconceived notion that you or any other Marine in this battalion is at fault or guilty of a violation of the Rules of Engagement. Am I making myself clear, Sergeant?"

"Yes, sir," answered Griffin dutifully.

"Good. Then maybe we can proceed. Captain Simmons," said Roberts, nodding toward the other officer.

"Very well, Sergeant. So you struck this Lebanese individual. With your fists I presume?"

Griffin nodded, "Yes, sir. With my fists."

"How many times, Sergeant? And to what effect?"

"Maybe four or five times, sir. And I knocked him down. After he went down I removed his weapons and the weapons of the other individual. I didn't hit the other guy, sir. He just surrendered his weapon without a fight," said Griffin, the contempt evident in his voice.

"Did you hit either individual with anything other than your fists?"

"No, sir."

"Why exactly did you feel compelled to strike the first individual, Sergeant Griffin? I'm still not completely clear on that issue," said Simmons.

Griffin sat for a moment, stunned that the captain was dwelling on this point, then asked, "Sir?"

"Why did you hit this individual, Sergeant? The question is plain enough, I believe."

Griffin looked at Roberts as if expecting an explanation. When Roberts again looked away he returned to face Captain Simmons and answered, "I hit him, sir, because he was in front of my squad, in a position to scout out our defenses, and he made a threat to me and to my Marines. And because he insulted the Marine Corps, sir."

"And then you proceeded to disarm him and the other man with him? Without any further provocation?"

Griffin looked at the captain and struggled to control his anger. He must be an idiot, thought Griffin, as he dutifully answered, "Yes, sir."

"This may all seem a bit inane to you, Sergeant, but I feel it is my duty to remind you that we are in a foreign country. We are not at war with its government, nor with any of the factions that face our lines or positions. And we have very specific rules defining the limits of our mission and authority while here. Am I making this clear for you, Sergeant Griffin?" asked Simmons.

"Yes, sir," answered Griffin. "But with all due respect, sir. My first duty is to ensure the safety of my Marines and the completion of the mission. Any actions I took that day, or any other day, sir, were to complete the mission as I understood it."

Simmons nodded, then continued, "Why don't you explain to us how a firefight was initiated that day?"

"Yes, sir," answered Griffin, not quite sure how he was going to proceed. He hesitated then continued, "A little after twenty-one-hundred Corporal Downs reported movement coming up the access road past his position. I had his fireteam at the rear of the building where they were in a position to see whatever came up that road. About twenty minutes after he reported movement we came under small arms fire. Initially the enemy force engaged the little gatehouse just in front of our position with small arms. Some spillover fire went through our position."

"Did any of your Marines return fire at that point, Sergeant?" asked Simmons.

"No, sir," said Griffin. "I had ordered them not to fire in the event of an attack unless I specifically ordered them to fire, or they felt they had to fire to defend themselves or our position." The captain nodded and Griffin continued, "Anyway, sir, they figured out that nobody was posted in the gatehouse and hit the front gate with small arms a few minutes after their attack started. We didn't return fire at that point until I was positive that they were trying to breach the gate itself."

"How did you determine that they were attempting to breach the gate, Sergeant?"

"I had rigged illumination flares in the area earlier that day and when we heard that gate rattling and our wire rattling we knew they had to be close. I ordered the illumination fired. Several of them were caught in the open and we took them under fire at that point, sir."

"Very well, Sergeant. Was that the first outgoing fire from your position?"

"Yes, sir. To the best of my knowledge."

"I see. You may proceed, Sergeant Griffin."

"Aye, aye, sir," said Griffin. "We took a series of rounds from small arms and an RPG. All fired from the area of the gate and gatehouse.

We returned fire and continued to illuminate the area and bring under fire any targets we could identify. We continued to press the attack without abandoning our defensive positions and inflicted casualties on the attacking force. We did not sustain any casualties and the enemy broke off and attempted to retreat down the hill along his route of advance. At that point Corporal Downs's fireteam brought them under fire on my orders."

"Were they retreating at that point, Sergeant Griffin?"

"They were falling back, sir. Off my position."

"If they were no longer aggressively attacking your position then why did you order Corporal Downs to fire on them? It seems to me this is a clear violation of the Rules of Engagement and disobedience of a direct order." Simmons stared at Griffin, waiting for his answer.

"I was holding an isolated position with only a reinforced squad, sir. I had just been attacked in force by an enemy unit of unknown size and capabilities, and I had a fireteam in position to inflict casualties on them as they withdrew. I took the opportunity to do just that, sir. With all due respect, sir, I was in no position to worry about hurting the feelings of the Lebanese government or anybody else. They had clearly made an attempt to overrun my position. For all I knew they were falling back to reorganize or bring up heavy weapons. In that position, sir, I did what I judged to be the tactically correct thing."

"Very well, Sergeant Griffin. Did you at any time radio the battalion and ask for permission to engage enemy targets?"

"No, sir. I did not," answered Griffin grimly, his face set in a mask of anger.

"Any reason why you didn't do that, Sergeant Griffin? It would appear from your own explanation of events that you had sufficient time to do so."

"I saw no reason to ask for permission to engage enemy targets, sir. They initiated the fire. We returned it according to the Rules of Engagement. My radioman made a contact report to battalion when comm was working and we requested supporting arms. Battalion had the required information in a timely fashion, sir. I am not required to get the CO's permission to return fire in defense of my position. Contact was inevitable, sir."

"I see," said Simmons. He knew from the testimony of others and the battalion's unit diary that Griffin had indeed made his contact report as required. He also knew that, due to the relatively low ground where the battalion CP was located, radio contact was frequently lost with units distant from the headquarters. Still, he was bothered by the apparent orchestration of the day's events. It had all been too neat, it somehow seemed to have been prepackaged by the Marines involved. Almost as if they had gone out looking for a fight and found one with the neighborhood toughs.

He wasn't ready to accept the first sergeant's explanation that Griffin was a renegade NCO who was just looking for an excuse to fire up the locals. He knew Griffin's reputation, and he had asked the Alpha company commander about him. All the reports had been favorable. He had looked at Griffin's personnel record and it too had been impressive. He had received meritorious promotion to corporal and sergeant, as well as letters of commendation and consistently high ratings for proficiency and conduct. He had been in the expected scrapes with the civilian police at LeJeune, and another fight on base that had resulted in an article fifteen, but nothing particularly detrimental.

Griffin was the sort of sergeant that any platoon commander was grateful to have in his unit. He was confident, capable, and aggressive. He had an impressive military appearance and Simmons liked the way he answered the board's questions. His own company commander had praised him as a dependable, hard-charging NCO.

Still, something was nagging at him. Slocum's failure to answer the board's questions was an issue, but Griffin didn't appear intimidated by the board. If he was guilty of some planned disobedience of orders then he certainly wasn't showing it.

Simmons decided that the real issue would be whether or not Griffin or Slocum, or both of them, had orchestrated the attack on the hill. Even that seemed to be reaching. After all, how could they bait the locals into making an attack? Possibly by Griffin beating the militia leader with his fists, but even that was making the assumption that the man he had struck was the militia leader. And the Lebanese, or whoever he was, had come up to their position and ordered them off the hill. No one could expect an NCO like Griffin to abandon his position under those conditions.

He began again, "Sergeant Griffin, I would like to move on now, to the morning after the firefight. What I would like to know is what type of resistance you encountered as you moved your men off the hill and back to the battalion. Just give it to us in your own words if you will, Sergeant."

"Yes, sir," said Griffin. "We came off the hill at approximately oh-eight-hundred on the orders of the battalion operations officer. We didn't encounter any resistance, sir. I did order the point fireteam leader to detonate a series of claymores as they egressed the position in order to clear any ambushes that might have been set on the withdrawal route."

"Very good, Sergeant. I am aware from previous statements given to this board by members of your squad and the dragon squad that you and Corporal Downs and the corpsman attached to your squad located one individual near the gate who was wounded, presumably in the attack the night before. Is that correct?"

"Yes, sir. That's correct," answered Griffin.

"And it is also my understanding that you and the corpsman administered first aid to this man. Is that correct?"

"I administered the morphine, sir," said Griffin, anticipating the next question. "Not the Doc. And I ordered him back to the squad position while it was done." Griffin swallowed hard and told himself to look Simmons in the eye. The hard questions were coming, he knew.

Simmons cocked an eyebrow at Griffin and asked, "You administered the morphine, Sergeant Griffin? Personally?"

"Yes, sir. I did," came the reply.

"Why you, Sergeant Griffin? Was there some reason the corpsman attached to your squad couldn't do it?"

"No, sir. I ordered the corpsman forward to check out the wounded man and give me a report on his condition. Only the point fireteam was in front of us and I ordered the Doc back to the compound because I didn't want to expose him unnecessarily to an enemy ambush. He was the only corpsman on the hill and I didn't want to risk losing him to treat an enemy soldier, sir."

"I see," said Simmons. "What was the corpsman's evaluation of the wounded man?"

"That he was past help, sir. He had multiple wounds from shrapnel to his abdomen. His intestines were literally spilling out of his uniform. The corpsman treated him and administered one stick of morphine to ease the pain. The Doc advised me at that time that moving the man, even to medevac him, would probably kill him due to hemorrhage."

"Did you attempt to call for a medevac bird, Sergeant Griffin?"

"No, sir. I did not," said Griffin as the members of the board noted his answer.

"Exactly what action did you take at that point, Sergeant?" asked Simmons.

Griffin knew that Simmons had him. If he refused to answer the question they would simply ask the Doc what had transpired at that point. Griffin assumed that they already had, and that the point of the current line of questions was simply to formalize his own admission. He stared at Captain Simmons and said flatly, "I determined the amount of morphine necessary to put the guy out of his misery, sir. I ordered the Doc to leave me a couple of sticks of it and clear the area. I then asked the wounded guy if he wanted it and he signaled that he understood it was enough to kill him. After that, sir, I administered the stuff to him myself."

A murmur of voices rose behind Griffin as the Marines in the room talked among themselves about this latest revelation. Griffin had practically admitted to murder. No matter how humane his reasoning, the officers would see it from another perspective. All the Marines stood in silence as the officers hurriedly conferred among themselves.

After a few minutes of whispered discussion Captain Roberts looked at Griffin and asked, "Sergeant Griffin, if I understand what you just told the board you decided to administer a lethal dose of morphine to this wounded soldier in order to relieve his suffering. Is that correct?"

"Yes, sir. That's about the size of it," said Griffin.

Roberts rubbed his chin and again addressed Griffin, "Sergeant Griffin, I feel it is my duty to advise you that you are admitting to a serious offense. You just don't have the authority to make decisions like that. No Marine, or corpsman, can decide to do what you did. It's just not allowed, son." Roberts hesitated, thinking quickly that maybe it wasn't too late for Griffin if he could stop him from saying anything further about the incident with the wounded man. He was sure that Griffin had done the only thing that he could, and equally sure that Simmons didn't want to court-martial Griffin or Slocum if it could be avoided without attracting a lot of attention from the higher-ups. "Sergeant Griffin," he began, "I think it is time for the board to confer for a few minutes. During that time I suggest that you reconsider what you have just told the board."

Roberts looked at Simmons who sat in silence at the center of the line of officers. He knew he had preempted Simmons's next series of questions but he couldn't sit there and do nothing while Griffin handed them the rope to hang him with. He was sure that Simmons had had no idea that Griffin had administered a lethal dose of morphine to the wounded man. The corpsman had been vague about the dosage and none of the officers had thought to ask in detail how many syringes of morphine were given to the man. The corpsman hadn't even mentioned that he had been ordered to return to the squad area, or that Griffin had ordered him to leave any morphine behind.

As the officers rose and filed out of the room Roberts's mind searched for a way to eliminate the wounded man from the equation. The whole point of the board had been to determine if the two sergeants had provoked a firefight, or deliberately disabled a vehicle in order to delay leaving the position and thereby encourage an attack on the Marine perimeter.

He just couldn't understand why Griffin had admitted to giving the man that injection. Obviously Griffin thought that the board already knew. Why else would he admit to doing it? That was the only explanation that made any sense. A scene from his first tour in Vietnam came to him, his own platoon sergeant shooting another Marine at point-blank range as the boy lay gasping for breath through lungs seared by flame. He understood now, but he hadn't then. Even if the boy had lived long enough to be put aboard a medevac flight he would have died on the flight back to the rear, and he would have suffered terribly in the interim. All the platoon sergeant had done was short-circuit the process and alleviate the boy's suffering. Thirteen months in Vietnam had taught him that sometimes life was so painful that it wasn't worth holding onto for another few minutes.

Roberts silently thanked God that he had never been forced to sit where Griffin now sat. The sergeant had tried to do the right thing, to make the best judgment call he knew how to make. Roberts was sure he would have done almost exactly the same thing had he been in Griffin's place. The problem now was that Griffin was going to be judged by another set of rules. A set of rules that applied better to the parade ground than the battlefield.

Roberts shook his head and closed the door behind him, the knob still in his hand as he looked at the others and said, "Why don't you excuse Captain Simmons and myself for a few minutes." As the others shrugged and filed out Roberts mumbled "Thanks." He looked at Simmons across the empty room and let out a long sigh.

"Jesus!" said Simmons. "Why the fuck didn't he just keep his mouth shut? If he hadn't said anything about the fucking rag-head we would just about be through with this bullshit by now. Christ!" said Simmons as he threw his hands into the air and stared out the window, "I can't believe I got stuck with this fucking board."

"All part of being an officer and a gentleman, I guess," replied Roberts.

"Yeah, right," said Simmons angrily. "I get selected to preside over this bullshit board because Alpha's first sergeant has a hard-on for a couple of sergeants who don't say 'Aye, aye, first sergeant' quick enough to suit his taste. What a fucking blow job this has turned out to be."

Roberts tried to come up with the solution to Griffin's problem. He was now certain that Simmons didn't want to see either Griffin or Slocum court-martialed. Except for the mention of the morphine and the wounded Lebanese he was convinced that the two sergeants would not have been charged. He decided to let Simmons answer the questions, after all he was the senior officer sitting on the board. "Okay, so it's a blow job. I think we've established that over the past few days. So what are we going to do about it? Being leaders of men, I mean?"

Simmons shot an angry look at Roberts and said, "What do you mean, what are we going to do about it? Their shit is fried now. At least Griffin's is, with that fucking confession about juicing the Lebanese. I don't see that we have any choice but to charge him. You got a better suggestion?"

Roberts hesitated for a minute and said, "Let's go see the Old Man on this. He's a fair man and he's been around a long time. I don't think he is going to be any too anxious to see one of his sergeants come up on a charge like this. Besides, what do you plan on charging him with? Murder? It's hardly that. From what he describes the guy was about to cash in his chips, all Griffin did was make it easy for him instead of leaving him there to die. There's got to be a way around this mess."

Simmons shook his head negatively and answered, "I don't see how you can say that after what you said in the courtroom about him not having the authority to do this. All of the testimony is recorded by the company clerks and I don't see how they could have missed a word of that. Between the two of us we have practically convicted him already.

Besides, the story will be all over the battalion in another half an hour. The first sergeant is sure to get wind of it and then wonder why we're not charging Griffin with something. I just don't see how we can get away with not charging him. I guess we won't have to charge Slocum, he doesn't seem to have had any role in this part of it."

"Look, we can explain it by saying that Griffin misspoke himself. That he thought he was giving the man an injection that would only alleviate his suffering, not be fatal. He's an infantry sergeant, not a hospital corpsman. How should he know the difference? We'll adjourn until tomorrow morning and in the meantime I'll go and speak with Griffin and the Old Man."

"There's still the first sergeant. What are we going to do to pacify him? The bastard will probably have Headquarters Marine Corps fry my ass for dereliction of duty."

"He might want to try," said Roberts, "but that would mean bucking the Old Man, assuming he buys our plan, and no first shirt in his right mind is going to do that to his own colonel. He'd be ruined no matter what the outcome."

"I don't like it," said Simmons. "Maybe you're not aware of this, but I'm an attorney. That's probably why the colonel selected me to head up the board. What Griffin did in the courtroom a few minutes ago has a legal definition. It's called a spontaneous utterance, and what it amounts to is making a legal confession as far as Sergeant Griffin is concerned. Legally there is just no way to avoid a trial. Questions have to be asked, and Griffin should have a defense counsel before he answers. If he had had one already none of this would have happened in the first place."

Simmons thrust his hands deep into his trouser pockets, a gesture proscribed for Marines in uniform but a habit from his university days. When he caught Roberts's eyes again he felt embarrassed at his oversight. He shrugged and said, "Sorry, guess I'm just a slimy civilian at heart. Look, I'd like to help Griffin. God knows I didn't ask any questions in there that I didn't have to. I don't see where Griffin is guilty of anything more than doing his duty and being a compassionate human being." Simmons hesitated and ran a hand through his hair. "I can understand your wanting to protect them. Neither of them deserves this, especially not Griffin. He's a good sergeant. But we can't just walk away from this as though nothing happened in there a few minutes ago. It's not legal. And it's not right."

Fifteen minutes later the board had been reconvened and Griffin and Slocum stood before it as Captain Simmons addressed the two Marines. "It is the decision of this board, after careful consideration of the testimony given before it, that Sergeant David F. Griffin, USMC, should be held for court-martial. Pending further investigation Said Named Marine will be formally charged and will be immediately appointed with appropriate defense counsel. Said Named Marine is not to remove himself from the confines of the battalion headquarters until such time as he is told he may legally do so. Do you understand this, Sergeant?"

"Yes, sir," answered Griffin flatly.

"Very well. It is the decision of this board that in the matter of Sergeant Robert P. Slocum that Said Named Marine is not bound over for court-martial and should be returned to duties forthwith."

"Am I understood, Sergeant Slocum?"

"Yes, sir," said Slocum.

"Very well then. This board is dismissed with the thanks of the commanding officer of the First Battalion, Eighth Marine Regiment. Gentlemen, thank you." Simmons waited for the four officers to file out of the room then once again regarded the two sergeants before him. "Dismissed!" he said and Griffin and Slocum about-faced and left the room.

CHAPTER

24

The Syrian squinted into the mid-afternoon glare and swept the windshield wipers over the windshield of the small Peugeot for the hundredth time that day. A fine grime of sand mixed with heavy diesel particles firmly adhered to the glass and served as a coarse abrasive that had scratched the windshield in a neat arc circumscribed by the wiper blades.

He cursed his luck at having found himself behind a convoy of Syrian military vehicles headed for Damascus. A three-hour journey in the cool of the morning had been turned into a full day of misery when he found himself pulling up behind the slow moving line of trucks and various other vehicles. Incredibly, he had been the only other vehicle on the highway, making him the first in line behind the huge Soviet-made truck that was at the end of the convoy. More than once he had attempted to pull into the other lane of the narrow highway and pass the convoy, thus relieving himself of the necessity of breathing air fouled by the exhaust of the truck. Each time he had pulled out of traffic he had been waved back by two of the soldiers riding in the rear of the truck's open bed. No doubt the bastards were enjoying their game, he grimly thought.

He had been tempted earlier in the day to just run by them in the car, trusting that the speed of the vehicle would carry him past before they had time to react. He had attempted to sweep the Peugeot around them only once. When he applied the accelerator the little car sputtered and refused to gain speed. After that the soldiers had smiled and patted their weapons. He had settled back for a long ride to Damascus and resigned himself to the fact that he would have to abort the first meeting and rendezvous with his control at a secondary location previously agreed upon.

He gained the outskirts of the city, pulling onto a smaller road and taking a circuitous route into the heart of Damascus. He parked the Peugeot in a lot behind a government building and walked through one of the crowded markets careful to observe the traffic behind him and see if anyone was following. When he was certain he was alone he went to a small restaurant he knew, discreetly located in an alley behind the fish market, and ordered a meal.

As he sat waiting for the food and reading the paper that had been brought to him he considered his situation. The delay caused by the convoy was an inconvenience but was actually little more than that. If he chose to meet his control tomorrow at the secondary rendezvous the man would act as though the things he would request were being paid for out of his personal account.

In reality the man was not so much of a control as a logistics officer whose mission it was to support the Syrian as he operated in the field. To accomplish this he had been given an air-conditioned office in one of the newer districts of Damascus and a staff of officers and senior enlisted men who understood the logistics system of the Syrian military and government. In actuality the man viewed his job as something of a reward for his years of faithful field service. The Syrian was sure that he and his staff operated a very lucrative black market operation with the goods they "removed" from government warehouses under the guise of supplying officers in the field. Very few questions were asked of men in the position of the logistics officer. His Special Branch identification would silence almost anyone who questioned him, and for those individuals not intimidated by his identification, a percentage of the earnings from the sale of the stolen goods would suffice.

The Syrian continued to read his paper, scanning the busy street for signs of his control officer. Precisely on the hour he saw the man making his way up the crowded street, frequently checking behind himself to ascertain if he was being followed. The Syrian watched with a bemused expression on his face as the man arrived at the appointed spot and checked his watch. Satisfied that he was indeed at the appropriate place and there at the specified hour the man began to pace up and down the sidewalk. The Syrian sighed in disgust. To even the most casual observer it would be apparent that the man was meeting someone. The only saving grace was that this fellow was so old, and so innocent looking, that no one would suspect him of being associated with an intelligence operation. The Syrian knew that anyone passing him on the street would be more likely to assume he was someone's grandfather, perhaps late for a luncheon with a favored son or daughter.

He decided then to wait until the man had remained at the rendezvous the specified quarter of an hour and then follow him away from the designated meeting place. This would allow the Syrian to determine if the man had been followed, and if so, by whom.

At precisely fifteen minutes past the hour the man turned and walked down the street in the direction from which he had arrived. The Syrian settled the bill and was pleased to note that no surveillance team followed the officer away from the area. For now, at least, he could be reasonably certain of the cooperation and support of his superiors, however unwillingly it might be given by some of them.

The Syrian casually followed the logistics officer down the street and out of the souk. With a few quick steps he was beside the man who continued on his way without noticing the Syrian. He took the man's elbow in a friendly gesture that attracted no notice from passersby. "Hello," he smiled. "It's always a pleasure to see you, my friend."

"Hello," said the man, and the Syrian thought he detected an undercurrent of fear in the man's voice. "Perhaps we could go somewhere it would be possible to have a quiet conversation?" the man asked.

He smiled again. "Of course. If you will follow me I think I know just the place." As he guided the man down the street he quickly ran his hands over the man's sport coat and located the small automatic pistol in a holster under the arm. He feigned a look of surprise and clucked his tongue, saying, "I'm surprised that you don't trust me, Mohammed. To think, a pistol?" He shook his head and added, "I should be offended were we not such good friends."

The officer quickly regained his composure and answered, "There are thieves about in these areas at night. You would be well advised to carry a pistol yourself, my friend." The Syrian searched the face of the older man and wondered if there were a not so subtle warning in the man's response. He was unable to decide if the man was being clever or merely trying to justify his having a weapon. He smiled and asked, "Is there a reason why you think I should have a pistol in Damascus? Other than the thieves?"

The man shrugged and the corners of his eyes crinkled. "There are always reasons for a man to carry a pistol. Some have better reasons than others, my friend." The old man hesitated then added, "Perhaps those of us in this business always have a reason to carry a weapon. You might be wise to do so, especially in these times when the thieves grow more clever." The Syrian smiled slightly, enjoying the exchange. "Would you mind terribly, Mohammed, if I borrowed your pistol for the time being? I seem to have left mine elsewhere."

Mohammed shrugged again and said, "It is as you wish. After all, it is my job to supply you as you ask. And you have so seldom asked for anything that I should feel ashamed not to give what you ask now. Particularly since it is so small an item." Mohammed turned down a dark narrow street as the Syrian guided him and then removed his holster with its pistol and two magazines. The Syrian nodded toward the street and they resumed walking along the crowded boulevard that was filled with men seeking their various pleasures.

They continued in silence for a few moments as the Syrian considered his situation. Finally he asked, "Will my current request be a problem for you?"

Mohammed sighed, "It is not a matter of the request itself being a problem. The materials you have asked for are in Damascus, and they have been packaged as you have asked. There is currently an ample supply of these materials, thanks to our Czechoslovakian comrades. I have arranged for you to take shipment of them at your convenience. All you have to do is give me the address of the destination, or arrange for their transport yourself."

"I understand," said the Syrian. "Perhaps arranging the shipment will be a problem for you. I can do that myself, through other channels. You have done quite enough, my friend. I am grateful to you."

Mohammed stared straight ahead, speaking softly. "I think, my friend, that you are not aware of just how grave the situation is in Damascus. Certainly you have been away a long time."

"You are suggesting that I return to Damascus?"

Mohammed shook his head. "No. That would not be wise at this time. But there are certain considerations that you should be aware of. Certain events that may concern you."

"I see," said the Syrian. "Perhaps you could be of assistance to me in this area. That is, if it isn't asking too much of you."

Mohammed shook his head and continued, "I am an old man. Soon I will be eligible for my pension. Life seems quite different from the perspective of old age. I would prefer to live to play with my grandchildren." He sighed and looked at the Syrian, then added, "I no longer have the energy or the inclination to hate my enemies. Perhaps it is my age, or just a lack of a certain indefinable passion for one's work. I am no longer as certain of things as I once was in my youth." Mohammed cast another furtive glance at the Syrian then continued, "You are a very good officer. Perhaps the best I have seen. Certainly the best that is currently in the field for us. It would be a shame for you to end your career so soon."

The Syrian was puzzled. Obviously the old man knew more than he was saying, and more than the Syrian had initially thought. The problem now was to extract the information in such a way as to not frighten him into silence. "Perhaps, my friend, you could help me to ensure that my career is not unexpectedly interrupted."

For a few minutes the two continued in silence. They walked together down the street dodging groups of men in their expensive foreign clothing and Western-style shoes. Without looking at the Syrian, Mohammed began, "You should be aware that the size of your request has created, speculation, shall we say, as to the nature of your next target?" The Syrian cocked an eyebrow as the old man continued, "This speculation has at times been somewhat less than friendly in its nature. It has not fallen on deaf ears at certain higher levels than you and I might normally be privileged to have access to. I believe you understand my meaning?"

The Syrian nodded. "Certainly," he said. "And am I to believe that this might create a problem in one or more aspects of the operation I have planned?"

"I wouldn't know any details. But certainly a man such as yourself, with the background and experience you have, would have an idea of the type of problems this might cause." Mohammed paused. "The possibilities, it would seem, are limitless given the current conditions in your area of operations. We have many enemies, and their vigilance is unwavering. You, too, should remain vigilant. It is the prudent course."

The Syrian nodded his head indicating that he understood. As he slowed his pace he turned toward a small souk where a number of taxi drivers waited for the young men who would exit the club district after a night of entertaining themselves. "I believe we will be able to find taxis for ourselves nearby," he said. As he walked the older man to a waiting taxi he kissed him on both cheeks in the Gallic manner and said, "Thank you, you have been very kind."

Mohammed shrugged and said, "It is as nothing, I am afraid. You have served well. Better than those who would not have you serve longer. I should be careful if I were you." As he entered the taxi Mohammed handed the Syrian a slip of paper and added, "The things you have asked for are located at that address. Others, who may not wish you to be successful, know of its location and are watching for you to retrieve it. An identical shipment is located at the address on the reverse side, and if you act quickly no one will know of its existence. I hope that you will need only one of the shipments to complete your mission. Good luck, my friend."

The Syrian stood impassively as the taxi pulled away from the curb with Mohammed inside. It was now quite obvious to him that his request for the extraordinary amount of explosives had attracted unwelcome attention. If Mohammed could be trusted, and the Syrian had no reason not to trust him, then his mission might indeed be in jeopardy. The problem now would be to get the bales of explosive safely from Damascus to his staging area in Beirut. Once in Beirut he was confident that he could move it to another area and construct the device that he would use against the Americans. The key would be to act quickly, Mohammed had made that plain enough.

CHAPTER

25

The Syrian had spent the early morning refining his mental image of the plan. Despite the warning given to him the previous evening by Mohammed he was determined to go ahead. He reasoned that his plan was sound, if anything it was so ambitious that no one would believe him even if he were to reveal the details of it.

He had decided, after much thought and his reconnaissance of the Marine compound, to load a large truck painted with the color scheme of the Oger Liban construction vehicles with bales of plastic explosive. The charges, each weighing some 250 kilos, would be individually wired with its own detonator. The detonators would be cylinders of explosive gas under maximum compression. By utilizing this scheme he reasoned that he could effect a virtual simultaneous detonation of the numerous individual bales of explosive, thereby taking full advantage of their destructive potential. His scheme called for the truck to arrive at the airport construction site early on a Sunday morning, a time when he knew the Marines to be least vigilant. As a further means of camouflaging the purpose of the truck he would cover the gas cylinders and bales of explosive with a layer of dirt. The truck would appear as no more than a delivery of fill dirt being brought into the construction site.

Although he had never before detonated such a large charge he could find no reason why it might not succeed. His real concern was the amount of explosive necessary to bring down the entire building used by the Marines as their headquarters. He had determined the amount to be used by extrapolating the amount used for the bombing of the American Embassy. After recalling his failure to destroy the entire embassy building, he had added another six bales of explosives as a safety measure.

He had decided to spend his day acquiring transport for the explosives to Beirut. After a light lunch he returned to his room and dressed in his uniform, smiling as he fastened the shoulder boards of a lieutenant colonel onto his uniform jacket. He also carefully pinned on the insignia that marked him as a member of one of the elite commando battalions of the Syrian Army. He was confident that with his rank, his commando insignia, and a little judicious bluffing he would acquire the necessary vehicles and personnel to transport his explosives without a great deal of inquiry.

By late afternoon the city was oppressively hot and most of its inhabitants were relaxing in the cool interiors of their homes or shops. Very little traffic crowded the normally busy street in front of the district headquarters of the army transportation corps. The Syrian walked toward the front gate and approached the sentry with a meaningful stride. The man stood to attention outside the small guard booth as the Syrian touched the brim of his uniform cap in salute. He paused briefly in front of the open door of the guardhouse and glared at the sergeant inside. The man was fast asleep, his feet propped on the small desk in front of an even smaller electric fan that buzzed noisily. Without waiting for the man to awaken he stepped inside the walled courtyard of the building and proceeded toward the front door.

He instantly decided he had been wise to change into his uniform. All soldiers respect rank, and that would serve him well with any luck. He approached the front desk in the lobby where three enlisted men sat behind a low wooden table. Returning their salutes he asked for the commanding officer. The senior sergeant present stiffened and asked if he could assist the Syrian. The Syrian froze his face in a mask of indignation and repeated his question. The sergeant held his gaze briefly then indicated a hallway leading off to the Syrian's left. He then asked if the Syrian would wait while he telephoned the office of his commanding officer. While the sergeant dialed the number the Syrian strode off in the direction indicated by the sergeant.

By the time he reached the office of the commander, whom he

noted was a full colonel, a second sergeant stood in front of the door leading to the commander's office. The Syrian locked his gaze on the man and asked sarcastically, "Sergeant, do you know how to greet a senior officer?"

"Yes, Excellency," said the sergeant as he locked his body in a position of rigid attention. As the Syrian started to move past the man he saw the sergeant's eyes shift warily to the doorway and the man hesitatingly move toward it. He looked again at the sergeant and raised an eyebrow. Obviously the man had been told to prevent him from barging in on the commanding officer. The Syrian glanced into the small anteroom before him and noted that it was empty. Only a small desk with a telephone and typewriter was in the room.

In the same instant that he began to move past the sergeant and walk into the office of the commander the Syrian understood why the man had risked challenging a senior officer. He nodded at the sergeant with the slightest hint of a knowing smile and said, "Very well, Sergeant." The man nodded in return and a look of relief spread over his face. The Syrian stepped quietly into the small anteroom and studied the equipment on the desk momentarily. He pressed the button on the intercom system and immediately the room was filled with the sounds of lovemaking from the interior of the colonel's office.

The Syrian held the button down and listened as he again looked at the sergeant. The man stood impassively near the outer door. He released the button and approached the sergeant. "Sergeant, you will remove yourself to the nearest guard post. Am I understood?"

"Yes, sir. Sir, if I may . . ."

"I am aware that this is your post, and I am sure that your commander appreciates your discretion. However, I am a senior officer and I have just given you an order. Do you need to be further instructed?"

"No, Excellency. It is just that . . ."

"Sergeant, I have given you an order. Are you questioning my authority?"

"No, Excellency."

"Then go. I will explain to your commanding officer."

The Syrian watched as the sergeant walked down the hallway and waited at a discreet distance. He glanced around the small office, noting the stacks of paperwork and the bulging file cabinets. The Syrian knew that any man who daily worked in such an office was more a bureaucrat than a soldier. That would make his task easier, he reasoned.

The colonel's office door opened and a young woman stepped into the foyer, straightening her hair and smoothing her skirt. The Syrian ignored her as she walked past. He walked directly into the colonel's office. As he closed the door behind him he glared at the colonel who attempted to act as though nothing had happened.

"Who are you?" demanded the colonel. "And what is the meaning of this intrusion into my office?"

The Syrian hesitated only briefly before throwing his commando identification card onto the man's desk followed by the set of orders he had created the night before. As he glared at the colonel, the man picked up his identification and studied the photograph of the Syrian. "The telephone number of the authorizing unit is on the last page of my orders, Colonel. Since I have been delayed somewhat by your activities this morning, I suggest you be prompt in securing whatever authorization you think is necessary before detailing the men and equipment specified by my orders. I do not have unlimited patience."

"How dare you address a superior in such a manner! Who is your commanding officer?" demanded the colonel.

The Syrian leaned across the colonel's desk, placing both palms on the man's papers and said in a menacing tone, "If you really want to know, Colonel, I suggest you telephone the number on my orders and ask to speak with Colonel Hasni. He will be more than happy to explain to you the necessity of my battalion borrowing one of your trucks for a few days. While you have him on the line, you might also explain why you have delayed one of his officers who has been sent to you to accomplish what would appear to be a task easily handled by a junior sergeant. Perhaps while you are dialing the number you can think about these things, and with any luck the colonel won't be too busy to take your call. I am sure he thinks highly of our comrades in the transportation corps."

He straightened up and backed away from the man, opening his palm and slowly indicating the telephone with his left hand. When the colonel made no move to pick the instrument up the Syrian added, "A judicious decision on your part, Colonel. After all, you have many trucks in your command, but only one career to think of. Am I right?"

The colonel said nothing but angrily picked up the orders and began flipping through them. The Syrian nodded as the man initialed in the proper spaces and signed his name to the last page, tearing away and keeping the correct copies for himself. As he finished, the Syrian said,

"Good. Now there is one further matter. I will require your discretion regarding my request for one of your vehicles. You will personally see to it that the men and vehicles are available promptly and that they are competent. No one is to know of my request," said the Syrian with obvious contempt on his face.

"Take whatever you need, Lieutenant Colonel. Then get out of my command. Don't think that every man in the Syrian Army lives in fear of the almighty commando battalions."

The Syrian smiled and said, "That is precisely what I intend to do. And let me assure you of one thing, my amorous little Colonel. If you so much as think about denying me the men or equipment I have requested for this mission, I can assure you that Colonel Hasni will be the least of your worries. Am I understood?"

The Syrian watched as the man slowly nodded. He didn't want to push him too far. For his plan to succeed, it would be necessary for this colonel to grant his request with as few delays as possible. While the authority to take the men and vehicle would be granted, if it were too slow in coming it might create problems. Problems he wished to avoid.

He checked the paperwork one last time to see that there were no errors that might prohibit the issuing of the men or equipment. Satisfied that everything was indeed in good order, he smiled at the colonel who sat behind his desk and said, "Very good, my Colonel. You have served the army well today." The Syrian spun on one heel and left the room, careful to close the door behind him.

He noticed the absence of the secretary in the small anteroom and passed quickly through to the corridor, noting the sergeant had returned to his post. He nodded and strode off down the corridor without further speaking to the man. As he gained the outer courtyard, he noted that the sergeant was still asleep in the guard post by the gate. He casually saluted the other guard, stepped through the gate, and flagged a taxi, confident that his plan would go forward.

CHAPTER

26

H e stood on the elevated walkway and surveyed the bundles of explosives. On each wooden packing sled a set of four crates filled with plastic explosive had been placed around a cylinder of compressed gas. Each cylinder was fitted with an internal detonator that could be electrically fired by a single switch.

Later today the technicians from Damascus would load the pallets of explosives and their detonators into the trailer using one of the small forklifts left in the abandoned warehouse by its previous owners. Once the trailer was loaded with its deadly cargo he would have it moved into the large dock area just outside the warehouse. There he planned on covering the explosives with a layer of earth, filling the trailer just enough so that the detonators remained exposed, enabling him to complete the wiring. He would do this under the cover of darkness lest the Americans and their satellites detected him during the operation.

After the cylinders had all been wired and the circuits checked he would cover everything with a few inches of soil. Although an observant sentry would question why earth was being hauled into the site, the driver could explain that it was needed to fill a portion of the excavation underway at the airport. The Syrian was betting that the vehicle would not be given more than a casual glance as it crossed the checkpoints and entered the airport terminal area.

If for some unforeseen reason he was forced to abandon the vehicle with its cargo of explosives, with the dirt acting as camouflage he at least had a chance of avoiding detection and recovering it intact. It would appear to the casual observer as nothing more than another vehicle left by its owner until it was needed. He was planning on acting quickly. The only delay had been training the boy to drive the large truck.

On the actual day of the mission he planned on entering the terminal area dressed as a maintenance worker. His plan called for an attack early on Sunday morning, a time when there would be few, if any, passengers in the terminal. No one would question an unkempt man in a dirty green smock carrying a broom and dustbin. After the detonation he could escape in the general confusion.

He had initially been concerned about entering the terminal area as the only road leading away from it ran immediately west of the Marine headquarters. He preferred to leave the area by walking away from the target, but in this instance that would not be possible. He would have to be in the terminal during the operation. It was the only public access building close enough to the target to ensure that the wireless detonator would not fail.

He had also been concerned about the effect of the blast. The amount of explosive was huge. Much larger than anything he had previously used, even on a test range. It would be difficult to place himself close enough to the bomb to ensure detonation without running the risk of injury. He would have to find some sort of shelter to use when the bomb was detonated. It would also be necessary to pack his ears with wadding to protect them against the concussion and noise.

He had reviewed the plan for the past week, looking for the faults. As always the weak point was the driver. There was always a measure of chance where a human being was concerned. He had toyed with the idea of detonating the truck as it passed near the Marine headquarters on its way south to the terminal entrance. He was sure that the explosion would greatly harm the building occupied by the Marines. There was little doubt that it would kill any Marines who happened to be exposed on the western side of the building, but he needed a larger victory. And he sensed that he could have it.

This must be his master stroke. If he succeeded in destroying the headquarters of the Marines and killing many of their officers then the political leaders would have to withdraw the rest of the Marines from Lebanon. The French and the Italians would follow.

He had already prepared a communiqué to be given to a friendly Lebanese journalist after the bombing. He would claim a great victory for Muslims everywhere in the name of the Ayatollah Khomeini. The American people had already been conditioned by their journalists and government to believe that Iran was little more than a seething cauldron of terrorists and religious fanatics who lusted for the blood of innocent Americans. They would be more than willing to accept one more terrorist incident committed by Iranians for the Ayatollah.

He envisioned himself returning to Damascus in triumph. There would be another promotion if he were successful. The thought occurred to him that should anyone ask him what reward he would like for having achieved such a brilliant success he would not know what to ask. He had no ambition beyond accomplishing the missions assigned to him and remaining far enough afield so as not to become one of the petty, squabbling bureaucrats that hovered around the military headquarters buildings in Damascus.

He smiled wryly to himself. He would probably just remain in Damascus and await the assignment of another mission. He realized that he was happiest when he found himself months into a mission and far removed from Damascus and all of its intrigue. He had become, if not a loner, then self-contained in almost every aspect of his nature. He wasn't sure if the change in his personality had been dictated by his assignment to the intelligence field or had just been a natural facet of his character.

In any event he had no desire to return to Damascus for any longer than was necessary. After the bombing there would be a few hours of confusion in Beirut. What remained of the Lebanese Internal Security Force would make a show of throwing up roadblocks and pulling civilians from their cars under the pretext of looking for the bomber. The ISF troopers would extort a sum of money from the unfortunate drivers and if the amount was sufficient the driver would be released unharmed.

He had no intention of being caught in any such random checkpoint. He would immediately go to ground in one of the villas he occupied in the fashionable Christian suburbs of the city. These areas would not be searched and he would wait there until the hunt was called off. At most it would last a week.

On the day of the attack he noted with a feeling of satisfaction the inactivity of the Christian quarter where he had taken up residence the past week. Sundays were an inviolable day of rest for the Christian residents of Beirut. He had watched the American Marines enough to know that they too observed the Christian Sabbath as a day of rest. That factor had been carefully weighed in choosing this day for the attack.

He dressed in the plain green smock that would identify him as a porter at the airport and drove quickly through a hushed city. He parked the car in an area north of the airport and walked the last few kilometers to the terminal. He had anticipated no difficulty in making his way to the terminal itself, and found to no great surprise that he was right. No one would think twice to check the identity papers of a simple janitor on his way to work.

The Syrian stood in front of the terminal in the early morning and made a pretense of looking for litter and cigarette butts that he swept into the bag hanging from his shoulder. The sun was not yet fully over the mountains and the morning air held a chill. From where he stood he could look north up the broad boulevard and past the Marine head-quarters.

He noted with satisfaction the casual attitude displayed by the young Lebanese standing their post in front of the terminal building. He had walked past the troopers in front of the Marine barracks on his way to the terminal earlier that morning and not one of the Lebanese had so much as given him a second glance. They were all very young and obviously had little experience in the military. He had reasoned that they were recent conscripts and accordingly had been given the early morning tour of duty when little traffic could be expected.

He had casually walked past their checkpoint in his dank smelling coveralls and eyed the Marine sentries posted along the fence separating the Marine building from the sidewalk and then the boulevard. They appeared alert and watchful, but he was confident that they would have no reason to fire on his vehicle when it drove past them in the next few minutes. It would appear to all the world as just one more construc-tion vehicle going about its business in a city trying to rebuild after more than ten years of civil war.

The Syrian had decided earlier that morning that the terminal offered no real position from which he could safely detonate the explosives. He would be forced to stand out front and trigger the device at the proper moment. He estimated that he was roughly five hundred meters from the point on the building where he expected the boy to place the truck. He would do his best to scramble into the lobby of the terminal at the critical moment, but he was worried about the distance between his transmitter and the receiver wired to the explosives.

At this distance there was a greater chance that the signal would be too weak to trigger the device. If the driver failed to do it himself the Marines would kill him while he sat fastened in the seat of the truck. That would force him to close on the truck and again try the remote transmitter, hoping that none of the Marine sentries noticed him edging closer to the compound.

He scanned the ground between the terminal and the Marine building for the hundredth time looking for a likely way to approach. All he saw was the broad boulevard stretching away to the north with its tree-lined sidewalks on either side. He would find precious little cover there. More likely a nervous sentry would shoot him before he could cover half the distance to the truck. Even if he got close enough to detonate the device, and he survived the ensuing blast, the debris falling back to earth would almost certainly kill him.

Without thinking he shook his head and smiled at the irony. To die at the moment of his greatest victory. The irony would not have been lost on Farouck, he knew.

He continued to sweep nonexistent bits of trash into his bin as the truck pulled slowly onto the boulevard heading due south toward the terminal. His first warning of its approach was a faint grinding of gears as the boy shifted into low and bore down on the LAF checkpoint.

The Syrian tensed and felt a current of fear stab through his intestines as the young guard stepped into the roadway and prepared to wave the boy to a stop. The big truck's engine compressed as the boy lowered the transmission another gear and the brakes emitted a dry scraping sound that was audible to the Syrian almost a full kilometer distant.

He silently hoped that the boy wouldn't lose his nerve and attempt to run the checkpoint. The Lebanese soldiers on duty weren't much older than the driver and certainly would not think to wake one of the older more experienced sergeants in order to check a single vehicle. His breath caught in his throat as another soldier emerged from the sandbagged shack that served as a guardhouse and stared in the direction of the truck.

He watched intently as the second man regarded the truck, apparently curious at its appearance so early on a Sunday morning. Ultimately success or failure rested on just such unpredictable moments of chance. Months of planning would be wasted if the guard decided to stop the vehicle and its inexperienced driver. The Syrian tensed, knowing that the guard had only seconds left in which to decide to let the truck pass unchallenged. He stood motionless. Recalling his last conversation with Ahmud, he heard himself breath the word *"Inshallah"* as he felt for the transmitter with his left hand. Before he could locate the trigger on the device the guard raised the red-and-white striped beam that served as a barricade and the truck glided past the checkpoint. The truck continued smoothly past the target building with its perimeter of Marine guards who watched it go by.

Inside the Marine compound Griffin turned his head as the big diesel approached, the straining of its motor breaking the quiet of the morning. He held up a hand to stop Slocum from speaking and said, "Just a second, Bobby." Slocum stopped eating his breakfast and followed Griffin's gaze as he focused his attention on the broad boulevard beyond the iron fence which surrounded the Marine compound.

"Where do you suppose he's going so early on a Sunday morning, Bobby?" asked Griffin, nodding to indicate the big Mercedes diesel that was grinding its way south on the boulevard.

Slocum looked up briefly from his eggs and cast a casual glance in the direction of the truck. "Probably just over by the terminal. The Lesbos got some kind of construction going on over there. Rebuilding one of the runways or something. They use those big trucks to haul away the concrete they're breaking up."

Griffin continued to stare at the truck as the driver shifted gears. He noted the strain of the engine to take the load and the heavy black cloud of smoke emitted by the exhaust stack. Griffin had spent enough time around the docks to know that this truck was fully loaded and the driver was struggling to accelerate. "Bobby, something ain't right here. That guy is loaded and he's headed into the construction zone. Besides, it's Sunday. Why is he here anyway? He should be off today."

Slocum again looked toward the big truck. "Maybe he's a Muslim. Don't they have a different holy day from us?"

"I don't know," said Griffin, his instincts telling him something was wrong, "but he's the only son of a bitch at work today. Nobody else is down at the construction site. There's nobody to unload this guy when he gets where he's going." Griffin moved from under the eaves of the building and stood on the bench seat of one of the tables to get a better look at the driver. He could tell that the driver was very young, probably still in his teens. He sat stiffly in the seat of the big truck and stared straight ahead.

Something in the demeanor of the driver triggered an alert in Griffin. He didn't have the casual manner affected by every other truck driver Griffin had ever known. Griffin could clearly see, even at this distance, that the driver had both hands on the wheel in the classic position of the novice driver. The thought immediately struck him that no novice belonged behind the wheel of a truck that size.

The vehicle began to draw abreast of their position as Griffin ran toward the fence hoping to get a better look at the truck and its driver. As he vaulted to the top of the low retaining wall and sprinted toward the fence the truck drew even with him and he stopped and stared at the boy. The machine gunner on duty had already noticed the truck and as it passed he slowly tracked it with his weapon.

With a mounting sense of dread Griffin concentrated on the young driver. He could now plainly see that he was a boy in his teens. His mind searched for a plausible explanation. The thought occurred to him that maybe the boy was driving the truck for his father. He glanced quickly again toward the construction site farther south and confirmed that it was devoid of any activity.

In an unconscious motion he took his rifle from his shoulder and loaded a magazine into the well. As he charged the weapon he saw the driver looking nervously in his direction. For a brief moment Griffin thought the driver was going to smile. Then he saw through the smile and detected the deadly purpose behind it. Griffin knew then that the driver wasn't smiling. He was laughing.

By the time Griffin brought the weapon into his shoulder the truck had accelerated toward the terminal and he no longer had a line of sight to the driver. He yelled for the lance corporal manning the machine gun to charge his weapon and follow. With relief he noticed that the man didn't hesitate to abandon his post and followed him at a sprint across the compound.

Griffin estimated it was forty yards back to the building and another twenty to a place where he would have an angle of fire on the truck if it pulled into the lot south of the Marine compound. As he ran he yelled for Slocum and the cooks to get their rifles and fire at the truck. He heard one of the cooks screaming for the sergeant of the guard as he cleared the corner of the building and saw to his horror that a series of plywood buildings erected by the battalion engineers to serve as foul weather chow halls now blocked his line of sight across the parking lot.

Griffin sprinted along the face of the building for a glimpse of the truck. As he drew even with the guard shacks some two hundred meters south he noticed the Marines on duty step outside the small sandbag bunkers and stare in the direction of the truck, obviously attempting to get a better look at the vehicle. Griffin guessed that the two young Marines now watching the big truck circle the lot and gain speed were puzzled by the appearance of the vehicle on a quiet Sunday morning.

He began screaming for them to fire at the truck and he noticed one of them turn to look in his direction. The sentry raised his radio above his head, obviously wanting to communicate with Griffin but puzzled as to why there was no response from him over the small radio. Realizing that the man would not be able to understand him at this distance Griffin settled his rifle in his shoulder and began tracking the vehicle.

He cursed as the driver took a course parallel to his own position and moved in and out of his line of sight. As he squinted into the iron sights of his rifle Griffin heard Slocum moving into place with the machine gun and the sentry he had ordered away from his post on the west end of the compound. He struggled to steady his breathing in order to level the sights on the truck. In the same instant he acquired the cab of the big truck he realized that once he fired the sentries on post would follow his example and begin firing.

He fired his first round and saw the windshield of the Mercedes diesel shatter. In a brief instant Griffin saw the driver reflexively duck, then recover and swing the truck in a steady arc toward the battalion headquarters. He settled his sights on the driver's chest and waited for his moment. As he waited for Slocum and the cooks to begin firing he fired his second round. Griffin briefly looked over the sights of the M-16 and saw that he had hit the driver high in the shoulder.

He again began tracking the truck with his rifle as the driver struggled to regain control over the vehicle and bring it back on a course that would roll it into the building. To his relief he heard the others begin to fire, the machine gun walking its rounds toward the big truck as it advanced on the Marine compound.

To his horror he realized that the machine gunner had quit firing almost as soon as he had begun. Griffin correctly surmised that the gunner was afraid the rounds would go wide and strike the sentries in the parking lot. Without taking his eyes from his sights Griffin screamed for Slocum to get the gun up. In his peripheral vision he saw Slocum advance on the gun and shove the gunner out of the way. As he fired his third shot Griffin distinctly heard the splatter of lead against the denser metal of the truck's grill and saw chips of paint fly from the front of the truck as Slocum's fire began to strike the vehicle.

The truck continued to swing wildly from side to side as it advanced on the headquarters building. Griffin was able to discern that the driver was seriously hurt by the fire of the Marines. As the truck drew to within fifty meters of the compound the boy was slumped over the wheel, his left arm hanging limply at his side.

Griffin estimated that he would have time for one more shot before the truck would strike the gate and roll the final few meters into the building. He had no doubt as to what the truck was carrying. He sighted carefully on the top of the boy's head, which rested on the large cream-colored steering wheel. Through his sights he could see the boy was still attempting to steer the vehicle through the gate. Griffin held his breath and began squeezing the trigger of his rifle.

An instant before the rifle went off Griffin saw the boy raise his head off the steering wheel and look in the direction of the building. He knew the boy was checking his heading and would attempt to make a course correction with his remaining good arm. A moment later the round from Griffin's rifle caught the boy at the base of his neck and flung him backward against the rear wall of the cab. The boy's body slammed into the metal skin of the cab, then rebounded forward onto the steering wheel.

The force of the body hitting the wheel altered the course of the truck slightly to the west, throwing it off its course for the center of the building. A mere fifty yards away Griffin was now sure that the driver of the vehicle was dead. He shifted the aim of his rifle for an instant toward the trailer, his mind rapidly rejecting the idea of firing into the load of explosives. Griffin knew that a detonation this close to the building would result in a terrific explosion that would probably destroy the battle-damaged building.

Realizing that his rifle would be useless against the truck he decided to take cover, screaming for Slocum and the others to do the same. As he ran east along the face of the building his eye caught the entrance to the building's basement.

Griffin turned in time to see Slocum and the others head west toward the boulevard and the sandbagged positions occupied by the sentries. He watched helplessly as the truck slammed into the iron fence some fifty meters from the headquarters building. The driver's side wheel caught the low stone footing of the fence and the truck jumped wildly over the low wall, tearing through the fence with a screech of metal. As first the cab and then the trailer cleared the fence Griffin saw the body of the driver being tossed limply from side to side. He ran for the shelter of the basement as the truck continued toward the Marines with only a slight loss of momentum.

CHAPTER
27

The truck cleared the fence and rolled across the compound, striking the building near its center and wedging itself under the concrete eaves. The driver's compartment of the cab sheared off on impact and allowed the vehicle to penetrate to the heavy metal bulkhead at the front of the trailer. The forward motion of the truck was arrested as this bulkhead struck the concrete that formed the roof of the first story and the floor of the mezzanine level.

The tremendous noise of the impact echoed heavily across the runway and Marines inside the building woke thinking the headquarters had suffered a direct hit from an incoming artillery round. A split second later the Syrian detonated the load of explosives, and the resulting blast vaporized the bulk of the vehicle instantaneously.

The shock wave sheared off the meter-thick concrete supports holding the building as the structure rose off its supports for a brief instant, propelled by the force of the explosion. Before the building could begin its inevitable collapse the shock wave had raced up the hollow interior of the building and further weakened what little internal support remained.

Marines standing post on the roof of the headquarters experienced the sickening sensation of rising rapidly for a few inches with the building before eardrums and sinuses were punctured by the concussion. As large chunks of concrete rocketed skyward the building began to descend into the void left by the disintegration of its supports.

The mezzanine level collapsed onto the cut granite flooring of the ground level, crushing everything beneath it under tons of concrete and decorative marble. The battalion armorers, cooks, and hospital corpsman not killed by the blast died in the first seconds after the explosion. The sergeant of the guard, who had seen the truck approach from his ground level post and run out of the building to fire on the vehicle, was blown clear of the building and came to rest near the gate through which the bomber had steered his vehicle.

The remaining three floors began to collapse onto the rubble of the mezzanine, as dozens of men were crushed to death in their sleep. Even those who had been awakened at the sound of Griffin's firing had not had time to don their gear and get out of the building. Entire platoons, billeted together in the custom of Marines since their inception, died in an instant before the sound of the explosion had rolled across the runways and reached their comrades in the rifle companies which ringed the airport in a protective semicircle.

Clouds of dust began to rise above the collapsing building as chunks of concrete blown clear of the building reached the apex of their flight and descended on the Marine compound with deadly force. Men billeted in sandbagged tents surrounding the Battalion Landing Team headquarters were struck by falling debris or deadly missiles formed by the shattering of the concrete walls and hurled horizontally across the compound. More than a few of these men were saved by the protective barrier of sandbags that had been placed around their canvas tents. Others suffered fatal wounds from the deadly projectiles.

The building began to settle onto the remnants of its foundation as a mushroom-shaped plume of dust, pulverized concrete, and debris rose hundreds of meters into the air. To the Marines standing watch on the perimeter of the airport the BLT appeared to have been hit by a small nuclear device. Men in the rifle companies, unaware of the extent of the damage to the battalion headquarters that disappeared in the growing cloud of dust, reported to their respective commanders that the BLT headquarters was under attack.

The alarm was sounded in the rifle companies and the troops roused and told to stand to general quarters as frantic company radio operators tried in vain to raise the battalion combat operations center over the tactical radio net. Fifteen minutes after the detonation of the Syrian's bomb a radio operator from the MAU headquarters building, located just one hundred meters north of the destroyed BLT building, broke onto the battalion net and advised the rifle companies and one battery of artillery that the BLT had been destroyed.

Company commanders unwilling to accept the word of an obviously shaken junior enlisted man then instructed the radio operator to have the Officer of the Day advise them of the situation at the BLT. To their horror the voice replied that he was indeed the Officer of the Day and that they should send Marines and any hospital corpsman ashore to the BLT area ASAP.

Platoon commanders quickly mobilized squads and sent them at double time across the runways of the airport. As the Marines in the relief parties drew near the building they were engulfed by a fine choking dust that made breathing difficult. The BLT continued to be obscured in this cloud until the squads were close enough to realize that the building was no longer standing. What remained was a pile of rubble approximately half the height of the building that had been there only minutes before.

The first Marines sent to the relief of their comrades left their company lines and headed west toward the cloud enveloping the BLT building. Company commanders listened over the radio net as officers at the MAU operations center called for the task force just offshore to send whatever medical personnel could be spared to assist with an unknown number of casualties.

Downs jogged at the head of first squad as they headed toward the BLT area. After concluding his testimony before the board of inquiry he had been returned to duty with the platoon. As the senior corporal in first squad he had been in charge of the squad in Griffin's absence. Like the rest of the battalion, Downs had been awakened that morning by the explosion, and stared in horror at the sight of what had been the BLT building. Within minutes of the explosion Staff Sergeant Whitney had ordered Downs to form up the squad and prepare to double-time across the runways to the BLT building and lend whatever assistance he could to the on-site commander. He had also been told to take two hospital corpsmen with him.

Downs glanced behind and looked at the two navy corpsmen. One of them was already struggling to maintain the pace of the Marines. Downs noted that his face was red and the front of his cammie blouse was soaked with sweat although they were less than halfway to the headquarters building.

Downs stepped out of the column and nodded for Ferris to maintain the pace as he fell back. From all directions he could see similar columns moving in the direction of the BLT. Here and there he heard the report of small arms fire or the echo of a shouted command. The airport remained strangely silent and Downs decided that the usually busy runways were either shut down due to the attack or there were no flights scheduled to arrive this early on a Sunday morning.

He looked at the hospital corpsman and noted the man's stumbling steps and ragged breathing. Glancing toward the cloud of dust that he knew concealed the BLT building, Downs judged the distance to be well over two thousand yards. A quick mental calculation told him the squad would have to cover a mile before reaching the compound. Even at its normal pace, not slowed by the corpsman, the squad wouldn't reach the area in less than seven or eight minutes. Already he could feel the pace slowing to that of the tiring corpsman.

He glanced again toward the company area and the distance covered seemed pitifully small. No sign of a jeep dispatched by the company commander to ferry the corpsman to the scene. Downs debated his options. If he abandoned the corpsman and jogged ahead with the squad they would reach the BLT a lot sooner. Given the looks of the cloud rising from what had been the BLT, a couple of minutes might make all the difference. There was also the possibility that the BLT had been hit by some sort of rocket fired at them by the Syrian Army. Maybe a SCUD or FROG. It might even be a prelude to an attack by local militia allied with the Syrians.

He also knew that there were going to be considerable casualties once they arrived. One corpsman could make a big difference in a situation like that. He looked again at the struggling corpsman and the man returned his stare. "I can't keep up, Corporal Downs. Can we slow it up just a little?"

Downs nodded at the man and said to Ferris who remained at the head of the column and continued to set the pace, "Bring it down just a little, Ferris. The Doc needs a break." Ferris nodded without saying anything and Downs realized that his eyes were locked straight ahead, fixed on the growing gray cloud. He knew that Ferris would slow the pace for only a minute or two, then he would gradually pick it back up to its previous level. Another glance at the struggling corpsman and Downs realized that the man would never make it to the BLT without long breaks to regain his wind.

He realized that just wouldn't be acceptable. Downs quickly searched his mind for an answer and caught himself asking what Griffin would do in a similar situation. He decided Griffin would automatically lighten the man's load. He turned and looked at Smith who jogged along smoothly behind the corpsman, "Smith, you and Samson take the Doc's gear." Downs noted the corpsman look at him and nod his head in thanks. Further back in the column was the other corpsman who had been detailed from second platoon and told to make the journey with his squad. Downs caught the man's eye and asked, "Can you make it if we pick it up?"

"Yeah, Corporal. I'm okay. I run almost every day. Let's get there, man." Downs grimly nodded his head and again looked at the corpsman. He detailed two Marines from the squad to escort the lone corpsman to the BLT area, instructing them to rejoin the squad after arriving. As the Marines and corpsman fell out of the small formation Downs said, "See that he gets to the BLT and then come find us. Don't kill him on the way over and if you see a vehicle heading across the runway for the BLT flag it down and throw him on board. Got that?"

The man nodded that he understood and Downs signaled to Ferris and the squad resumed its pace. When they were within a hundred yards of the wall of dust they heard the low rumbling coming from the building as tons of concrete continued to settle on itself. As the squad entered the cloud, fine particles of concrete pelted their helmets and flak jackets and clouds of dust made breathing difficult.

Downs ordered the squad to slow to a walk and gave the command to form a skirmish line. He was not sure of the situation at the BLT as the building continued to be hidden by the cloud of dust. One hundred yards into the brown fog Downs spotted the first Marine. The man was walking drunkenly toward them and Downs realized that he was suffering from shock. Without any order being given the remaining corpsman began to treat the man.

He halted the squad as the corpsman treated the young Marine. Downs squatted on his haunches by the man and noticed for the first time that a fine gray powder covered the ground. He touched his hand to the powder, hoping that it wasn't some chemical agent delivered by a Syrian warhead. He raised a finger to his nose and gently sniffed at the powder. He noticed Ferris staring at him and shrugged.

"What is it, Steve?"

"I don't know. But if it's some sort of chemical or something I'm a fucking goner. Try not to touch the shit, man. There's no telling what it might be."

Tiger rubbed his hand across the front of his flak jacket and said, "It ain't no chemical agent, Steve. This is concrete dust. I can tell by the smell. Besides, the air is full of it. If it was a chemical agent we would all be dead by now."

Downs realized instantly that Tiger was right. As the corpsman continued to treat the casualty he peered into the fog and wondered what his next move should be. He searched his memory and tried to recall the layout of the battalion headquarters and its perimeter guard posts. He knew that a wide boulevard ran north-south along the western limit of the compound. A battery of 155mm howitzers was set up north of the compound beyond the MAU headquarters and he guessed that they would send their own patrols down to report the situation at the BLT. The southern extreme of the BLT area was guarded by a line of sentries and beyond that was the terminal building at the southern end of the boulevard.

Downs decided to sweep slightly south along the southern end of the BLT compound and work his way west to the fence marking its western limit at the boulevard. He ordered the patrol forward and then remembered the casualty. "He'll have to come with us, Doc. I can't stop here. Just bring him along. Got that?"

The corpsman nodded and the patrol moved off. The stench of burning rubber overwhelmed them and they could plainly see several vehicles on fire near the heap of rubble marking the eastern edge of the BLT compound. As the small patrol drew closer to the BLT their pace quickened and Downs found himself virtually running forward.

The wind began to break up the cloud of dust that had settled over the whole area and Downs knew he would have to abandon his original plan. It was obvious that the BLT was down. From two hundred meters away he could begin to see the extent of the damage. He signaled for the radio handset and instantly keyed the mike. "Alpha Six, Alpha Six, this is Alpha One. Do you copy? Over."

"Roger, Alpha One. This is the Six Actual. Go ahead with your sit rep."

Downs instantly recognized the voice of the company commander, Captain Ward. He continued to keep pace with the squad and said, "Sir, the BLT is down. Everything, sir. The building has apparently been hit by something that just about destroyed it. We're two hundred meters out and we can see dead and wounded all over the place. We're proceeding toward the building now. No enemy in sight, sir. Over."

The young captain almost two kilometers distant peered across the runways and tried to see through the brown fog that blocked his view. One of his junior corporals had just confirmed what had been reported earlier by the MAU officer of the day. Still, it couldn't be as bad as they had reported. Both of them were making the situation out to be something close to total destruction of a four-story building by a single hit. He tried to imagine what kind of weapon could deliver that amount of destructive force and could only think of some sort of missile. He was fairly certain that the Syrian army had been pushed out of missile range by the Israeli army some weeks before.

His eyes searched the eastern sky for the telltale vapor trail that would mark the flight of such a missile. He saw none and wondered instead about Corporal Downs. Maybe he was just one more young NCO who was witnessing combat for the first time. It was possible that he had encountered some casualties and was already bordering on a state of shock himself. It happened. They were all young, the Marines in his command. The oldest of them might be twenty-four or twenty-five. He guessed Downs to be no older than twenty-one.

He thought carefully of what he would say next to Downs. He remembered also that Downs had evidently handled himself well at the firefight on the hill and at the embassy. The realization struck him like a physical blow. He felt his stomach turn to ice water as he realized that the BLT building had probably been struck by a car bomb. It was going to be the embassy all over again. Only this time it would be dead Marines stacked on the sidewalk, not dead civilians. An image of the burned hulk of the U.S. Embassy blazed across his mind's eye.

He looked around the tent that served as his company command post. Already he knew that he would have to send whatever men and equipment he could reasonably spare to help at the BLT. His eye came to rest on the company first sergeant. He would have to put the first sergeant in charge of whoever he sent to assist at the headquarters compound.

Ideally he would have been able to send his company executive officer. The XO was his second in command and as such was in the perfect position to command a relief force. But the XO had come down with some form of local flu the past week and had been flown out to the ships just offshore. He didn't want to pull a whole platoon out of the line and thereby weaken his defensive perimeter. He preferred to gather together whatever men he could spare from the company headquarters and send them in a group under the command of the first sergeant. That would preserve the integrity of his rifle and weapons platoon and at the same time provide a substantial relief force to aid the BLT.

He grimaced as he thought of placing the first sergeant in charge of his Marines. The man had done more to demoralize his company in six months than he thought humanly possible. He had constantly been at odds with him over his attitude toward the Marines in his command. And then the incident with Griffin and Slocum. He had been tempted to punch the man when he found out he had gone to other officers and senior enlisted men in the battalion and pushed for their court-martial. They had had one heated exchange and since then they had barely managed to exchange military courtesies.

He gritted his teeth and keyed the handset, "Alpha One, Alpha One, this is Alpha Six Actual. Do you copy? Over."

"Roger, Six Actual. Go Ahead. Over."

"Move into the BLT area and establish a perimeter. Assist the wounded and keep me informed with a sit rep every fifteen minutes. Do you copy, Alpha One? Over."

"Roger, sir. I copy. Be advised, sir, that there are lots of wounded and KIA. We are going to sweep south and move to the western extreme of the BLT compound. The MAU and the one five-five battery will probably be sending patrols down from their positions. The MAU building appears to be up and I can see Marines moving in and out of it, sir. Do you copy, Six? Over."

"Roger. I copy you loud and clear. Proceed with your current course of action and give me those sit reps. I'm sending you a relief party. If we lose comm reposition yourself and reestablish comm. Is that clear? Over."

"Roger, Alpha Six Actual. Alpha One, out."

The captain handed the handset to the company radio operator and signaled for the first sergeant to approach. "First Sergeant, it seems that the BLT has been hit seriously by some sort of explosive. I've got Corporal

Downs and a squad from First Platoon there now and the initial sit reps don't look good. From what he says the whole damn building is down. What I want you to do is get all the people together from the company admin section and whoever else isn't assigned duty in a rifle platoon and head over there. Take one radio and some extra batteries with you. Are you clear on that so far?"

"Yes, sir," answered the first sergeant tightly, "I'm following you, Captain. But I wouldn't worry too much about the BLT being hurt real bad. I know Corporal Downs and he's a shit bird if I ever saw one. Chances are when I get over there it won't be all that serious, sir. I'll form the men up and let the Captain know the situation when I arrive. Will that be all?"

The captain struggled to control his temper in front of the Marines in the headquarters tent. He glanced quickly around at the others, then lowered his voice and said, "Now you listen to me, First Sergeant. I don't give a damn what your opinion of Corporal Downs is, or any other Marine in my company for that matter. As soon as we get back to the States you can consider yourself relieved. I'm done with you. In the meantime just form up a detail and lend whatever assistance is needed at the BLT compound. Am I understood?"

The first sergeant glared at the company commander, then broke his stare and looked at the young Marines in the tent who were trying to give the appearance of not having heard the exchange. "Yes, Captain. You're understood. Will that be all?" asked the first sergeant.

"One more thing, First Sergeant. As soon as I'm able I'll be sending someone over to the BLT to relieve you. When that man arrives you are to return here and report personally to me. In the meantime you will not redirect Corporal Downs or any other infantryman from this company or any other unit on how to best employ the Marines under his charge. Have I made myself plain?"

"Yes, sir."

"Good. Carry on, First Sergeant," said Ward.

CHAPTER

28

Downs watched as the squad settled itself along the fence marking the western perimeter of the BLT compound. Most of the sentries on duty had remained at their posts after the explosion, anticipating an attack about to be mounted against them. When the attack had failed to occur individual Marines began to leave their posts and attempt to aid their comrades in the downed building. Only a few, manning every third position along the perimeter, now remained.

Most of the men manning the wire would normally have been considered walking wounded and pulled from the line. To a man they had suffered punctured eardrums, and a few had been wounded by flying debris from the explosion.

Downs scanned the boulevard for movement and then the positions of his fireteams. He was satisfied that he had placed them in defensible positions in the event of an attack. He realized that the two corpsmen had been detailed to a hastily designated battalion aid station and that he wouldn't see them again until the wounded and dead were treated or tagged. Already a long row of bodies had been placed at the southern end of the compound just inside the fence. He looked quickly in their direction, trying to will himself not to look again, but the sight of the poncho-covered forms lying sedately on the dirty concrete captured his gaze.

Downs counted silently to himself the number of bodies in the growing row. When he reached twenty he stopped. He waited for the anger to come and realized somewhat apathetically that it wouldn't. He wondered if he knew any of the dead Marines, then realized that virtually the entire H&S company of the battalion must have been killed by the explosion. He was certain to know most of the dead men.

Already, heavy equipment from the MAU Service Support Group was beginning to arrive and Marines were being directed to stand clear of the rubble while engineers attached cables and attempted to lift the larger pieces of concrete. Men working in the wreckage of the building were quickly covered by a fine powder and took on a sickly light gray appearance.

In several places Marines were digging furiously with whatever tools were available, attempting to open air shafts in the hopes that those trapped below would not suffocate while the rescue work progressed. On what had been the western face of the building Downs had seen a Marine crawl into the rubble to emerge grimly a few minutes later shaking his head negatively. The squad had watched the man's entry into the rubble, then issued a collective moan when it became apparent that his attempt had failed to locate any survivors.

Downs continued to watch the rescue effort as an engineer in greasy green coveralls walked purposefully in his direction and spoke with one of the Marines at the far end of the line. Downs watched as a Marine pointed to him and the engineer nodded and headed in his direction. He stood as the man approached and nodded hello.

"Morning, Corporal. I need some help if you can give me a couple of your men. We opened a shaft on the other side of the building and we can hear somebody down there but we can't get to him. The hole is pretty small and there's no way to make it any bigger right now."

Downs nodded and asked, "Okay. What do you need from me?"

"I need any of your men that are small and will go down the shaft and help dig. We're trying to enlarge the opening or dig past some concrete, but it's so tight down there only the small guys can get to it. It's pretty hard to breathe down there, too. They don't last long once they've started. Think you've got anybody I could use?"

Downs looked down the line of Marines that formed his squad. Only Tiger would have any hope of getting into a small opening between tons of concrete. "I've got one guy. Let's go and get him." Downs strode off toward the center of the squad where he had positioned Tiger's gun.

He noticed that Tiger and Samson had opened extra cans of ammunition and laid out their fields of fire, coordinating this last action with the machine gunner from another squad that had arrived and positioned itself north of their squad.

Downs approached Tiger and said, "Tiger, give your gun to Samson and let him designate one of the riflemen to be the new assistant. This corporal needs you on the other side of the compound for a while."

Tiger opened his mouth to speak, then looked at Downs who spoke to Samson, "Get whoever you think can handle it, but get someone and have the gun back up in a hurry. If you need me, come find me. And make sure whoever you get knows how to change a hot barrel and clear a jam, especially a failure to extract. When this gun gets hot it'll do that every once in a while, so go over the procedure with him. Got that?"

Samson nodded his assent and Tiger began to climb from his sandbagged hole. The corporal from MSSG looked at Downs and said, "Hey, Corporal, this is kind of risky. I won't force anybody down one of those tunnels, you know? Maybe you want to tell the lance corporal what I need and he can make his own mind up."

Downs grabbed Tiger by the wrist and pulled him from the hole. When Tiger was up he looked at the other corporal and nodded, "Okay, that's fine," he said. "This is the deal, Tiger. The corporal here is from MSSG and they are moving heavy equipment in to lift the rubble off. Before they can do that they are tunneling down to the survivors and wherever they think there might be some people left alive to make sure they have air. There's a guy on the other side of the building that they've found in the rubble, but the shaft down to him is so small only the little guys can get down it to work. I told the corporal you are the only guy from my squad who could help. Any questions?"

Tiger looked at the MSSG corporal and asked, "Is he still alive?"

"He was a few minutes ago. We want to try and tunnel down to him and bring him up so we don't shift the rubble and crush him with the heavy equipment. It's really tight down there, and there isn't a lot of air, so you'll only be able to work a few minutes at a time."

Tiger looked back at Downs and shrugged. "I'll be back as soon as I can, Corporal Downs. Make sure Samson goes over the extraction procedure like you told him."

"Yeah. Just do whatever you have to, then get back here. I don't want an inexperienced crew on this gun if we get into the shit. Okay?"

"Yep. I'm clear. I'll be back in a little while. Soon as I show these guys how to dig a hole. See you, Corporal Downs." Downs nodded to the other corporal and watched only briefly as Tiger and the other Marine crossed the compound in the direction of the building. Without giving Tiger another thought, Downs jumped into the hole with the M-60 and ran his eye over the weapon. He noted that Tiger had set the gun up on its tripod and weighted each leg with sandbags. In that configuration Downs knew that the gun could deliver a deadly accurate fire by control of its traverse and elevation mechanism. All the gunner had to do was swivel the weapon in the direction of its intended target, fire a burst, and wait as the assistant gunner adjusted the mechanism to correct elevation and bring the rounds into the target.

Downs noted the field of fire designated for this gun and nodded to Samson, who a few minutes before had been Tiger's assistant gunner. "You clear on what I want?"

"Yeah, Corporal. I got it. Pick a new assistant gunner and show him the extraction and barrel changing procedure. Anything else?"

"Yeah," said Downs, "don't forget to show him the designated fields of fire and be sure he understands how the traverse and elevation adjustments work. The principles, not just the mechanical adjustments. I want both of you to know how to do everything. Practice feeding the gun with him. You've got time to show him everything while nothing's going on. If the shit hits the fan we're going to need this gun to be up and it'll be too late to break him in then." Downs hesitated, looking into Samson's eyes in an effort to see that his instructions had registered. "Understood?" he asked.

"Yeah. I'm clear. I'll get somebody who's familiar with the gun."

"Okay," nodded Downs. "Let me know if you have a problem or if Tiger gets back." Downs climbed out of the hole and strode off to find the radioman. After making his situation report to Captain Rock he jumped into a hole with Ferris and Smith. "How's it going," he mumbled not really expecting an answer. The two cousins shifted to acknowledge his presence but said nothing.

From across the compound Downs heard the shouts of "Incoming!" and watched as Marines took cover. He glanced at Ferris and Smith and said, "Helmets," as the three of them donned the heavy steel pots and lowered themselves into their hole. Downs crouched on one knee and looked over the lip of the hole as the first mortars impacted the compound, the explosions leaving greasy clouds of black smoke in their wake.

The first series of three explosions was quickly followed by three more which straddled the rubble of the downed headquarters building. Downs heard Ferris mutter "motherfucker" and wasn't sure if it was due to the fact that wounded Marines were being shelled or because the gunner was walking his rounds in their direction. He lowered himself into the hole and crouched against the damp dirt walls waiting for the explosions. They came quickly, followed by three more that were all long shots over the compound and into the street beyond. Downs heard the metal fragmentation pinging against the iron rails of the fence to their front and silently willed the gunner to shift his aim.

Downs cringed waiting for the next series of mortar rounds as the air was torn by a volley of 155mm fire from the Marine artillery to his north. Before he realized that the fire was outgoing and directed at the enemy mortar position a second volley had been fired and Marines were on their feet and cheering. Across the compound Marines broke from their cover and screamed with a mixture of rage and pleasure as two more volleys were fired by the battery.

Downs looked on without emotion as the radio crackled to life in his pocket, "Corporal Downs, this is Samson. Do you copy?"

Downs pulled Smith back into the hole with one hand and keyed the mike with the other. "I copy, Samson. Go ahead." He shot a glance at Smith and said, "Stay down, you asshole."

"We're takin' sniper fire up here. Two rounds already during the mortar attack. Do you copy?"

"I copy. Anybody get hit?"

"Negative. But this guy can shoot. He almost got my A-gunner. We think we know where he's at though. We saw some movement in the buildings across the street. Those office windows just west of our position. At the top of the MEA hangar. You know the one I'm talking about?"

"Roger," said Downs, resisting the impulse to lift his head over the rim of the hole and look at the building. He looked quickly at Smith and said, "Samson's got a sniper across the road in the big hangar building. Load your grenade launcher with a smoke round and make ready to assault the building. After we lay down two rounds of smoke the three of us will cross the street and go after the sniper or whoever is in that building. Load with bee-hive for the assault, Smith. I'll be first out of the hole, then Ferris, then you. Everybody clear?"

The two nodded and checked their gear as Downs explained the situation to Samson, then shouted orders for the rest of the squad. On his command the three squad grenadiers fired smoke rounds from their grenade launchers and all three of the squad's corporals threw a smoke canister directly in front of their position.

Downs waited for the smoke to reach its maximum density then lunged out of the hole and sprinted for the other side of the street as the rest of the squad laid a suppressing fire on the building where they thought the shots were coming from. As the three ran across the street Downs saw a flicker of movement in the windows of the tallest building. Any doubts about the origin of the movement were erased a split second later as a round cracked past, then struck the concrete of the roadway and whined off.

The three reached the safety of the far side of the street and flattened themselves against a hanger wall. Without looking back Downs instructed the other two, "I got him. He's in that building just ahead of us. He was on the top floor as we crossed, but he's bound to have some sort of security down below. On my command let's put some 40mm on that door and then we'll rush it. I'll take the point. Smith you reload while we cross. Clear?"

"Let's do it, Steve. That guy can shift positions and either get an angle of fire on us or get out of the building."

"Yep," said Downs, "let me ready the squad." Downs again spoke with Samson via the small radio in his flak jacket pocket. "Samson we're going to assault the hangar you said the guy was in. We got some movement on the way across and drew some fire. When you hear Smith's 40mm go off lay down suppression fire on the face of that building. Be careful not to go too low, we're going to enter from the south side. If you copy, acknowledge. Then pass the word to the rest of the squad. Over."

"Roger, Corporal Downs. I copy suppression fire on the upper stories of the hangar after we hear your grenade. Give me thirty seconds to pass the word and we're set. Over."

"Okay," said Downs, "that's it then. Smith get up here with that grenade launcher and give the door a round of HE on my command. As soon as it goes Ferris and I will rush it. You two set?"

"We're ready, Steve," said Smith. "My reload is bee-hive. I'll be right behind you."

Downs edged away from the wall and took a quick glance at the door some forty meters away. He noted the absence of windows in the flat hangar wall and the single small window in the door. Failing to detect any movement he motioned Smith up and said, "Do it."

Smith stepped quickly away from the wall where the three had been sheltering and aimed his rifle with its 40mm grenade launcher at the small door. He eased back on the trigger and the grenade sailed toward the door in a low arc, arming itself on the third rotation. The bulbous aluminum nose of the grenade struck the door high in the center and blew it off its hinges. Before the smoke had begun to clear Downs and Ferris were running toward it.

Downs gained the wall two strides ahead of Ferris and threw himself against it. He paused, momentarily listening for any movement inside the building. Hearing nothing, he stepped inside, the acrid smell of the explosive stinging his eyes. He realized instantly that he was in a stairwell that led to the upper stories of the building. Roughly finished concrete steps led upward to the office spaces of the huge hangar. Downs guessed that this must be a service entrance and that it probably had doors opening onto a central corridor on each floor of the office space that served the huge hangar.

He eased himself away from the wall, his neck arched as he looked up the darkened stairwell. The only light filtered in from windows in the exterior walls, and Downs's eyes slowly adjusted to the dim interior light. He edged closer to the steps and continued to strain for any sign of movement. Hearing nothing he gained the center of the small room and peered up the rectangular space between the flights of stairs. As his eyes became fully adjusted to the dim light he heard the empty metallic ringing of a grenade spoon hitting the concrete flooring on one of the upper stories. Without hesitating he took two quick steps back toward the door and collided into Ferris. Catching him full in the chest with his rifle, Downs shoved with his arms and succeeded in throwing Ferris back out the entrance. Both rolled away from the open doorway and sheltered behind the concrete wall as the grenade exploded and threw its deadly shrapnel in every direction.

Before the smoke could clear Downs had regained his feet and was again in the small room. He carefully settled his rifle in his shoulder and aimed it almost vertically, then slowly advanced toward the stairs. Checking to ensure that the sights were aligned, he positioned himself under the steps and again looked for movement in the space between the flights of ascending stairs. Downs continued to look over his sights until the top portion of a head appeared in the narrow rectangle of light. He waited a fraction of a second longer, then shifted his focus to aim the rifle through its sights, acquiring his target and squeezing the trigger in the same instant.

The report of the rifle seemed deafening in the concrete confines of the stairwell and in the back of his mind the tinkling of the expended brass casing on the floor dimly registered. Downs continued to eye the upper flights for any sign of movement, then signaled Ferris and Smith into the room. As soon as the two cousins surmised what he had been doing he bounded up the steps to the first flight.

Downs gained the first landing and was confronted by a heavy gray metal fire door. He debated the wisdom of trying the door to see if it would open, then decided not to. The noise would only alert anyone who was waiting for him, either in the corridor or higher on the stairs. Reasoning that he had the initiative, and knowing that he had inflicted at least one casualty, Downs knew it would be better to remain on the attack. The problem with any advance up the stairs was that it would allow the defenders the first shot at him, or they would simply throw another grenade down the steps, at the very least forcing him out of the building.

Downs quickly decided to try the door. The knob spun freely in his hand and he slowly opened the door and peered into the empty corridor. He brought Ferris and Smith up to the first landing and explained his plan to them. Since it was logical that the sniper and the rest of his comrades were on the top floor and they were expecting an attack up this stairwell, Downs would cross to the far side of the building and ascend the stairwell on that side. In that way he would maintain the initiative and have a reasonable chance of attacking the enemy position from an unexpected direction.

He moved the selector lever on his rifle to full automatic and stepped into the corridor, his back pressed against the wall. Moving from door to door in the long hallway he quickly gained the far end where he observed a door identical to the one at the other end now guarded by Ferris and Smith. Downs leveled his rifle and reached for the knob, expecting his entry into the stairwell to be met by a hail of fire from an unseen adversary.

Easing the door open he could not detect the presence of anyone in the stairwell and turned to give a thumbs-up signal to Ferris who nodded nervously. Downs softly shut the door and began ascending the steps. He paused every few seconds to listen for movement from above. Remembering the small radio in his flak jacket pocket and fearing that it might emit a burst of static or a friendly transmission he felt for the knob and turned it off. Downs realized that he was now completely isolated from the squad. Even the act of communication would have to be preceded by turning the radio back on and hoping the signal would penetrate the concrete walls of the building.

He thought of the possibility of his rifle jamming and paused long enough at a landing to fix his bayonet. The click of the handle locking onto the lug on his rifle seemed to be deafening. He again began to ascend as the sound of a shot rang out from above. He was now convinced that the sniper would be on the top floor of the building, and that the man was aware of his presence.

Realizing that his squad was under fire and that the sniper had enough daring and presence of mind to fire even after he had seen them cross the road to assault his position, Downs began to grow angry. He crouched against the wall and debated his next move. Once he gained the top flight of stairs he would almost surely be confronted by the sniper's security force. He guessed that they would number between two and four men, probably poorly trained militia. As he sat debating his next move he heard the door two flights above open and an exchange take place in Arabic.

The men continued to talk as Downs rose and began to quickly but silently ascend the steps. The pungent aroma of sulfur floated down to him as the man struck a match and undoubtedly lit a cigarette. Downs hesitated one flight below, just out of sight of the men. He had heard only two voices, and now the men were probably enjoying a smoke. He tried to imagine the scene above. They would be standing by the door, cigarettes in their hands, not expecting him to materialize on the landing below.

He knew the cigarettes could only last a few moments more, and all his training told him that this was his moment. Without further thought Downs swiftly rose and rounded the corner, his rifle already in his shoulder, his feet seeking the steps that would bring him into the view of his prey.

The two men came into his view as Downs pointed his rifle at the chest of the nearer one and squeezed off three rounds. The man's mouth formed a perfect circle and the small deadly projectiles slammed into him with terrific force. The sound of breaking glass reached Downs through his excitement as the second man released his small coffee cup and reached down to pick up his rifle that was leaning against a wall. Before the man's hand met the weapon Downs fired and the man slammed into the wall, the rifle clattering noisily to the floor.

Without hesitating Downs raced up the remaining steps and flung the door open. Two men stood in the narrow hallway looking in his direction and he quickly fired a long burst at them. Both fell and Downs ducked back inside the door and changed magazines. Without exposing himself he pointed the rifle around the door jamb and into the hallway and emptied a second magazine in the direction of the men.

He quickly changed magazines, careful not to let the empty drop to the floor and alert any remaining militiamen to his predicament. Praying that Ferris and Smith would not now assault the other end of the hallway he stripped a fragmentation grenade from his flak jacket and laid it carefully on the floor next to the door. He then switched on the small radio in his pocket and said, "Samson, this is Downs. Do you copy?" His heart stopped as he waited for Samson's reply. After a few moments of silence he again said, "Samson, this is Downs. Can you copy me?"

His second request was met by a long burst of static followed by silence. Downs detected movement in the hallway and fired twice down the corridor. He then stripped a smoke grenade from his vest, pulled the pin and tossed it into the corridor. A heavy curtain of yellow smoke began to fill the hallway. Downs again keyed the small radio and said, "Samson, this is Corporal Downs. I'm on the top floor of the hangar and I've got the sniper pinned between me and Ferris. If you can hear me I want you to put down some suppression fire on the window where you think he's at. You should be able to see yellow smoke any second now. If you copy give me three short burst on the radio. Over."

Mercifully, the radio crackled three times with a heavy cloud of static and Downs muttered "shit" under his breath. As Sampson began to fire the machine gun at the window where he imagined the sniper to be, Downs crawled down the corridor, grenade at the ready. Rounds from Samson's firing penetrated the walls and ricocheted wildly down the corridor. Fearing that one of the stray rounds would hit him, Downs rose to his feet, trotted down the corridor to the door where he knew the sniper to be, and tossed the grenade in through the transom window. He backtracked down the hallway and gained the safety of the stairway, fighting the urge to cough and gag on the acrid smoke that filled the hallway.

The grenade went off with a resounding explosion and shattering of glass, blowing the door completely off its hinges and tearing ragged holes in the smoke. Downs again keyed the radio and ordered Samson to quit firing. In a few seconds the firing stopped and Downs strained to hear any indication of movement in the corridor.

Hearing nothing he leaned out of the doorway and glanced briefly at the scene in the darkened corridor. The bodies of the two militiamen remained where he had last seen them, and a heavy pall of smoke hung in the passageway. Ceiling tiles were strewn across the floor and electrical wiring hung in loose loops down the walls in several places. Downs inserted a fresh magazine and stepped into the corridor, his eyes fixed to the front, searching for the slightest movement.

In the back of his mind a warning came to him that militiamen might still be behind the other doors along the corridor. He decided that the best course of action would be to clear the room where the sniper had fired from, then return to the other rooms and clear each one individually. He silently hoped that no doors connected suites, but logic told him otherwise.

Downs gained the edge of the door and eased around it as it flopped lazily on its broken hinges. The interior of the room emitted a sharp, acrid smell from the explosion as Downs froze just outside and listened for any sign of life. With one quick movement Downs rounded the door and stood in the broken frame, sweeping his rifle from one side of the room to the other. In an instant his eye took in the crumpled form of the sniper against a far wall, his rifle smashed against the overturned desk he had improvised as protection from the fire of the Marines below.

Downs quickly drew back into the corridor and checked to see that none of the doors had opened to reveal a rifle muzzle pointed in his direction. The corridor remained a silent scene of devastation. In the next instant his mind's eye replayed the scene in the ruined room and Downs knew that he had gotten a glimpse of a half-opened connecting door and a large blood trail leading into the next room.

Downs searched for the proper solution. If he reentered the room and followed the trail he was very likely to walk straight into an ambush. A wounded enemy might still be alive and waiting for him on the other side of the doorway. Downs had no desire to confront such a situation.

He also reasoned that the rest of the Marines across the street would be watching the window for any sign of movement and would fire at the slightest provocation. Using the radio to let them know would be impractical as he wasn't sure that they would be able to clearly copy his transmission.

The obvious choice was to assault the room through the door that opened onto the corridor. This would still leave the wounded man with a number of advantages. He would hear the door being opened and simply shift his aim to that entry point. Even assuming that the door was unlocked, or could be kicked in, Downs was no better off with this point of entry. It also occurred to him that perhaps the man in the other room wasn't wounded at all, but had merely taken a wounded comrade across the room after the grenade had exploded. Downs realized that the man might have been in the other room when he threw his grenade and had not been even slightly wounded.

Without further hesitation Downs decided on his course of action. He couldn't descend either flight of steps as he had already alerted any other militia in the building to his presence. Ferris and Smith would have to hold their position while he cleared this floor himself, then he would signal down to them.

Downs took two quick steps across the open doorway and again glimpsed the shattered interior of the office. He edged away from the wall and peered into the room, focusing on the partially open door with its menacing trail of blood. Downs searched the grimy floor and an icy chill ran through his stomach as he saw the footprints in the powder of dust on the floor tiles. There had been another man in the other room and he had moved his comrade to safety.

The plan now hardened in Downs's mind and he removed another fragmentation grenade from his flak jacket and shifted his rifle to his left hand. Reaching through the trigger guard of his rifle he removed the pin of the grenade, holding the spoon fast to the cool metal canister. Downs's lips moved slightly as he muttered the word "Jesus" to himself and he grasped the spoon with his left index finger and began counting down the seconds of the grenade's fusing device.

With the peculiar coordination born of a thousand summer days spent on the ballfields of his hometown, Downs stepped away from the wall and into the doorway of the room, all the while facing the half-open door leading to the connecting office. His left boot made a slight crunching noise as he planted his foot eighteen inches inside the room and his right arm moved forward in a low graceful arc toward the opening between the door and the wall. As Downs rolled the metal sphere off his fingertips he knew intuitively that the grenade would strike the wall just where he had aimed and bounce obliquely into the next room. If the grenade had been fused correctly it would explode in the room, hopefully while it was still in the air.

After hesitating a fraction of a second to watch the grenade sail toward the wall Downs shoved off with his left foot and spun out of the room and back to the far side of the wall. He knew the blast from the grenade would send shards of glass and metal debris through the door and the concussion would echo around the room searching for an outlet. From this side of the doorway he would at least be out of its direct path. As he knelt to cover the other doors in the hallway with his rifle Downs heard an exclamation from inside the room.

The explosion ripped through the room, sending a shower of debris through the two doors. Before the concussion had fully subsided Downs was on his feet and racing for the corridor door that had mercifully been blown open. He stepped around the metal door and fired a quick burst into the room. Realizing that Samson would shortly open up on the front of the building he knelt and peered into the smoke along the floor. Seeing two bodies Downs quickly pumped rounds into each of them, then swept the room with fire before retreating to the corridor. As he flung himself against the wall Samson began to rake the front of the building with fire from his machine gun. Downs prayed that the grenadiers from his squad and the other squads would have enough presence of mind not to put rounds through the windows of the offices.

Within a few seconds Samson had sprayed the entire front of the building with fire from his machine gun and Downs reentered the small room with the bodies of the two men prostrated obscenely in death. His eye followed the muzzle of his rifle around the room looking for any sign of life. Seeing nothing Downs backed into the corridor and keyed the small radio, "Samson, this is Downs. Do you copy?"

"Roger, Corporal Downs. I copy. Go ahead. Over."

"Hold your fire on the top floor. I just cleared the room the sniper was in and I'm in the corridor now. If you see movement up here it will probably be me. I don't want you to fire on me by mistake. Make sure the other squad tied in on your north knows I'm up here. Got that?"

"Roger, Corporal Downs. I copied your last. Also be advised that a squad from Bravo Company is across the street and sweeping the building bottom to top. They are aware of your position and Smith and Ferris have already made contact with them. Their squad leader wants you to move to the top of the southern ladderwell and sit tight. He says they'll come up to get you. Do you copy? Over."

"Yeah. I copy. The southern ladderwell. Tell him I'll be there, Samson. Unless you have further traffic for me I'm going to move now. Over."

Downs quickly stepped inside the room and checked the two bodies for movement. Both of them lay in the exact position he had last seen them and the office was barren other than overturned and shredded furniture. Downs debated disabling the two rifles carried by the men then quickly decided not to. He realized that to break them he would have to put his own weapon down, a thought he didn't relish since other rooms in the corridor might still hide some militia. Before leaving the room he grabbed the long Soviet-made sniper rifle and slung it across his back, then headed for the southern end of the building.

He opened the door at the top of the stairs and peered at the deserted landing through the narrow crack between the door and the jamb. Assured that the landing was empty he stepped through the door and listened for movement. His heart froze as he detected sound below. He waited for a few moments before deciding that it was the squad from Bravo Company moving up the ladderwell. Downs could now hear the team leader directing his Marines up the narrow concrete steps.

He edged the door open and stepped back inside the hallway. He prepared to yell down to the other Marines but was afraid that a nervous rifleman might fire straight up the ladderwell, the rounds ricocheting wildly off the concrete walls. Leaving just a crack in between the door and the jamb Downs said in a loud voice, "Hey, Bravo Company. Is that you down there?"

A long pause was followed by a voice echoing up the concrete, "Yeah. Who the fuck are you?"

Downs suppressed a chuckle and answered, "Corporal Downs, First Platoon, Alpha Company." Another pause followed and Downs detected murmuring below as the four Marines no doubt discussed their next move. He struggled to remember a name of someone in Bravo Company that he could use as an identifier. The same voice came back to him, "Okay. If you're Corporal Downs, then who is the baddest fucking Marine to ever live?"

Downs knew he should give the pat answer of Chesty Puller or Dan

Daly, but instead he said, "I'm the baddest motherfuckin' Marine you'll ever meet. Are you comin' up here or not?"

He heard laughter below followed by, "Okay, smart-ass, then who is the biggest asshole in the battalion?"

Downs smiled and answered, "Easy. The Alpha Company First Shirt."

"Okay. Don't move. We're on our way up," said the voice. Downs stepped back inside the stairwell and lowered his rifle to point at the flight of steps below him. If some militia were trapped between him and the Bravo Company fireteam he wanted to be ready. To his relief he saw the helmet of one of the Marines appear, followed by the three others.

Downs smiled at the corporal and said, "I'm glad to see you. This corridor still hasn't been properly cleared. There's rooms off both sides of it and only two of them have been cleared. What's the rest of your squad up to?"

Without hesitation the corporal answered, "We're clearing all the floors by working south to north. All we have to do is hold here until they tell us the floors underneath have been cleared. Then they'll come up and we'll clear this floor. Any hostiles left will be pushed toward the northern ladderwell and allowed to go out the north side of the building. We've got a fireteam in place down there for when they make their exit."

"Yeah, that sounds pretty good. I don't think anybody is left on this floor, but you can't tell. They could be hiding in one of the rooms. Are your guys securing the doors down below us?"

The corporal nodded and said, "Yeah, and we're using your two guys to hold one of them. Did this guy get one of your fireteam? You're short a man."

"No," said Downs, "we came over with only three." Downs motioned toward the door and said, "Let's open that up and put your rifleman there in case anybody breaks for the ladderwell on the far side or has any ideas about assaulting us. At least we'll see them coming."

"Yeah, sounds good." He nodded toward the door and the rifleman and grenadier opened it and took up positions observing the corridor. "You can head back down if you want, Corporal. We'll take it from here."

"Okay," said Downs. "Why don't you use your radio to let them know below that I'll be coming down."

"Yeah. Good idea. See you later." Downs paused while the corporal notified the fireteam leaders on the lower floors that he was coming down, then nodded and descended the stairs. When he reached the second story he found Ferris and Smith had already been relieved and were waiting for him outside.

Downs nodded to them and the three crossed the street back to the compound in silence. The great shattered mass of rubble that had been the BLT headquarters building loomed over them as they reentered the compound. Downs walked directly to Samson and asked, "Any of ours get hurt during the shooting?"

"No," said Samson. "One of the guys from Bravo Company got nicked, but he didn't even come off the line. The round just passed between his flak jacket collar and his web gear."

"No shit," responded Downs. "He's a lucky bastard."

"Yeah, that's for sure." Downs indicated the M-60 with a nod of his head and asked, "The gun give you any trouble?"

"Nope. Worked just fine."

"Well, that's yours until further notice, Samson. Understood?"

"Yeah. I'm clear," answered the big Marine. "Uh, one other thing, Steve," said Samson as Downs turned to go.

"Well, what, Samson? I need to go check the squad and see how Tiger is doing."

"Yeah, I know." Downs stood by and watched as Samson shuffled his weight from one foot to the other. "They found Sergeant Slocum over by the fence line there," said Samson. "They need an NCO who knows him to go over and ID the body. I guess he's pretty fucked up."

Downs struggled to control his thoughts. He let a long sigh out and asked, "Where is he?"

"They've set up a temporary morgue in front of the BLT for all the bodies without positive ID. NCOs are required for the ID, then they tag 'em I guess. He's over there on the fucking ground, man. Not even a poncho on him." Samson wiped his face with his hand and continued, "This is just all fucked up, man. You know? They wouldn't even have known it was him except he had a dogtag laced into his boot."

Both Downs and Samson reflexively looked down at the dog tags laced into their left boots, the silent emblem of the infantry. "Why don't they get one of the NCOs from Dragon Platoon to ID him? Jesus, what the fuck is going on around here anyway? Sergeant Slocum left the platoon before we even deployed."

Samson shook his head and said, "It won't work, Steve. Dragons were billeted in the BLT building. They all bought it, man. Maybe some of them are alive in the rubble, but they ain't gonna be in no kind of shape to ID him even if somebody can dig down to them. One of us has to do it. H&S company is gone, man. Fuckin' wasted. The whole company. Can you believe it?"

Downs turned and silently regarded the mound of rubble. Marines swarmed over it carrying whatever tools they could find to dig and break away rubble. On the north slope of the dirty mound a cluster of men were gathered in a tight circle around several huge slabs of broken concrete. Cables and ropes stretched away from the circle of men and were attached to a truck at the base of the north face of what had been the BLT building. Downs nodded to indicate the group and asked, "What's going on up there?"

Samson shook his head and spat. "There's a guy trapped up there between the sheets of concrete. They say his legs are pinned and almost cut off by the weight of the concrete. They're afraid as soon as they lift it away from him he'll bleed to death before they can tourniquet what's left of his thighs. Right now they're just givin' him morphine to ease the pain." Both Downs and Samson turned to look at the group before Samson continued, "Awhile ago he was screaming for them to kill him, then he started asking for his mother. This situation is totally fucked, man. We ought to form up and go out in the ville and kick some ass. I've had all the bullshit I'm gonna take from these assholes. Fuck the Rules of Engagement, I say we get some payback. ASAP."

The two stood in silence for a moment before Downs asked, "Where did you say they had Sergeant Slocum?"

"East side of the building. Over by the access road is what they told me."

"Okay, then. I'll go and get it done. You make sure everybody here stays in their holes and alert. Don't let anybody pull us out of the line for any reason. From the way it looks we're the only thing between the battalion and the whole fuckin' city."

Downs turned to go then added, "Hey, Samson. One more thing, and pass the word on this. They probably hit the BLT with the same type of car bomb they used on the embassy. So any vehicle moving down that boulevard is fair game. None of that bullshit about waiting to be fired upon before engaging. Just fire the fucker up and don't worry about asking any questions."

Samson shook his head and said, "No shit, man. Fuck 'em anyway with their stupid rules. They passed the word a little while ago that the French headquarters got hit this morning, too. Jesus, this is crazy."

Downs strode off and headed south of the BLT building planning to stop and see Tiger. As he made his way past piles of rubble and twisted hulks of jeeps and other vehicles that had been parked in close proximity to the BLT building Downs began to get a better idea of the destruction. The building itself was now less than one third of its original height, the upper stories having collapsed onto the lower ones. Huge slabs of concrete ringed the mound and Marines had strung ropes to enable them to pull themselves up the sides.

All over the rubble men were burrowing between the slabs and attempting to locate comrades. Less than an hour after the explosion wounded men were being pulled from the rubble and rushed to the Battalion Aid Station that had been hastily erected and staffed by whatever corpsmen and doctors could be scrounged from the rifle companies and the fleet offshore.

Everywhere the ground was littered with the debris of the five-hundred-odd men who had been billeted in the headquarters or had slept in the tents and temporary shelters around the base of the building. As he made his way to the far side of the compound Downs stepped over the remains of magazines, web gear, clothing, official documents from the battalion administration section, and letters from wives and families back home.

The thoroughness of the destruction began to sink in. Samson had been right. H&S company had ceased to exist. The Marines who had comprised the company were now dead or trapped in the rubble. The battalion's tactical planning section was destroyed, as was the communication section, and the specialized combat units like the dragon and TOW missile platoons. The navy corpsmen who made up the bulk of the battalion's medical personnel would also undoubtedly have been lost. The rifle companies were now without direction. They would act with whatever coordination they could manage, but the system for the operation of the battalion had been effectively destroyed within seconds of the explosion.

The residue of the lives that had focused around the building was strewn over the area and dusted with a fine gray powder. Downs stared in disbelief as he walked past huge pieces of the building's concrete flooring that now rested precariously on the rubble pile. From each piece of concrete, steel reinforcing rods extended, stripped of the masonry that had surrounded them by the force of the blast.

Downs reached the far side of the compound and approached a long line of bodies laid side by side along the road. He nodded to a dazed lance corporal and said, "I'm Corporal Downs, First Platoon, Alpha Company. One of my Marines said you needed somebody to come over and ID one of our old NCOs, Sergeant Slocum."

Downs waited for the boy to answer but he said nothing. Downs took in the vacant look on the boy's face, then realized he was in shock. He looked around and saw an older Marine who looked in his direction after a moment and asked, "Came to ID one of 'em?"

"Yeah," answered Downs, "I'm looking for Sergeant Slocum. He was with the dragons. You know where he is?"

"Couldn't tell you, Corporal. Just look for yourself, and when you find him let me or one of the other staff NCOs know. We'll set you up with a toe tag and you'll be on your way."

"Okay," said Downs as he turned to confront the silent line of young men laying before him. Not wanting to lift the cover off the faces of those with ponchos over them he began to walk down the row of bodies and read the names on the tags laced into the dead men's boots. When he reached the one imprinted with "Slocum, Robert, P." he stopped. Downs silently peered at the body, searching for some sign of the jaunty, wise-cracking boy he had known. He knelt by the dead man's feet and again examined the tag. He was sure that there were no other Slocums in the battalion, and it was logical that Sergeant Slocum would have been in the area at the time of the explosion. Downs hesitated, not wanting to again look at the boy's face. He didn't see Slocum there.

"That him?" called out the staff sergeant.

"Yeah. I think so," answered Downs. "It's kind of hard to tell."

The staff sergeant walked over and offered Downs a small paper tag with a string laced through it. "Do you recognize him, Corporal? We need to have a positive ID if you can."

Downs began to fill out the blanks on the tag with Slocum's personal information. "The tag's his," said Downs, indicating the small metal disc bearing Slocum's name and laced into his boot. "And he's the right size and all. But Jesus, he's so fucked up I can't tell for sure." Downs stood and handed the tag back to the staff sergeant. "That's the best I can do, Staff Sergeant."

The older Marine nodded. "You said he was in dragons, right?"

"Yeah," said Downs, "he transferred over from our platoon during the past year."

The staff sergeant nodded knowingly and added, "Well, I don't expect that too many of dragons platoon is going to be left alive. It's more than likely him. We'll go ahead and tag him as your sergeant."

"Yeah. Okay, Staff Sergeant. Anything else you need from me?"

"Not unless you see somebody else you recognize that hasn't already been tagged."

"No," said Downs quietly, "I should be getting back to my platoon."

"Okay, Corporal. Thanks for your help."

Downs headed in the direction of the squad, making his way along the south side of the building so that he could stop and see Tiger on his way back. Men and equipment continued to swarm over the rubble in increasing numbers as the intact units of the battalion reacted to the loss of the BLT building and its Marines.

Spotting the same corporal that had earlier asked him for his smallest men to tunnel into the rubble, Downs walked up to the man and nodded hello. Downs stood silently by while the corporal gave orders for an earthmover to pull away a huge section of concrete. When the job had been done the corporal turned to him and said, "Your man is down there now. I hope you don't need him back because we're shorthanded as it is and we really need the little guys."

"No," said Downs. "I just came by to see how he was doing."

The corporal shrugged and answered, "Stick around about five minutes and you can ask him for yourself. I've got them on twenty minute shifts and your guy is due to come up in a few more minutes."

"Yeah, I'll wait for a while," said Downs, glancing apprehensively in the direction of the squad.

"Suit yourself," said the corporal. "I'll be over here with the heavy stuff if you have any questions."

Downs stood idly by while Marines around him moved equipment into position or attached cables to pieces of rubble. He spotted three smaller men stripped to the waist, sitting in a group away from the rest of the Marines working on the rubble. Downs surmised that these were the men who were working shifts with Tiger in the shaft. He walked over and asked one of them, "Are y'all the guys working in the tunnel?"

"Yeah, Corporal. Don't tell us you got somebody in another part of the building?"

"No," said Downs. "The other guy who's down there now is one of my troops. Tiger."

Two of them nodded and the third again answered, "Yeah, he's down there now. We'll go and get him up in a couple of minutes."

Downs noted that at the mention of Tiger's name one of the others checked his watch. He guessed that this man would be Tiger's relief. He looked in the direction of the building then back to the smaller Marine. "So how is it coming down there?" The boy shook his head and took a long pull from his canteen, then spat the water out on the ground. "Not too good, Corporal. The tunnel is really tight and it's got a couple of nasty turns in it. One of us has to stay at the bend just to help get the dirt we dig around the corner, otherwise the rope gets hung up and the guy who's diggin' has to back out and free it."

"Are you getting any closer to getting the guy out?" asked Downs.

"Maybe. It's hard to say. Every time we think we're close we run into another big chunk of concrete and we have to tunnel around it."

"Is he still alive?"

Downs noted the exchange of glances between the Marines. After a moment the one shrugged and said, "He was last time I was down there. But he's hurt pretty bad, you know? He keeps passin' out and we lose him for a few minutes at a time. You never fucking know if the guy bought it or what."

"Does anybody know who he is?" asked Downs.

"Yeah," answered one of the other Marines. "He's the guy they had up here for a court-martial, Sergeant Griffin. I think he's from one of the rifle companies. You know him?"

Downs swallowed hard and tried to digest the information. It all began to fall into place. Griffin would have had to have been in the building at the time of the attack, Downs knew. He was being held for court-martial. Where else would they have held him? He had been relieved of duty.

He turned away from the others as he felt the bile rise in his throat. He tried to imagine Griffin trapped below the surface, pinned by tons of concrete and unable to move in the choking dust and grit. Downs asked the group, "Where is the entrance to the tunnel?"

"Right over there," pointed one of the Marines. Without hesitating Downs set off for the entrance. At least he could find out from Tiger if Griffin were still alive and what kind of shape he was in.

He arrived at the entrance to find it manned by two Marines who were pulling sandbags of dirt and debris from the hole at the end of a long rope. He walked over and asked, "How much longer until Tiger comes up?"

One of the boys turned to face him without losing his grip on the rope and answered, "A few more minutes. What's the hurry?"

"Nothing," said Downs, "I'm his squad leader."

The two Marines looked at each other. The one who had spoken shrugged and said, "Let's bring them up. They been down awhile." As the two finished bringing up the next sandbag of debris one of them grabbed a metal mess kit and held it over the entrance to the tunnel. He beat on it with a short piece of pipe and Downs knew the sound would travel down the tunnel to the two Marines working below. The prearranged signal resulted in Tiger and another Marine emerging from the tunnel a few minutes later, both filthy and bleeding from scratches along their faces and arms.

Tiger emerged cursing and spitting and then spotted Downs. "How you doing, Corporal Downs?" he asked.

"Okay, Tiger. How's it going down there?" Downs handed Tiger one of his canteens and waited while Tiger alternately drank and spat water, splashing some over his hands and face.

"You heard?" asked Tiger, not looking at Downs.

"Yeah. Are they right?"

Tiger poured the remainder of the canteen over his head and answered, "Yeah. They're right. It's Sergeant Griffin. We got close enough to talk to him a few minutes ago, then he passed out. He's fucked up, Corporal Downs. He don't even know who I am half the time."

Downs looked at Tiger and asked, "Can you tell what kind of shape he's in? I mean, is there any way he'll make it if we get to him?"

Tiger turned and cast a furtive glance at the other Marines who remained near the entrance to the tunnel. "Let's take a walk. Okay?" Downs nodded and they began to walk away from the others, Tiger continuing in a subdued voice. "He ain't got a chance, Corporal Downs. He is all fucked up, man. Before he passed out I asked him how bad he was hurt and he started laughing and told me not to bother digging, just pass him a forty-five and he'd save me the trouble."

Downs considered the information for a moment then shrugged and said, "That's just Sergeant Griffin. He's a tough motherfucker and he just won't give in like that. Besides, if he can talk he can't be hurt that bad, right? And if you're close enough to talk to him how much longer can it take to get him out?"

Tiger shook his head negatively and continued, "Listen to me, Corporal Downs. I been down there and I know what it's like. The only reason we can talk to him and see a little bit of him is that there is a crack between two big pieces of concrete. We have dug almost all the way around it and there ain't no way to get to him without lifting the shit off from the top. Are you following me so far?"

"Yeah," said Downs.

"Good," continued Tiger, "the other problem, and Sergeant Griffin already has this figured, too, is that the pieces of wire they used to reinforce the concrete are exposed and have him pinned to the stuff below. As soon as we touch the stuff above him we'll move the rebar that's stickin' him and he's a goner. He'll bleed to death while we're up top screwing around with the heavy equipment and tryin' to figure a way to get it off of him without moving the wrong piece and causing an avalanche down below." Tiger shook his head again and said, "He said it himself, he's fucked. The only thing now between him and buying it is the pain from havin' that iron stuck through his abdomen."

Downs walked on in silence for a few steps before asking, "So what's the deal, Tiger? What are we supposed to do now? Just sit up here and wait for him to die?"

Tiger grabbed him by the arms and spat, "Hell no! He ain't no wimp, but this is too much. The fucking guy is gonna die, man. He knows it, I know it, and you know it. He already asked me to get him a forty-five, so let's do it and let him go out without all the extra pain. What's the point in letting him suffer? So he can live a few extra minutes down there?" Tiger looked around at the scene of destruction before him and wiped his face with a hand. "It's fucked, Steve. It's all fucked, man. Look at this shit. H&S is gone."

Downs stood by in silence for a few seconds. His mind brought to him an image of Griffin trapped below in the darkness. Tiger's argument made sense to him. If what he said was accurate then Griffin was as good as dead and even he knew it. He shuffled his feet and looked toward the entrance to the tunnel as Tiger said, "You're his friend, man. What are you gonna do?"

"The right thing, Tiger. I'm gonna do the right thing for once in my life without worrying about the consequences." Downs turned to face Tiger and asked, "There's no doubt in your mind that we can't get to him in time?"

"No way in hell, man."

"Okay then. Can you get back down there out of turn without causing any attention?"

"Yeah. People aren't exactly fightin' to get down there. Anyway, the other guys know I was in Griffin's platoon. They heard me talkin' to him down there. They'll just think it's cause I want to help out a buddy."

"Good, that'll help."

"We still gotta have a forty-five. Where are you gonna get that?" asked Tiger.

Downs shrugged and said, "I know where I can get one that won't be accounted for, if that's what you mean." Downs glanced across the compound at the long row of dead men. "I'll take care of it, Tiger. Just wait here and I'll be back in a few minutes. I'll meet you over by the water bull and you can tuck it under your flak jacket and go down with it like that. Will that work?"

Tiger considered for a few seconds then answered, "Yeah, it sounds good, but let's hurry up. The longer we wait the more he pays down there and the more officers and staff NCOs are gonna be nosing around up here." Tiger glanced back toward the tunnel leading down to Griffin. "Let's just do it and be done with it. It'll be better for everybody that way."

"Meet you by the water bull in ten, Tiger," said Downs as he strode off in the direction of the morgue.

CHAPTER

29

Downs walked past the long row of dead Marines and into the tent that had been set up to serve as a triage center. Spotting the staff sergeant he had spoken with earlier Downs nodded and asked, "Staff Sergeant, got a minute?" The older man regarded him for a moment then a look of recognition crossed his features, "Sure. Alpha Company, right?"

"Yeah, Staff Sergeant," answered Downs not wanting to repeat his name. "I thought maybe I would come for my sergeant's gear. I know his family and all and I'll probably write to them and see that his stuff gets home. That all right?"

The staff sergeant glanced quickly at a navy lieutenant who was working over a wounded man and asked, "That okay, sir?"

"What's that, Staff Sergeant?" the man asked absently.

"The Corporal here has come for the personal effects of one of his men. Will it be all right if he takes them, sir?"

"Yes, yes. Of course. See to it, Staff Sergeant," answered the lieutenant without looking at Downs.

The staff sergeant nodded in the direction of the bodies and Downs said, "Thanks, Staff Sergeant," and exited the tent.

Downs walked over to Slocum's body and quickly went through his pockets removing his wallet and other personal effects. Trying not to look at Slocum's face, Downs removed his pistol belt with its forty-five automatic and two magazines. He inserted one of the magazines into the empty well of the pistol then worked the slide, chambering one of the short stubby rounds. The other magazine he stuffed into a cargo pocket of his utility bottoms. Without standing, Downs fastened the leather holster onto the front of his web belt so it would appear as a normal piece of his gear. He would discard it later when nobody was around.

He walked out of the tent, nodding to the staff sergeant, who continued working inside. Downs measured the distance to the water bull where he could see Tiger waiting. When he was halfway there he heard the voice of the Alpha Company first sergeant ringing across the compound, "Hold it right there, Mister Downs! Where the fuck do you think you're going with that weapon?"

Downs spun to face the first sergeant who was barreling down on him from across the compound. He noted the starchy newness of the first sergeant's uniform in stark contrast to the dinginess of everything else around him. As the first sergeant approached him, Downs reflexively locked himself into a position of attention.

"I said just where the fuck do you think you are going with that weapon mister!" screamed the first sergeant as he placed his face within inches of Downs's. "Well, I expect an answer," he spat.

"I was headed back to the squad area, First Sergeant," Downs lied automatically.

Without warning the first sergeant reached out and grabbed the muzzle of the sniper rifle Downs had taken from the militiaman that morning and slung across his back. The first sergeant jerked the weapon violently off his shoulder, Downs resisting only slightly. "And where did you manage to pick this up, Corporal? And what makes you think you have the right to strut around my battalion with it slung over your shoulder like fucking Davy Crockett?"

Downs glared at the man, then answered, "We were engaged by an enemy sniper this morning, First Sergeant. We assaulted the ambush according to standard infantry tactics and within the Rules of Engagement. I took the rifle from the hostile sniper after he was KIA to prevent it from falling back into enemy hands."

The two continued to stare at each other defiantly, then the first sergeant lowered the weapon's muzzle and attempted to pull the bolt to the rear and clear the chamber. Downs looked on smugly as the first sergeant struggled with the weapon whose action refused to budge. As it became increasingly apparent that the first sergeant did not know how to clear the weapon, Downs smiled. The first sergeant caught his smirk and instantly dropped the rifle and grabbed Downs by the collar of his flak jacket.

The first sergeant tightened his grip around the material of the flak jacket, saying "I'll teach you to laugh at me, you wet-behind-the-ears little motherfucker." With one motion Downs thrust his knee into the soft flesh of the first sergeant's testicles. He stood by as the first sergeant collapsed onto his knees, then placed the flat of his boot in the middle of the man's chest and pushed him over onto the ground. "Fuck you, asshole," said Downs. "I'm sick of your shit. You want a piece of my ass, then now is your chance. Come and get it."

Marines nearby stopped their work and waited. Downs glared at the first sergeant while the man waited for the nausea to pass. When he had regained his breath the first sergeant hissed, "You're finished, mister. Place yourself under arrest. You're relieved, just like your buddy Griffin. You struck me without provocation and I'll see you in the brig for it. I hope you enjoyed yourself, mister, because you're going to pay me for it. Now, get out of my sight."

Downs stared for a moment then spat on the ground. "You don't deserve to wear the uniform, you piece of shit," he said and turned to walk away. Still shaking, he found Tiger by the water bull.

"Hey, nice move on the first shirt, Steve. I'll be sure to visit you in the brig," said Tiger.

Downs attempted a smile and replied, "Yeah. Well, the asshole had it coming, that's for sure. Anyway he would've found something else to bust me for. At least this way I had the pleasure of kicking him in the balls."

"Must've been an awful small target," laughed Tiger.

Downs smiled. "Yeah. It was, now that you mention it." The two shared a conspiratorial laugh then Downs asked, "Tiger, are you sure there is no way to get him out alive? I mean really sure? If you're close enough to hand him the pistol can't you pull him out?"

Before Downs had finished, Tiger was looking at the ground and shaking his head negatively. "I told you. There just ain't no way. He's jammed in between a bunch of huge slabs of concrete. We're busting the edges off of a couple of slabs and we can get a hand through to him but it's impossible to clear a real opening against all that hardened concrete without a jackhammer." Tiger looked in the direction of the ruined BLT building. "Jesus, last I checked they were trying to get him to put his hand through the opening so they could give him a stick of morphine in one of his fingers."

"Maybe the morphine will help him hold on long enough for us to free him?" asked Downs hopefully.

Again Tiger shook his head. "No dice, Steve. He's refusing the morphine. Says he doesn't want it." Tiger paused. "You know why, man. He knows the morphine will only make him pass out for a little while, or just fuck up his coordination. He knows he has to stay clear to do himself. He's a gritty son of a bitch, but nobody can blame him for wanting to end this. Nobody could take this, man."

Downs took a deep breath and drew the pistol from its holster and handed it to Tiger. "I guess there just isn't any way out of this, is there?"

"You said it yourself, Steve. We've got to do the right thing. He's a decent guy and he ain't gonna make it no way."

Downs nodded in acceptance. "Yeah. I know. Just I never thought anybody would get Sergeant Griffin. You know, Tiger?"

"Yep. The fucker is bigger than life in a lot of ways," said the diminutive Marine. Both of them looked toward the looming mound of rubble. "Guess there's nothing left now but to do it."

"Yeah," said Downs. "Tuck it under your flak jacket in the front and nobody will notice."

"Good idea," answered Tiger as he put the muzzle of the barrel into the front of his trousers and hid the butt of the large pistol under his dirty flak jacket. "See you," he said as he turned to go.

"Hey, Tiger," called Downs. "Tell Sergeant Griffin I said," Downs hesitated, wondering what message he could send to Griffin down below in the rubble and choking dust. "Shit," said Downs. "Just tell him I said hello, man."

Tiger paused. Wiping his face with a dirty hand he turned and faced Downs, "Fuck that, Steve. I'm gonna tell him you kicked the first shirt right in the balls and you're going to the brig." Downs smiled crookedly, not trusting his voice. Tiger made a slight thumbs-up motion and said, "Semper Fi, motherfucker," and strode off in the direction of the tunnel.

CHAPTER

"Reckon they'll have him out in a few minutes more, Corporal Downs," said the staff sergeant. "Damn shame. He was a fine boy."

Downs nodded silently. The past seven days had been a nightmare of digging for survivors interrupted only by mortar attacks and sniping from an unseen enemy. The grim reality of the attack had emerged as they continued to pull bodies from the rubble night and day for a full week. Now nerves were frayed and tempers routinely flared at the smallest provocation.

A rifle company had been air-lifted over from Camp LeJeune along with a replacement H&S company and the battalion had resumed normal operations within hours of the attack. The new H&S company had assumed tactical control of the rifle companies and dug itself in along the western runway.

Downs and the squad had remained in place at the BLT compound in order to provide perimeter security and to assist in the rescue effort. For the initial forty-eight hours they had worked around the clock, dividing their time between digging and standing watch on the line. After the last survivor was pulled from the rubble, and the death of Griffin, the squad had grown dispirited. With each man pulled from the destroyed BLT building they had withdrawn further into themselves. By week's end they were a group of individuals operating on sheer nerve, no longer responding to anything with real emotion.

As the motor on the crane throttled up and lifted the last piece of concrete off, Downs caught a glimpse of Griffin. He silently signaled Samson, Smith, and Ferris to follow him down into the crater. The four worked in silence to put the body into the green plastic bag, then carried Griffin to the lip of the huge hole. As they gained the summit a Lebanese rescue worker reached out to take one of the handles from Downs and assist him up. Downs angrily shoved the man's hand away and clambered out of the rubble.

The rest of the squad stood by in silence as the staff sergeant nodded in the direction of the morgue and said, "Take him over to the tent, Corporal Downs. I'll be along in a minute or two to see after his personal effects." Downs and the others proceeded across the compound and laid the body bag outside the tent that had served as a morgue for the dead.

All four edged away from the bag before Downs began, "Come on, Samson. Let's go in the tent and get a toe tag from one of these guys. We can fill it out while we wait for Staff Sergeant Whitney." Samson followed Downs toward the dark interior of the huge tent. As they stepped inside they both paused in the entry to allow their eyes time to adjust to the dim interior.

Objects inside the tent slowly came into view and Samson and Downs could make out the rows of bodies, some not yet covered by ponchos. Downs also took in the first sergeant, his back to them, bent over a dead Marine collecting the man's personal effects. He motioned to Samson to be quiet and the two edged farther into the tent along one of the canvas walls.

They watched as the first sergeant removed the man's wallet and letters from a cargo pocket in his utilities, then rifled through its contents. With a feeling of rising disgust Downs looked on in silence as the first sergeant removed the money from the wallet and added it to a large roll he extracted from his own trouser pocket.

A glance passed between Downs and Samson before the bigger Marine removed his rifle from his shoulder and said, "You've had it, motherfucker. I'll goddamn do you myself. Not even a fucking grave digger steals from the dead." Downs glared at the man in silence as Samson leveled the muzzle of his rifle at the first sergeant.

The first sergeant spun on one heel to face his accuser as Samson snapped the bolt forward on his rifle, chambering a round. "Who the fuck do you think you are, mister?" hissed the first sergeant. "How dare you enter my tent without asking permission! Get the fuck out. Now!"

"Fuck you, asshole," said Samson, the rifle menacingly coming to point at the first sergeant. "I'll go to Leavenworth the rest of my life, but you ain't gonna walk away from this. Besides, Downs saw you take the money. He can be my witness. We'll just say you rushed us with your pistol. I saw the size of that roll. When they find that on your fuckin' corpse they'll know damn well what you been up to. You got more there than a first shirt pulls down in a year."

Downs watched as the first sergeant began to rise and move toward the far wall. "Okay, son. Now let's all just calm down. Put that rifle away and I'll forget this happened. It's been a tough week for all of us. All of our nerves are frayed." The first sergeant smiled somewhat hesitantly, and Downs realized that he had never before seen the man smile. "Come on, Corporal Downs," he continued, "you must know that the lance corporal is making a mistake. You may not like me but you know I wouldn't steal from a fellow Marine. Especially a dead man. No matter what you think of me you must know I wouldn't do that. Right, son?"

Downs crossed his arms across his chest and said, "I know what I saw. But why don't you go ahead and give me your explanation. I'd sure as hell be curious to hear it." Without losing eye contact with the man, Downs added, "If he even looks like he's going for that pistol, or if you hear anybody coming Samson, just fuckin' grease the piece of shit. He doesn't deserve to live. Besides, I bet if we look at the paper for these guys' personal effects not one of them will have more than twenty bucks listed to his name."

Downs saw a hunted look pass across the first sergeant's eyes and knew he was right. The first sergeant shifted his gaze from Downs to Samson. Downs knew the man was trying to figure the odds. Attempting to gauge whether or not Samson would pull the trigger. "Oh, he'll do it First Sergeant," said Downs. "And nobody will question it much after the fact. Wouldn't it just embarrass the shit out of the Marine Corps to have to admit that one of its lance corporals shot a senior staff NCO that he caught stealin' from the dead in Beirut."

Downs laughed cynically, "I can see it now in the after action report.

First Sergeant Schmucatelly was killed by the accidental discharge of another's Marine's weapon. That would save everybody a lot of embarrassment."

"Fine with me, Steve. I say we do the fucker right here and now." Something in Samson's tone let Downs know that he was deadly serious. From the periphery of his vision Downs was aware of Samson's rifle tracking the first sergeant as he moved closer to the far wall of the tent. "Far enough, motherfucker," said Samson, "you don't need to get any closer to that hatch. And don't worry, First Shirt. I got no problem with shooting you in your back if you try and make a break for it."

Downs looked on in silence as the first sergeant swallowed hard and began, "Look now, guys. Its not like I was really stealin' from these Marines. I was gonna take the money and see that it got back to their families. You boys don't know how long things like that can be tied up in the red tape once we hit the States. It could take months for those families to see any of their money if I just sit back and allow it to go through channels. I was just trying to take a few shortcuts for the sake of the families. That's all. You must realize that I wouldn't steal from these dead men."

Samson gave a short laugh and tightened his grip on the trigger. "You must think we're the two stupidest sons of bitches in the Marine Corps if we're gonna buy that load of crap," he said.

"Yeah, First Shirt. Maybe you better try again. Make us believers in the fucking Band of Brothers you're always preaching about. Go ahead," taunted Downs. "We got a few minutes to hear you out."

The first sergeant wiped his brow and straightened up to his full height. "Okay, boys. So I was fuckin' up and you caught me at it. What's the harm? These guys don't need any money where they're going. I got a wife and three kids back at LeJeune. You two got no idea what that does to a man's resources. I have to scrimp and save for every nickel. All I was trying to do was pick up a few extra bucks without hurting anybody. None of these men is even married. So mom and pop back home won't get Johnny's last paycheck to blow on beer and pretzels. They got thirty-five thousand coming from Uncle Sam anyway for a death gratuity. They'll never miss a few bucks the kid had in his pocket to play poker with on Saturday night."

Downs and Samson stood impassively while the first sergeant continued, "Look guys, it's not like I'm not willing to cut you two in on it. Now you guys been out on the line and you're tired and so maybe you're not thinking as clear as you normally would. You shoot me, Samson, and the best you can hope for is leniency from the court-martial board. Probably both of you will do a pretty long stint in the brig. What good is that going to do for anybody here?''

The first sergeant looked from one Marine to the other, then continued, ''What I'm proposing is that we all benefit from this. I've got quite a bit of cash here and I'm willing to split it equally between the three of us. We'll all go home winners in a few weeks and nobody is the wiser. And nobody gets hurt. Not really. The families got more money coming than they'll be able to spend. Think about it guys. Is it worth it to shoot me over something like this and ruin the rest of your lives because you don't like me?''

The first sergeant opened his palms and displayed a large roll of bills. ''It's just business boys. We don't have to like one another to do business, do we? Besides, what Marine likes his first shirt? Come on, guys, you must know they pay me to be a prick. That's part of running the company. It's the system, it's the way things work in the Corps. You guys been Marines long enough to know that.''

Downs looked at the first sergeant in disgust. ''So how are we going to split Sergeant Griffin's money, First Shirt?'' he asked. Before the man could answer Downs said, ''Do the motherfucker, Samson.''

Samson smiled and slowly brought the M-16 to his shoulder as the first sergeant attempted to back away from the rifle muzzle. Before the weapon could complete its travel to his shoulder Staff Sergeant Whitney entered and said, ''Put that rifle down, Samson. I've heard enough of this shit to make me sick for the rest of my life.''

Without taking his eyes from the first sergeant Samson said, ''No way, Staff Sergeant Whitney, I'm gonna waste this motherfucker. I can't stand the sight of him any longer. If I don't do it he'll just beat the rap.''

The staff sergeant took in the look on the big Marine's face and his grip on the rifle. He noted that neither Samson nor Downs had shifted their gaze from the first sergeant when he had entered and spoken. ''It's over Samson. If you shoot him now it's just murder, plain and simple. He's no Marine, son. He'll go to the brig, then they'll drum him out short of his retirement like they never knew him. Don't ruin the rest of your life over this. He's not worth it, boy.''

The staff sergeant continued to study Samson, looking for some sign on the boy's face that he was making a decision. As he watched him the staff sergeant knew that Samson's decision was made. He intended to kill the first sergeant. "Don't do it, Samson. Don't, son. Nothing is worth this. Do you think any of those men on the deck there would expect you to go to the brig for the next ten years to set this right?" The staff sergeant waited for an answer, but the big Marine gave no indication that he had heard.

The staff sergeant glanced at Downs who continued to glare at the First Sergeant with his arms folded across his chest like a judge. "Help me out, Corporal Downs," he said.

Downs shook his head slowly from side to side, his eyes never leaving the first sergeant. "I can't, Staff Sergeant," he said. "This is beyond me."

The staff sergeant again turned to Samson. "It won't do any good, son. If you shoot him he'll die but you'll end up in the brig. Samson, nothing is worth ten years in Portsmouth Naval Prison. It won't bring them back to life," said the staff sergeant, gesturing to indicate the dead men. "And worst of all a year from now your sacrifice will be forgotten by a battalion that's made up of new men from other units."

The staff sergeant took a hesitant step toward Samson. "Come on, son. Give me the rifle and we'll walk away from this. I'll make sure the bastard gets what he deserves. Nobody is going to doubt all three of us."

Samson tightened his grip on the rifle and edged away from the staff sergeant. "Get back, Staff Sergeant. I know what you're thinking. It ain't over yet." Samson shifted his attention to the first sergeant. "Drop that forty-five, First Shirt. And I'd really like it if you try something smart after you clear that holster. It'd give me an excuse." The three Marines stood as the first sergeant gingerly pulled the pistol from its leather holster and lowered it to the floor of the big tent. "Now step away from it," said Samson.

After the first sergeant had backed away from the weapon the staff sergeant again asked, "Give me the rifle, Samson. It's over, son. It has to end here."

"It ain't over till Corporal Downs says it's over," answered the big Marine, the rifle leveled at the first sergeant's chest.

"Corporal Downs?" asked the staff sergeant.

Downs hesitated, then said, "Let's go, Samson."

CHAPTER

31

The Syrian casually glanced at his watch and noted that he had ten minutes before the final call for his flight. He rose, left some bills on the table to pay for the coffee and paper, then picked up his small overnight bag and attaché and walked toward the boarding gate. Within minutes he had boarded the MEA airliner for Athens, taken his seat in the business class section, and begun reading his paper.

He glanced out the small window as the pilot guided the aircraft toward the runway. He noted, without emotion, that after two weeks the American Marines had almost completely cleared away the rubble left after the bombing of their headquarters. What was left had been pushed into huge conical mounds lining the western runway, and trucks similar to the one used in the bombing were waiting in line to haul these away.

He had spent the past two weeks observing the Marines as they went about the task of conducting rescue operations and sorting through the rubble for clues as to the identity of the bomber. He had become a faithful reader of the daily papers, and noted with satisfaction that every editor left in the city after ten years of civil war had righteously concluded that the bombing was the work of an Islamic fundamentalist sent to Lebanon from Iran.

The single call he had placed from the lobby of a hotel in west Beirut to a Muslim editor had sufficed to lend sufficient credibility to his contact so that the man was widely copied in the other Lebanese papers. It had been only a matter of hours before the Western wire services, all of which depended on local reporters for their information, published their own version of his claims. As was his experience with previous actions, he found that all the papers were willing to publish the version of events being promoted by their competitors in lieu of credible versions of their own. Once the story had taken root it had assumed an energy of its own, and through repetition gained greater credibility. As was often the case, it was totally irrelevant to the wire service correspondents that they had absolutely no way to verify either the information provided by their own sources, or those of their competitors. Very often, he knew, the sources were actually the same.

It had been almost too easy. He had worried for some days if he had not been tricked in some fashion. He waited for the Marines to conduct foot patrols into the Muslim villages surrounding their lines, to flush out any of the militiamen who had fired on them as they conducted their rescue operations. Instead he had been puzzled as they continued to wait behind their barbed wire and sandbags. He had observed, through his binoculars, the movements of the American warships in the Mediterranean. On occasion they would maneuver closer to shore, but they did not fire into the city as he had expected.

He had been so alarmed by the lack of a response that he surmised that the Marines had gotten intelligence from the Israelis indicating that a lone agent was to blame. For several days he moved continuously, never sleeping in the same place and spending his time in various public places searching the crowds for faces he had seen behind him the day before. After a week of such activity he had come to two conclusions. The first was that the Americans were caught off balance by the attack and were not going to mount an effective response to it. The second was that his own nerves were wearing thin and that he had to leave Beirut before he began to make mistakes that even a junior field agent did not make if he wished to survive.

He had concluded that the safest way out of Beirut would be the most brazen. As soon as the local papers reported that the Marines had again opened the airport to international travel he booked a flight to Athens. As he had expected, his stolen Lebanese passport saw him safely through official checkpoints. A few French francs got him past all the militia barricades between his hotel and the airport. He had been careful to travel with only a few thousand francs so as not to make too tempting a target to some militia hoodlum. The bulk of his funds he had wire transferred to various European accounts prior to the action.

He leaned forward in his chair as the airliner accelerated toward takeoff. As the airplane gained speed he noted the condition of the Marine positions lining the western perimeter of the airport. They were dug in along the small natural rise in the ground and their armored vehicles were in defilade. They were good soldiers, but they had learned too late. They had paid a price for their negligence, just as Ahmud had paid a price for his foolishness. The next time it would not be so easy for him. The Israelis were proof of that.

When he arrived in Athens he immediately booked a flight for Geneva, where he planned to relax for a time. He would give the bureaucrats and administrators in Damascus time to write their reports and make their evaluations.

He waited in the crowded boarding area of the terminal until his flight had been called twice. When the attendants were boarding the final passengers he crossed the terminal to a public telephone and dialed, from memory, the number for the Syrian Embassy in Athens.

The phone rang twice before a clerk in the security section of the embassy picked it up and answered with a simple "Hello." Without hesitation the Syrian spoke, "Listen very carefully. My name is Samir, I am a businessman from Aleppo. You are to telephone Youssef, in Damascus, on my behalf. You will tell him that I have been delayed, but that I expect to return to Damascus before the feast days in my village. He can expect to see me then." The Syrian paused, listening to the movement of the clerk's pencil over his notepad. "You have made notes, very good. You must be precise when you deliver my message."

The Syrian watched the second hand move around the face of his watch as the clerk read back the message. Once he was satisfied the man had it right, and before the call had gone into its second minute, he placed the receiver back in its cradle. He crossed the terminal and boarded the flight, already planning his first meeting in Geneva with his bankers regarding the recent deposits made to his accounts there.

CHAPTER

32

Downs lowered himself farther in his hole as the three helicopters swung over the landing zone and beat the morning air with their rotors. He turned and watched briefly as the machines hovered some fifty feet off the ground and lowered their slings. Marines dashed out and attached hooks to the netting and the pilots coaxed the loads off the ground and headed for the ships offshore.

The morning had been a steady progression of men and equipment toward the beach some four kilometers to the rear. Now the men of first platoon stood in a thin semicircle between the village to their east and the airport to their rear. Two hundred yards away, across an empty field of brown grass, Downs could see a few dozen Lebanese civilians who had come out of their homes on the cold February morning to watch the departure of the Marines.

Three more helicopters landed in the big field as another platoon from Bravo Company dashed out and climbed aboard. Downs turned his back to the machines as the rotor wash blew over him in a cloud of dust and debris. He watched the Lebanese through slit eyes as some of the children waved at the departing helicopters with their loads of Marines. Most of them stood impassively as the pilots smoothly lifted their machines into the air, then lowered the noses of the helicopters and fought to gain altitude.

As the last of the Bravo Company Marines was lifted out Downs looked in the direction of the staff sergeant who pumped his fist twice. The platoon struggled to its feet, clumsy under the weight of their packs. The squads formed up and began to withdraw toward their next position, leapfrogging backward so as to maintain at least one squad in place with its front toward the village.

After they had gone one hundred yards past second squad Downs set them into an extended skirmish line along an abandoned railroad track, the Marines automatically arranging themselves behind the remains of the elevated roadway. He watched as another squad leader and his Marines ambled past with their gear. Few of the Marines spoke, although they had all been anxious to leave Lebanon in the months after the bombing.

He glanced along the track, noting the position of each man, satisfied that they were properly set in. To his right a radio crackled constantly with traffic from the other units already at the beach. "Anything for Alpha Company, Staff Sergeant Whitney?" he asked.

The staff sergeant shook his head. "Nope, not really. All the usual fuckups. We'll probably be delayed gettin' to the beach from the way it sounds." Whitney paused for a moment, gazing in the direction of the Lebanese village, then said, "It sure doesn't get any easier the second time around."

"What's that?" asked Downs.

"Leavin' like this. I did it once before. From Vietnam. You might have heard of that one somewhere in the past," smiled the older man.

Downs turned and faced Whitney. He noticed for the first time that the staff sergeant seemed older. Downs realized that he liked the man. "Yeah, Staff Sergeant," he said with a low laugh, "I've heard it mentioned someplace."

"I figured as much." The two stood in silence again for another few minutes as the squad continued to hold its position, the other squads moving past it in the direction of the beach. "I don't much care for retreats, Corporal Downs. They're bad for morale, among other things."

"Is that what this is?" asked Downs, cutting off the staff sergeant. "A fucking retreat?"

"No, but I almost wish it was," said Whitney. "Sometimes you gotta retreat. To save yourself or something. This is a hell of a lot more like just plain quitting, and I like that even less. I generally finish what I start, and I always keep my word. Seems to me we're a little short in both instances here."

Neither man spoke for a minute, then Downs said, "I never thought we'd quit, that's for sure. But Jesus, just look at us. It looks to the whole world like we're running. What do you make of that?"

"Well, I could see how others might come away with that impression. But I guess what you and I have to decide is what really took place here. I mean, really, what did happen here? Do you know?"

Downs shrugged. "I think I understand all the political maneuvering, Staff Sergeant. I just don't care for it at my expense. They're making us look like we weren't good to our word. As Marines, I mean. We came here to do something and now we're leaving before we've been allowed to accomplish the mission."

"Yeah, that about sums it up," agreed Whitney. "I felt like shit for any number of years because of the way we abandoned the Vietnamese." The staff sergeant caught Downs's look of disbelief. "That surprise you, Corporal Downs?"

Downs shrugged again. "Yeah, maybe. I just didn't figure there was any love lost between you and the Vietnamese. You know?"

Whitney smiled and nodded his head. "Let me ask you something, Corporal Downs. And take a minute to think about it before you answer. Do you hate anybody over there?" he asked, nodding to indicate the Lebanese village.

Downs thought for a few moments then answered, "I don't think so. Shit, Staff Sergeant, I don't even know anybody there."

"Yep," agreed the older man, "that's the way it is for me too. I did two tours in Vietnam, Corporal Downs. Finished both of 'em, too. I saw my share of action all right. You name it and we did it in those days. It was getting that way here, too."

The staff sergeant paused, obviously choosing his words. "I guess the point is that once the shooting stops a man has time to think. And among all the things you think about is the fact that you killed somebody who really hadn't done anything to you." He stopped again and laughed, "Well, maybe nothin' other than being in his own country and carrying a rifle and tryin' to kill you or your friends, who are trying to kill him in the first place."

Whitney shook his head and winked at Downs. "You'll be doing some thinking in the future, Corporal Downs. About what went on here, and the things you did and the things you didn't do. That's natural. It's gonna happen, and when it does there will be days when you feel real shitty about all of this and everybody connected with it."

Downs nodded without answering and continued to stare at the Lebanese village. "Sometimes I think about Vietnam and all that went on there. Even now." Whitney let out a long breath and continued, "I'm not real good at stuff like this, Corporal Downs. But I know what it's like to come back home and stew about these things. Doesn't seem to bother some men, and others don't ever forget."

"Yeah, I see where you're going with this, Staff Sergeant," said Downs.

"Maybe you do, Corporal Downs. But there is another matter I wanted to talk to you about." Downs looked at the older man expectantly and the staff sergeant continued, "The Captain and I are aware of what you did the day the BLT went down. He put you, Smith, and Ferris in for awards."

Downs shrugged. "I'd heard that from a guy in the company admin section, Staff Sergeant. It doesn't really matter a whole lot to me right now. But thanks anyway, I appreciate it."

"Yeah, son, I can understand how you might feel that way." Whitney hesitated, rubbing his chin with a hand he continued, "Unfortunately for you and me we live in funny times, Corporal Downs. I'm ashamed to say it, son, but those awards are going to be denied. Something about higher headquarters not wanting to admit it's a war over here by handing out medals back home."

Downs laughed and looked at the staff sergeant. "Now why doesn't that surprise me?" he asked.

"Well, God knows it shouldn't," said the older man. "But I know what took place up there, Corporal Downs. It took courage. Real courage."

Downs scraped a boot into the red clay of the embankment, and stood in awkward silence for a moment, saying quietly, "I don't think so, Staff Sergeant. I'm not being modest either. It wasn't courage, it was apathy. There's a difference, but maybe they look alike from a distance."

"Maybe, son, but I don't think so," said Whitney. Downs felt his throat tighten as the staff sergeant continued, "Sometimes it matters more that you did the right thing when it was your turn than getting an award or a medal. Ultimately, it's the kind of man you know you are that matters most. Not the ribbons and badges. Remember that, Corporal Downs."

"I will, Staff Sergeant. Thanks," said Downs.

Whitney looked around him at the Marines making their way rearward, toward the beach, with its waiting landing craft and myriad of activity. He slapped Downs on the shoulder and said, "Well, off to do my duty. Keep your squad alert, Corporal Downs."

Downs grunted a reply, then turned back toward the civilians who remained at the edge of their village, as Whitney joined up with the other squads. Within minutes first squad was back on its feet and headed for the coast road. Downs knew the squad would pause there while other units that were delayed were lifted off the beach.

The ground began to take on a gentle rise and Downs knew that they were close to the beach road. Already he could detect the faint smell of salt spray in the chilly air. Rounding a curve in the road the ground fell away and he could see the beach with its confusion of activity.

Flags marking sectors of the beach for the bosuns flew at regular intervals and the flat-bottomed LCUs periodically grounded themselves in their assigned places and took on loads of men and equipment. The ships of the fleet had pulled in as close to the shoreline as they dared and a steady stream of small craft swam between them and the beach.

On the beach, pockets of men rested in neat rows waiting for their transport to the ships. Everywhere there was movement, most of it centered around the two temporary causeways as units edged their way closer to this common departure point. From the center of the activity the beachmaster screamed commands into a megaphone from atop his tower, attempting to lend order to the confusion.

Downs searched the scrub along the dunes and found the tanks. They were sitting low in the sand, their chassis dug into prepared positions, the main guns pointed menacingly toward the coastal highway. On the nearest tank he could make out the crew attaching the fording gear. He reasoned that they must be nearly through with the back-load if the tanks were preparing to pull off the beach.

Helicopter gunships swung low overhead and swept the length of the beach as Downs calculated the time remaining. The back-load would take most of the day. He would arrive on ship sometime in late afternoon or early evening. In the meantime all he had to do was stay alert and wait. He settled farther into the sandy depression he had found between two mounds of saw grass and drew his field jacket tight over his chest.

His mind began to wander and he thought of how good it would feel to get a real shower on ship. Clean, hot water and a hot meal. He would sleep in a real bed for a change, one with sheets. The voyage back to Spain would be easy. They would stop for a few days at the naval base in Spain, clean vehicles and gear, and then they would be on their way back to the States.

He tried to think of her and realized suddenly that he hadn't thought about her in weeks. He tried to visualize her face, but nothing would come to him. He forced himself to think of the times they had spent together. Long summer evenings on the front porch of her house when they had talked about nothing for hours.

He realized with a start that the scene was familiar to him. The soft summer evenings, the muted voices from inside her house, the quiet moments when they had sat in silence and held hands, but he could not focus on her. No image of her came to him, and no sense of loss for her.

Before, when he had daydreamed of her, it was as if she were there. For a few moments he would be lost in his reverie and he could smell her perfume or feel the warmth of her face pressed against his. He closed his eyes and struggled to remember her. To recall her walk, or the way she laughed, something she had said to him on some long-ago night spent with each other in the darkness. He tried to remember the way it felt when she touched his neck, or the softness of her voice in the quiet.

He ran his hand inside his pocket and brought out her last letter. He looked at the worn envelope, its edges frayed and soft from months in his pocket. He took the letter from the envelope and began to read the words there. Without finishing the first paragraph he knew that it was over. He no longer hurt when he read her words.

Downs sighed softly and looked at the neat script, the pages beginning to come apart where she had folded them. He scooped a hole in the sand with one hand then put the letter inside it. As he brushed the sand over the envelope he thought once very quickly of her and smiled softly to himself, then shook the sand from his hand and rose to check the squad.

EPILOGUE

They shall not grow old, as we that are left grow old:
Age shall not weary them, nor the years condemn.
At the going down of the sun and in the morning
We will remember them.

—Lawrence Binyon (1869–1943)

She smiled softly and turned to look at him. He sat there quietly in his blue suit, looking straight ahead. Next to him sat their youngest daughter, a mass of golden hair encircling her face, her hands tucked into the crook of his arm.

She looked past him to the stately brick buildings lining the quadrangle, their sturdy white columns freshly painted. The lawn had been cut the previous day and the smell of fresh mown grass drifted up to her as the sun began to climb over the roof of the building behind her. The neat rows of folding chairs were filled with the parents of the graduates, and cameras flashed here and there in the crowd as students accepted their diplomas. She looked back to him and knew that he was gone again. He's going to miss it, she thought. He'll be daydreaming. As the next row of students rose to accept their diplomas the little girl plucked her father's sleeve and said, "Look, Daddy!"

"I know," he said quietly, and she watched to see that he noticed their oldest daughter approaching the stage to accept her diploma. She saw him tug at the sleeve of his suit coat, pulling it over the faded scar on his right wrist. She had seen that gesture a thousand times. As if by hiding the scar from view he could erase it from his mind. But you can't, can you, Steven Downs? The best you can do is push it down inside and never show that part of yourself to anyone. What happened to you over there? You were so sweet and innocent before. And now there is a dark part of you that you are afraid to let me know. They took a part of you from me, and they have it still.

Something in her resented this part of him that he refused to share with her. It had been difficult in the beginning. He had come back and she had been away at college. She had dated other boys. She had been happy. And then she had seen him. All the old feelings had come rushing

340

back to her in that brief instant when she glimpsed him across a crowded street. Standing on the sidewalk that day long ago, among her friends, she knew that she had been wrong to hurt him.

It had been awkward at first. Eventually they had started seeing each other again. She had hoped that things would return to the way they were before. Everything seemed normal enough. They dated. He transferred to her university in order to be closer to her. Everything seemed fine. Friends said how good it was to see them together again.

She knew that she made him happy, but it wasn't like before. He had changed. He was no longer the open honest boy she had known all her life. At first she had waited for him to come to her, to tell her of his hurt, what had happened to him. He had never spoken of it to her and eventually she had asked him about it. His answers had been evasive and noncommittal. She had felt as though he was deliberately hiding something from her so as to punish her. She came to believe, and she had held the belief for a number of years, that he was keeping a part of himself separate from her and from their relationship.

For a long time it had lain dormant between them. But it had been there. After they were married she would find him sitting alone in a darkened room in the middle of the night. She asked for an explanation only once. He had turned the light off and said ''no.'' The sadness and resignation in his voice had been enough to keep her from ever asking again. And so it had been for the twenty-odd years of their life together. In her mind everything was separated by the time before he went away and the time since his return. She had no idea what had happened to him during his months in Lebanon, and no way of asking him about it. She had come to accept that it was private, and that he had no intention of sharing it with her. She had accepted his decision because she had no choice. She had always loved him, and she knew that he loved her.

The birth of their first child changed him for the better. He was enthralled by the little girl. With his child he lost his reserve and she saw the old innocent Steven shine through the mask he wore. The terrible sadness she sensed in him faded when he played with his daughter. When the little girl had started talking he had begun taking her for long walks. They would be gone for hours sometimes, just the two of them. She sensed, more than knew, that the child was having a healing effect on his soul. Steven had always favored her, although not obviously, and she knew the little girl had touched him in a place she could no longer reach.

They both watched as their oldest child crossed the stage and accepted her diploma. She put her hand on his, covering the faded scar on his wrist, and as he turned toward her, she smiled.

GLOSSARY OF TERMS AND ABBREVIATIONS

ACTUAL: Used to designate the commander of a unit as opposed to the radioman who would normally relay commands. "Six Actual" designates the actual unit commander, with "Six" representing the commander.

AK-47: Infantry assault rifle issued to various armies, including the Syrian Army. Carried by many militia organizations in Lebanon.

AL LAYLAKAH: A suburb of Beirut just east of the airport in the southern portion of the greater Beirut area.

ALPHA COMPANY: Designation for the first company of the first battalion of any Marine Infantry Regiment. Other companies in the first battalion of any infantry regiment would be Bravo, Charlie, Headquarters and Service Company, Weapons, etc.

ALPHA SIX: Designates the commander of Alpha Company, with "Six" being the designation for commander of the unit.

AMAL: One of several political groups formed by the Lebanese Shiites. Amal is also the Arabic word for "hope." Various militia groups and organizations were formed by Amal throughout its history.

AMTRAC: An amphibious tractor, official designation Landing Vehicle Tracked Personnel-7 (LVTP-7). An armored vehicle capable of ferrying approximately twenty-four Marines from ship to shore. Lightly armed with a .50 caliber machine gun, its primary role is that of an amphibious armored personnel carrier. Once ashore it can be used as transport for small units.

BACK-LOAD: Term used to refer to the removal of men and equipment from positions ashore to shipboard.

BATTALION AID STATION (BAS): The unit comprised of USN hospital corpsmen and other medical personnel and attached to a USMC

343

battalion. Individual hospital corpsmen are attached to companies and platoons as needed and accompany Marine patrols to treat casualties.

BATTALION LANDING TEAM (BLT):   A designation for a task-oriented unit formed from various smaller units and built around an infantry battalion. Composed of, among other things, an infantry battalion, a unit of amphibious tractors, a small unit of tanks, combat engineers, etc.

Also used by Marines to designate the building in Beirut where the BLT Headquarters unit and personnel worked and were housed.

BEE-HIVE: Slang for a 40mm antipersonnel fragmentation round fired from an M203 grenade launcher.

BEIRUT INTERNATIONAL AIRPORT (BIA):   The large airport located in the southern portion of the city of Beirut. The USMC took up defensive positions here and enabled the airport to resume operations during the USMC deployments.

BEKKA VALLEY: A fertile valley east of Beirut and separated from it by a mountain range. During the period of the USMC deployments in Lebanon it served as a staging area for various militias, as well as being in the operational area of the Israeli Defense Force and Syrian Army.

BELLEAU WOOD: World War I battle where the Marines of the 5th and 6th Marine Regiments distinguished themselves and earned the nickname "Devil-dogs" from their German foes.

BOOT: Term used to describe Marines new to the Fleet Marine Force.

CAMP GEIGER: USMC base co-located with Camp LeJeune, North Carolina. During the period of the Lebanon deployments it was the home base for the 8th Marine Regiment.

CAMP LEJEUNE: USMC base located in Jacksonville, North Carolina. The 2nd Marine Division is based here. Elements of the 8th Marine and 6th Marine Regiment, 2nd Marine Division, served in Lebanon during the 1982–1984 deployments.

CAX: Combined Arms Exercise. A military exercise that integrates various units such as infantry, air, armor, and artillery units.

CHRISTIAN PHALANGISTS: One of the numerous factions of Lebanon. Composed of Christians as opposed to Muslims, the Phalange was relatively well armed and at times allied with the Israelis.

CLAYMORE: An antipersonnel mine that can be remotely fired on command or fired by means of a trip wire.

CO: Commanding Officer. Also referred to as the "Old Man."

COMM: Short for radio communications.

CP: Command Post.

DAMOUR: Site of a massacre of Lebanese civilians prior to the USMC deployments of 1982–1984.

DOC: Slang for hospital corpsmen who accompany USMC infantry units.

EAS: End of Active Service, the discharge date for Marine enlisted personnel.

EIGHTH MARINE REGIMENT: One of the infantry regiments that composes the 2nd Marine Division. The 2nd Marine Division is also composed of the 2nd, 4th, and 6th infantry regiments, as well as the 10th Marine regiment (artillery).

FERRET: A lightly armed, highly mobile armored vehicle used by the British units in Beirut.

FRAG: Fragmentation Grenade. Using a grenade to kill an individual is known as "fragging."

FRENCH FOREIGN LEGION: French military unit that served as part of the multinational force with the USMC in Beirut. On 23 October 1983 French paratrooper units serving in Beirut suffered a similar bombing at one of their positions, losing fifty-eight men.

FROG: Designation for the Soviet made Free Rocket Over Ground. A portable, crew-served weapon capable of carrying a variety of warheads. At the time of the Lebanon deployments this weapon system was in the inventory of the Syrian Army.

GOLAN: The Golan Heights are a mountainous area captured by the Israelis from the Syrians during the 1973 Yom Kippur War.

GRUNT: Slang term for infantry Marines. Used with a degree of pride by most Marine infantrymen.

H&I FIRE: Harassment and Interdiction Fire. Intermittent fire, usually from small artillery units used to harass the enemy but not expected or designed to cause great damage or casualties.

H&S COMPANY: Headquarters and Service Company. One of the companies composing any Marine Battalion. This unit contains headquarters personnel and other specialized units of a Marine Battalion.

HAMRA: An area of Beirut noted for its shops and affluence.

HAY-EL-SALAAM: One of the southern suburbs of Beirut in close proximity to the Beirut International Airport. Its residents are primarily Shiite Muslim.

HE: High Explosive.

HOOTERVILLE: Slang term used by Marines in Beirut to mean the villages in immediate proximity to the USMC positions east of BIA.

INDIAN COUNTRY: Slang for territory controlled by enemy forces.

INFANTRY TRAINING REGIMENT: Refers to the "school" at either Camp Geiger, North Carolina, or Camp Pendleton, California, that all Marines attend after Boot Camp to learn basic infantry skills.

INSHALLAH: Arabic for "If God wills it."

INTERNAL SECURITY FORCES: A paramilitary unit of the Lebanese police force. Easily recognizable by their khaki uniforms and red headgear. Among the first units of the Lebanese government to resume operations after the entry of the Multi-National Force.

IDF: Israeli Defense Force. The army of Israel that operated in Lebanon during the period of the USMC deployments.

IWO JIMA, battle of: One of the Volcano Islands in the northern Pacific. Iwo Jima was the scene of a bloody battle between the U.S. Marines and Japanese forces during February and March of 1945.
The battle is now synonymous with valor and courage among Marines.

IWO JIMA, USS: Designated by the USN as a Landing Platform Helicopter (LPH) and capable of carrying various helicopter and Vertical and Short Takeoff and Landing aircraft (VSTOL) such as AV-8B Harriers. One of the amphibious support ships that made up the squadron of amphibious ships transporting Marine Units to the Mediterranean. The *Iwo Jima* and her sister ships supported operations ashore.

KAFFIYEH: Traditional Arab headdress. Worn by Arab men as a symbol of pride and culture, or to designate an affiliation with a particular group. Varying patterns on different kaffiyehs may represent various organizations, military units, or peoples.

KHALDEH: A village south of Beirut and within sight of the USMC positions at the BIA. It was also a military post for the LAF.

KIA: Killed In Action.

LAAW: Light Anti-Armor Weapon, a small shoulder-fired weapon carried by individual Marines and designed for use against tanks and light armor vehicles.

LAF: Lebanese Armed Forces, the army of Lebanon. After the civil war in Lebanon it was largely ineffective. During the period of 1982–1984 attempts were made by the U.S. government to rebuild it with assistance from Marine and U.S. Army units and advisors.

LCU: Landing Craft, Utility. USN designation for the small, flat-bottomed craft that ferry men and equipment from larger ships to shore and vice versa.

LEBANESE AVIATION SAFETY BUREAU: An organization of the Lebanese national government whose office building was shelled and otherwise damaged during the civil war and subsequent Israeli invasion. It was this building that became the headquarters for USMC Battalion Landing Teams deploying to Lebanon and was later largely destroyed by a truck bomb on 23 October 1983 killing 241 USMC, USN, and USA personnel, and wounding 70. Various units were barracked in and around this building at the time of the bombing.

LESBOS: Slang term for Lebanese used by Marines. Not meant to be a pejorative.

LP: Listening Post. A post manned at night, usually by a small unit such as a fireteam, for the purpose of detecting enemy movement or actions.

LZ: Landing Zone. An area designated for the landing and takeoff of helicopters.

M-16: Standard issue assault rifle of the USMC.

M-60: Light machine gun carried by Marine units.

M-203: 40mm grenade launcher that attaches to the forearm of M-16 rifles. Each fireteam in a Marine rifle squad has one designated grenadier armed with an M-203.

MAU: Marine Amphibious Unit. A task-oriented unit composed of a Battalion Landing Team and other units. Various MAUs were deployed to Lebanon from September 1982 to February 1984 to include the 24th, 22nd, 32nd, and 31st. The MAU acts as higher headquarters for the BLT during deployments. Headquarters for the 24th MAU during October of 1983 was in a one-story building immediately north of the BLT headquarters building.

MEA: Middle East Airlines. Civilian airline that operates from BIA.

MM: Millimeter. Such as a 40 millimeter grenade launcher.

MEDEVAC: Medical Evacuation. Personnel wounded or killed in action would be medevaced. Usually done by helicopter.

MNF: Multi-National Force. The organization composed of USMC, French, Italian, and later British military units that was sent to Beirut in 1982 to evacuate the PLO and later returned to keep the peace.

MOS: Military Occupational Specialty. One's job within the USMC. Any Marine infantryman has an MOS within the "03" field, 03 being the designation for infantry. Intelligence MOSs are designated by 02, Logistics by 04, etc.

MOTOR-T : Motor Transport. The unit and Marines assigned to operate, service, and repair a Marine unit's vehicles.

MRE: Meal Ready to Eat. A complete meal packaged and easily transported, served to Marines in the field. MREs replaced C-rations during the 1980s.

MSR: Main Supply Route. Designates the principal artery used by a military organization to supply its units.

MSSG: MAU Service Support Group. A USMC unit that provides support in the form of engineering units and other essential services to MAUs and BLTs ashore and afloat.

MED: Slang for Mediterranean Sea.

MOSSAD: The Israeli Intelligence agency.

NAVY ACHIEVEMENT MEDAL: An award given to Marines for superior performance of their duties.

***NEW JERSEY,* USS:** One of the Missouri class battleships constructed during World War II. Its armament includes 16-inch naval rifles that were used in support of Marine units ashore.

NEW RIVER: A salt estuary that runs through Camp LeJeune, North Carolina.

NIS: Naval Investigative Service. Investigative agency of the USN charged with investigating serious crimes.

NJP: Nonjudicial Punishment. Also commonly called "Office Hours," this is the lowest form of court-martial. Once a Marine enters a plea of guilty to a low level infraction of the UCMJ or other regulations a company grade officer may determine punishment by using this system. No jury or trial is afforded the guilty party.

OCS: Officer Candidate School. One of the schools attended by officer candidates. Located at Marine Corps Developmental and Educational Center, Quantico, Virginia.

OFFICER OF THE DAY: OD, also OOD. The officer assigned to guard and other functions by unit commanders in every Marine unit.

OGER LIBAN: A Lebanese construction company operating in Beirut and making extensive repairs to the facilities at the BIA during 1983–1984.

OLD MAN: Slang for commanding officer. Also "CO."

OP: Observation Post, an outpost manned during daylight hours usually by a small unit such as a fireteam. The purpose of an OP is to detect enemy movement.

PANHARDS: A light, mobile armored vehicle. Used by various forces in Beirut, including the LAF.

PARRIS ISLAND: The oldest training center for Marines, Marine Corps Recruit Depot Parris Island, is located on Parris Island, South Carolina.

PLO: Palestinian Liberation Organization. Name given to a collection of smaller civil entities and military organizations and nominally headed by Yasir Arafat. Prior to the June 1982 invasion of Lebanon by the IDF, the PLO had numerous offices and military organizations in Beirut and at other points in Lebanon.

POS: Position. Location of an individual or unit.

PRC-68: A small handheld radio used by Marines for communication between members of a squad or other small unit.

PRC-77: A large man-portable radio used for communication between Marine units.

REACT: The reactionary force. Normally held in reserve, this force is used at the discretion of a commanding officer to relieve units in jeopardy.

RPG: Rocket Propelled Grenade. A Soviet-manufactured shoulder-fired weapon similar to a bazooka designed for anti-armor and antipersonnel missions.

RULES OF ENGAGEMENT: Marine units operating in Beirut and those on standby offshore were issued specific Rules of Engagement to which they were required to adhere while in Lebanon. These rules, in addition to standing General Orders, governed the conduct of units and individuals ashore. Individual Marines of all ranks were expected to know and understand these rules without fail.

SABRA: An area of Beirut, north of BIA, inhabited by large numbers of displaced Palestinians. It was therefore known as the Sabra refugee camp, although most of the structures there were permanent in nature by the time of the USMC deployments.

SEMPER FIDELIS: Latin motto of the USMC, "Always Faithful."

SHATILLA REFUGEE CAMP: An area of Beirut, located north of the BIA, and home to many of the Palestinian refugee families. Despite its being called a refugee "camp" the area had been inhabited for so many years by the Palestinians that most of its residents lived in permanent structures.

SHATILLA WOOD: An area of Beirut, located north of the BIA, that was the home for numerous Palestinians refugee families. Located next to Shatilla Refugee Camp and sometimes considered to be a part of it.

SHELTER HALF: A canvas covering that is standard issue to Marines. When buttoned to another shelter half carried by a fellow Marine it forms a small, two-man tent used for shelter by both Marines.

SHIITE: One of the many sects or branches of Islam, the religion founded by the prophet Mohammed.

Many of the Shiite residents of Beirut lived in the southern sections of the city, well within the USMC area of operation. Despite being the most numerous segment of the Lebanese population the Lebanese Shiites are among Lebanon's poorest citizens and during 1982–1984 did not have political representation representative of their share of the population.

SHIT BIRDS: Derogatory term for Marines who do not perform their duties with skill or enthusiasm. Slackers.

SHIT CAN: Term used to describe a garbage can. Can also be used to designate something that is to be thrown away.

SIT REP: Situation Report. An abbreviated report following a predesignated format. Normally relayed via radio.

SIX-BY: The large utility transport truck used by the USMC.

SOP: Standard Operating Procedure.

SQUADBAY: The large open barracks used to house Marines ashore. Squadbay specifically refers to the area where the Marines sleep, and store their personal and military gear.

SUNNI: A sect of Islam, the religion founded by the prophet Moham-med. The Sunnis were among the more influential Muslim citizens of Lebanon. During the period 1982–1984 it was widely believed that the Sunnis were second in both political power and wealth only to the Lebanese Christians.

TARAWA: One of the Gilbert Islands in the central Pacific. Tarawa was the scene of a fierce battle between U.S. Marines and Japanese forces during November 1943.

TOKAROV PISTOL: A Soviet-manufactured pistol with an action simi-lar to that of the Browning pistol.

TOW: A crew served antitank missile. TOW gunners launch their weap-ons from fiberglass tubes then sight the weapon with an optical system while it is in flight. The launcher can be mounted on a variety of vehicles or be free-standing on the ground. TOW missiles are also used in the anti-armor role by helicopter gunships such as the Cobra.

TRIPOLI: A city in modern Libya, it was once located in the Barbary States. A small force of U.S. Marines captured it in response to depredations on American shipping made by the Barbary States during the early part of the nineteenth century.

UCMJ: The Uniform Code of Military Justice. The set of laws and regula-tions governing all members of the United States military.

VAL PACK: A canvas or nylon carrying case used by officers and Staff NCOs to transport personal belongings, uniform articles, etc.

VC: Viet Cong.

VILLE: Slang for village, town, or city.

XO: Executive Officer. The second in command of a unit.

ZEROS: Slang for Officers. Officer pay grades are designated 0–1 (Sec-ond Lieutenant) through 0–6 (Colonel). Hence enlisted Marines sometimes call them "Zeros."